My Husband Next Door

CATHERINE ALLIOTT

PENGUIN BOOKS

First published by Michael Joseph 2013
Published in Penguin Books 2014
003

Copyright © Catherine Alliott, 2013
All rights reserved

The moral right of the author has been asserted

Typeset by Jouve (UK), Milton Keynes
Printed in Great Britain by Clays Ltd, St Ives plc

ISBN: 978-1-405-91392-8

www.greenpenguin.co.uk

For my sister-in-law, Chris,
with love

Prologue

The first time I knew I was in any sort of trouble was this time last year, when I ran out of church, disastrous flowers in my hands, straight into Ludo. I was running from some very formidable women at the time, chief amongst them Celia Harmsworth, and the flowers were ones I'd been asked to arrange in the vestry. Celia had rung the week before to see if I could stand in for Venetia Rivers, who was heli-skiing in Argentina, like you do of a Monday morning in June. Although I sniggered with my friend Lottie about women like Celia and Venetia, pretending not to want to join their gang, we jolly well jumped if they asked us to do something. Or at least, I did.

'It doesn't have to be grand,' Celia had barked down the phone from Longhorn Manor, or Foghorn Manor as I liked to call it – had she barked from childhood, I wondered? When did one start? Adolescence? 'But it does have to be yellow and white,' she'd concluded. 'That's the theme. Just do two arrangements, keep it simple, and we'll do the rest. And don't attempt to place them yourself. Just drop them orf on Friday in the vestry and the gels will place them on Saturday for the wedding.'

Slightly miffed at not being trusted to place my own arrangements I'd put down the phone, cravenly agreeing I'd do as she asked. Well, naturally, I'd forgotten. The flowers, the yellow and white theme, the wedding – everything. Had picked up my pencil and gone straight back to my sketch pad, all of it cleanly wiped from my brain. Some days later, though, sauntering back through the village from coffee at Lottie's, I'd passed the exquisitely pretty Our Lady of Mercy's and, mid weighty decision about whether to treat myself to a Creme Egg or a Walnut Whip from the shop, had halted and gone cold. I'd flown home and fled down the garden to the only conceivable spot where something – anything, let alone yellow and white – might be blooming, but unfortunately Curly the goat, who escaped on a regular basis, had beaten me to it. He regarded my flower bed as a convenient fast-food bar and was even now licking his lips by the demolished roses, dribbling petals and moving seamlessly on to pansies for pudding. I cursed him roundly, which he took equably on his hairy chin, and ran inside. In panic, I rang the local florist. No problem, said one-eyed Susan, replacing her dentures audibly and probably her glass eye too. And actually, she said, she'd be chuffed. She knew the young couple who were getting married, and it'd be a pleasure. I promised to pick the flowers up later.

I had quaked slightly when I collected them because I hadn't meant for Susan to arrange them, just provide the stems: I'd planned to at least do that myself. I stole very quietly into the empty church to leave them – anonymously, of course – in the dark vestry and was just tiptoeing away, when I was halted in my tracks.

'You cannot *possibly* be serious, Ella!'

Celia herself emerged from the shadows brandishing a pair of secateurs and half a tree. She was tall, whippet thin and wore a white apron rather like a butcher. She gazed down in horror at the two arrangements I'd laid on the stone floor, one of which spelled KAREN in white carnations, the other PAUL in yellow.

'Y-yes – I mean – no. No, of course not. I'm really sorry, Celia. Susan did them, but it wasn't her fault. I wasn't – you know – specific enough.'

I shrivelled under her steely gaze. One or two of her henchmen had materialized from the shadows too, aprons efficiently tied, secateurs raised menacingly. I recognized Annabel Marsh-Price and the comedically named Puffy Trumpington.

'You got them from one-eyed Susan?' Celia's eyebrows went into her hairline. 'I meant you to pick from your own garden! We don't get arrangements from florists – how *utterly* ridiculous. What on earth would be the point?'

'Yes, no, quite. I do see, except – except there wasn't very much. There isn't really at this time of year, is there?' I stammered. It was fragrant midsummer. 'I mean – at least, in mine.'

'Well, gather flora from the hedgerow, then,' Celia bellowed in cadences sufficient to be heard at the back of an abbey let alone a village church. '*Anything* is better than that. Take them back and tell her they *simply won't do.*' She straightened her bony back, a gimlet gleam to her eye.

Well, obviously I didn't have the nerve to do that – one-eyed Susan could turn quite nasty – but as I hurried out of the church with the wretched arrangements I ran straight into Ludo in the lane. He was at the wheel of his open-topped Land Rover, paused at the village crossroads.

'Someone died?' he asked, eyeing the huge floral tributes in alarm.

'Oh, no, quite the opposite. Oh God, Ludo, listen.' I explained, breathlessly, about Curly and Susan and Celia.

He threw back his head and roared. When his face came back to me it was bright with delight. Blue eyes shone in a tanned, lean face. 'So bony bum's livid?'

'That barely covers it,' I hissed, terrified she was coming up behind me and would hear, not daring to look.

'Well, do her good to get her blood up. I don't suppose she gets much excitement in her life. This will tweak her up no end. Anyway, hop in. Let's see what we can do.'

He leaned across and swung the door wide for me.

'Really?' I clambered in gratefully beside him, slinging the arrangements in the back. 'You mean from your garden?'

He gave me an apologetic smile as he shifted the gears. 'No, I'm afraid that's out of the question. Eliza would be deeply unamused if I so much as pinched a dahlia, but we can still carry out General Celia's orders.' He grinned and tapped his nose. 'I know a bank where the wild thyme grows.'

'Ah,' I said as we took off at speed, roaring down the hill. I had to clutch the top of the door for balance. '*Under Milk Wood*.'

His mouth twitched. 'I'd go for something a little earlier but let's not quibble.'

Feeling like an extra in *MASH* I hung on to the side of his beaten-up convertible jeep as we sped down to the bottom of the lane and splashed through the ford at the bottom, forking left through the valley. We took off into the sun. I don't know about Celia but this was the most excitement I'd had in a long time and, rather uncharacteristically, I gave myself up to it: to the speed and the exhilaration, the wind in my hair, Ludo's brown arms and steady hands on the juddering wheel beside me. This man was in complete control, something woefully lacking in my life. I didn't glance at the slim-jeaned legs, knowing that would be a mistake, but I did sneak sidelong glances at his profile, noting the dihedral of his straight nose and the shock of blond hair whipping back from a high forehead. The noise from the engine precluded much speech but we yelled to one another, turning to exchange vivacious smiles. As ever, I thought, he exuded happiness. Every time I saw this man, I felt his optimism, his enthusiasm. He buzzed up the windows so we could talk properly. His eyes, busy as he drove, sparkled over everything, taking it all in. None of it belonged to him, but I felt his gaze to be proprietorial nonetheless.

'I hate going past this farm,' he said, as if to illustrate. I turned to look at the ponies I passed many times, standing by the gate, up to their hocks in mud. 'He's got plenty of paddocks at the back,' he told me. 'Could easily move them when it's wet, but he can't be bothered. So they get mud fever every year.' He shrugged, irritated.

And I'd just thought: muddy ponies. Hadn't considered it.

'You know this area like the back of your hand, don't you?' I called, wiping hair from my mouth where it had stuck to my lips. Happily I'd managed to apply something adhesive that morning, although it had originally been for Celia.

'Should do. I grew up here. Well, just over the hill. Rudolph and I scrambled through every ditch, dammed every river and climbed every dry-stone wall. I've still got the scars to prove it – mostly from farmers who don't take kindly to the right to roam.'

'Your brother's called Rudolph?'

He turned and grinned. As usual giving it both barrels.

'My mother was terribly suggestible when she was pregnant. She had a crush on Ludovic Kennedy when I was born, then she saw Nureyev dance at Covent Garden when she was pregnant with my brother. Poor Roo. He's learned to dread Christmas. And Red Nose Day, of course. She'd been weeping copiously at the end of *King Lear* when she was about to pop with my sister, Cordelia.'

'Oh!' I stared delightedly into the sun, imagining her hugely pregnant in the audience. 'I love that she wept.'

'Oh, she's a sucker for a tear-jerker. So's my dad. He's seen *Casablanca* countless times. We tease him he wells up in the Hovis ad. It's funny because he sees tragedy on a daily basis – stillborn lambs are an occupational hazard for him – but take him to a tragic play or film and he's limp.' He smiled ruefully. 'Actually, we're all horribly emotional.'

'I like emotion.'

He glanced at me in surprise. 'So do I,' he said, with a wistfulness that took me back a bit. 'A lot, in fact. Without feelings, what else is there?'

Our eyes locked for a moment longer than was absolutely necessary and I turned away quickly, trying to think what to answer. By the time I'd decided, it was too late. The silence became a bit deafening and I was grateful for the noise of the engine. I knew Ludo socially, as a friend of my sister's, but mainly because he worked in my garden, and if that sounds grand, it isn't. First, I'd hesitate to call Ludo a gardener; he's a landscape designer – a Chelsea Flower Show exhibitor, no less – and most of his work starts with a pencil, although recently, with the recession, he'd been doing more with a spade. He gardened for me these days as a favour, but my garden isn't big and it obviously shouldn't have taken seven months to complete. It certainly shouldn't be an on-going project.

'Lucky your parents hadn't been watching *Dumbo*,' I hazarded lightly.

He threw back his head and gave that barky laugh I loved. I liked the fact that I could make him laugh. People always think the other way round is more seductive, but I'm not convinced.

'Or *Lassie*?' he ventured.

I laughed myself. There. Both ways. I sank back happily in my seat. 'Your parents sound heaven.'

He looked across, surprised. 'I suppose they are.' He jerked his head to the right as we rattled along the valley floor. 'If you had x-ray vision you'd see them across there, through two banks of hills, just behind Jake Walter's place. Right now Dad'll be coming in from the fields and they'll be settling down to *The World at One*, the *Telegraph* crossword, bread and cheese and Mum's pickle. You can set your watch by them. And yours?'

'What d'you mean?'

'Heaven too?'

I hesitated. 'They have their moments. Dad does, anyway.' I felt disloyal. 'And my mum, of course.'

I looked away, letting the wind whip through my hair and take my head with it, feeling the sun on my eyes as I half shut them, using my lashes as shades. If only this drive could go on for ever.

'Where is home, Ella?'

I knew he meant in the essential way, not where I lived now. 'Commuter-belt Buckinghamshire. Practically the suburbs. Dad commuted to London.'

'Don't apologize; someone has to.'

'But not you any more.'

His face broke into a radiant smile and he kept his sparkling gaze straight ahead. 'No. Not me any more. As you know, I ran away. OK, here we are.'

He swung the jeep sharply into the side of the lane and we slid smoothly to a halt. The engine stopped and I was struck by the sudden quiet. A skylark whirled above our heads, a wood pigeon cooed softly to another, but, other than that, silence prevailed. A high hedge grew on both sides of the narrow lane so not much was visible other than a slim green corridor. In a moment, Ludo was out of the car and slamming the door. In another, he'd disappeared. Downwards, I realized.

I got out and went round the front of the jeep to the verge, looking after him. 'What is this, *Through the Looking Glass*?' I called.

'Just bother to stoop a bit and you'll find the ground gives way.'

I gazed down. So it did. Into a huge sort of hole. I lowered my legs gingerly into it. Then I slid down on my bottom into what I imagined was some sort of earth. It felt like a water shoot I'd been to once with the children. Would I ever come up again? Did I care? I crouched and ducked forward and my head popped out on the other side into an enormous field. I realized I'd gone under the hedge. A sea of poppies stretched as far as the eye could see.

'Oh!' I stared about. 'Now that's quite something.'

'Isn't it just?' He gave me a hand and I clambered out, hopefully in an easy, at-home-in-the-country sort of manner. I brushed myself down and glanced knowledgeably behind. 'Badger sett?'

8

'No, ancient culvert, old drainage ditch. Foxes do use it, though, and you wouldn't want to come here at night – they take exception to visitors. But there's no gate to this field from the road, so this is the only way in. The gate's over there.' He nodded into the distance.

He stood for a moment with his hands on his hips, taking in the scene, which was certainly glorious: a swaying ocean of thigh-high grass just on the cusp of bleaching to hay, seed heads bobbing, sprinkled with jewel-like flowers. In amongst the poppies were ox-eye daisies, buttercups, speedwell and cowslips.

Ludo crouched down and cradled something pale and bell-like in his hand. 'See this?'

'What is it?' I crouched beside him.

'Fritillary. Conditions have to be incredibly pure for this to thrive. I'm not sure I've seen it anywhere else but here. There are orchids too, only tiny ones, but exquisite. Anyway,' he said, straightening up, 'this is your palette.'

He began to pick carefully, stooping low to gather right from the base of the stem anything yellow and white, blooms of which hue, along with the poppies, were abundant. I followed suit, but, out of the corner of my eye, I kept watch on the elegant cotton-picker beside me, bending gracefully down then arching up tall and slim to add strategically to his bundle. We kept apart but parallel, working our way across the field, ending up with a great armful each, and then I told him Celia had only asked for two arrangements.

'Oh, right.' He turned. 'I thought you meant the whole church!'

No, I was just enjoying myself too much to stop the roundabout, I thought, but I didn't say it.

'Oh, no, sorry,' I called, 'just a couple. She said that she and the other gels would do the rest.'

'Well, then this will probably do us.' He missed my quip and I hoped he didn't think that was the way I said girls. Too late to rectify because he was already talking as he came towards me, shirt as blue as the sky, hair not far off the buttercups, arms full of flowers.

'Now what you're going to have to do, Ella, since they're wild, is sink them in tepid water the moment you get home, right up to their necks in buckets.' He demonstrated with one hand cupped under his chin. 'Leave them like that overnight and let Celia do the rest in the morning. If you don't, because they're organic, you'll have dead weeds on your hands tomorrow.'

'Got it, sir. And surely you don't arrange wild flowers, anyway? Just bung them in a vase?'

'Something a little more careful might be in order for a wedding, but I know what you mean. I can't bear formal arrangements, either. And as a matter of fact I know Karen; she helps Mum in the farm shop. She'll love these. It'll go down much better than anything stiff or stylized.'

I took the bundle he handed me into my arms. 'You're a star, Ludo, and I can't thank you enough. You've completely saved me.'

I hadn't meant to say anything profound but I think we both knew this could be taken on many levels. It was entirely possible Ludo could save me; I certainly needed saving. Even to the most casual observer, my life was terribly complicated. So complicated, in fact, that the entire village would doubtless have views on the topic. Go into huddles outside the shop. One thing was for sure, though. It would take more than a bunch of flowers to rectify it.

'And they won't mind?' I asked, lurching off at a tangent to protect myself. We were walking back towards the lane. I was that aware my response to this man was very potent. That I needed tangents.

'Who?'

'Up at Highgrove. I didn't know you worked there too.'

'You've lost me. I don't.'

'But you know the gardeners?'

'Some, why?'

'This is Highgrove land, Ludo. Prince Charles. Didn't you know?'

He stopped. Looked shaken. 'Since when? It always used to be Dick Baker's field. Set-aside.'

'No, he sold it, apparently. On account of all the wild flowers. Can't you see the secret service men in the bushes?'

He did actually turn to look, but it was only a glance. He was back to me in an instant, his face both outraged and delighted. He threw back his head and hooted up to the heavens. He was good at being teased and I loved that he didn't try to pretend he hadn't been had.

'Witch!' he roared, impulsively throwing an arm round my shoulders and giving them a squeeze. I leaned in, laughing. It was only an arm and a squeeze and a lean but the current took us both by surprise. He dropped his arm quickly and we walked on. I gazed fixedly at the tall hedge ahead, knowing it was terribly important to keep doing that. To watch the pendulous, creamy, elderflower heads swaying in the breeze. Ludo prattled on easily enough, about the importance of fields like this, and how other farmers should at least manage just a few acres of organic land without pesticides, but I knew we were both jolted. We'd been alone before, of course, but this was different. Up to now we'd been in professional mode, within legitimate parameters. For just as an office affords a screen to a burgeoning romance, so the workplace of my garden did it for us. We'd hide behind pruning decisions, stare purposefully at herbaceous borders or recalcitrant iris bulbs, managing to keep ourselves safe. This poppy-strewn meadow with its high-hedged seclusion was the equivalent of a city wine bar after hours: last orders called, the place deserted, except for two people alone at the corner table, no colleagues for ballast, no meetings for protocol, no structure for protection.

As I said earlier, I knew I was in trouble when I ran out of the church and got impulsively into his car. Knew it was pivotal. As we achieved the hedge I had an overwhelming urge to give in. To stop him right there in his farming chat and tell him how much I liked him. He later told me he'd wanted to kiss me. Neither happened. We slipped easily back down the culvert, out the other side to his car, and back into the real world. The world of work and money worries and domesticity: of children and husbands and wives. But when we drove home it was in an unlikely silence, and when he dropped me off there was something soft and heavy to his eyes as he said goodbye. I watched him drive away and stood for a good few moments in the empty yard after his Land Rover had gone. I knew it was the start of admitting things to each other, things we'd hardly dared to admit to ourselves. The turning point in our friendship. For a long time I'd been aware that this man brought order, not just to my garden, but to my life.

Joy, too. And I'd been joyless for too long. I'd begun to recognize the sound of his tyres on my drive, to glance quickly from my sketch pad through the attic window to make sure it was him. But thus far I'd tried not to make my eyes light up when I handed him a cup of coffee, tried not to let him see I'd seen a light in his. After this day, I didn't try any more. And neither did he.

Chapter One

The swimming-pool man came today. That's the sort of world I live in. I'm being facetious, of course. It's my sister Virginia's world; I just stray into it from time to time. Pool man, French-polishing man, wood-chopping man – you name it, she's got a man for everything: a man for all seasons. The only man who comes to see me is the milkman and even that relationship is in a state of flux since I failed to comply with his last monthly contract, stuffed aggressively, and for the third time, into one of my empty bottles.

I watched him now, this pool-cleaning chappie: white shorts, tanned legs, navy T-shirt, a cliché if ever I saw one, his handsome face as empty as the vacuum he was skimming the water with. I was reclining poolside – although I might have been mountainside for all the attention he was giving me – on one of Ginnie's smart teak loungers that she never sits on, but hurries out every day to rearrange and cover with chic cushions. God, I thought, lifting my white legs slightly under my sundress so they didn't look so fat, and flipping the pages of *Harper's*, I'd sit on them, but Ginnie just laughed and said it wasn't the same when it was your own. 'You wouldn't run a hotel and rush out to sit by the pool every day, would you?' Probably, I'd thought, if I wasn't busy, and the guests didn't mind; but that was no doubt where I was going wrong in life. I didn't have Ginnie's towering sense of responsibility, her capable nature, her organizational skills. Which was also probably why she'd ended up living in a vast house like this with a man like Richard, whilst I lived in a house like mine, with a man like Sebastian. Or not, as the case may be.

Sebastian and I had, as my mother would tell her bridge four with an over-bright smile and unamused eyes, a marvellously modern relationship. (Cue corners of the mouth lifting.) Modern in that we were no longer married in any physical sense, but, since we couldn't afford to get divorced, we cohabited, albeit separately and, to most people's minds, weirdly. He was in one of the converted outhouses in the grounds of what had once been his family home, and I was in the crumbling farmhouse itself, whose very dovecotes and dog kennels were listed, not to mention the small dark farm itself. 'A National Treasure,' Pevsner gushed obsequiously, going on to ask rhetorically: 'Is not this surely one of England's little gems?' Well, it depended how you liked your little gems. Personally I wouldn't mind them sparkling in my ears occasionally, not falling damply around them with dodgy plumbing and duck manure strewn about for good measure. And since Sebastian was regarded by many as a national treasure himself, I'd ended up being not just chatelaine of one, but nursemaid and guardian to both.

I sighed and rearranged my pasty limbs, watching the tanned Adonis's steady progress as he sucked the detritus from the bottom of Ginnie's already immaculate turquoise tiles. Everything about Ginnie's life was immaculate: her gutted and revamped manor house – the interior re-designed for contemporary living by one of the leading architects of the day, complete with loggia, orangery, domed hall and sky-lit kitchen – as well as her groomed acres beyond the ha-ha, her horses, her rare-breed cows, even, damn it, her children, whom I adored but who were a rare breed in themselves and couldn't have made a more marked contrast to my own. Hugo and Araminta: the former an ex-head of house at Harrow, all-round sportsman and captain of the first eleven, currently reading Classics at Cambridge, and Araminta, slim, white-blonde and flawless, who spent her weekends home from boarding school trotting off to Pony Club events and winning all manner of best-turned-out rosettes before practising her oboe in the evening. One shouldn't make comparisons, of course, they were bound to be odious, but neither seemed to be afflicted by any of the grunting, spotty, comatose-inducing hormones which mine had embraced with gusto.

Seeing Araminta in the distance popping over a log on Smartie, her pony, made me whip out my phone and text: 'Are you up?' Not quite daring to ring, of course. To be on the receiving end of an outraged: 'Whhaaaa—?' Or, 'It's the holidays, right?' I pocketed my phone quickly. I didn't mind so much when I was there, in fact I found I could get more done with them snoring quietly upstairs and not lolling round my kitchen suspiciously sniffing the milk, but, sheep that I was, I had a major panic attack when I was here, knowing Ginnie wouldn't countenance such sluttish behaviour. She'd be pulling the duvet off at nine and encouraging a hive of teenage industry by ten.

'All done!' the pool man said suddenly, jerking me back to reality. He withdrew his hose and turned to me with a smile.

Ah. Clearly he had been aware of my existence. Just hadn't thought it worth acknowledging.

'Excellent.' I swung my legs round and went to get athletically to my feet, but my sunglasses fell off my hot shiny nose in the process. I lunged for them chaotically.

'And you can tell her I've fixed the automatic pool cleaner too.' He gestured at the snake-like suction, roving menacingly round the bottom of the pool.

'Oh, good, because she did say it moved but didn't suck,' I said, scrambling for my specs. 'Or did she say it sucked but didn't move?'

'Sounds like the ideal woman,' he quipped.

I straightened up and blushed in surprise as he grinned. 'Yes, well, anyway,' I rushed on, flustered, 'thanks so much. I'll tell her.'

'What's she like to work for?' he mused as I gathered my magazine and pushed my feet into espadrilles to walk house-wards with him.

'Oh – I, er, no. I'm her sister.'

He looked taken aback. Then downright horrified. 'God. Sorry. It's just I've seen you here a lot and I thought . . .' He reddened, clearly regretting his lewd joke.

'Yes, I can see how you might think that,' I agreed breezily, not seeing at all but wanting to rescue us.

Actually, it was an easy mistake to make, I thought, as I rooted in my handbag on the terrace table for Ginnie's cheque and paid him (seventy quid! Blimey, perhaps I should clean pools), because Ginnie didn't just employ men here, but women too. Clever women, who, in order to raise children, had given up their careers but then wisely cultivated another, one that afforded them interesting and stimulating days – restoring pictures, binding books – but still allowed them to cradle a drink with the husband by the Aga when he returned from work, and one they could turn off in the holidays too, leaving them free for the children.

'Which is what *you* could do,' Ginnie would insist, 'if

you went back to painting properly and had an exhibition. Instead of flogging a dead horse for a woman you hate.'

It was loyal of her to suggest I could still paint properly and make a living from it, and I appreciated that. It was also a fair portrait of my relationship with Bonnie, my editor. It should have been the ideal job, illustrating children's books – part time and from home – and for a while it had been and I'd enjoyed it, even though it wasn't what I'd gone to art school for. But recently the bottom had dropped out of the Gloria the Glow Worm market and no one wanted to know how Horace the Hedge Pig buffed his prickles with an old chamois leather until they shone. It was all Debbie the drop-out at eight, with an alcoholic mother and a dope-fiend boyfriend.

'Children want books they can relate to,' Bonnie had told me gently when I'd taken my ideas for the Brenda Beetle range to her, all in dreamy pastels with rhyming couplets. 'And children don't really read poetry,' she'd said more dismissively.

'What about *The Cat in the Hat*?'

'That's a classic,' she'd said firmly, putting me in my place.

'They sing songs, don't they? Nursery rhymes?'

'That's different,' she'd said, looking at her watch. 'Now, how about something on bullying? Something contemporary?'

Bullying. I'd gone home depressed.

'Publishers want nice illustrations of syringes,' I'd tell Ginnie gloomily. 'Not Doris the Dormouse in her spriggy apron.'

'Oh, nonsense,' she'd snort. 'My children were brought up on that sort of thing!'

'Maybe I could draw Doris the *Depressed* Dormouse?' I mused. 'Coming home from work in a gloomy heap? Or Sid the Self-harming Snail rubbing his shell against sharp grasses?'

'You're deliberately missing the point. I'm talking about proper painting again, selling pictures. The trouble with you, Ella, is you don't want to compete. Don't want to join in. You're sulking.'

Ginnie knew which buttons to press. And kept her finger right there. And up to a point, she was right. It did all seem a bit vulgar, somehow. Showing off. Bad form. This shinning up the greasy art pole. You couldn't just leak pictures out quietly like you could a children's book, just happen across it in a shop and smile secretly. No. You had to hire a gallery with bright lights and say: Ta-da! This is me. Please buy! Allow me to apply my red stickers! But there was a myriad of other reasons Ginnie didn't know about which kept me from my oil palette, all of which ensured that I carried on drawing hedgehogs for no one – with the occasional adolescent drop-out thrown in for Bonnie – and supplemented my meagre income by running holiday lets from cottages in the garden. Well, outhouses, really.

But holiday lets didn't change their own sheets and right now I just wished Ginnie would hurry up. I went inside and gazed out of her kitchen window at the empty gravel sweep. I couldn't just walk out, though. Ginnie was on an important mercy dash to see the parents in Buckinghamshire, where Dad, by all accounts, had done a dizzy. She'd very much expect me to stay and wait patiently. Hear it all from the horse's mouth.

'A dizzy in what sense?' I'd asked, alarmed, when she'd

summoned me to oversee the crucial pool suctioning. 'Has he had a fall?'

'No, no, nothing like that. He's just . . . behaving very oddly, Mummy says.'

I could get no more out of her. But then she and my mother had always had a sort of coded communion, a secrecy I couldn't penetrate. It could mean Dad had refused to take the rubbish out, or drawn the line at yet another church choir practice and taken up refuge in the shed, and who could blame him? My mother's sharp tongue and exacting standards were not for the faint-hearted. In another age she'd have run her own bank or company. Instead, she'd been the ultimate corporate wife and pushed. And Dad had got there, to the top of his stock-broking tree in the City, where he'd been an amiable figurehead – liked enormously, but perhaps not that respected – in the affable-buffoon mould. These days, of course, he wouldn't have survived. Now he'd retired, though, he thought he'd like to enjoy himself, which didn't necessarily mean shooting and playing bridge.

'Quite right, Dad,' I'd agreed, surprised when he'd voiced this to me recently. My father liked both of these things. 'What does it mean?'

'I'm not sure,' he'd said thoughtfully.

And then a few weeks later, Mum had rung, in something of a state for her, saying Ginnie had better come quickly, and since Linda, Ginnie's daily, was having a day off, here I was, but now I really had to go. It wasn't just the sheets in the cottages, it was that Ludo had said he'd pop into my studio, and I dropped everything for Ludo. A year after I'd jumped impulsively into his car our relationship had tiptoed quietly on, to the extent that I'd begun to wonder if this gentle, wry man was the one I should have married at nineteen, instead of Sebastian. Sadly, though, Ludo was already married: to Ginnie's best friend, Eliza. So no, I hadn't slept with him. Hadn't even kissed him. And never would, should the situation remain the same, which it very much looked like doing.

Eliza, once an attractive blonde, was now a rather cross-looking one – apparently because she'd married an accountant who'd chucked it in for a much less lucrative soil-tilling career – and known locally as the Ice Maiden. She'd rarely un-frost for a dinner party let alone for her husband, who she found as frustrating as everyone else found charming and delightful. So Ludo was left to decorate the gardens of the local gentry – now that the recession had deepened, his spade got even more use – and I was sure many a housewife panted for him as he leaned on his fork in his faded chambray shirt that matched his blue eyes, advising them, in his mellifluous voice, to go for bigger beds, but he claimed not. And, even if they did, he loved his two girls too much to do anything about it, except stroll around the sunken garden with me now and again, wondering idly whether, if we were to lie in the shade of the pear tree together, it would still look like a working relationship.

I texted him now, telling him not to bother to come over, that I was held up. Asked where he was.

He texted back:

I'm Puffy Trumpington's bitch today. Shame. I wanted to show you my etching. x

I smiled and pocketed my phone. He didn't really want to show me an etching; that was just his excuse for coming to see me. If he was feeling bold he'd bound up the stairs to my attic, botanical print in hand and we'd gaze feverishly at one another over it. Eyes locked in excitement we'd pretend to discuss framing options.

'What exactly are the mounting possibilities?' Ludo would murmur and I'd dissolve into giggles, then go through the motions of showing him cardboard mounts.

Later, over a cup of tea, he'd hold my hand across my drawing board and we'd idly spin dreams of one day being together: one day being when Eliza had finally succumbed to the charms of her tennis coach – Ludo encouraged tennis coaching even though they couldn't afford it – or perhaps her personal trainer.

'We'll sail off to sea, somewhere hot.'

'Oh, I don't do water, Ludo.'

'Really? Icky-poo?'

'Almost immediately. I was once carsick, airsick and boatsick all on the same trip,' I told him, almost proudly. 'They ran out of sick bags on the boat.'

'What an extraordinarily seductive picture you paint. I'm so glad you never try to be mysterious. Does anything happen on a train?'

'Not a thing.'

'Great. I'll see you there, then.'

He ducked as I threw my pencil at him.

All this, of course, however innocent, was nevertheless reprehensible, and kept firmly from the outside world, and in particular from Ginnie, who, although desperate to find me a man, might not be that desperate.

'If you could just kick your ex-husband out it would be a start,' she'd snap. And I'd agree that it would, although where Sebastian would go worried me. How would he manage? He could barely tie his own shoelaces.

'Anywhere!' she'd shriek. 'Upper Ramsbottom, for all I care, but you *own* that house now, Ella, you bought him out. Richard saw to that. How he has the gall to stay there I don't know!'

She knew that by invoking Richard, I'd feel indebted to her, which, in a way, I was.

'Because it's his home, I suppose,' I'd say, nibbling the skin round my thumbnail. 'Not just our home, but the one he grew up in. Doesn't seem quite right to ask him to leave.'

'But you'll never forge a relationship while he's there, don't you see? And is that what you want? To end up alone?'

I'm not alone, I'd think: I've still got Sebastian. And, even more privately, I'd think: I've got Ludo.

Neither of these would have counted in my sister's book, of course, even had I voiced them. A cantankerous estranged husband who roared and spluttered his way out of bed at midday to stumble downstairs, horribly hungover, to his studio, where he painted angrily before destroying the canvas, and a celibate relationship with a married man? Oh, no. Having a man meant marriage, or at least cohabiting, even if it was in a cold marriage bed like the one I was sure my parents had shared for years.

At that moment I heard tyres on the gravel outside. Ginnie's green Range Rover shot by the window then disappeared down the side of the house to park. A car door slammed, then moments later, the back door too. Out of habit, I instantly looked busy, washing up the plate I'd had toast on earlier, refolding a tea towel on the Aga rail. The two dogs, classy, well-trained Labradors, got to their feet politely, not rushing and crashing into her legs yelping loudly, as mine would have done, but wagging courteously, waiting for her to shed her coat in the boot room, then come in and dump her handbag on the island, looking – even for Ginnie – harassed.

'Nightmare,' she hissed, eyes flashing manically at me as she kicked off her shoes. 'Complete and utter nightmare.' She strode across the room to sink down in the sofa by the French windows, arms and legs splayed out like a starfish for emphasis. Ginnie never underplayed anything. She was also a countrywoman through and through and didn't pander to make-up during the day or anything poncy like that. She wore county-fair fashion, the well-bred sort you found at Badminton Horse Trials or the CLA Game Fair: jeans, Joules polo shirts in pink or blue – collar up – that was her uniform, and, at night, a sparkly Indian coat thrown over velvet trousers. Her short, mousy-brown hair stood vertically on end having probably not seen a hairbrush this morning, her unpainted mouth hung open.

'What?' I said impatiently, knowing her hyperbole of old. Most things were a complete and utter hair-tearing nightmare, from the sheep having too many lambs to suckle, or the cows – which she'd been known to milk herself *in extremis* – having mastitis, or the piano tuner not turning up. All were disappointing but not the stuff of Hades.

'Daddy, OK, has totally and utterly lost it,' she informed me, her eyes huge and fixed.

'In what way?' I said defensively, instinctively on his side.

'He's taken up with another woman. A floozy.'

I stared at her. She looked back at me hard, unblinking.

'Oh, don't be ridiculous!' I said at length, when I'd finally found my voice. 'He can't have done!'

Nevertheless I gripped the tea towel I was holding, realizing suddenly that Ginnie couldn't talk she was so distressed: she was swallowing hard. My heart clenched with fear.

'It's true,' she told me eventually, in a much smaller voice. 'Or at least, he hasn't gone off with her yet, but he's parading around with her, for God's sake, for all the world to see. Lunch at the Rose and Crown, dinner at the King's Head, dog walks in the woods, and then he goes back to Mummy as if nothing has happened! And when she complains, he says mildly: I'm just having a nice time, Sylvia. Enjoying myself. Enjoying my retirement.'

'Oh!' My hand shot to my mouth in shock. Ginnie nodded, mute.

I groped my way round the kitchen to perch beside her. 'But . . . but that's so un*like* Dad. So . . . strange. He's so straight.'

She nodded silently again, this time down at the floor. Unable to utter. I stared at the same terracotta tile she was gazing at, trying to take it in.

'Who is this woman?'

'A dog therapist, by all accounts,' she snorted, briefly regaining some of her equilibrium, injecting the words with venom. 'Can you believe it? Some ghastly phoney who runs counselling sessions for recalcitrant dogs. Well, you know what Buster's like. Daddy spoils him rotten. So he took him along to see her. The mother of that ghastly little thing Hugo's seeing recommended her, apparently.' Her eye twitched compulsively at this, the only chink in her armour.

Hugo, otherwise known to my children as Perfect Cousin, had recently rather daringly broken out of his mould to conduct his first serious relationship with a girl he'd met whilst working at the pub near my parents. A girl whom Ginnie – smile tight – had hitherto described as not *necessarily* being out of the same drawer, having not gone to the right schools, but a sweet little thing nonetheless, even if the picture Araminta had shown her on Facebook did look a little over-pierced, the hair a strange bottled colour. Now, it seems, she was a ghastly little thing. The gloves were surely off. I tried to get my head round this.

'So . . . this girl's mother . . .'

'A mad woman called Jennie, with six dogs, for heaven's sake. Who has six dogs!' she spat.

'Well –'

'She suggested Daddy take Buster along, because it had done wonders for one of hers, the mother of this pack of wolfhounds. And Daddy did, and they got on famously, and now look!'

'What's her name?' I asked, wondering what on earth she could be like. A dog therapist.

'No idea. Mummy just calls her the Dog Woman.' She shuddered. '*So* naff,' she said heatedly. 'So *very* suburban. Wouldn't happen in Gloucestershire.'

I thought of Ludo holding my hand over my chipped Asiatic Pheasant teapot, my eyes, too. She'd be shocked to hear it went on whether the heir to the throne lived around the corner or not.

'But this woman and Dad, they're not . . . you know . . . lovers?' I could barely say it.

'No, no,' she said instantly. 'At least, Mummy says not.' She flinched. 'Can you imagine such a thing?'

'No,' I said quickly.

'They haven't had the chance. Well, what Mummy

means is, he hasn't spent the night away. Just wining and dining brazenly around the village. Poor Mummy.'

Yes, poor Mum. For all that my mother and I didn't quite see eye to eye, I could see this was a horrendous humiliation. To be queen bee of the community, matriarch of all she surveyed. To run the church rota, be head of the parish council, ex-JP, wife of an ex-high sheriff. To be Sylvia Jardine, married to Angus, erstwhile director of a big City firm, who assessed people and intoned quietly of those who didn't match up: 'Not boardroom material, darling.' To be so publicly shamed. It would be a crushing blow and I feared for her.

Ginnie and I sat shocked and silent on her mossy-green sofa. A dog hopped up beside us, sensing distress. Ginnie absently stroked the Lab's dark head.

'Anyway, she's on her way now,' she said eventually, and with a massive sniff. She fished up her sleeve for a tissue, blinking hard.

'She's coming here? To stay? Oh, good. That's good.'

'No, no, not to stay. She's leaving him. She's taken the dog, too. Says she's not staying there to be humiliated, and she's certainly not leaving Buster behind to be Daddy's Big Excuse. Says he'll have to find something else to hide behind if he wants to see the Dog Woman again.'

'Oh! Quite punchy. So she's coming here?'

'Good God, no. Richard would never sanction that. You know what he's like. Anyway, Linda and Mike are in the cottage, and we haven't got any other suitable accommodation.'

I stared. The dog slid off the sofa and went to whine at the back door, ears flattened, sensing trouble now.

'No, we thought she could come to you, Ella. After all, you've got your holiday lets.'

'Two!' I yelped. 'I've got two holiday lets!'

'Exactly, because the other ones are occupied by half of your ex-husband's family. They're the ones taking up all the room, Sebastian and that barking aunt of his, Ottoline. It's only right you have some of your own family too, don't you think? On your patch? Oh, do stop whining!' This to the dogs, who were both whimpering at the door now, looking stricken. She got up to let them out and they disappeared, sharpish. She turned back to me. 'She's got to go *some*where, Ella.' She crossed the room to straighten a tea towel on the Aga. 'And, anyway, I don't suppose it will be for ever.'

Chapter Two

I realized I was spluttering. Dribbling, even. At length I found my voice. 'But, Ginnie – Ginnie – no. Just, NO! I mean, how on earth –' splutter splutter.

'It's simple.' Calmly. 'That outhouse next to Sebastian's, the one before you get to Ottoline's. She can have that one.'

'But I've got a family coming into that next week, the Watsons. They're taking it for three weeks. It's my busiest time!'

'Well, she'll pay, Ella. She doesn't want charity. We've already talked about it. She knows you depend on your rent, and Lord knows you don't get any from Sebastian, so she'll pay the going rate. Whatever the Watsons were paying.'

They'd already talked about it. Already discussed the logistics, about how my mother would live with *me*, without even consulting *me*.

'You might have bloody asked!' I snorted.

'I am,' she said evenly. 'I'm asking you now.'

'Telling me, more like!'

'Well, if you're not happy, Ella, I'll ring Mummy and tell her it's no go. It's not a problem.'

'Why can't you have her?' I squeaked, knowing that of course it was a problem. That we couldn't possibly do that.

'I told you,' she said patiently. 'She needs to be independent, as if she's actually left him. Shock him into realizing how stupid he's being. It's no good if she's just in my spare room, is it? She's in there enough as it is.' I could see the logic in that. 'Just imagine,' she added. 'Richard would go mad.'

'I'll go mad!' I yelped.

'Yes, but at least we're family. Richard finds her – well, you know.'

Yes, I did. Snobbish, picky, demanding, nosy, critical – oh, *so* critical. I felt faint at the thought. Clutched the sofa arm. Yet, at the same time, she could be kind. And, occasionally, funny. When that mask softened. And it would be so crushed right now. So . . . buckled.

'What will I tell the Watsons?'

'Leave that to me,' Ginnie said magnanimously, sensing defeat. 'I'll call them. Tell them you're ill, and that the whole place is riddled with some ghastly infectious disease and I haven't even set foot in the place. And, anyway, Millie Saunders has holiday lets. I've already rung her and she's got a slot free next week.'

God, she really had thought it all out, hadn't she? Got very busy with her hands-free in the car. As usual, she and Mum, behind my back, had schemed. Outmanoeuvred me. Except . . . that wasn't really fair. They'd had to think of something. Side by side in the kitchen at the Old Rectory, perched on stools at the counter with the faded blue tiles. Mum, white-faced, a bit thinner than usual; Ginnie, forced to come up with something, some modus operandi. Whilst Dad – who'd normally be polishing the silver, perhaps, or doing some job Mum had found him, whistling through his teeth as he worked – was where? In the Rose and Crown with his bird? Yes, they'd had to hatch a plan. And I was the obvious choice. The one with the holiday accommodation. One of which was occupied by my husband, who had no money and therefore couldn't pay, one by Ottoline, who certainly *did* pay, too handsomely, and who'd have paid Sebastian's rent as well if I'd let her, and now one by my mother, who, much as I disliked the idea, would have to pay if I didn't want to go under. And it was nothing to her. My parents were well off. In fact, when the money had run out six years ago and I'd started the lets as a way of keeping our heads above water, Dad had wanted to buy them outright, to give me some capital, keep them in trust for Josh and Tabitha. But I hadn't let him. I'd felt so much like a failure anyway – failed marriage, failed career, with my shining sibling, so successful by comparison, on the other side of the hill – that I hadn't wanted him to bail me out. Rescue me. Had wanted to do it myself.

Somehow I'd borrowed the money from the bank – under the guise of a business plan which Richard had helped me to write – and Dad had applauded that. Richard had also got round the planners, who'd been a nightmare about the listed buildings, which were little more than shacks. And Dad had come over to help me paint them once they'd been converted. Had beamed and said, 'Well done, darling,' when we'd put the final touches to the skirting boards in the ones we called the Stables. One of which Mum would be in. What was he *thinking* of? What had possessed him?

'He's flattered, I suppose,' said Ginnie, breaking into my thoughts, reading them too. She turned and opened the Aga lid, then reached for the kettle and banged it on the hob. 'She's about fifteen years younger than him, apparently, and you know what they say: there's no fool like an

old fool. Makes him feel special or something, I imagine.'
She sighed wearily, raking both hands through already vertical hair.

'But he was never *like* that, Ginnie. Never unfaithful. I
mean, he certainly flirted, loved a party . . .' I remembered
him of old, working a room, roaming convivially, chatting
up the prettiest of Mum's friends, rocking back and forth
in his brogues and tweed jacket, a spotty hanky billowing
from his top pocket, Trumper's aftershave. 'But it was all
so light-hearted. Just a bit of fun.' I wanted to go on to say:
'He always loved Mum', but a bit of me felt that was a
bridge too far. It was more that he was an honourable man.

'Well, quite. And, actually, Mummy rather liked him
playing the rogue with her mates, they all loved it. Just a bit
of harmless flirting, she called it, but this is something
entirely different. She says it's as if he's got blinkers on.
He's very calm, very polite to her, but very definitely off
for lunch at Carluccio's in Bicester Village, for God's
sake – wild horses wouldn't have dragged him there
before – wearing a new cashmere blazer he bought in
Hackett, a pink shirt, a peacock-blue tie and a jaunty felt
hat. He looks . . . rather dapper, Mummy says.'

Yes, he would. My father was a good-looking man. And
Mum . . . well, had been beautiful in her day and was certainly still attractive, but women didn't age so well, did
they? It wasn't entirely fair.

'Right, I'll have her,' I said decisively, getting to my feet
and making for my handbag on the dresser. 'And I'll ring the
Watsons, too. I'd rather see to that myself, Ginnie. Just give
me Millie Saunders's number. I'll clinch it with her first.'

Ginnie moved very quickly, rushing gratefully to the
dresser for a pen and a pad of paper.

'Thanks, Ella. She'll be so grateful.' I declined to answer, knowing, as we both did, that this was unlikely. 'And I won't leave you stranded, I promise. She's spending tonight with us and then I'll come across with her tomorrow. Be constantly back and forth. Take her off to plays, National Trust gardens – that type of thing. I'd have the wretched dog for you, but you know what Richard's like about me having two dogs in the first place. He certainly won't sanction –'

'Yes,' I interrupted suddenly, swinging to face her. 'Have the wretched dog for me, Ginnie. Get round Richard. I've got three dogs myself and Maud's in season. And he's a randy little bugger.'

'Right,' she said after the briefest of pauses, knowing she was cornered. And that, very occasionally, I wasn't a complete pushover.

'He can sleep in the stables,' she said stoically. She raised her chin bravely. 'We'll muddle through somehow.'

She'll muddle through, I thought incredulously as I said goodbye and left. She had a small, elderly dog, already banished to the stables, whilst I had Dragon Lady living with me. As I drove down the drive I put my foot down peevishly, nearly colliding with horse-lunging man, who was coming up it.

I drove down the lanes which wove through a seeming maze of identical dry-stone walls enclosing small green fields, but which I could navigate with my eyes shut. Over the hill I went and then down into the valley the other side. Around the next bend, on a thin, straight ribbon of road, a rash of sleepy grey villages erupted one after another, with barely a church, let alone a pub for distinction. Finally, after a particularly fast stretch, the road narrowed and plunged again, taking me around slightly less picturesque fields which featured the odd abandoned caravan, burned-out car, or corrugated-iron shed. We were entering my own muddy valley: my own, less-manicured patch. As I turned at the end of a dead-end lane into my farmyard, the scale of the place struck me too, as it often did when I'd been to Ginnie's – or Torrington Towers as my children called it, that being her name by marriage. Tiny. And much more prosaic. Only at a stretch, on a sunny October day at about four o'clock in the afternoon, could it be called charming. I say four o'clock because by then the sun would be low enough to be blinding and one might not notice the crumbling walls or the patchy roof tiles, just a compact, low farmhouse with small, dark, mullioned windows, believed to date from the thirteenth century – oh, yes, ancient – surrounded by the ubiquitous dry-stone walls that gave onto open countryside beyond.

To one side of the not-quite-cobbled yard, at right angles to the house and behind a tangle of mulberry bushes, was the first and most curious of the stone outbuildings. Curious because circular, with a conical slate roof. This was known as the Dairy, which Sebastian and I, when we were still madly in love and had lots of money, had converted, rather well and under the eagle eye of English Heritage, to a one-up, two-down. It was here that Ottoline had created a beautiful and quirky home for herself. Beyond that were the Stables, which looked as they sounded: two converted loose boxes with hay barns, now bedrooms, one imaginatively called Number One, the other Number Two. To the east of them, and therefore opposite the farmhouse, was the Granary, a square, stone building with a pitched roof, raised on a series of triangular stones, which in the old days kept the foxes from the grain. Inside was an open space, which, since he only lived to paint, functioned purely as Sebastian's studio, although there was a sofa in the corner that he sometimes slept on if he didn't make it to the gallery upstairs, which – as much as there was a bed in it – served as his bedroom. These eclectic buildings, clinging together with bits of old mortar and flung randomly about what had once been a functioning farmyard, comprised a sort of commune, with the children and me living in the farmhouse, the largest, but only by comparison.

In the days of Veronica, my mother-in-law, the whole place had been cutesy and bohemian, and whilst not a working farm, very definitely a hobby one. She'd work tirelessly in the vegetable garden, elegant in long skirts and a floppy straw hat, and was a tower of strength to 'Dear Bob', her rich but hopeless husband. She was a tough act to follow. She'd be horrified at her vegetable garden now, I thought, as I came to a halt in the yard and spied it through a gap where the wall had tumbled down. I made a mental note to throw the overgrown courgettes onto the muck heap, which was probably not what Veronica had meant when she'd written in a recipe book: Twenty Things To Do With Courgettes.

I got out of the car exhausted. Exhausted because the old Volvo I drove overheated if it had to loiter in traffic and I'd have to sit for ages by the side of the road until it cooled down. This wasn't normally a problem in the Cotswolds, but today I'd come up behind a farmer driving his sheep down the middle of the lane and, if I didn't want to overheat, this involved a detour, and then road works, which had caused me to dive down a tiny track and out of my way again. On the point of swinging into the yard I'd spotted a creditor standing by his van staring speculatively up at the house, hands in pockets. Horrified I'd driven round the village until I was sure he'd gone. Wishing I had some money, in which case of *course* I'd give it to the Electricity Board, although I might buy a new car first, I'd finally made it home.

By now it was past one o'clock and the upstairs curtains were still drawn, although that didn't necessarily mean the inmates were asleep. If my children couldn't see, they simply turned on lights. Sure enough, as I shoulder-barged through the front door, a blaring television down the hall suggested a few vital signs. Stooping to collect the post from the mat which they'd have seen as they came down but, on the grounds that it wouldn't be for them, not collected, I simultaneously answered the telephone, which was being ignored on the same basis. Just an annoying noise. Rather different to the days of racing to beat the parents before they barked at one's friends, I thought, as I clocked an automated message telling me what to do if I was in debt, before slamming the receiver down.

As usual, the sitting room resembled an old people's home at Eastbourne. The residents were slumped at either end of a sofa, feet up on low stools, tartan rugs tucked over their knees. One poor soul had her rug right up to her chin, her pale face peeking out just enough to view the flickering screen. The curtains were shut; the air was fetid, stale and institutional. Plates and mugs from the night before, which the staff hadn't had a chance to get to this morning, festered happily, although the dogs had made a pretty thorough job of licking them clean. The dogs, in fact, were the only hint that this wasn't a geriatric establishment: both were on the sofa with the residents.

They leaped to greet me – the dogs, that is – jumping up my legs in delight, howling a welcome as I marched across the room, drawing the curtains ruthlessly. The children blinked in horror at this rude and unwelcome intrusion. Josh's hand went up to cover his eyes.

'Shit, Ella.'

'It's ten past one, for heaven's sake!' I swung round, hands on hips. 'Are you going to stay here all day?'

They regarded me with disgust, as one would a jailer.

'God. Why so stressy?' Josh shot me an incredulous look as he pulled his father's old felt hat right down over his eyes and sank deeper under his rug.

'Move, can't you?' asked my daughter, craning her head round my legs as I stood in front of the television.

'No, because it's coming off!' I said, rather boldly for me. I might usually have negotiated for the end of the programme. I lunged to press the button and plunged us into silence. The residents, too weak to get to their feet and protest, simply sank back in silence.

'She's been to see Ginnie,' Josh observed bitterly.

'Picking up tips,' said Tabitha, shutting her eyes. 'Getting a crash course in helicopter mothering.'

'She doesn't need tips; she's there already.'

By now I was getting very busy opening windows, wrestling with a rusty catch as I threw it wide, spotting a pile of bantam poo behind the sofa which I'd have to deal with later. 'I'll have you know, Araminta sets her alarm for eight o'clock in the school holidays,' I stormed, roving around the room picking up empty mugs, a lemonade can, a winding and still-damp towel employed to dry my daughter's hair, putting tops on an array of evil-smelling, putrid-coloured nail varnishes. 'She's been picked for the Areas and she gets up early to learn her dressage tests!' I swooped on a soggy, well-licked Smoothie carton under a chair.

'Don't say Areas like you know what you're talking about,' Tabitha said coldly. 'Like you're a horsy mother.' She was on her BlackBerry now, texting expertly. If only that lightning thumb action could spread to all her digits, be translated to the piano, the viola or something, I thought, watching it fly across the keys.

'No, but we don't need horses to have a hobby, do we?' I said in a chummy voice. 'Why don't you go for a bike ride or something?' Then, quickly: 'Or walk the dogs?'

'Dog-walking isn't a hobby,' said Tabitha. 'Unless you're a depressed, middle-aged housewife.'

But my son wasn't so easily deflected. 'A *bike* ride?' Josh had staggered to his feet on the sofa, felt hat on his head, rug wrapped round him like a Shakespearean cloak, and was regarding me with delight. 'A *bike* ride, Ella? This sister of yours in her ivory tower is not just misguided she's downright dangerous! Is that what cousin Hugo does? Goes for a *bike* ride? Dear God, where will it all end? Does he rub brass, perchance? Collect stamps?' He got down from the sofa and circled me in disbelief. 'And is that what you'd like me to do? Swap my Abyssinia for his Czech Republic, enquire eagerly after his German First Editions before getting on my bike and popping round to compare? That way weirdness lies, Ella, you suggestible old bag, you.'

'That will do, thank you, Joshua,' I snapped. 'Lift. LIFT!' This to Tabitha, who had her legs on my best and only cashmere jumper. I jerked it out.

'Give it a few more years and it'll be a hollow chest and a bedsit for me if I go down that path. No friends, of course, because no one else will share my interests, so dinner for one in the microwave, and then, before you know it, it'll be the long mac and the dirty magazines.' He was still circling me but I ignored him, swooping on another lemonade can. 'No girlfriends to speak of, just the almighty crush on the woman at the library where I work, The One Who Wheels The Book Trolley, with the moustache and the thighs that rub together in a nylon whisper . . .' He shut his eyes and swooned. 'And who I lust for at night, under the sheets, magazine at the ready –'

'Josh . . .' I warned

'But who sadly turns out to be shagging the chief librarian, um . . . Derek! Derek, my only friend – *or so I thought*!' His voice lowered to a sepulchral whisper and he clutched his rug tragically at the neck. 'Plunging me into even deeper despair, and through the basic desire for human touch, homosexuality –'

'Josh, I mean it, stop now!'

He stopped still and blinked. 'Well, golly, Ella, I'm just trying to point out to you where all this prolonging of childhood innocence gets you. Where all Ginnie's pony rides and cycling will lead. Although I think you're misinformed. Rumour has it the bike Hugo's riding has neither wheels nor peddles.'

His sister sniggered, never for one moment abandoning her texting.

'All right, that will do!' I said sharply, turning my attention to the sofa cushion where Josh had been sitting, plumping it viciously, removing crisps from down the side. 'Ginnie says she's a lovely girl, actually.'

'Ginnie hasn't met her,' Josh told me. 'So she's talking out of her arse, as usual.' He dripped out of the room still draped in his rug.

'Have you?' I asked, regretting it instantly.

He stopped abruptly. Hunched his shoulders in mock dismay and turned back. 'Oh, the inquis*ition*,' he groaned. '*Al*ways the prurient interest in the teenage sex life. Go on Facebook, Ella, if you must. Uncover our passwords, like Ginnie does, if you must live vicariously through your children. If you have no life of your own.' He shuddered in horror, ever the actor, and shuffled on.

I watched him go, a slight gleam to my eye. Had he turned, it might have betrayed the perverse pleasure I took in my son's bullying, which undoubtedly kept me on my toes. Happily it went unnoticed. Instead he stopped in the middle of the kitchen and spread his arms wide, the rug forming a perfect square from behind.

'Why is there never any food in this house? Why? No cereal? No peanut butter? No staples?'

'Peanut butter is not a staple and there's plenty of food,' I told him.

He opened the fridge door and drank apple juice straight from the carton, his head tipped back. Then he belched loudly, shook the carton, which was clearly empty, and replaced it. 'You're poisoning us with all this concentrate – you know that, don't you? It's full of sugar.'

'Sophie's mum won't have anything other than Tropicana

in the house,' Tabitha informed us, her eyes still on her BlackBerry. 'She says it's pure. Not like ours.'

'Well, eat a sodding apple!' I stormed. 'From the frigging tree outside!'

'Ooooh . . .' Josh staggered backwards. 'Temper.'

'And there's plenty of cereal in the cupboard,' I seethed. 'If you just look!'

I'd followed him in and started setting about the chaotic kitchen, throwing plates in the sink, feeding the dogs, answering the phone to yet another automated voice who wanted to know exactly *how* deeply in debt I was, trying in vain to shoo the cockerel out.

'Now, Ella, you know that's not true,' Josh said sternly. 'It's all stale.' He was riffling in the larder, ignoring packets he knew to be soft and inedible.

'Because *you* two don't shut the packets properly.'

'So . . . hang on.' He wrinkled his brow. 'In some warped war of attrition, you're not buying more? Is that it? Is this the Rich Tea Biscuit Crisis all over again? Bought in the knowledge that they were loathed and wouldn't be eaten, but gave the impression of a burgeoning larder? Of being a good mother?' His eyes widened.

I pushed past him, reached behind the flour tin and thrust a hidden packet of brand-new Coco Pops into his hands. 'There. But if you don't screw the packet down properly and close the flap –'

'Yeah, yeah,' he said amiably, giving my shoulders a quick squeeze as he passed.

At the tinkle of fresh cereal in a bowl, Tabitha was sparked into some sort of Pavlovian response. She came slowly in her dressing gown, still texting. Together they perched at the tiny island, and for a while, aside from the bantam cockerel crowing from the top of the dresser, all that could be heard was contented slurping as the sugar hit some spots. Tabitha, who got up relatively early – ten-ish as opposed to Josh's twelve-ish – had already had a good few hours of solid cathode-ray treatment before Josh came down, judging by her gormless expression, but if I tried to shoo her from the room at midday she'd say it wasn't fair, Josh was still watching, and if I tried to switch it off Josh would say *that* wasn't fair, he'd only just got up. They knew their rights and their quotas, my children, and argued them vociferously from positions of strength, like trades union officials. Tabitha stopped abruptly, mid-slurp.

'How old is this milk?'

'Today's, why?'

'It's not very cold.'

'That's because someone didn't get it off the step and put it in the fridge. I've only just picked it up,' I said pointedly, but they ignored me. They wouldn't want to eat anything out of date, even though they were quite happy to poison their systems with copious amounts of vodka and nicotine. Josh was gazing blankly down the garden.

'You want to plant some stuff out there,' he said suddenly, waving a laconic arm to where my depleted flower beds lay. 'Bulbs, or something.'

'Daffodils,' agreed Tabitha, following his gaze.

On perkier days I might have told them what I thought of them finding *me* jobs and how about *them* doing some digging – not to mention the seasonal difficulties of achieving daffodils in August – but I had other things on my mind.

'Listen, darlings –'

'Or those white things,' Josh offered.

'What white things?'

'I dunno. Snowdrops.'

I licked my lips, wondering where on earth I'd gone wrong, and ploughed on regardless. 'Um, listen, darlings, Granny's coming to stay.'

'Is she?' said Tabitha. 'Why?'

'Well, because she wants to. Just for a bit.'

'What, on her own?'

'Yes, just for a while. Needs a break, I think.'

'From what?'

'Well . . .'

'You mean, without Grandpa?'

'Yes. For a bit,' I said, wishing I'd thought this through before I'd embarked on it. They ate on, digesting this news in silence. I busied myself at the sink, my back to them.

'Where's she going to sleep?' my daughter enquired. The fourth bedroom in our house was used as my studio.

'In the Stables, I thought. Number One.'

'I thought you had a family going in there?' I could feel Josh's eyes on my back.

'Yes – I did, but that's OK. I'll cancel them. It'll be all right. Millie Saunders has got room. They'll be fine.'

'You mean, you won't get the rent?'

'Well, no, I will, because . . .'

'What, Granny will pay?' This did shock them. I turned. Spoons were lowered.

'Has she left Grandpa?' asked Tabitha, in a smaller voice.

'No. Well, at least . . .'

'Come on, Ella,' Josh said. 'What's going on?'

I took a deep breath. 'Well, the thing is . . . Well, I suppose, yes, in a way. You see, the thing is, Grandpa – well, Grandpa has met someone.'

They blinked. Stared at me.

'Who?' asked Josh.

'I'm not sure yet. At least, I only know that she's a dog therapist, or something. But it's just a flirtation, you know. He hasn't left Granny, or anything. They've just had lunch together. That's all. Dinner. But Granny feels – well, a bit left out.'

'I'm not surprised!' Tabitha's eyes widened.

'And wants to come here for a bit.'

They regarded me in silence. Then ate on.

At length, Josh spoke. 'Fuck me. The old dog.'

'No – no, he's not an old dog,' I said quickly. 'Because I told you, it's not like that. Just – you know, the odd drink at the pub. Friends, that's all.' I felt a bit breathless suddenly.

Tabitha got up and took her empty bowl to the side. She remembered something else too, something fuzzy and indistinct, so she picked it up and moved it to the dishwasher. I watched her open the dishwasher, which was full of clean, not-yet-emptied china. This perplexed her. The thought processes which had instructed her to do something must surely be wrong, because she couldn't do that. Not all that china: mugs, plates, knives and forks. She put the bowl in the sink as a perfect compromise.

'When's she coming?' Josh asked.

'Tomorrow, I think.' Bending down I pulled a stack of clean sheets from the tumble dryer, noticing Ottoline had kindly done a load of ironing and left it on the side. I straightened up and handed the top section of pressed linen to Josh as he made to go out of the back door and across the yard. I wasn't keen on him smoking in the house.

'Take those to Dad, would you?' I handed him the pile.

'He won't be up yet.'

'I know, just leave them inside the door.'

'He won't change them.'

'I know, just leave them, Josh, OK?'

Leave me with the pretence that I might wash my husband's sheets, but I don't actually change them for him, even if that's not the reality, hm? A moment of silent communion took place between mother and son, before Josh accepted the sheets and traipsed out, leaving the door wide open.

The dogs and the cockerel accompanied him. I watched his tall, bony figure, feet bare, hat perched on his head, tartan draped, like some modern-day Hamlet. Tabitha went back to the sitting room to her laptop, snuggling down under her rug. As I went to put more sheets in the washing machine, I noticed the answering machine was flashing. I played the message. Ginnie's voice filled the airwaves, loud and breathless.

'Hi, Ella! Just to say, you are *such* a star to have Mummy, and also to say that I obviously haven't told the children. All I've said is that Granny's been feeling a bit down in the dumps and we thought we'd treat her to a few days away. A few stately homes and a spot of theatre, which isn't Daddy's cup of tea. Presumably you've done the same with yours? See you soon – toodle-oo!'

I sighed as I pressed the erase button. When I looked up, Sebastian was coming down the steps of the Granary, scratching his head like a bear emerging from its lair. Tall, thin – too thin, old jeans frayed at the bottom, a crumpled checked shirt, feet bare, blinking in the daylight. Craggy and unshaven, his eyes hooded, his face lined. He was no longer handsome, although perhaps just a hint in the right light. Where once he would have held a paintbrush, now he held a wine glass, brimming with something red and strong, the first, and by no means last, of the day. Josh picked his way gingerly across the cobbles towards him with the sheets and they exchanged a few gnomic words. I saw Sebastian grunt. If he saw me at the window he didn't acknowledge me, but turned and followed Josh back inside. They'd smoke for a bit, the two of them, at either end of the sofa, before beginning the business of the day: my son finding another screen – probably in the empty holiday let where no one would bother him – and my husband, an easel with a blank canvas. Around this he'd circle and prowl all day, cursing it with furious, flashing eyes, eyes that had once been so gentle. He'd taunt it, too, with his glass, which emptied and filled continuously, ever in a state of flux, whilst the whiteness of the canvas remained the same.

Chapter Three

I first met Sebastian when I was nineteen. I'd dropped out of St Martin's art school on the basis that all I wanted to do was draw, and they wanted me to work with mixed media – express myself in stones and seaweed and old Coca-Cola cans – and looked startled if I so much as suggested something as bourgeois and predictable as sketching from life with a pencil. Having withdrawn, I stayed in my tiny apartment and drew the pigeons on the window ledge instead; chimney pots, too, with vast restless skies rushing behind them, which seemed to capture my mood. My parents, who'd considered art school dropping out in itself, and nothing like as useful as the Montessori course Ginnie had done, were unaware I didn't attend classes, so I had a happy, if fairly solitary, time in my studio flat. It belonged to my father's Aunt Hilda, who lived mostly in Bath, and was in a genteel but dreary mansion block off Cadogan Square. I was on the third floor and below me was a dentist called Mr Sharp, which amused me, and on the floor above, an elderly Russian lady with an enormous white Pyrenean Mountain Dog. Above her was a rather up-and-coming artist called Sebastian Montclair, who was dark and dashing and handsome and had a lot of noisy parties. I'd passed him on the stairs once or twice and he'd flash me a smile, but no more than that: he always seemed in a hurry, leaping to mount the remaining flights, taking the stairs boyishly two at a time.

To make ends meet I washed brushes for quite a famous portrait painter called Magnus Simpkins, who was a terrible old letch and who, if I wasn't careful, chased me round tables. Somehow Sebastian discovered I worked for him and as well as flashing me the smile, once said: 'Still running round after old Magnus?' to which I'd prosaically answered: 'Yes.' It was our only exchange, but I treasured it, wishing I'd had the presence of mind to say: 'No, actually, he's running round after me.' Occasionally I'd pass a beautiful, sleepy-eyed blonde, tripping her way down from the top floor in kitten heels, and she'd give me a contented, bed-sated smile, wrapped in a huge fur.

Mrs Elgar, the Russian lady, was devoted to her Pyrenean Mountain Dog, Putchkin, and when she went back to Russia that summer for three weeks, she asked me to look after him for her. Putchkin was old and massive and she must have seen me hesitate.

'Oh, don't worry, *Liebling*, I know he is old, and if he dies I hold you not in the least responsible. We all go sometime, you know, and he has had a good life.'

She was a dear old thing and she'd also offered to pay, which clinched the deal, and so Putchkin came down a flight of stairs to live with me. Perhaps it was the shock of moving, or missing his mistress, but at any rate, sure enough, on the fourth morning I awoke to find him dead and stiff in his basket. Horrified, but relieved Mrs Elgar had voiced the possibility, I rang the vet, from a card she'd given me, and told them what had happened. The receptionist said it would cost a shocking twenty pounds for someone to pick him up and have him cremated, but a mere quarter of that if I brought him in myself.

I gazed at the motionless mound of white hair in the

corner. He was huge, but I didn't have twenty pounds: I barely had five.

'I'll bring him in,' I told her.

Mrs Elgar, I knew, had an enormous ancient leather suitcase on top of her wardrobe, because she'd once shown me her old evening gowns in her bedroom: sparkling, chiffon creations which she'd held against herself and twirled about with, telling me dreamily of balls in St Petersburg. I bounded upstairs with her key, found it, emptied it, brought it back down, and, with a certain amount of difficulty – and snivelling, I was fond of Putchkin – got him inside. I had to sit on the case to shut it, and then heaved it down the three flights of stairs – no lift – then down the front steps and out into the street. It wasn't far to the tube so I set off, wishing the case had wheels – it was unbelievably heavy – when Sebastian came up beside me.

'Going somewhere?' he asked in surprise, looking down at the case.

'Oh, er, no, not really,' I mumbled, marching on, but of course not really marching. It was such an effort and took two hands.

'Here, let me,' he said, taking the case from me.

'No, no –'

'Yes, yes.' He laughed. 'I insist. God, it's heavy. Where are you headed?'

'Victoria,' I muttered. 'But, honestly, don't worry. I can manage.'

'Oh, well, I'm going to Victoria, too. There's a gallery in Ebury Street I need to have a look at. I'll help you.' And he fell in beside me with his long, easy stride, one hand carrying my case, the other impatiently brushing his longish dark hair out of his eyes. He flashed me another of those devilish smiles.

'Christ, what have you got in here? It weighs a ton.'

My mouth was devoid of saliva and my tongue seemed much too big for my mouth all of a sudden. We passed an antiquarian bookshop.

'Old books,' I told him quickly. 'My – uncle – is a . . . collector. A dealer.'

'Oh, right. In Victoria?'

'That's it.'

He frowned, then his face cleared. 'Oh, yes, it's at the far end of Ebury Street, isn't it? Marlborough Books? It's practically opposite the gallery.'

'No, no, that's not it,' I said, feeling rather hot. 'He – my uncle – works from home.' No. No good. He'd want to find the house. 'From his flat. In a block. A mansion block, with a lift. So that's good,' I finished lamely.

'Oh. Right. Well, at least I can get you to the door.'

And so he did: taking my case on the tube, heading for my fictitious uncle in his book-lined study – kindly and grey, no doubt, with bifocals and elbow patches on his cardigan – chatting away companionably the while, asking me about art school. He wanted to know why I'd left, telling me he'd been to St Martin's and loved it, and that maybe I should persevere because the second year was better; you got to choose what you wanted to do. Mind you, he said, that was a good ten years ago. Twenty-nine, I calculated quickly in my head. I managed to ask what he was doing now, and he told me landscapes, oh, and some seascapes. And skies. He just loved windy skies. 'So do I,' I said, glancing up in delight. And so we travelled on, rattling away on the underground: me, Sebastian, and a dead dog.

As we got off the tube he told me about an exhibition he was having, saying he was apprehensive. It was the first time he'd had a one-man show and not collaborated, as it were, and he felt the spotlight and the pressure rather keenly: an empty gallery, surrounded by one's work, waiting for the first person – the first critic – to arrive. I agreed that would be a nerve-wracking moment; but not as nerve-wracking as the one I was experiencing now as we reached the top of Victoria station steps, emerging into the sunlight, and he asked me which way the antiquarian book dealer lived.

'He . . . lives that way,' I said, swinging round to point in the opposite direction to Ebury Street, where I knew the gallery to be. 'But, honestly, I can manage from here, I –'

It was no good. He was off.

We walked along, my eyes darting about wildly in search of large mansion blocks, which were thinner on the ground than around Cadogan Square, but, eventually, I spotted one in the distance. Telling him firmly that Uncle Michael was a bit of a recluse and didn't like strangers, and that anyway it had a lift, and was now literally moments away, I went to take the case from him. At that moment he let it go, which resulted in both of us dropping it. Naturally, the inevitable happened.

The case was old, with weak fastenings, and as it thudded on the ground it simultaneously sprang open. An awful lot of hairy white dog spilled forth onto the pavement.

Sebastian stared in horror. I did, too. Putchkin was vast.

'Don't tell me,' he said at last, as I stood by, mute and helpless. 'You're actually an Arctic explorer and you're taking a polar bear cub to the zoo?'

'No,' I said wretchedly. 'It's Mrs Elgar's Pyrenean Mountain Dog. I was too embarrassed to tell you. I'm taking it to the vet.'

His eyes widened. A few people in the street were turning to stare as they passed.

He lowered his voice. 'Well, I hate to tell you, but I think going to the vet is optimistic, now. Had you thought of walking him there on a lead?'

'Oh – no! I didn't put him in alive,' I explained, then snorted suddenly, as the idea of squeezing a live Putchkin into a suitcase threatened to overtake me. I had to lean against a wall to regain some composure. 'I knew he was dead,' I told him between unattractive wheezes, 'but it was cheaper. I mean, than having him collected.'

When my mirth had subsided, I was surprised to find him still there, regarding me with some amusement.

'No Uncle Michael, then. Do you often make up stories like that?' he asked, his eyes narrowed speculatively.

'All the time,' I admitted, wiping my eyes. It was a relief to tell the truth. 'Literally, all the time. I'm frightfully creative.' I began bundling Putchkin back into the case.

After that he invited me upstairs quite a lot. I'd walk around his canvas-filled studio in silent wonder, a drink in hand, marvelling at his portraits, his landscapes – skyscapes mostly, as he'd said – vast swathes of grey and white, the sort of thing I longed to do but wouldn't have the scale of personality to attempt, on huge great boards. Many were unfinished, but just a few were perfect. Absolutely perfect.

'You're a genius,' I said, without thinking, when I was crouched in a corner, going through a stack of canvases, and coming across one of a cornfield, so evocative and billowing and powerful it had made me say it.

He'd laughed, pausing a moment at his easel, paintbrush in hand.

'Hardly. And that was done years ago. I was really charged at the time. It helps, of course.'

'Of course.' I stared at the painting. 'Who was she?'

He looked at me thoughtfully. 'Someone at art school. Kohl-blackened eyes, long dark hair, very slim figure. Very slim personality, as it turned out, but at the time I thought she was everything I wanted.' He jerked his head at the painting. 'As you can see.'

I could. The galloping clouds, the rush of wind through the corn, everything triumphant and in full flight.

'Celeste is very slim, too,' I observed. Celeste was the sleepy-eyed blonde I used to pass on the stairs, and whom I still passed, but who these days looked a bit more tear-stained than bed-stained.

'Don't fish,' he said, without taking his eyes off his picture.

'I'm not, I'm just saying –'

'You're just saying I don't go for much flesh on the bones and the fact that you have a little more than, say, the girl who inspired the cornfield, or Celeste, must surely provoke me to say – oh, but you're lovely as you are – or some such twaddle.'

I flushed darkly. 'Absolutely not. No way was I looking for a compliment!'

I straightened up and, feeling more than a little foolish, drained my drink and stalked back down to my own floor. I thought I heard him laugh as I went.

Some weeks later he offered me an easel in the corner

of his studio. It was an immense area, taking up the whole of the top floor, with floor-to-ceiling windows. He said that the solitude was what he disliked most about his profession; that up until recently a friend had shared the space; that, years ago, painters had always worked together, as a movement, and that's what he'd loved about his time at art school, the group classes, the discussion. He said that, in his experience, painters worked better like that. He happened to have one of the best north lights in London and I had an extremely dingy corner of my aunt's kitchen. Why wouldn't I want to work up there? Of course I would. But I can't tell you how quickly I hustled my palette, my paints, and my easel upstairs.

Funnily enough, Sebastian was right. It became a mutually beneficial arrangement, and as the weeks went by I started producing paintings the like of which I'd never thought myself capable, digging deep and somehow coming up with a reciprocity of scale to suit my grand surroundings and my juxtaposition to this great talent beside me – a modern master, in my view. Sebastian, meanwhile, created what he was kind enough to tell me later were the best paintings of his career. In our respective corners we painted in companionable silence, sometimes pausing for a cigarette and a chat, but otherwise working all day and some of the night. The rest of the night, when I'd disappeared, I knew was reserved for Sebastian gently winding down what remained of his relationship with Celeste.

'She wants to get married,' he'd said gloomily one morning as he squirted cobalt blue onto his palette, his eyes heavy with fatigue.

'Ah,' I said sympathetically, not knowing what else to

say. I'd want to get married to someone like Sebastian. Who wouldn't?

'She's nearly thirty and we've been together for four years. So, you know.' He shrugged.

I felt desperately grown-up, being treated thus, as if I were an agony aunt. Behind my easel I cocked my head to one side. 'That'll be the biological clock,' I said sagely – not such a hackneyed expression as it is now; indeed in those days rather an edgy one.

He shot me a look. 'Everyone thinks it's just women who want babies,' he said bitterly, which surprised me, because everybody did.

'Right, well, you know how she feels, then,' I said lightly, but not feeling light. I picked up my brush.

'Of course. But it's got to be right, hasn't it? I just wish she wasn't so . . .'

'What?'

'Desperate.'

Desperate. Didn't he know love had made her desperate? That she didn't know what to do with herself she was so consumed with wanting him, and wanting to have his babies, and that once he'd said yes she'd go back to being the bubbly, fun, joyous Celeste of old? Didn't he know that? Why were men so stupid? I didn't say that, though; wasn't intensely loyal and supportive of Celeste, because I had my own agenda. Again, I'm not really a girl who has an agenda, but love had done that to me, too. Made me calculating, just as it had made Celeste desperate.

I became a person who was extremely unavailable, even unreliable: anything, in my immature way, that I felt was the opposite of Celeste. Thus, when latterly I'd gone up every morning early, chatted happily over a cup of coffee as we cleaned our brushes before painting, laughed at stupid jokes, and maybe groaned in despair at yesterday's offering facing us on the easels, now I took to coming in late, so that Sebastian was already in full flow. The reality was that he didn't actually notice. So I took to refusing supper invitations at the bistro down the road, where we sometimes ate, under the mistaken impression that it would somehow make him fall in love with me.

Of course it didn't: he treated me as the nineteen-year-old art student I was, asking me if I was out with a Nigel, or one of my Sloaney friends. By this time he'd met Ginnie, who was going through a big Hermès scarf and Laura Ashley stage, coming into the studio with Richard, whom she'd now married and who was in the army. Sebastian couldn't quite believe Richard was real, clicking around in shiny brogues, a brass-buttoned blazer, regimental tie, hands behind his back. There had been a Nigel – a Henry, in fact – an on–off boyfriend from school, whom I'd ditched the moment I'd met Sebastian, but who I now reinvented, agreeing he was taking me out that night, so that it became a running joke.

'Where's Henry taking you, then?' Sebastian would ask as I packed up early, leaving him still painting, and as Celeste would appear, looking rather rattled not to find him alone. 'Somewhere nice?'

'Oh, yes, the Ritz or somewhere, I expect,' I once said naively and he'd roared, knowing no one ever took anyone anywhere like that unless they were over forty or could charge it to an expense account. Certainly not a couple of nineteen-year-old babies. But I didn't know why he was laughing and scurried away as Celeste looked at me suspiciously. As I shut the door I heard her say: 'Why do you let her work with you?'

I didn't hear his response as I crept down to my flat. Then I didn't like to have the television on in case he heard it and knew I wasn't at the Ritz at all, which, of course, he knew already.

On the night of Sebastian's one-man show in Ebury Street, I thought I'd die of pride. The gallery was lit up like a stage set in the gloomy October night and acted as a beacon in the fog: taxis drew up outside as it hummed with people spilling out onto the pavement, cameras flashed, journalists took notes. There, in the midst of the scrum, was Sebastian: tall and impossibly handsome, his narrow, sensitive face earnest as he talked to the press, his dark hair curling on a navy-blue velvet collar. Celeste hung on his arm in a slinky, gold lamé dress. All over the walls were the fabulous sweeps of colour and drama, the abstracts, the still lifes, the seascapes that documented his life, raw and exposed for everyone to see. They were more breathtaking, as one journalist in *The Times* put it the next morning, and more brilliant and exciting, than anything this country's art world had seen for a long time.

Richard was in Northern Ireland at the time, and not wanting to be alone amongst all Sebastian's arty friends, I'd persuaded Ginnie to get a babysitter and come with me – but I'd made her ditch her Hermès scarf at the door. Even she had been bowled over by the scale of his talent.

'He's good, Ella,' she'd said in grudging wonder, gazing at a rolling vista of hills in purples and mauves, clutching her handbag to her chest almost in self-defence. 'I almost feel I'm in that glen with him, staring up.'

'I know,' I'd said, trying not to purr. He wasn't mine, after all. Not even the tiniest bit.

Later, though, when Ginnie had gone, and all the press too, when there were only a handful of us, in fact, left in the gallery, he'd come across to me, quietly, just as I was draining my glass and thinking I couldn't decently, or even indecently, stay any longer, and asked if I'd like to have supper with him.

I blushed. 'Aren't you going to have a party or something?' I swept my hand around at what must be close friends remaining in the room, all older, of course, one or two of whom had turned and caught my eye in curiosity.

'I don't really feel like a party. I'm too exhausted.' He was watching me closely. He didn't look exhausted. He looked exhilarated.

'Well, what about Celeste?'

'Celeste's gone. She went a while ago.'

I knew. I'd seen her go. I was being disingenuous. Again, hopefully not like me.

'I asked her to come tonight because I felt it would be unfair and humiliating not to have her here, but she knew on what basis. We're not together.'

Suddenly I felt very sorry for Celeste. She'd looked beautiful tonight, and had no doubt spent hours at the hairdresser's and a lot of money on a dress, but her heart must have been breaking. Supporting her handsome, talented man who was no longer her man. Smiling hard. Making it until about nine o'clock, when I'd seen her slip away, supported by a girlfriend. I'd spent a lot of the last few months wishing Celeste wasn't so beautiful, so thin; that she could have a modelling assignment in New York, be vaporized by a passing UFO. But now I hoped she'd find a kind and wealthy investment banker to marry and have many children with, and live in a tall Chelsea town-house, which somehow, I felt, would be a fitting end, and one that, until I'd met Sebastian, I wouldn't have minded for myself. It was certainly what my parents had in mind. Now I'd be very happy in a one-bedroom studio flat, which, after supper at the usual Italian and after we'd held hands across the table and gazed at each other and not eaten anything at all, was where we repaired to.

'You're lovely,' he'd said later that night, leaning over me, propped on one elbow and gazing down, his dark eyes full.

'No, I'm not,' I'd said, hastily pulling up the sheet, knowing I was slightly overweight and that although my face was often deemed pretty, it was rather full at the moment. I sucked in my cheeks. Celeste had serious bone structure.

'Yes, you are.' He'd grinned. 'If I was a poet I'd say something cheesy about a rose that's about to bloom, just waiting for the right drop of sunlight to fall on it.'

It was poetic enough for me. Fall? I tumbled, knowing he was that drop of sunlight. And I knew too that, in part, it was my youth he was falling for, as perhaps I was falling for his maturity, but I also knew it to be love.

We spent the next few months in a tremendously bliss-ful state, mostly in bed, but also finding the time to walk in parks, eat in cosy restaurants – we regained our appetites after so much horizontal activity – and during that time I think both of us produced some of the best pictures of our careers. I even sold some of mine. We painted fever-ishly, quite often late into the night, before tumbling into bed exhausted, laughing that in the morning we'd hate what we saw on our easels, but we never did. And Sebastian would marvel at mine as much as I did at his. 'That's bloody good, Ella!' He'd stand back, close one eye. Cock his head. 'Bloody good.' And I'd lie in bed and smile contentedly, looking as much at his naked back as at my easel. Life was perfect, in so very many ways, but not according to my parents.

In their view there was absolutely nothing to recommend the situation. In fact, they were vociferous and shrill on the subject. Particularly my mother, and particularly when I went to see them in leafy Buckinghamshire three months later, parking in the carriage driveway, hearing the electric gates shut softly but firmly behind me, then walking under the Georgian archway and across the flagstone hall, to tell them we were getting married.

'You're nineteen years old!' Mummy shrieked, in the drawing room of the Old Rectory. She was perched on one of her white sofas and I was opposite her on the matching one. They resembled tombstones, so shiny and cold were they, just as she was: fresh from the hairdresser, hair stiffly set in waves, taupe cashmere cardigan draped over thin shoulders, one hand gripping a large gin and tonic. 'And he's thirty years old, for crying out loud! A dirty old man, practically. What's he doing? Can't he get someone his own age?'

You'll be pleased to hear Sebastian wasn't with me, although that's not to say she'd have tempered her language if he had been. Perhaps she didn't realize how insulting she was being to both of us. My father came in from the garden through the French windows, secateurs in hand, hovering behind me in his old Husky jacket. Truffle, our Labrador, came too and put her nose in my hand.

'She says she's getting married to the painter chappie,

Angus, the one who lives above. And don't think we don't know that you've dropped out of art school. You think St Martin's wouldn't write to tell us? And all because of this – this *Lothario*, who's seduced you! Obviously using every cad's trick in the book. Oh, I knew you were too young to have that flat on your own. You should have gone into the hall of residence like everyone else, but your father let you have your own way – as usual!' Always 'your father' when he was in the wrong. A distancing technique. Never 'Daddy'.

'Ginnie had it,' I argued, glad to get off the subject of Sebastian.

'Yes, but Ginnie was sensible,' she spat. 'Had nice little dinner parties, entertained properly, met Richard and his friends from the regiment. She wasn't lolling around with a bohemian set in some drug-fuelled haze.'

I blinked hard. 'I don't take drugs, Mummy.'

'Oh, I wouldn't put it past you! Smoking marijuana in an artistic huddle. I always knew art school was wrong.' She shuddered. 'All those drop-out types, and living the life of Riley in Knightsbridge, too!'

'You wanted the girls to have the flat,' Daddy pointed out mildly. 'Said it would give them an edge.'

She had. Had thought it would set me apart from the arty types on the Euston Road, whom she had no intention of having as prospective sons-in-law, with their earrings and joss sticks and long hair. Had thought plonking me in the middle of Belgravia would mean I might paint by day, but, on my return, would be sure to meet an estate agent called Justin on his way to Peter Jones in tasselled loafers and a pristine Barbour. She had no idea she'd planted me under a ticking time-bomb of a fully grown drop-out, who, despite me telling her he was famous, she'd never heard of, of course.

'I suppose you have great sex or something seedy,' she hissed alarmingly, clutching her pearls, clearly hugely upset.

Daddy and I flinched. Sex was never mentioned in our house.

'Sylvia,' he muttered.

'Oh, that's what it's all about,' she said, turning fiercely to him. 'Make no mistake about it. Her head's been turned because she's only ever been with fumbling nineteen-year-olds, but now she's met a man who knows his way around the block and her eyes have been opened – not just her eyes, either!'

'Christ, what are you on?' I stood up, horrified.

'Oh, don't get all prissy with me, young lady. I know the lie of the land.' She was shaking now. Dad stood by, help-lessly. 'You young people think you invented it. Well, great. Marvellous. Have your steaming affair with your older man. You can even mistake it for love, for all I care, but you don't have to marry him, for Christ's sake! You don't have to have his –'

She broke off as if hit by a falling branch. I was still standing before her, still red with anger and humiliation, in a prime position to watch the penny drop. You could almost hear its descent, echoing around the eau de Nil walls of my childhood. Mummy's eyes changed from sparkling fury to glazed horror. Her hand went to her throat. There was a ghastly silence.

'You're pregnant,' she breathed.

'Yes.' I swallowed, letting it sink in. Letting Dad take it in, feeling him go rigid behind me. Giving us all a moment. 'Yes, but that's not why I'm marrying him,' I said, in a low, quivering voice. 'I love him, and he loves me, and I'm not getting rid of it.'

She stared at me for a long moment. And then her face crumpled. I couldn't even turn to look at Dad's. And surprisingly, or perhaps not to me, because I'm her daughter and know her to be human and not a cartoon monster, she didn't rant and rave. She didn't spit about what a hussy I was; she just looked devastated. Crushed. And I felt dreadful. For giving her a nasty shock like that. I went to sit beside her. Dad sat down opposite, where I'd been sitting. After a long while, he spoke.

'But it was an accident, love? You obviously didn't plan to get pregnant?'

'No. I mean, yes, it was an accident. But we both –' I struggled to explain the gamut of emotions Sebastian and I had gone through when we'd found out. When I'd told him, very fearfully. How the shock in his eyes in moments had turned to joy, how his joy had instantly transmitted itself to me, and how, as he took my hand and looked at me with untrammelled delight, we'd both known this had to be, was meant to be: was the happiest thing that had ever happened to either of us. How to convey this to my parents? Who just saw their slightly headstrong, nineteen-year-old daughter, knocked up by an older man. Some ghastly predator.

'I love him,' I said simply, not knowing how else to put it. 'And he loves me. Why else would he want to marry me? He hasn't even suggested I get rid of it.'

Silence. My parents digested this, and when I eventually met my mother's eyes, and saw her shattered face, I felt only sorrow. My mother hadn't had a career. Her career had been her husband and her children and she'd poured her considerable talents and formidable strength into both. With Ginnie it had been easy, because Ginnie believed in everything Mummy believed in: a good marriage, children (I was with them so far), money, prestige, a large house, dinner parties with the right people (this was where I strayed), and the unspoken knowledge that none of this could be achieved properly without some sort of submission of self. She'd always known she might fail with me, that it would be a challenge, but to fail so soon, and so drastically, without me even limping through a few hoops — a few dinner parties arranged by Ginnie, perhaps, one or two suitable young men — this was a crushing blow. But for all her disappointment about that, and for all her snobbery and pretension, I firmly believe her sorrow was primarily, and genuinely, for me. I was, after all, her darling daughter, and I was pregnant. My life was going to be very different. My youth was over. And somehow, because she was Captain Sylvia, and in sole command of this ship, she felt she'd failed me.

I took her hand and she let me. It looked older, and more fragile, than I remembered. It's huge diamond ring a little looser than it had been. I sensed defeat in her tractability; she knew that, like my father, occasionally, when I said something, I meant it.

After a bit she straightened her back. Looked my father right in the eye.

'There are worse things than a tiny baby,' she told him firmly.

Dad met his wife's gaze and nodded briefly. Taking her lead, as usual. But sadly.

She turned to me. 'What did you say his name was?'

'Sebastian Montclair.'

'And he's famous?'

'Yes.'

'Look him up, Angus,' she snapped.

And with that she got stiffly to her feet and left the room.

After a bit, Daddy went to the book case in the corner, bending down to the bottom shelf where, aside from cookery books in the kitchen, Mummy kept the very few books she owned (all the others were my father's): *Dr Spock*, *The Good School Guide*, *Who's Who* and *Debrett's*. These were the manuals of her trade. Daddy put aside his gardening gloves, tucked his secateurs in his Husky pocket and drew out *Who's Who*. I had no idea if Sebastian would be in it, but as he pulled up a low, tapestry stool, found his reading glasses in the top pocket of his shirt and put them on to see more clearly, and as I listened to Mummy, slowly ascending the stairs to her room and making her way across the landing to lie down on her bed, it occurred to me that courage took many forms. This was their form, and as I sat quietly by, on the tomb-like sofa, I silently applauded it.

Chapter Four

The following morning, however, my mother was not so submissive. Not so shattered. In fact, she was downright punchy. Eight hours' sleep, courtesy of a couple of Mogadons and an eye mask, had enabled her to gather her strength, retrench and condense her arguments.

'None of your friends will have babies. You'll be lonely and isolated. This is not a decision to be taken quickly or lightly, Eleanor. Please think about it. Just for a week. Just for me.'

She knew I had a week or two to make my decision. Knew she had some leeway with the dates.

'My decision is made,' I told her firmly over the gingham tablecloth, the Cooper's Oxford and the boiled eggs.

'This isn't the nineteen-fifties, Ella,' Ginnie said quietly. 'You're not in the L-shaped room.' Oh, yes, Ginnie had been drafted in, like the 7th Cavalry. She'd arrived from London early, falling into line seamlessly. 'One or two people I know – friends of mine, even – have had abortions. You don't have to have it.'

'I know,' I told her coldly. 'Melody Pitt-Andrews, for one.' Mummy flinched, shocked. 'But I want to keep it.'

'To keep him?' Ginnie said gently. 'Sebastian?'

I looked at her in horror. 'That's about the most unkind thing a sister could say!'

'I know. But it has to be said. Are you worried that if

you don't have the baby and marry him, in a few years' time he'll be off? Seeing you as a minor diversion?'

I stood up. Realized I was shaking.

'Sit down, Ella,' Dad said gruffly, his hand on my arm. 'These things have to be said. Mummy and I just haven't the heart for it.'

I sat, trembling. Gave some thought to what Ginnie had said. Knew that, for all our differences, she'd be on my side. I tried to work out if it was the truth.

'OK,' I said eventually to my assembled family. 'OK. I hear what you're saying. And maybe a tiny part of me agrees that I love him so much I'm actually very happy I'm getting married so quickly and having his child. But as for trapping him . . .' I shook my head. 'A couple of days ago he said that if anything happened to the baby, if for any reason I miscarried or whatever, he'd want to marry me anyway.'

This silenced my family. They looked at me in silent awe, rather as I had looked at Sebastian, when he'd said it in bed that night, his hand on my stomach.

'Why?' I'd said in wonder. 'Why do you want me so much?'

'I don't know,' he'd admitted. 'Maybe I see something in you I wish I had myself. It's not your youth, it's not that simplistic. It's more indefinable. We don't have a word for it – rather tellingly have to borrow *joie de vivre* from the French – and even that's not quite right. Sounds like you're skipping around Paris waving flowers. It's more . . . more to do with your acceptance of the world as it is. With no desire to change it. Just to live in it, paint it, and be happy in it.'

I'd thought about this. I did paint life as I saw it, and

Sebastian, I knew, painted as he idealized it, as he wanted it to be. The passion many critics had seen in his work was often anger at the way the world was, whereas my work was more optimistic: more jubilant.

'You like the way I paint?' I'd joked.

'I like you. I like your lack of cynicism and your ability to take everything and everybody at face value. You're like Diblet. A tail-wagger rather than a bottom-sniffer.'

I'd giggled. Diblet was our puppy. A mongrel we'd rescued from Battersea Dogs' Home. A tiny brown rat of a pup that Sebastian had given to me after I'd stretched luxuriously in bed one night and declared myself as happy as a girl could ever be. Without, that is, owning a dog.

'Owning a dog?'

'Yes.' I'd blinked up at him in surprise. 'Don't you like dogs?'

'Yes, of course I do, but it's not something I think about. Not something I'm pining for, the lack of which renders me incomplete.'

'Really? Oh, it does me. It was the only reason I hesitated about leaving home. Leaving Truffle.'

I had gone on to tell him the legion of other names I had for Truffle: Truffly-wuffly, Truffy-woo, big-bad-Truff, and then the song I'd made up in her honour, howling during the chorus. I'd been at that sublime stage of in-loveness with Sebastian, the stage of no-holds-barred, silly voices, crazy names – Mr Bear in his case, Miss Prissy in mine for reasons too embarrassing to go into – when anything went.

The following evening, Sebastian had bounded up five flights of steps and burst through the door as I stood at my easel – and there he was. Peeking out from behind the lapel of his overcoat. Two huge, anxious brown eyes in a little pointed face. My heart had melted instantly – as much at the gesture as at the adorable bundle – and Diblet had become part of our lives, sleeping in a basket in a corner of the studio; playing with old paint tubes and brushes; being taken for walks by Mrs Elgar, who, saddened at the loss of Putchkin but too old to take on another dog, had adopted Diblet with delight; then, when Sebastian and I needed a break and took him out ourselves, striding up to the round pond in Kensington Gardens, the wind in our faces. Amongst the Pekes and Chihuahuas of the mink-swathed gentlefolk of our mansion block he struck a comical chord. Most were haughtily suspicious of him, for, as Sebastian said, Diblet was a bit of rough, with a metaphorical cigarette butt sticking to his lower lip.

"'Ello, darlin', fancy a shag?' he'd say in a low undertone as we passed the Peke belonging to Mrs Sharp, the dentist's wife.

The baby, we'd decided, would complete this happy band.

A few weeks later I passed the point of no return, and my parents, realizing it was a fait accompli, naturally also came around to the idea of marriage. In fact, they embraced it really rather enthusiastically. For imagine the alternative?

My mother, who, given her head, can go from nought to sixty in seconds, roared into action. Literally the morning after all bets were off she called a meeting at the Old Rectory, which we meekly attended. It would be the first time she met Sebastian and I was dreading it, but Mum surprised me, as she often can; never one for sulking, once beaten she takes it gracefully. We arrived at the house to find not only Ginnie and Richard – with Hugo toddling around by now – but assorted uncles and aunts, a proper lunch laid in the dining room, the table groaning with silver and crystal, flowers everywhere, classical music playing softly, champagne chilling in the fridge.

'Darling!' Mum greeted me at the door, arms outstretched, a kiss on the cheek that was surely genuine. 'And you must be Sebastian.' She extended her hand to him with the loveliest of smiles, eyes twinkling, absolutely nothing betraying what she might really be thinking, and actually, perhaps wasn't, by now. My mother can persuade herself of all sorts of things. She also has charm and as she led us through the sparkling, flower-filled, music-humming house, French windows flung wide to the sweeping lawns and river beyond – all of which said: This is who we are, Sebastian; cultured, prosperous, intelligent people – everything about her own smiling demeanour as she introduced him joyfully to the assembled relatives said: And this is my prospective son-in-law. Aren't I lucky?

'You know, Sebastian's frightfully famous,' she was telling Aunt Hilda – I noticed we had Hilda from Dad's side and not cosy, shawl-wearing, toffee-sucking Auntie Doreen from hers: Mum, like most crashing snobs, didn't have much in her closet to brag about. 'He's been written up in *The Times* and the *Telegraph*. Apparently he's the next Howard Hodgkin, and Miles Spender in the *FT* says he's Tate Britain's only hope of having someone genuinely experimental, talented and indigenous.'

I looked at her in awe as Sebastian blinked in surprise. Two weeks ago she wouldn't have known who Howard Hodgkin was, let alone an art critic called Miles Spender, but, boy, had she done her homework. Once, years ago, when Ginnie had failed rather a lot of O-levels but expressed a vague interest in photography, my mother, within hours, had not only uncovered some friend of a friend with a London studio, but, before Ginnie could blink, had her on a train rattling off to deepest Shoreditch. We learned not to have a vague interest in anything much.

So contemporary art, conceptual in particular, encompassing most English artists from 1960 to the present day would not be a problem for Mum. She'd have it under her belt in no time, bothering librarians in those pre-Internet days to let her look through old copies of *The Times*, sourcing reviews, charting the career of an up-and-coming artist called Sebastian Montclair and discovering, to her delight, that things were not so bad at all.

'His grandmother was Lady Louisa Radcliff you know, great friends with one of the Mitford girls,' she purred to Hilda, whose back straightened visibly. She was in the same over-thin, well-preserved vein as Mum.

'Was she?' Sebastian looked stupefied, and so adorable with his long, freshly washed hair and his floral shirt, brown eyes soft amongst these sharp-eyed relatives assembled round our dining table.

'You didn't know she was a Lady?' Mum was astonished.

'No, the Mitford bit.'

'Oh, yes. She was in Austria with Unity,' my mother assured him, as if Unity were a close personal friend. 'It says so in Debo Devonshire's letters. And his *grand*father,' she went on importantly, as if Sebastian wasn't there at all – Ginnie shot me a sympathetic look over the asparagus – 'was one of the greatest painters of his generation. Just as, one day, Sebastian will be of his!'

'He was also one of the greatest drinkers,' Sebastian

told her with a laugh. 'Let's hope I don't emulate him on that front!'

Mum was on the point of making her famous face at this, but Dad roared, so she quickly changed her lemon-sucking demeanour to one of a frightfully gay avant-garde hostess and gave a tinkly laugh instead.

'Oh, I'm *quite* sure you won't do that, Sebastian, particularly now you've got the little one on the way.'

It was the first reference to the baby – executed in Mum's typically euphemistic, lower-middle-class way – but she hadn't meant it snidely. That too had gone from being a shameful secret to a much-lauded triumph. Her friend Angie, who lived down the road at the Manor, told Ginnie that Mum had arrived for bridge the previous week saying: 'Marvellous news, Angie. Both of my daughters are pregnant. Soon I'll have *three* grandchildren – aren't I lucky?'

'Oh – and I've had a little thought,' Mummy told us ominously over the lunch table, raising a well-manicured finger. I braced myself. Mum's little thoughts were generally anything but. 'More hollandaise, Sebastian? No? It's home-made? I thought – why not get married in the village church? After all, Ginnie did.'

'No, Mum,' I said firmly, glancing at my father for support. He gave me a quick nod. Sebastian had gone a bit pale. 'I am not waltzing down the aisle six months pregnant like a ship in full sail with a crowd of little attendants behind me.' In her head, I knew my mother had already chosen the flowers in their bouquets, their silk sashes. 'We've already decided we're going for a registry office, just family and close friends.' As her face fell I put her out of her misery. 'Chelsea,' I added.

To see it rise again like one of Delia's soufflés, which

she executed so beautifully and was handing around even now with a little green salad, was almost a joy to behold.

'Oh, yes, *Chelsea*,' she purred as Mick Jagger and Bianca and countless other arty but famous folk clearly sprang to mind. She paused a moment in her soufflé-doling and I could see a whole screenplay playing out in her head as I no doubt stood in some dated Ossie Clarke number with a floppy white hat, Sebastian in some terrible, seventies, flared suit beside me.

In the event, I wore a cream lace dress from Warehouse with Ginnie in pale lemon as my bridesmaid, whilst Sebastian looked divine in a biscuit-coloured linen suit and open-necked shirt. My parents were obviously there, Sebastian's were long dead – but his Aunt Ottoline came, a divorcee who'd been close to Sebastian as he grew up. I took to her at once. Small, round and with shrewd eyes in a tanned, nut-like face, she immediately filled me in on all the gossip in Sebastian's family – his mother had been pious and a pain, his father, mild but bullied – but she also told me I'd got the pick of the bunch in my new husband, who was a complete honey. How could I not love her instantly?

Apart from that, relatives were thin on the ground and the small throng of people showering us with confetti as we came down the registry office steps, blinking into the sunlight, were either friends of mine from St Martin's, or Sebastian's from the art world. To be honest I don't remember much about anyone in particular, which perhaps speaks volumes about how I felt that day – I was in a complete and perfect bubble with Sebastian.

I remember holding his hand as we stood laughing at each other in the street, passers-by turning to smile at our happiness. And I remember thinking, as the photographer snapped away: surely this is the girl who has everything? Two weeks prior to our marriage Sebastian had held his second one-man show in a prestigious gallery in Cork Street. It had been a resounding success both critically and commercially. The newspapers had called him 'the cream of his generation', and the money he'd made would enable us to buy a proper flat – a house, even – and no longer live in an attic. The emotion we'd felt on that day as everyone finally left the gallery and we'd hugged each other with glee, toasting our success with a glass of champagne, was akin to the happiness I felt as I gazed up at my new husband in the street and his eyes, full of love, gazed down. We had everything. We had each other, we had the baby, we had ambition, and we also shared a special bond: something no one else knew about and which was as binding, in its way, as the gold ring on my finger. It only served to bring us closer together; it was another expression of our love. We felt complete.

Despite the bright midday sunshine the photographer wasn't taking any chances. His camera bulb flashed madly and the young couple caught laughing into the lens and captured in the photographs I later put proudly in a leather-bound album look like any other pair of shiny-eyed newly-weds on their wedding day. Any other young couple who have found each other, are blissfully happy, and can't quite believe their luck.

To this day I can't bear to look at them.

Chapter Five

I was at the kitchen window, elbow deep in suds at the sink, when Ginnie drove into the yard on Wednesday morning in her green Range Rover. Mum was in the passenger seat beside her. Even at this distance I could see that Ginnie had her over-bright face on and was chattering away gaily, exclaiming and pointing at the ducks as one would to a child. Mum, beside her, in a printed summer dress and navy cardigan, looked grim and tight-lipped. She clutched her handbag on her lap and regarded her surroundings suspiciously. I felt my spirits sink into my Ugg boots. As I pulled the plug in the sink, something nasty and slimy, probably a piece of old pasta, wound itself round my finger. My heart, too, it seemed. What had I agreed to? What?

The dogs were clamouring to be let out. Stupidly I opened the back door and they shot out, barking furiously at the car. As I dried my hands on a tea towel, my face, I realized, was already plastered with a replica of my sister's fixed smile.

'Hello, there! How lovely!' I called, determined to get this off to a good start. I went to greet Mum as she attempted to descend from the dizzy heights of the Range Rover passenger seat, which is not designed for elderly women, and not helped by the dogs, jumping up to greet her. Ginnie ran round to help but my mother waved her away furiously and then there was a moment when we all got thoroughly mixed up with the dogs, the car door and her heels sticking in the muddy, cobbled yard. She sorted herself out and made determinedly for the house, accompanied by two barking dogs and two daughters shrieking at them to 'Be QUIET, can't you!'

'Mum! What a treat,' I gasped breathlessly as I came in after her and shut the marauding dogs out, just about letting Ginnie squeeze in behind me. 'Did you have a good trip?'

An inane question because she'd only come from Ginnie's, but I was nervous. My mother wasn't. Head high, back straight, hair stiffly waved, she kissed me lightly as I lunged, never quite touching my cheek.

'This is very good of you, Ella,' she told me, ignoring my prattle. 'And it won't be for long, I assure you. Just until the painters have finished redecorating upstairs. You know how I can't bear the smell, and of course your father couldn't care less.'

I glanced incredulously at Ginnie. She shrugged sheepishly back.

'No. Quite,' I muttered as Mum swept past, spotting Tabitha in the playroom.

'Hello, darling, how are you?'

'Oh, hi, Granny.' Tabitha got up off the sofa to kiss her.

'Is that the party line?' I hissed, when she was out of earshot.

'That's what she's telling everyone, yes.'

'But surely she knows I know?'

'Well . . .' Ginnie scratched her leg uncomfortably.

'Oh, Ginnie, for heaven's sake!'

This was so like my family. Everything tucked away under wraps for form's sake. No feelings vented, no emotions expressed; everything to keep up appearances and save face.

'Tabitha needs some slippers,' Mum scolded, coming back into the kitchen. 'Her feet are freezing. And what on earth is she doing watching television at this time of day? Is she ill?'

'Oh, no, this is early for Tabs,' I told her breezily. 'She doesn't usually surface before ten. Josh is still in bed. That's teenagers for you, I'm afraid. And, actually, it's well documented. They do need more sleep than we do.'

Start as you mean to go on, Ella, I told myself firmly. This is your house. Your rules. Or lack of them.

'Not in my day they didn't,' she said tartly. 'If you or Ginnie were in bed after nine o'clock I'd pull the covers off!' Ah, so that's where my sister had inherited it from.

'Be my guest,' I said brightly. 'Now, Mum. Cup of coffee? Then I'll take you to the cottage.' I said it as if installing my mother in one of my holiday lets were the most natural thing in the world.

'I had a cup at Ginnie's. And of course she makes it far too strong. What on earth is that chicken doing up there?'

I glanced up to the top of the dresser. 'Oh, that's Ladyboy, and he's not a chicken he's a bantam. Or she is. She started as a hen but then got feathery legs and a comb so he's sort of a cockerel now. The others bully her – him – so he comes in here.'

'How thoroughly unhygienic!' She shuddered. 'Where does he go at night?'

'Oh, outside,' I lied weakly, obviously not starting as I meant to go on. Ladyboy was often to be found with the dogs in their basket.

'Well, thank heavens for that.' She pulled her cardigan protectively round her bony shoulders. Made a disapproving face. 'I think perhaps I'd like to see the house now,' she declared, for all the world like a prospective purchaser waiting to be escorted to a property by an estate agent.

I felt my dander rising. Noticed too that Ginnie was keeping very quiet. Guilt, probably. Plus twenty-four hours of the same treatment.

'Right. Jolly good. Well, I'll just get the key.'

It wasn't hard, because it was in my pocket, but it was something to say. I brandished it as if I'd discovered the Holy Grail and we trooped outside. We crossed the yard in silence. Sebastian's curtains were still drawn in the Granary but Ottoline, his aunt, who'd lived on the farm in one building or another for years, was sitting in a wheel-backed chair on her doorstep in the sunshine. Her legs, in jeans, covered with an apron, were planted firmly astride as she carefully painted her mugs, which were ranged before her on a little table.

'Good morning!' she called cheerily, as I waved from a distance. Mum swung round, not having spotted her.

'Oh. Good morning, Ottoline,' she said stiffly. Then: 'Is that woman still here?' – not bothering to go and greet her properly, and not really bothering to lower her voice. 'I thought there was some mention of her going to Newlyn? Doing her pottery thing down there?'

'There was,' I said evenly. 'And she went down there for a bit but she didn't like it. Missed Netherby. And I missed her. I like having her here.'

My mother made one of her faces. 'Gracious. It really is like a commune, isn't it?'

It is now, I thought.

'And Sebastian hasn't seen fit to move out yet, I suppose?' She glanced at the Granary.

'No, he hasn't,' I said shortly. 'Apart from anything else, he's got nowhere to go.'

'Well, I don't see that that's your problem,' she snapped.

I just about kept myself in check.

'Right, here we are,' I said brightly, as we approached the little stone cottage. I put the key in the latch and pushed open the blue stable door. Inside I'd painted the walls a pale shell-pink, the bare floorboards a white gloss and strewn them with plenty of colourful Kelim rugs which overlapped. All the lamps were on – I'd bought a few new ones in IKEA – and the wood-burner I'd lit that morning, even though it was summer, glowed warmly in the corner. I'd been in here a good couple of hours already and hadn't needed a key, but I'd wanted her to see that she'd got privacy and security. A pair of creamy sofas fitted snugly, facing each other either side of the stove. Between them on a low table were the newspapers I'd nipped out to buy earlier and, on a whim, *Harper's*, which she loved. The glazed door at the far end of the room was open to the tiny garden, its checked curtain fluttering in the breeze.

'Oh, Ella, it's sweet!' enthused Ginnie, genuinely impressed. 'I haven't been in here for ages and you've done so much. You've really made it cosy, hasn't she, Mummy?'

My mother sniffed, looking around.

'And you've got a few new pieces too,' Ginnie swept on, sensing frost. She stroked an old chest of drawers, which had a bit of woodworm but was otherwise quite unremarkable, in the corner.

'Lottie got it for me,' I told her as we both watched our mother, anxiously. Lottie was my best friend in the village – in the world, come to that – and she dabbled in antiques. 'She picks up things like this for a song at Kempton and offers them to me first, before she puts them on her stall.'

'A song is all they're worth,' said Mum, coming across and opening a drawer of the chest. It got stuck as she tried to push it back. As Ginnie went to help she almost slapped her hand. Ginnie shrank. 'I hope she doesn't overcharge you, Ella. You always were a soft touch.'

'Yes, I was, wasn't I?' I said lightly, feeling myself coming to the boil.

'Oh, Mummy, do look at the dear little kitchen,' Ginnie broke in gustily, shooting me an imploring look. 'It's got one of those darling little butler sinks you love.'

'Must you sound like a character in a P. G. Wodehouse novel?' Mummy enquired as she marched the few paces it took to get around the bar that divided the sitting room from the galley kitchen with its duck-egg-blue cupboards. She pulled out one drawer, then another. Happily they both slid back perfectly.

'Yes, very nice,' she said grudgingly. 'You've done it up well, Ella. Although I'd be tempted to take a few of these rugs out of the kitchen area; they'll only get things spilled on them. And there's nowhere really to sit and eat, is there? I suppose one could sit at this bar, but I like to get my feet under a proper table. No room, I take it. Ah, well. The view's pleasant enough and one could always sit outside, I imagine. If it was nice.'

'One could,' I agreed. 'If one was so inclined. And if one didn't mind seeing the commune from there.'

My mother caught my tone immediately. A muscle twitched in her cheek.

'It's very kind of you, darling,' she said stiffly. I wished for all the world that I hadn't said it. The mask had slipped instantly and the pain was there for all to see.

'It's a pleasure, Mum,' I said gruffly, wishing we were the sort of family who could hug each other now, when words wouldn't do. Or even *find* words. '*Sorry, I'm being a cow.*' '*No, I'm sorry. I'm the cow.*' But we weren't.

There was an awkward pause. 'Well, I think I'll be on my way. I've got to pick up Araminta from a sleepover,' Ginnie said breathlessly. She lunged to kiss Mum clumsily, who stood like a rock.

'And I'll pay the going rate,' she said, ignoring Ginnie. 'Whatever the Watsons were paying, I'll pay.' Dignity was restored and she was going for the crown of thorns.

'Yes, I know you will,' I said miserably, wishing I didn't have to take it. But I did. My mother's chin rose stoically to accommodate the crown.

'All the bills too.'

'It's included in the rent,' I said wretchedly.

'Bye, then, Mummy,' plunged on my sister. 'I'll come by and take you to Woodstock soon. You wanted to see Blenheim, didn't you? The gardens are glorious, and the lake. Tomorrow, if you like?'

'Well, give me a couple of days to settle in, Ginnie,' she said impatiently. 'There's no mad rush, is there?'

And Ginnie agreed there most certainly wasn't. Giving me a guilty peck on the cheek, she slipped away, in the manner of a woman, I thought, watching her scurry to her car, who's just planted a small bomb.

It reminded me of when the children were little and had a nasty cold, sometimes even a bit of a bug, but I'd take them to school anyway: deposit them guiltily in the playground – and run, desperate to get to my easel. Of course, they'd detonate at about lunchtime and I'd get a call from the school, have to drop my brush and go and get them. Naturally there'd be no question of Sebastian going, I recalled, spotting a curtain finally open at the top of the Granary. It always fell to me. Just as had the shopping and cleaning and everything else to do with the two houses we'd ever lived in – this one, bought from Ottoline ten years ago, the one in London before that – but that was how I'd wanted it. I'd wanted to be the wife of the famous painter who dabbled a bit herself: 'Who is that beautiful girl? Oh, really? Sebastian Montclair's wife? Mother of two? No.'

And I'd loved every minute of it. Had played the part to perfection. Had often felt I was in a film, in fact, racing down the King's Road in a tiny skirt with Diblet on a lead and Josh riding on the back of Tabitha's pushchair, all of us laughing as I dropped her at nursery, then him at school, kissing them both goodbye. Running home to Flood Street via the little grocer's on the corner to pick up a baguette, fruit, cheese, possibly a bunch of daffodils. Pablo, the shopkeeper, would stand in his doorway in his long white apron, shaking his head and calling: 'Slow down! You do too much!' I'd laugh and brandish my daffodils. Back I'd dash to my studio, my husband, my easel in the corner, only a tiny part of me divorced from the action, feeling like a spectator who's wondering uneasily what's going to happen next. Knowing things are not quite right.

And slowly, insidiously, as the children grew older, this film did begin to get stranger. A bit jerkier, perhaps, before lurching on in its merry, rom-com way. The scenery was unfamiliar now, the action taking place in the country.

Removal lorries arrived at a farmyard, and the young couple, last seen living at a house in Flood Street, emerged cautiously from a car as their children jumped joyfully, with their dog, to explore. And then it got more peculiar, this film, as unfamiliar people appeared. Like Isobel. Isobel, bottle-blonde and buxom, who wasn't introduced slowly, maybe in a crowd scene at a party, or perhaps by implication with a shot of Sebastian reeling home drunk from the pub where she worked, lipstick on his collar – but with a bang, when I'd come back from shopping mid-morning, the children at school. I'd dashed upstairs thinking I had a good two hours at my drawing board in the attic – by now I'd abandoned the easel and was illustrating children's books – and had popped to the bedroom en route to dump my bag. Stopped in my tracks. There he was, in bed with her. Waiting for me, almost. Looking me straight in the eye as I burst in, as if to say: It doesn't matter how wonderful you are, Ella, what a bloody good job you do of managing things, of splicing together this delightful footage, I can still bring it to a shuddering halt, just like that. I can still press the nuclear button. Have done, too.

Hadn't he just?

'Is this gas?' My mother was saying. She bent over and fiddled with the knobs on the cooker, sniffing hard. If it was she'd be out cold by now.

'No, electric,' I told her, going across to demonstrate. I held my hand over the ring. 'It just takes a moment or two to warm up. There's no gas in the village. We're not on main drains, either. In fact, the septic tank needs emptying; it's a bit whiffy at the moment.'

'And you have to do that, do you?'

'Well, not personally,' I said, momentarily diverted at the idea of prising open the vast lid and shovelling tons of neat sewage into barrows. 'A tanker comes and siphons it away. I'm just saying that it might be a bit more rural round here than you're used to.'

'I don't frighten easily, Ella,' she told me crisply. 'I was brought up in the country, don't forget.'

'Of course,' I said, realizing I probably had been trying to scare her. Hoping my woodworm and raw sewage would send her scuttling home, back to Dad. Except, of course, Dad wasn't there. On a date, no doubt. All at once I couldn't cope with the subterfuge.

'Mum,' I blurted suddenly, 'I know about you and Dad. Ginnie told me. I can't carry on pretending I don't.' She looked me frigidly in the eye. I blinked first. 'Do you –' and this was brave – 'do you want to talk about it?'

Her eyes glittered briefly. 'No, I do not. And in any event, you'd hardly be the best person for the job, would you? With a failed marriage behind you? And for your information, even if I were the sort of woman who wanted to settle down for a cosy chat and a weep about such things, it wouldn't be about me and Dad, as you put it. It would be about your father and his floozy. This has abso-lutely nothing to do with me.'

And leaving me standing in the middle of my own holi-day cottage, she sailed through the open French window to inspect her tiny garden, for all the world as if she were Lady Many Acres.

As I said to Lottie later that afternoon, in her cottage across the stream on the other side of the village, it was as if she were doing *me* a favour. Not me her. We had a pot of tea between us and had already demolished an entire packet of chocolate digestives.

Lottie looked pensive: the delicate skin of her forehead crumpling like tissue paper as it did when she was deep in thought, her china-blue eyes reflective. She tilted her chair back precariously and deftly flicked another packet of biscuits from the larder to fortify us. 'Except she's hurt, don't forget. So she's bound to lash out. People like that always do. It's their first line of defence. Was that all?' she asked, opening the packet.

'Well, no,' I told her. 'Because, obviously, I was seething. So, obviously – stupidly – I followed her out to the garden shrieking: *I was only trying to help!* I did manage not to add: you ungrateful old bag – but I was literally shaking. She turned to me and said, "Help, Ella? Help whom? I'd be the vulnerable one, wouldn't I, having shared and wept? You'd have the edge. That's why people go into the so-called caring profession of counselling, you know, to make themselves feel better. To be able to say: Gosh, poor you, in comparison to me."'

Lottie threw back her head and howled. She was a counsellor herself, amongst other things. I dunked my biscuit miserably, letting her roar. No one could laugh like Lottie: sides shaking, face quivering.

'God, she's sharp, your mum, isn't she?' she said eventually, wiping her eyes.

'As a blade,' I said glumly. 'I told you, she should be running BP. I thought you'd be livid.'

'Not in the slightest,' she said, helping herself to another biscuit. 'There's an element of truth in what she says. Counselling is definitely a two-way street, and, actually, she's right – it would have helped your relationship, wouldn't it?

If she'd settled down for a chat and a sob? You could have squeezed her wrist and offered her a tissue, and then the next time you saw her, when you took over a flask of soup or something generous, she'd find it hard to be quite so abrasive, having let her guard down.'

'Abrasive? Repulsive, you mean.'

'OK, repulsive. But it would make life easier.'

'But why shouldn't it be bloody easier?' I said petulantly. 'I'm the one having her to stay.'

'Yes, but she's the one with the problem. She hasn't come to help *you* out, to make *you* feel better; she's come to sort herself out. Anyway, don't get too bogged down. She won't be with you for long. I should just grit your teeth and get on with it. If she wants to be ignored, flaming well ignore her. Let Ginnie be the one pussy-footing about and wringing her hands and getting swatted away for her pains. As you say, you're making the biggest gesture by having her. If you ask me, it's only a hiccup in a very long marriage. God, they must have been together for donkey's years. She'll be back with your father within a twinkling, you mark my words.'

I did. Had always marked Lottie's words, for she was not only my best friend, but my wisest by far.

'You think?'

'Of course. Matter of weeks. Days, even.'

I breathed out gustily. Was genuinely heartened as I straightened my back in her creaky old Lloyd Loom chair, and even resisted the new packet she opened. Lottie didn't, but then Lottie didn't really care about weight, just bought something a bit roomier next time. And she was only a couple of sizes too large, anyway. And pretty too, so one didn't really notice. Silky-straight blonde hair to her shoulders, that soft peachy skin, bright blue eyes like a doll and the most unlined face of a woman her age I'd ever seen. 'At our age,' she'd say, 'you choose between your face and your bottom.' No prizes for guessing which she'd chosen.

She lived on the opposite side of the village to me, in a tiny blue terraced cottage, which was picture-postcard perfect on the outside, and terminally damp within. Especially in the winter when the river crept right up the path to her door. Lottie made do with sandbags and a cheerful smile and swept the water away. Her neighbours rang the council, put up For Sale signs and fretted – but she shrugged it off, saying it would soon be spring. She'd arrived on my doorstep just after we'd moved into the farm, with a bunch of tulips. 'If you're anything like me,' she'd said, 'you'll be in a state of complete and utter chaos, so I thought I'd offer tea and sympathy at my place. It might cheer you up to see a house that's been lived in for four years but is even more chaotic than your own.'

I'd smiled and thanked her for the flowers. And then the following week, when everything in my house was pretty much where it should be but nothing felt any better in my heart, I'd popped round for that cuppa, wishing Sebastian would talk to me and knowing I needed a friend. I discovered that Lottie was not exaggerating. Her house, as she cheerfully put it when she opened the front door, was indeed a tip.

'The trouble is, if I clear up, I can't find anything,' she'd wailed.

She'd led me back down the obstacle course that was her hallway, strewn with finds from car-boot sales which would eventually appear on her Saturday stall in the market.

We wound our way round pretty broken bird cages, delicate three-legged chairs, and an assortment of elegant yet wireless lamps, to arrive in her kitchen, where what looked like a full-scale model of HMS *Ark Royal* was being assembled on the table. Lottie – or Hamish, her husband – always had a project on the go. Always a big idea that was going to make their fortune. Hamish had once built half a boat in the garden shed. Almost all were cheerfully abandoned halfway through as a bad idea, whereupon they'd embark on the next.

The present scheme involved a mountain of wool and an electric knitting machine, found at a boot sale. It was in perfect working order apparently and they were going to run up adorable baby bonnets and booties to sell to the smart boutiques of Cheltenham. I couldn't quite see it myself, but I didn't comment because it had been Hamish's idea and hopefully that meant he was doing the knitting. A good thing. As Lottie freely admitted, being addicted to beautiful things, she certainly hadn't married him for his brains: he was the bearer of few. In his youth he'd been an exceptional cricketer: tall and elegant, with chestnut curls and an aquiline nose, he'd gracefully send sixes and fours down the crease to the boundary, behind which Lottie sat, panting and adoring, clapping hard as lots of inside leg was displayed. Unfortunately he'd proved not quite good enough to play at county level so, newly married, they'd cast around for other things. Insurance, advertising, watch and car sales and carpentry had all had a brief mention on his CV, but he'd always been politely moved on – no one could ever be rude to Hamish with his easy smile and relaxed manner. Projects were now his thing, whilst Lottie brought home the real bacon.

To be fair, Hamish was currently appearing in under-wear ads for thermals on the back of the *Sunday Express* – if you've ever wondered who those lantern-jawed, greying-at-the-temple chaps are, now you know. But it was Lottie who left the house at eight and returned at seven. She was an acupuncturist at the local Holistic Centre, where I was quite sure her clientele came as much for her words of wisdom as her skill with the needle. This, she'd assured me, was just as well. She'd recently retrained – acupuncture being more lucrative than counselling – and hadn't quite found her feet. Occasionally, nerves struck. I'd assured her this was completely natural. She'd only just started.

'I'll have only just finished soon,' she'd said glumly. 'When word gets about that the new acupuncturist can't pin the tail on the donkey, let alone cure clinical depression. I literally have to *see* the needles and my hands start shaking.'

'Only at the very beginning. When you first started,' I consoled. 'Not now.'

'Remember when I kept saying: "Just a little prick"?'

I giggled.

'The women used to laugh. Found it amusing.' She sighed. 'The men didn't, obviously.'

'Obviously.'

'And then I got that complaint . . .'

'Only one.'

'I know, but the management said I was too frivolous. I didn't tell them it was to calm my own nerves and that I had to laugh my way to the semi-naked body on the slab. And now? Oh, God, I don't know, Ella, I just can't seem to get it right.' She shot her hands through her hair. 'Can't seem to be *con*fident about it. It all seems so crucial some-how, to get the sodding needle in exactly the right place.'

Well, it is, rather, I'd thought uncomfortably. But I didn't say anything. Wriggled nervously instead. Personally I reckoned she'd be better off going back to the counselling, which she was so brilliant at, but Hamish was keen for her to keep going with the acupuncture and, one day, have her own practice. Here, at home, he thought.

He was outside on the terrace even now, painting some terrible old garden table, which evidently had all the makings of the new reception desk. Apparently it was destined for the narrow hall, the one you currently had to limbo-dance down.

'Have you tried talking to him?' she asked, watching Hamish lope to the garden shed for more paint, moving with his long, easy stride. She was still so much in love with her husband it often made my heart ache to see them. She turned back. 'Your father?'

'Oh.' I came back to her. To reality. And my mother in my back garden. 'No, I haven't. But Ginnie has. It wasn't an unqualified success.'

Lottie grimaced. 'I can imagine.'

She and my sister didn't always see eye to eye.

'So I thought I'd ring him up tonight,' I went on quickly, not in the mood to hear her views on Ginnie's shortcomings as a suitable emissary. 'I was going to ring yesterday, but then thought – no. Give him a night or two alone in that house. He might be sadder than he imagined, knocking around on his own.'

'Good thinking.' She sipped her tea. 'After all, it's one thing to entertain dreams of an extra-marital fling, but quite another to have carte blanche to go ahead with it when your wife's disappeared. I'm sure a few nights of a solitary boiled egg will take the wind out of his sails.'

'Exactly,' I said, immensely cheered. I wasn't sure Dad could even boil an egg. I even wondered if I should call the Watsons and say that if anything fell through with Millie Saunders, they could come back? Extend my ad in *The Lady*?

'What about yours?' I asked, dunking what I determined really was the last biscuit of the day. 'Speaking of problem mothers?'

Lottie's mother was a formidable and ferocious ex-head mistress. She'd recently lost the plot a bit but refused to go into a home, even though she ate the cat food and emptied buckets of water from bedroom windows, splashing her neighbours.

'Terrible.' Lottie's shoulders hunched in terror. 'Much worse. And so *rude*.'

'But not coming here?'

'No, thank God.'

Lottie, to her credit, and to Hamish and the children's dismay, had offered to have her, but she'd refused to go anywhere. Had bellowed down the phone to Lottie: 'Who, pray, in their right mind, would want to live in your house?'

Lottie had replaced the receiver murmuring: 'Well, you're not in your right mind, so I'd thought you might.'

'Hamish took a call this morning from Abdul in the Spar, where she does her shopping. He left me this note.' She pushed it across gloomily. It read:

Abdul rang. Your mother smashed a bottle of ketchup in his shop this morning. Sadly her attempts to clear it up with her bare hands were not entirely successful. No doubt frustrated, she then ran her hands through her hair. Terrified Shoppers Ran From Blood-Soaked Woman!

'Oh, God.' I passed it back, shocked. Wondered if in thirty years' time Lottie and I would be such a problem to our own children. Or even fifty years' time. Weren't we supposed to live to a hundred now? What on earth would we do after the age of eighty? Potter round going gently gaga, being an emotional drain on our families? Or nimbly play bowls with ancient but toned brown legs in white shorts? The latter, I hoped.

'Shoot me,' Lottie told me firmly now. 'If I ever show signs of turning into my mother. I give you full permission.'

'I thought that was my job?' Hamish came in through the back door, bending his head to accommodate his great height. 'I thought I was the one wielding the shotgun?' He stooped to kiss my cheek, flashing that famous smile. 'Hello, doll.'

'Hi, Hamish.' I grinned up at him.

'You can both do it,' she told us. 'One of you with a blank bullet, like in a firing squad, so neither of you knows who's the executioner.' She beamed, clearly immensely pleased with this. 'And, anyway, if I lose my job down at the centre, there'll be an altogether different sort of firing going on.'

'Don't be silly,' Hamish snorted. 'You've just got that job. You're not going to lose it.'

'Don't be so sure. I had a pig of a day yesterday, as you know. No one rang, did they?' she asked anxiously.

'Only a Mrs Harper. I said you'd ring back later.'

'Mrs Harper?' She froze. 'Oh, God – that's her!' she hissed in sepulchral tones.

He blanched. 'Is it?'

'Yes! That's the one!' She clutched at the front of her dress with both hands, terrified.

93

'Who?' I asked, mystified.

'This enormous woman,' she turned wide blue eyes on me, 'who I did yesterday and lost the needle.'

'Where?'

'Down her buttocks.'

'Oh, God!' I gasped.

'She makes me so nervous, Ella, because she's so big. I'm never quite sure I've got the needle in the right place. There are so many places I *could* get it in, if you get my drift. So many rolls. So my paws are shaky anyway. I dropped it right down her crack.'

'Lordy,' I said inadequately. 'What did you do?'

'Tried to pick it out, but it slipped further. And the thing is, her bottom is so big, I had to kind of . . . *open* it.'

'No!'

'I know!' she wailed, shaking her hands in the air. 'I had to use tweezers in the end. Thought I'd have to ask her to get up and shake – but, no, I got it out. Thank God. And she was sweet about it. Said it didn't matter a bit. But, oh – now she's *rung*.' She looked wretched. 'Perhaps she's talked to her husband? Decided to sue? I have a feeling he's a lawyer.' She gripped the table top with both hands. 'Tighten your belt, Hamish. I see another age of austerity coming on. Another winter of gruel and discontent.'

'Nonsense,' he said cheerfully. 'She sounded quite delightful on the phone. I asked if she was ringing about the baby bonnets, because you know I put an ad in the local shop, and she said no, but she was terribly interested. Her daughter's about to have her second. You might want to run some up in white, as well as pink and blue, hon. I said we would. Some people like the choice.'

'Oh! Really? Oh, yes, good idea. I'd better. Oh, I'm *so*

glad she wasn't cross. You're sure she wasn't cross, Hamish? I'll ring her back later. Talk baby bonnets with her. Distract her. I'd better get cracking.'

And so saying she got hurriedly to her feet, stashing what remained of the biscuits away in the cupboard – cramming a last one into her mouth – before brushing crumbs from her front and sliding the mountain of wool with both arms back to this end of the table. Then the knitting machine. It was my cue to leave and I was going anyway. I bid them both farewell. Hamish gave me a cheery salute and sauntered back outside to the reception desk, which, he told us, had had its first coat, and needed to dry, something he clearly thought best achieved by settling down next to it with the newspaper. His wife, meanwhile, settled herself at the knitting machine at the kitchen table.

It was interesting, I thought, as I made my way back through the quiet, slumbering village, crossing the little stream by the footbridge which divided the cottages, how it was always assumed that Lottie should be the worker bee in that family. Why hadn't Hamish trained to be the acupuncturist? With Lottie on reception? Surely he'd be just as adept with a needle? More so, probably. After all, he was a cricketer. Had a good eye. I'd voiced it once, lightly, and Lottie had laughed and said, 'What a waste! With Hamish being so gorgeous!' And it was true in a way. Imagine what a hit he'd be, reading the paper, glancing up to flash lovely smiles at lonely housewives as they came in. Why shouldn't he play to his strengths? And not being quite so gorgeous, perhaps Lottie saw it as her role to play to hers? To be industrious?

Interesting how neither of them found that emasculating, I thought, as I followed the lane home to the farm, the sun warming my cheeks. In my marriage, both of us would have done. Did. Was that because Sebastian had once been so successful? Or because he was older? He'd always looked after me, and I'd assumed he always would. Not now, of course. Now I was doing whatever I could – illustrating books, changing sheets, unblocking loos – but was it all too late? I wasn't sure. It did occur to me, though, as I brushed the graceful crocosmia heads in the hedgerow with my hand, that had our marriage been more like Lottie and Hamish's from the very beginning, with no preconceptions, no codes of conduct – albeit unwritten – it might have been happier. I looked up to the glittering heavens. Might even have been the happiest under the sun.

Chapter Six

Sebastian's final exhibition had opened on a hot summer's night back in his glory days of feverishly penned previews in all the major broadsheets, interviews in Sunday colour supplements, and a glossy catalogue to stop doors with. It had been another acclaimed success and he'd made a great deal of money. Collectors and dealers from all over the world – New York, Paris and even China – had come across to snap up his work: it had been a sell-out. Naturally he deserved a break. Exhibiting a staggering forty-six paintings had been no mean feat and Sebastian worked slowly, anyway: it was a gigantic effort. Also, we didn't need another exhibition. We were in a sweet little house in Chelsea, Joshua was in a private school, Tabitha at a Montessori down the road; money was no object. Sebastian had a floor to himself at the top of the house, a huge studio with a domed glass ceiling designed especially, which flooded with light, and although I still painted a bit, two young children were hard work and took up most of my time. I was happy just being a mum and, of course, a wife to my famous husband. And Sebastian *was* famous, and feted for being so. We were asked to all the right parties, first nights, glittering events at the Royal Academy or the Tate Modern. Society hostesses loved to throw us into the mix at their dinner parties, amongst the boring bankers and bellowing barristers.

'Do you know the Montclairs? No? Oh, Sebastian's

frightfully successful, exhibiting in Paris next year. Oh, not next year. But you've got a picture in the Pompidou Centre, am I right? And the Musée d'Orsay?' She'd glance ostentatiously at one of his canvases on her wall, above the fireplace.

Mum, as you can imagine, was in heaven, claiming she knew all along what a star he'd be, what an overnight success. She bored all her friends rigid with her gloating. Even Dad was deeply affected and at the end of one of his book-club meetings, when everyone was deciding what to read next, one of the more amusing members, Peggy, I believe, had drawled: 'Why don't we read the Jardines' son-in-law's reviews?'

The critics loved him, the public loved him – chiefly because he was good-looking and accessible, not weird – and Javier, his agent, naturally worshipped him, but Sebastian, it seemed, could not love himself. He'd become increasingly quiet and withdrawn. I came back from shopping one day to find he'd slashed a hole in one of his more recent canvases: a difficult picture he'd been working on for some months, a nude, which he usually found so relaxing, but couldn't finish, and, in his frustration, had ripped. He hadn't meant to. Had meant to scrape paint off with a palate knife, but it had gone right through, which had shocked him, I think, for Sebastian was the gentlest of men. But there were a lot of canvases he couldn't finish. They stared at him, like unfinished taunting testaments, stacked around his studio walls. Years later, when I finally told Lottie this bit of our story, she'd said: 'Of course. Because it's all about confidence. On a much smaller scale, and much less creatively, it's me with my needles.'

This had made me go cold: the thought of Sebastian losing so much confidence so quickly. Back then, I just thought privately that he needed to get a bit of perspective, look at how much he had achieved, not dwell on what he wasn't doing. And maybe not start the next painting, I'd say, looking on in alarm as he abandoned a perfectly lovely, half-executed landscape, until he'd finished the last?

His eyes would travel round to me in despair, and if I hadn't been so knee-deep in young children and all that went with it, I might have given it more thought; persuaded him not to paint for a while, not to pick up his brush so quickly. Hindsight, of course, is a tremendous thing. As it was he continued to paint furiously, just as we continued the relentless round of parties, with Sebastian being told how marvellous he was and him thinking – he'd say knowing – he wasn't, and then coming home to a baby-sitter and a dark house with an even darker studio upstairs, where he'd always go before bed, turning on the light, to be surrounded by the mockery of his unfinished creations. 'Mockery?' I'd say. 'That's what it feels like,' he'd answer. Of course, the demons are always much worse at night. Later, when I hadn't slept either, I'd creep upstairs to find him sitting slumped and dejected on the floor in the corner, his handsome face hollow and sad, an empty bottle beside him, quite drunk.

In those early married days I'd cradle him and cajole him to bed, and we'd make love, even though he was in no fit state: talking for hours, making plans, bolstering his pride. But even then, looking back, I think we both knew he was in trouble.

By the time Joshua had started at a pre-prep school and

Tabitha was at an adorable little establishment down the road – complete with Mary Jane shoes, a cape and a straw boater – the rot had really set in. By now he hadn't exhibited for years and although he painted all day every day, he achieved very little. The parties had stopped – the invitations dried up – but that wasn't the problem. Money was. Although I was illustrating madly now – as much as I could, making something of a name for myself in the children's fiction market, Puffin in particular, and in a completely different medium to the oils I was used to – it wasn't enough. The mortgage on a house in Flood Street doesn't pay itself and the children were in the sort of schools which were mortgages in themselves. Admittedly Sebastian's pictures had sold for a great deal, but he'd been thoroughly ripped off by Javier and the galleries and our reserves were drying up. Although we'd kept a certain number of beautiful paintings for ourselves, one or two of which I still own and will never sell, we knew we'd have to sell a few, if something didn't happen fast.

Happily it did, in the shape of Ottoline. She still lived at Netherby, but had decided it was too big for her. Had she? Or had she seen what was happening – she adored Sebastian – and swooped to the rescue? Either way, she offered it to us at a knock-down price, on the understanding that she'd live in a cottage in the grounds. The Dairy, to be precise. To say we snatched at it like a drowning man being tossed a lifeline would be an understatement. Or at least, I did. Sebastian was compliant in those days, I thought, looking back guiltily now. Happy to take a lead from me, who ran the show like . . . no, *not* like my mother. I dug my nails fiercely into my hand. Anyway, he agreed. And I felt it was definitely the way forward. To take him out of the unforgiving spotlight of London, away from the probing journalists asking when Montclair's next exhibition would be, wondering aloud – and in print – if he was a busted flush. Away from the queries from friends, the genuine concern, but also the gloating Schadenfreude of other artists – oh, it's a bitchy world, the art scene – who were secretly pleased the enfant terrible was no longer painting them off the canvas.

Later, Sebastian said our swift exit from London looked and felt like running away: that maybe we should have stayed. I was horrified when he voiced this some years after we moved, thinking: Why didn't you mention it at the time? But he just said: Oh, you were so sure of yourself, Ella. As you always are. It wasn't said with any malice, just a statement of fact. But I shrivelled. I'd wanted to protect him, had felt like a tigress with her cub. But he'd felt I was embarrassed, ashamed of what he'd become. Never. *Never.* Then, he was still my beloved Sebastian, art or no art. As far as he was concerned, though, he'd been a failure for a long time.

And failures, or people who see themselves as such, are hard to live with. Where once he couldn't bear not to be solely in my company, would hustle me away from a glittering Belgravia party saying, 'I just want to be with you, Ella. Don't want all this razzmatazz. Let's get back to Josh, just be the three of us', now, it seemed, he couldn't bear to be with me.

The minute we got to the farm he adopted his studio. Not the one I'd envisaged and designed as a surprise, at the top of the house, with the only money we'd salvaged from selling London, but in the dark little Granary across the way. That hurt.

'But I had it specially done for you, got an architect and everything. It's got a north light. I thought you'd love it!'

'You have it,' he said, slurring his words very slightly even then. 'Have your desk under the window and scribble away for your precious editor. Which I'm sure you've imagined yourself doing, but then felt even better for giving it up for me: for Sebastian to work in. Doing the right thing, as usual.' He surely knew how to wound. 'I'm not going to be on the receiving end of your charity, Ella. I'll be the disreputable, discredited drunken has-been across the yard if you don't mind. Tell your friends I'm a tramp or something, if you wish.'

My eyes flooded with tears. I watched him go: his once-tall, athletic frame stooping slightly, his dark head flecked with grey. As he turned to shut the door to the Granary, the handsome face was craggy, the eyes, latterly so deep and soft, fuzzy with disappointment and red wine.

The children were more knowing, by then. At a state school now, of course, in the next village, they'd come running back from school, it being literally across the fields, and race to say hello to Daddy in the Granary. Then, suddenly, they'd check themselves. Glance back at me quizzically as if to say: Is it a good day? Can we go? And I'd nod if he was on form, watching from the kitchen window as he enveloped them in bear hugs when they ran into his studio, dropping everything he might be doing – or not, as the case would more probably be – asking them about their day, looking at the paintings they were clutching. Sometimes, though, I'd shake my head and say: 'I think Daddy's tired, darlings. See him later.' By this I meant tomorrow, not wanting them to see him lurch towards them from some dark corner of the studio, head low and swinging like a bear's, giving incoherent answers to their prattling.

Surprisingly, though, he wasn't an alcoholic. I'd thought he was, and had begged him to see someone. A doctor, then AA or the equivalent, and he'd done both. Returned triumphant.

'The fact that I can go for long dry periods and don't drink steadily through the day means I'm just a heavy drinker, Ella,' he told me on one of his completely sober days. 'I hope that doesn't come as a great disappointment to you? That we have nothing to hide behind?'

I'm telling you the worst bits, the very darkest times, the roughest side of my marriage and his tongue, because, oddly, although people say you remember only the good times, I disagree. I remember the imperfections and the lows. The terrible rows. Me, tearful and often horribly shrill, him silent and brooding. But if I'm honest, and really give it some thought, there were many happy times too. Times when we'd lock the studio door, say: Forget it! And take the children to the river, with a picnic, to paddle. Holding up shorts and dresses, they'd catch tiny fish and tadpoles with Sebastian beside them, trousers rolled, their delighted smiles catching mine and saying: This is lovely, why can't we always be like this? And when they'd run off to find Diblet, who escaped constantly now, loving the freedom to chase as many rabbits as he could, Sebastian and I would lie back on the grassy bank, the sun on our faces. We'd talk in hushed voices about how much better it was going to be. How we'd work through this muddy patch, how our love would see us through and how everyone had their peaks and troughs.

'I love you, Ella,' he'd say, tracing a fingertip down my

cheek as I turned my head towards him. 'And you know what your tragedy is? You love me too much.'

'No such thing,' I'd whisper, knowing it was true. 'Ah, but there is such a thing. If you subjugate your own self. If you're forever the supporting act and never the player. You can't dedicate your life to saving someone.'

'I'm not saving anyone. I'm loving someone. And, anyway, you're not just anyone, you're my husband.'

He'd smile: that lovely, slow, creasing smile that started at his eyes, led to his mouth, then enveloped his whole face. 'You should have married someone your own age, Ella,' he'd say, as the children ran back with Diblet on a lead. 'Someone you could have set out on a journey with. Not someone who was ahead of you already, and who's supposed to be at the peak of his career, but is actually sliding down the other side.'

I did sometimes wonder if this was the problem. If, in marrying, we'd placed too much responsibility on his hitherto carefree shoulders. If that sudden need to provide for a very young family had sapped his creativity. But surely that was the same for any man? Except, not many men marry nineteen-year-old girls. I wondered if he felt he had three children.

We'd go back to the house happy and buoyed up after a day like that in the fresh air. When the children were in bed, we'd fall contentedly into ours, always our balm, our salvation, the place where we could make everything better, where we could find peace.

One particular morning, though, after a river trip, flicking through the fashion pages of the *Daily Mail*, I'd seen Celeste modelling Chloé's latest collection in Paris. It had given me a start. Not that I hadn't seen her in the papers before, I had, but I wondered . . . if I'd let them be, hadn't intruded, might that have worked? If he'd married someone more his own age, who was pursuing her own career on the catwalks of Milan or Paris, someone who didn't make him aim so high because he didn't love her quite so ardently, might he have relaxed more? Not set himself such high standards to fulfil her happiness? That, I sometimes felt, was the problem. That he felt too responsible for my life: that his own expectations of himself, to satisfy mine, were too exalted.

I don't remember clearly when it was that Sebastian moved permanently into his studio. Certainly he was painting there – or not – all day every day, prowling round his easel, flicking through canvases propped against the walls, and occasionally falling asleep on the sofa, but it was Ottoline who brought it to my attention. By now she'd made the Dairy her own, in her slightly eccentric but intrinsically stylish way, just as she had once done with the farm. When I'd first seen Netherby, visiting with Sebastian years before, I'd been delighted by the unusual décor: the navy-blue sitting room, oversized lamps placed low on Moroccan trivets, huge cushions on rugs, everything dark and pretty much at floor level, so unlike the brightly lit, vanilla-coloured walls of my childhood. Ottoline herself had been potting away at a wheel in a corner of the Russian Red kitchen, a kiln in the old pantry, which she'd wallpapered with old newspapers, the downstairs loo book-lined to replicate a tiny library.

'That's where you get it from,' I'd told Sebastian sagely on the way home to London in the car. 'The arty side. It must have been on your father's.'

He'd laughed. 'Don't confuse arty with artistic. Ottoline

makes very nice pots and I like a lot of her glazes. She undoubtedly has style, but she can't draw.'

'Just as I can draw but have absolutely no style,' I'd mused.

He hadn't answered. Because it was true. I found dressing hard enough, let alone dressing a house. And once Ottoline had moved out her furniture and belongings, I saw the farm for what it was: a rather ramshackle collection of small dark rooms topped by a few gloomy bedrooms. Yet it had looked so cool and interesting in Ottoline's time. Foolishly, I'd turned to my mother and sister for help.

'Oh, we'll have it fixed up in no time!' they'd chortled, and within a twinkling I had ditsy Colefax wallpaper, chichi sofas with fringes and some china rabbits by Herend. I was appalled, but, having more or less commissioned them, I could hardly take it all back. Sebastian thought it was hilarious.

'I'm not sure what's worse, your mother's faux Sloaney style, or Ottoline's arty pretension!'

'I'll change it,' I'd muttered, throwing a rug over a yellow sofa and taking a bronze figurine off the bookshelf.

'And replace it with what? Everything you do says something about you, Ella. It's inevitable. Every cushion you place, every word you say. It all leaves an imprint.'

I knew this to be true and to be the root of my problem. And he knew it, too, and was telling me as kindly as he could. Not to adopt anyone else's persona – Ottoline's, my mother's – but to be my own person. The trouble was, I didn't know who that was. All I ever did was copy other people: the way they dressed, the way they designed their houses, sometimes even the way they spoke. I was a chameleon. Sebastian said he could tell who I was on the phone to by the way I was talking. I didn't know how to be me. Even my illustrative style was closely modelled on one I'd seen before, admittedly in France, therefore far enough away – charming, bloated ducks waddling to ponds, rabbits with pot bellies and droopy eyes, deer with bandy legs – and I'd only glimpsed it in a second-hand bookshop in Aix, hadn't even bought the book, but it had been enough. My memory was pretty photographic for certain things and I'd reproduced it at home with swift, confident strokes, much to the delight of my publisher and the ignorance of Madame de Courcy, dead these twenty years, but surely left with a flattering legacy. The implications I swept under the carpet.

The day Ottoline pointed out that there was something else I'd swept under the carpet must have been about five years into our occupancy at the farm. I was in my attic studio, sketching away, making Sally Squirrel spring-clean her house for a visit from Harriet Hare, when Ottoline came through the door behind me, wearing her usual fisherman's jumper over tatty old jeans and a puffa jacket. I always thought it was a blessing her style didn't extend to her clothes as I'd surely have copied those, too. She plonked herself down in a creaking basket chair in the corner, her short legs planted firmly apart, and lit a cheroot, the small, dark cigars she smoked, knowing I didn't mind. I put down my pencil, turned and waited, knowing she wouldn't interrupt unless it was important.

'When did you last see your husband, Ella?' she asked, cutting to the chase.

'Isn't that the name of a play?' I said lightly, playing for time.

She shrugged. Didn't answer. If I was going to play silly buggers she wasn't going to join in. Her dark eyes held mine: not unkindly, concerned.

I sighed. 'A few days ago, I suppose. He said he'd rather eat at the pub. And of course, now he's got that bed upstairs . . .'

The little gallery above his studio had once hosted a table and chairs. Now he'd moved a bed in. A double one.

'Does it bother you? That he's moved out?'

'He hasn't moved out, Ottoline.'

She snorted. 'Well, when's he coming back?'

'I don't know,' I said quietly. 'I haven't asked him.'

'And even if he has moved out, he hasn't gone very far, is that it? And, actually, the house is more peaceful with him over there. No one's treading on eggshells wondering what sort of mood he's in. And, in a way, it's sort of easier for you and the children?' I didn't answer. She sighed. 'It's the thin end of the wedge, Ella. Ask me, I should know. I told myself things like that, too. Told myself I didn't like the diplomatic circus, that was all. Not every wife did. Traipsing from one hot country to another, all those parties – that it was nothing to do with me and Humphrey. Told myself it was the life I hated, not my husband. Or the fact that he didn't want children.'

Ottoline had been Humphrey's second wife. He had children from his first; said he didn't want any more. Sebastian and I had imagined that's why she'd left him, but she later told me it wasn't. That though she'd ached for children for a while, what she really wanted was a man who loved her enough to give her something she ached for. That man clearly wasn't Humphrey. She'd come home, thrown away all her cocktail dresses and told Humphrey it wasn't a ploy: she wasn't going back. Although Humphrey was apparently distraught at the time and made a few trips home to try to persuade her, she wouldn't budge. And Humphrey remarried within the year, which, as she said, rather proved her point. Rather than being bitter, though, she'd thrown herself into helping her brother run the farm, which they'd jointly inherited, started potting, and pretty much brought Sebastian up, in place of his fey, selfish mother. Humphrey had been her great love but also her great disappointment. Even more so when his third wife had given birth to twins.

'Ottoline, I've never asked you this,' I said suddenly, as she puffed away at her cheroot in my basket chair, 'but do you ever wish you'd twisted Humphrey's arm like that? Like his next wife did?' We both knew what I was talking about.

'Sometimes,' she admitted candidly, after a pause. She blew smoke in a thin line up to the ceiling. 'Usually in the small hours. Or on a cold, January morning. And I suppose that's what I've come to say to you today. Don't be afraid to arm-twist, if you have to. Sometimes people don't know what they want until you give it to them. And then they're delighted. Apparently Humphrey's thrilled to bits with his two boys.'

'Ah.'

'Just as Sebastian might be, if you told him you wanted him back here, with his family, where he belongs. Not across the way.'

I picked up my pencil, turned and bent my head to add a feather to Harriet Hare's bonnet. Ottoline watched me draw in silence.

That had been then. And Ottoline hadn't opened up to me since, not being the type for a heart to heart, even though we were very good friends, the best, despite our age difference, along with Lottie across the way. Nor was she the sort to interfere, and having said her piece, she left it at that. Sebastian stayed where he was.

As I say, that was some years ago. He'd been in the Granary ever since and I'd been here, in the farmhouse, in, some would say, an ideal marriage. I had a husband, but I didn't. He couldn't live with me, yet, it seemed, he couldn't live without me, even though he'd toyed with the idea when a cottage came up for rent in the next village. Without meeting each other's eyes we'd discussed him living there and letting out the Granary, which would cover the rent on his new cottage. Come to about the same thing. I was in terrible pain as we discussed, effectively, separating. I don't know if he was in pain too. I do know it never happened. I also heard through the grapevine that he went to see other cottages, in other villages, but never clinched the deal. Instead we lurched on in our chaotic, some would say bohemian, fashion – although bohemian sounds exotic it just feels like a muddle – and the children adapted as children do. It has to be said that him staying put and not moving away was much better for them. They had both of us. The only time sparks flew – a saucepan, as it happened, full of cold stew – was when Ludo, as Sebastian put it, 'came sniffing around'. Actually, he'd sweetly brought me raspberries and sweet peas from his garden when he'd known I was having people to supper on my birthday. Sebastian found them on the doorstep. I hadn't said a word when I'd discovered Isobel. It had hurt terribly – after all, he'd meant it to – but I hadn't said anything. Certainly hadn't thrown pans. Perhaps I didn't feel I had the right. And I'd cleared up that stew without a word of reproach, either. Wiped the walls in silence.

Chapter Seven

Ludo was Ginnie's property really, not mine. Or her set's property, at any rate, Ginnie being the sort of woman who had a set. Not that he'd be aware of it – part of Ludo's charm was that he was oblivious to his own – but she and her friends found him quite delightful. After all, he might be a blue-collar worker but he was educated and well-spoken and the collar was linen and came from Ralph Lauren. Given half a chance, Ginnie and her girlfriends would sit around breathing heavily about him and going a bit hot, albeit with absolutely zero intent.

'Gorgeous,' they said, setting down their bridge hands, the one and only time I'd been rushed across to make up a four. Celia Harmsworth had cystitis apparently, and even though I'd learned at my mother's knee, in such rarefied company the cards slipped from my hands I was so damp with nerves.

'Such mahvellous eyes,' brayed Helena McCauley, going a bit misty and forgetting her fistful of trumps for a moment.

'Mahvellous,' her partner agreed, sipping her Chablis.

'Can't think what Eliza's *doing* letting him roam around the country like that.'

'Well, she doesn't care. You know what Eliza's like. She thinks he's never been good enough for her. And now that he's a gardener, she's positively dismissive.'

'Silly girl. Someone will snap him up if she doesn't want him, you mark my words. I get palpitations every time I *see* him in my courgette bed!' declared Helena.

'I don't think he's like that, though,' someone else mused dreamily. 'I think he's actually a really rather nice man.' Fond imaginings of walking holidays in the Fells in this particular head.

'Nice or not, the next time he bends over to tend to my radishes, I swear to God I'm going to have trouble restraining myself,' Helena retorted, and everyone dissolved into giggles at her boldness, knowing she was joking. Infidelity belonged to the city sisters: women to be talked about and tutted over. Of course, it happened out here too, but not to women like *them*, to which Sebastian would say: because they looked like horses, and who knew what their commuter husbands were up to in London?

Smug, he told me they were, and there was indeed a certain self-righteousness about them. I didn't particularly want to join their big-house, dinner party gang – I knew my sister and I needed to have different friends if we lived close by, and that Lottie and Ottoline wouldn't be her cup of tea – but I was occasionally hurt that I'd never even been invited to lunch, or to play bridge properly.

'Not that you'd want to,' Lottie had pointed out.

No, but I hadn't been courted.

Except, it would transpire, by the object of their fantasies, which was something of a coup, I suppose. He'd arrived on my doorstep, back when things were particularly dire and my credit card had been cut up, in the form of a present from Ginnie. A very sweet and thoughtful one, as it happened, and which more than made up for the lack of invitations.

'Apparently your vegetable garden's a bit of a disaster,' he told me, as he leaned languidly on my porch in a crumpled white shirt and jeans. A crumpled smile too, devastating blue eyes and that shock of unruly blond hair. 'And your greenhouse could do with some attention. And, although you'd like to live off the land, you actually live in Waitrose.'

'Tesco,' I said absently, thinking I'd never seen anyone of that age – he must be at least forty – look so absurdly boyish.

'I think your sister has visions of neat rows of cabbages and runner beans marching triumphantly into the sunset, does that sound about right?'

'It sounds absolutely terrific,' I agreed eagerly. 'And so, so kind of her. Hang on, come in. I must just ring.'

He followed me inside and I bustled around getting him a coffee – not instant, I decided, dusting off the percolator – as he patted the dogs, not forgetting Diblet, I noticed, ancient and arthritic in his basket. Meanwhile I rang Ginnie, thanking her profusely. Saying he was just what I needed.

'I mean – the gardening,' I said, blushing and wishing I'd washed my hair that morning. Ginnie purred and told me exactly what I was to do with him, whilst Ludo stood at my kitchen window cradling a mug and gazing out at the chaotic mess that was my garden, his back to me.

'New potatoes,' she was saying, 'because they're absolutely delicious if you catch them early enough, but don't go mad because you have to dig the bloody things. And courgettes are brilliant, but beware marrows. Forget broad beans because the children won't eat them, but any soft fruit is tremendous. They'll eat them straight from the canes. Oh – and tomatoes, obviously. OK?'

'OK,' I told her breathlessly, thanking her again and wondering how much it had cost her. Wondering too, for the hundredth time, how much Richard must earn. I put the phone down.

'I thought you might want an asparagus bed and some baby onions,' Ludo said, turning his head towards me. He gave me that smile. 'They're lovely in salads. But let's see what you've got out there already, shall we? It may be that just a bit more planting is in order, or it could be we have to start from scratch.'

'Oh – start from scratch,' I said fervently, wanting hours and hours of this. I plunged my feet into my wellies by the back door and glanced in the cracked little mirror for long enough to see that my cheeks were flushed, which at least added a certain brightness. 'I'm quite sure nothing can be salvaged.' I added firmly.

As I told Lottie later, when I popped round excitedly to see her, it had been all I could do not to turn into a *Carry On* character, so thick and fast had come the double entendres

'Your sprouts have gone to seed,' he observed sadly.

'Haven't we all?' I cackled stupidly.

'And your dill's a bit leggy.'

'Oh, that the same could be said of me!' I even flourished a short little leg in a wellie, knowing it was hairy under the woolly tights.

'And your cabbages need a good seeing-to.'

Happily I didn't respond. It would have been shameful and deeply regrettable later.

But I did now know how Helena McCauley felt.

'Talk about frustrated housewives, Lottie, I was absolutely in there amongst them. And the trouble is, he makes everything sound so sexy, even though I'm sure he doesn't mean to. He took a look in my greenhouse and said my cucumbers were much better than his, and that his were perfect one minute but grew like mad the next. He said that, right now, he had a massive one. It was all I could do not to run snorting from the greenhouse. I felt about fourteen!'

'It's well documented, of course,' Lottie said, breaking cotton with her teeth as she sewed a name tape into her youngest, Matthew's, school shirt. 'It's all to do with the soil and the seductive texture of the earth. Getting one's hands dirty and getting right down amongst the loam and the worms. See Lawrence on this. Mellors was a classic example.'

'Except he was a gamekeeper,' I reminded her.

'Yes, but it's all that pastoral stuff, isn't it? Being at one with nature.'

'I think you'll find he was killing nature. Or raising birds to be killed.'

'Just as you're raising vegetables to be boiled. When's he starting?'

'Next week. He's going to create some raised beds, and naturally all I could think about was a huge four-poster with me springing athletically into it. He's not really a gardener, he's a garden designer, but he obviously realizes I don't have anyone to do the spade work, as I'm sure the Helenas of this world do. Perhaps Ginnie's told him? Anyway, he says he wants to handle mine properly.'

'I bet he does!' Lottie cackled dirtily. Then looked horrified. 'Oh, God. Barbara Windsor.'

'You see?' I told her in triumph.

'It is fairly irresistible,' she admitted.

'Certainly seems to come naturally to me.'

She eyed me with interest. 'And is he really like that, d'you think? Nudge nudge, wink wink, how's about getting a bird's-eye view of yer marrows from the bedroom window, missus?'

'God, no, not remotely. Given the slightest opportunity he talks about his children. Goes completely dewy-eyed. He even referred fondly to Eliza.'

'*Poisonous* Eliza?'

'Well, obviously, he doesn't think so.'

'Or he's being terribly loyal.'

'Yes. Yes, he is loyal,' I said thoughtfully. 'When I was drafted in to play bridge, Helena told me quietly – when Ginnie was out of the room – that he would never entertain the fact that he's made a terrible mistake. Has always maintained he has a lovely wife and a perfect marriage.'

'Because that's what he wants to believe.'

'I suppose. And you know, she could be perfectly sweet?'

'She's not,' Lottie said shortly. Eliza was a patient of hers, and although medical professionalism prevented her from telling me anything about the in-depth, one-hour consultation she kicked off with before the needles, I knew she'd been curt and abrupt to Lottie. Had thought it impertinent that an acupuncturist should be asking her anything personal, saying: 'I only came here to have my migraines sorted out, so kindly stop asking me about my private life and get on with it!'

I recalled Ludo telling me how Eliza liked to grow blackcurrants at the bottom of their orchard, because the smell reminded her of her childhood in Devon: what a sweet and wholesome image he'd created of her. How I, in turn, had talked about Sebastian being so inspired by the colours this spring, which wasn't true either. Sebastian had said he couldn't wait for autumn, when at least everything had a death-like quality, which was how he felt. How we protected them.

'And does he always work in his studio? Not outside?' Ludo had asked as we returned from our inaugural inspection of the vegetable garden that day, nodding across to the Granary which, mid-morning, still had the bedroom curtains closed and which he politely didn't draw attention to. Of course he knew, though. Everyone around here did. The famous painter who'd lost his bottle. Found another.

'Yes, mostly. Well, pretty much always, actually.' I'd never seen Sebastian with an easel in the fields. 'He's doing portraits at the moment, which is something of a departure for him, and by its very nature tends to be inside.'

'Oh. Right. Do you sit for him?'

'I haven't yet,' I said lightly.

Hadn't been asked. The children both had, and Ottoline did, quite a bit. But not me. Was he afraid of what he'd see, I wondered? Once, in one of our more bitter moments, I'd voiced this.

'I think I'm more afraid of how I'd interpret you,' he'd said, giving me a cold look. He'd apologized the next day, saying he hadn't meant it, but I carried it around with me nonetheless. Even unto the vegetable garden with Ludo.

'He's hugely talented,' Ludo said reverently, and I realized I was in the presence of an enthusiast. A fan, even.

'He is,' I agreed.

'I went to art school. Would have loved to have gone down that route and done fine art. Been a proper artist.'

The sun caught his startlingly blue eyes. 'But I wasn't gifted, not like that. I followed the design route instead and somehow ended up in landscape gardening, which at least combines art with fresh air.'

'I heard you were in the City once?' I asked shyly as we walked. He'd realize he'd been discussed, but hey.

'Oh, yes, I was,' he said, surprised. 'When Eliza and I were first married. I felt I should provide properly, have a proper job, so I retrained. Sat all the exams and got a job courtesy of one of her relatives. But I hated it. Had to get out.'

'And Eliza was supportive?' I prompted naughtily, feeling pretty sure she hadn't been.

He looked uncomfortable and I wished I hadn't said it. 'Of course,' he answered finally, lying.

I liked him for it.

That was back then. These days, however, eighteen months since he'd arrived as a gardener and well into our rather more ambiguous relationship, Ludo and I were more honest with each other about our spouses. I knew, for instance, that Eliza was sharp and sarcastic and capable of wounding him deeply with her taunts, her rages about lack of money, just as he knew Sebastian could hurt me, but for different reasons. We'd discuss them in hushed tones as we ostensibly inspected the greenfly on the gooseberry bushes down by the duck house on the river, as far, geographically, as we dared go without arousing suspicion.

Today, though, as we strolled around the runner-bean canes closer to home, canes which now positively dripped with bounty thanks to his green fingers, I didn't want to talk about Eliza or Sebastian. I had something else on my mind. Along with the fruit and flowers Ludo had left on the step recently for my birthday, he'd given me another present: a Mulberry handbag, which once, in an idiotic moment, whilst we'd been flipping through a magazine in my studio together remarking on the sleek celebrity hand luggage, I'd laughingly said I'd go to my grave without owning. He'd handed it to me in the orchard the following week, wrapped in pink tissue paper with a velvet bow. I'd actually dropped it I'd been so touched.

'I love it,' I told him now as we walked in the sunken veggie garden together, out of view of the farm. 'More than you'll ever know and for so many different reasons. But it's far, far too generous. You'll have to take it back.'

'Don't be ridiculous, I'm not doing that.'

'But, Ludo, you can afford it about as much I can.' I'd nearly fainted when I'd gone on the website.

'Who cares? And, anyway, I'm not going back to that shop; it frightens the life out of me.'

'Which shop?'

'Harvey Nichols. All those terrifying women armed with sprays ready to zap you as you walk in, wanting to know if I use moisturizer. I was in a muck sweat by the time I reached the handbag department.'

'You went all the way up there?' I said in wonder.

'I have been to London before, you know. Don't just chew a straw in a cabbage patch. Anyway, I had lunch at my club.'

I stopped in my tracks.

He laughed. 'Important to keep you on your toes, Mrs Montclair. No, I had lunch in Pret A Manger.'

I imagined him eating his sandwich with the handbag safely stashed under the table in a stiff white carrier bag. Glancing at his watch as he waited to get the train back. Felt a warm glow.

'Thank you.' I breathed, happily. We stopped in the shelter of the crumbling wall and he put his arms round me, holding me close. We were hidden from sight but a bit of me thought: Who cares?

'It's beautiful,' I told him.

It was. And it went everywhere with me. To the loo, to the bath – sitting on a chair well away from splashes but where I could gaze at it – and once to show the sheep. Josh hadn't noticed, of course, but Tabs jolly well had. I told her I'd won it in a raffle.

'A raffle!' she'd shrieked incredulously, riffling through it with all the efficiency of the drugs squad, searching for the magic label. 'Where!'

'At some charity do,' I'd said blithely, hiding my flaming cheeks in the fridge as I pretended to clean it. Oh, the tangled web . . .

'But, actually, there is a condition to the bag,' Ludo told me now as we emerged up the garden steps and walked back towards the house. I glanced at him, alarmed.

He hooted with laughter. 'Oh, no, not that! Although, actually – good point – why not? Whip your kit off, would you?' I shot him a withering look. 'No, it's just – I had a thought the other day. Why don't you start painting again? You know, properly?'

That old chestnut. The one everyone who cares for me asks eventually. I didn't tell him I couldn't bear to set up an easel in the fields and splash away in front of Sebastian's nose, that I loved him too much to do that. Or even to be up in the attic in a smock, happily stacking up the canvases. I knew I told him more than I'd told most people already. This man with his kind smile and his frank blue gaze.

'Yeah, I might do,' I agreed breezily. 'Too busy getting a

guaranteed income from my punters at the moment, though.'

'And does Sebastian help a bit more with said punters these days?' Ludo asked lightly as we passed the Granary, almost at his Land Rover.

I glanced at him quickly, knowing I'd promised to ask. 'Not really,' I said shortly.

He didn't press it. He knew Sebastian could barely give my paying guests more than a curt nod when he passed them in the yard, lugging their cases into the cottages, let alone help, and had begun to realize there wasn't much point in asking, either. Why couldn't Sebastian lend a hand, though? Do a bit of grouting or decorating? Didn't he know these were the people who put bread on his table and, more to the point, liquor down his throat? Or maybe that's why he was rude. Because in some convoluted way he despised them for being the means of his inactivity. I sighed. Life was so complicated these days. I sometimes longed for the Cadogan Terrace days, before children. Before responsibility. For simpler times. I was still only thirty-seven, but sometimes it seemed more like fifty-seven. I felt ancient, careworn and exhausted. Probably looked it, too. I straightened up a bit, un-creasing my forehead.

Tabitha emerged from the house in her old Barbour, the one with the big pockets which housed her cigarettes, and which she knew I knew about but tacitly didn't mention. Joshua was one thing, but I wasn't going to give carte blanche to my fifteen-year-old.

'Hi,' she said shyly to Ludo.

The three of us chatted a moment as he asked her about school – the same one as his daughters – and which subjects she was doing, and then he said he had to go, as indeed he did. I watched his long, slim back with regret.

Josh came out of the kitchen in bare feet as his sister sloped off to the river. Ludo's Land Rover reversed in the yard then swung out through the gates.

'There he goes,' Josh said, pulling his rug round his thin shoulders. He squashed his felt hat further down on his head. 'Oblivious to the chaos he causes.'

'What d'you mean?' I asked, turning sharply.

'Ludo. Ginnie's lust generator. Araminta says Ginnie puts on perfume before he comes round. Isn't he the one getting the juices flowing amongst the menopausal set?'

'Don't be ridiculous. And, anyway, I'm nowhere near menopausal!'

'No, but Ginnie is. Anyway, we weren't talking about you. You do look a bit flushed, though.' He peered into my face. 'Have you got Tabs's lippy on?'

'Of course not!' I lied. I had, in fact, nipped to the loo before Ludo arrived and pinched my daughter's Hot Pink Surprise, which had been sitting on the shelf. When I put it on, my face had looked even more surprised, but it had been hard to rub off.

'Looks remarkably like it. Hardly your usual Pearl 'n' Shine.' I flushed as he regarded me with ironic eyes. 'Hope you can handle yourself, Ella. You're at that dangerous age.'

'What d'you mean?'

'When the spark has gone out of your marriage and your children are growing up and getting boyfriends and girlfriends of their own. Exploring their own sexuality. You look around and think: Is this all there is for me? All that's left? Domestic drudgery? And all the time the hormonal soup bubbles up inside you and ebbs and flows, ebbs and flows . . .' He swayed back and forth in his rug, lurching like the tide. 'Sloshing this way and that –'

'Joshua!'

'Hot and cold . . .' He swayed, his eyes half shut as if in a trance. 'Tearful and moody –'

'That will *do*, thank you!'

Josh wanted to be an actor and was not without talent. He was currently rehearsing George in *Who's Afraid of Virginia Woolf?* and took every opportunity to be as caustic and In Character as possible. He stopped swaying and looked mock-affronted. Readjusted his rug.

'Well, shit, Ella, only trying to help. I mean, you could pop down to Lottie's funny farm – sorry, Holistic Centre – and get one of her cronies – sorry, alternative therapists – to sort you out, but why bother when you can get it all here for free? In your own back yard? Any little niggles, any loss of identity – the disappearing-woman syndrome, I've read all about it in the *Daily Mail*, any – pant pant – inappropriate hankerings?' He winked. 'You just bring it all here to Uncle Josh. We have a remedy for most things down on the farm.' He grinned. And then, tweaking my cheek affectionately, he ambled off, no doubt for a smoke with his sister by the river. I watched him go as he picked his way carefully in his bare feet, tartan rug dragging, the dogs and Ladyboy at his heels.

Chapter Eight

That little exchange with Josh stayed with me. Jocular though it had been, I thought about it on and off, and later that week, as I drove through the Buckinghamshire countryside en route to see my father – Ginnie had decided I was the best man for the job, the perfect envoy – I considered my children's position. Reconsidered, should I say, because, let's face it, I examined it often, from every angle. Of course it hadn't escaped their notice that their parents didn't actually live together let alone sleep together. They weren't stupid. Teenagers thought about sex a great deal – every four minutes for boys, according to Radio 4 – so they were bound to notice these things. And even though they'd been relatively young when their father had the affair with Isobel, that wouldn't have passed them by, either. He hadn't exactly been circumspect about it. Hadn't exactly slipped off to Brighton to conduct a secret dalliance with her – no, he'd conducted it reasonably publicly from the local pub, under everyone's noses. Admittedly this was where Sebastian spent a great deal of time anyway, but not as much as that. Not all night. She was the barmaid – or publican, I suppose, since she owned the Fox and Firkin – and she sat for him a lot, too. She was attractive, in a streaky blonde, throw-your-head-back-and-roar, slightly raddled sort of way, but no tremendous shakes.

Sebastian liked a sitter like this. Not a raving beauty but

someone who'd seen a bit of life. He liked to get that in a face. Bring it out. So she sat, and sat nude, for weeks; and he'd make charcoal drawings and many sketches, but I never actually saw a finished picture. When the light faded – Sebastian could only paint in natural light these days, which made him a nicer person to live with in the summer than in the winter – the curtains upstairs in the Granary would close and Isobel's car would remain in the yard. All night, on occasion. You'd have to be a very unusual sort of person, a very unusual *child*, not to notice that. I forgave Sebastian a lot over the years because I loved him – I even forgave him the time I found them in our bed together, knowing he'd been making a point: 'We're finished, Ella' – but I couldn't forgive him that. Such blatant tossing of his infidelity in his children's faces.

Usually, after an episode of sleeping rough for a while at the Granary – in those days it had only a sofa bed – he'd wander back to the farmhouse eventually. But after Isobel, I locked the doors. I didn't even have to change the locks. He tried only once to get in, found the back door locked, and sauntered back to the Granary. It was as if he'd wanted it to happen. Had forced my hand and was – if not happy – accepting of the outcome.

I went to see him after that, knowing Isobel wasn't there. Stood shaking in his studio. I told him that if he wanted to have an affair could he please do it elsewhere. Sebastian had been sober at the time and had agreed that he could indeed conduct the affair elsewhere. He said he had no desire to hurt the children and since he'd finished his portrait of Isobel – not quite true, he never finished it – he'd be happy to bed her exclusively in her flat above the pub, and would do so with the utmost circumspection.

Looking back, I saw it was his way of ending our marriage, but as we glared at one another that day, alone in the studio, me with fists clenched, still trembling, all I remember is the strange guarded expression in his eyes as he regarded me and the hurt and love I was afraid might show in mine. To this day I couldn't see Sebastian slouching across the yard barefoot, paint-splattered shirt hanging out over frayed jeans, without my heart turning over, and sometimes, as I saw him look at me, feeding the chickens or running to chase an escaped sheep, I liked to think I glimpsed his heart tipping too. Not spilling, but tipping. Not recently, though. I gripped the steering wheel as I wound down the snaking lane that led to my parents' village. Recently there'd been hate there as well. He'd said to me snidely the other day, as I'd taken his sheets across: 'I see that johnny gardener is still circling, Ella. You're obviously giving him what he wants.'

I'd turned to him in outrage as he stood at his easel, brush in hand. 'I'm giving him precisely nothing except the run of the garden, the digging of which you clearly think is beneath you! I wouldn't be so tacky as to dirty my own doorstep, like you and Isobel.'

Such was the mud-slinging we'd descended to. He'd regarded me coolly out of the corner of his eye as he'd carried on painting.

'You know, weird as that is, I think I believe you. You wouldn't want to lose the moral high ground, would you? Wouldn't want any grains of that precious terrain to slip through your fingers.'

I'd thrown the sheets on the floor and stalked out, tears stinging my eyelids, knowing, in a sense, he was right. Even had I wanted a proper affair with Ludo – which

I increasingly did – I wouldn't want to live with the person I would then become. As Sebastian so often said, it was all about appearances with me. But what he hadn't also said, but perhaps knew, was that my not having a physical relationship with Ludo was my way of keeping my family together. Viscerally I knew that if I descended to Sebastian and Isobel's level, that would be it. The farm would have to be sold and the children would lose their father across the way. My resistance was all that kept us tottering along in the precarious position we found ourselves.

No such restraint for my father, though, I thought in alarm as I purred through the picturesque village of my childhood and approached the Old Rectory gates. They glittered back at me in the sunlight, black and glossy between attractive stone walls dripping with purple aubrietia. The man himself was whistling his way back cheerfully from the village shop even now, looking like the cat who'd got pints of cream. I watched as he approached, oblivious to me. The *Telegraph* was tucked under one arm, a silk hanky flowed even more luxuriantly than usual from his tweed jacket and his cheeks were ruddy and flushed. Hopefully from the wind, I thought with a sudden qualm.

As the gates opened electronically and I crunched up the gravel drive ahead of him to the pretty Georgian facade, he recognized the car.

'Darling!' I heard him call behind me as I parked.

I tried not to, because he was categorically in the doghouse, but I couldn't help grinning broadly as I got out. Normally we'd both be looking around nervously for Mum, but as he swept his hat from his head and gave me a huge bear hug, my feet lifting off the ground, it was a relief to know that for once – and for the first time in years – we were not under the censorious gaze of Mum or Ginnie. They'd wonder if we weren't being too frivolous and silly. Too over the top. I loved my dad in a way I could never love Mum because I could be completely at ease with him, without wondering what would come next or how I should form my next sentence. The extra squeeze he gave me as he set me down told me he felt this too, and as I linked his arm and went inside I had to remind myself I was not here to have a good time with my father. I certainly wasn't to go to the pub with him, share a few drinks, or have a laugh, like two naughty schoolchildren. I was on a mission and should adopt a serious expression and get down to it, pronto.

'This is a surprise, darling,' he was saying, already rubbing his hands with delight as he shut the front door behind us. We went through the lofty, stone-flagged hall and he headed straight to the sherry decanter on the far side of the sitting room. 'Drink?'

'No, thanks, Dad. I'll have a coffee,' I told him firmly.

'Sure?' He turned with surprise from the drinks tray on the Pembroke table. 'Nothing stronger? Bloody Nuisance, perhaps?' Dad's name for a Bloody Mary, on the grounds that it involved him finding Worcester Sauce and slicing lemon, et cetera.

'Quite sure,' I said primly, perching on the tomb-like sofa. He looked disappointed. 'And perhaps you shouldn't, either,' I scolded. 'Mum wouldn't be too thrilled to see you drinking so early, would she?'

'Well, she's not here, is she?' he scoffed belligerently, pouring himself an extra-large one.

Error. I'd thought by introducing Mum early, I'd bring him up short. Remind him where his duties lay. Historically he'd have adopted a shamed expression, put his tail between his legs and got straight in his basket. Not today. His eyes gleamed at me alarmingly from the other side of the room.

'Not here to tell me when to get out of bed, whether I can tune the radio to a station I like, or if it's too loud. Not here to tell me not to whistle when I shave. Not here to tell me what time to get my paper, or if I can have a few biscuits – let alone a drink. She can't even give me permission to go and prick out my dahlias in the greenhouse. I can't tell you how liberating it is, Ella. Her coming to stay with you has been the most tremendous success. I can't thank you enough. Given us all some much-needed space.'

I blinked. 'Well, except me.'

'Oh, quite. Except you. And you're simply splendid to have suggested it, darling,' he said admiringly.

'I didn't!' I squeaked. 'Ginnie did.'

'Oh, did she? Oh. Right. Got the wrong end of the stick there.'

Clutching a veritable bucket of sherry he came across and sank happily into the armchair my mother forbade him to sit in, the most comfortable, pale-pink squishy one, on which his Trumper's hair oil, she said, made a nasty mark. Was it my imagination or did he give his head a little rub as he settled into it? This wasn't going quite as I'd envisaged.

'You mean . . . you don't mind she's gone? Mum, I mean?'

'Good Lord, no. Blessed relief,' he said with feeling. 'All she did was nag. Nag nag nag nag nag.' He waggled his head from side to side. 'And I'm quite sure she needed a holiday.' He gulped his drink.

'Well, it's more than a holiday, Dad,' I said sternly. 'She's moved out.'

He looked unmoved. Shrugged. 'Whatever.'

I flinched. My father didn't say things like 'Whatever'.

I ploughed on, my face very grave. 'This is deadly serious, Dad. You're in a real pickle here. There may be no way back. Honestly, between you and me, I think there's a very real chance she might move out for ever.'

'Oh, for ever is such a nebulous concept, isn't it?' he said airily, waving his hand in the air. 'Especially at our age. Good heavens, one of us could go tomorrow!'

I frowned, sensing the nub. I narrowed my eyes at him. 'Is that what this is all about? Sensing mortality round the corner and all that? Getting to a ripe old age and wondering if you've really lived? I mean – you know – emotionally?'

He widened his eyes at me in surprise. 'Well, I haven't, have I? I've been here, with your mother.'

There was no answer to that. I opened my mouth. Shut it. Swallowed hard. Tried a different tack.

'Daddy – Daddy, look. She's desperately sad and tremendously upset about all this. Humiliated, too.'

'Well, I certainly don't mean to humiliate anyone.' It wasn't said with any great contrition, though. He sipped his drink thoughtfully. 'Maybe it's best she's gone. If she feels like that. Has a little break from the village.'

'Well, she could hardly stay, could she?' I burst out. I slipped out of my coat, which I'd yet to remove, and flung it down beside me, folding my arms briskly. 'Not with you carrying on like this for all the neighbours to see!'

He blinked. 'That doesn't sound like you, Ella,' he said in mild surprise. 'Sounds more like the other females in my family. And, anyway, I'm not Carrying On, as you put it.

I'm just having a lovely time with a cracking girl.' He leaned forward eagerly. Set his drink aside and rubbed his knees with both hands. 'And she *is* a cracking girl, Ella!' he assured me, eyes twinkling.

I sighed, knowing the knee-rubbing of old. He wanted to divulge. Share. I sank back into the sofa feeling utterly defeated. Round one had definitely gone to him already. 'Go on, then,' I said bitterly. 'Tell me all about her. I can see you're dying to. And, actually, I might have that sherry after all.'

'Oh, she's one hell of a good sport,' he said, getting up with alacrity and bustling to pour me a drink. He helped himself to a little more at the same time. 'A real gem. She trained Buster, you know, which is no mean feat, as I'm sure you'll agree. But she had him walking to heel and sitting on command – even lying down and waving his legs in the air!' A hideous image of my dad doing much the same sprang to mind and I hid my face in the drink he handed me. 'And just as Buster fell for her charms, well, blow me if I didn't, too! I found I couldn't wait for the next training session to come around. I hustled over there with old Buster like nobody's business, I can tell you. I'd love you to meet her, darling. She's frightfully jolly. You'd like her enormously.'

'Dad . . . I'm not sure that would be entirely appropriate, would it?' I said, giving him an incredulous look as he sank back down in the pink armchair, sherry sloshing because his glass was so full. It was lost on him.

'Eh?' He looked blank. 'Oh, well. As you wish. You'll just have to take my word for it.'

'Won't I just?' I said witheringly, wondering what on earth had got into the man. I was also wondering why this wasn't going to plan. Or perhaps that was the problem, I thought suddenly: there hadn't been a plan. Let's face it, I'd been far too engrossed with thoughts of my own marriage, I realized guiltily, to formulate one about my parents' on the way down. I was rather glad Ginnie wasn't here to witness the mess I was making of this. She surely would have had bullet points, I thought, going hot. She always did. Swore by them. Written in her precise hand on a pad of snowy paper as she picked up the phone to do battle with a teacher, a carpenter who'd overcharged, friends, even, who she wanted to persuade to come to some charity lunch. She didn't move without them. I avoided my sister's gaze in a framed, black-and-white studio photo on the side.

'She's popping over later,' Dad told me breezily.

I jumped. 'Ginnie?'

'No, Maureen. If you change your mind you can stay for lunch.'

'Dad!' I was genuinely outraged now. 'Dad, you can't!'

'What?' He looked startled. Drink paused en route to lips.

'Well, have her here, in Mum's house! Having lunch together, in her kitchen, at her table. You just can't, it's *so* disrespectful.'

He regarded me openly now: candidly, like a child. Set his drink aside carefully. 'Ella, you have no idea how I've suffered. How I have had to measure every word, every phrase, every moment, in your mother's presence. Surely I can have someone to lunch, in what is, after all, my house too? The house I've paid for?'

I couldn't think what to say to that. He made it sound so innocent as well. Perhaps it was? I licked my lips.

'But, Dad,' I persisted, trying a different approach, 'this isn't what you want long term, surely? I mean, on any permanent basis? To replace Mummy with this dog-handler?'

'Maureen is more than a dog-handler and I resent your tone. She is an exceptional woman. Exceptional. And as to replacing your mother, no, of course not. Your mother is your mother. If she'd like to live here, that's fine. As you say, it's her house too. Maureen and I can go elsewhere.'

I went cold. 'You mean . . . you're definitely leaving her? For Maureen?'

'Well, I wasn't going to, darling, but she's moved out, hasn't she? And if you're saying she won't come back if Maureen is around, then of course we'll accommodate her. I was very happy with the situation the way it was, frankly. Don't know why she had to change it.'

Had he a screw loose, this father of mine? I stared. 'What – you carrying on with Maureen, and still living with Mum?' I exploded.

'Well, it's no different to the way you and Sebastian live your lives, is it, love?' This was said gently. His old grey eyes were soft. I gazed at him. Of course it wasn't. There were some very pertinent parallels. Was he aping us? Like some child, repeating learned behaviour? My tweedy father going all bohemian, because we were?

'Of course, I know there are differences,' he said, seeing my face. 'But there are as many complications here, in this house, as there are in yours. That's what I'm trying to say. Who was it said every happy family is the same but every unhappy one is unhappy in its own particular way?'

'Tolstoy,' I muttered.

'Exactly. There are reasons, love. This is not just bonkers Dad having a late-life crisis and going off the rails. Sugaring off with a buxom wench down the road because the opportunity presented itself. I was driven to this as much as Sebastian, for whatever reason, feels he was.'

I felt myself quiver inwardly. My mouth was dry. 'We must all take responsibility for our own lives, though, surely, Dad?' I said with as much self-control as I could muster. 'Our own actions? No one told you to marry Mum, to work in the City, play bridge, shoot. You made all those decisions. If your life became restricted within those – those traditional parameters, it was presumably because you let it be?'

My father and I had surely never talked like this before. He regarded me sadly.

'Yes, I did. I was compliant. Complicit, even. Because it was easier. Men are often like that, you know. We get coerced.'

'Yes. I know. Because you're nicer,' I said quietly.

'No, just . . . lazy, I think. More apt to give in. Give way. For an easy life.'

We were silent a moment. I thought of how Mum had undeniably bullied and coerced him for years, and how, in one brief passage of time – in the space of half an hour, perhaps, after a dog-training session at Maureen's, Dad hanging on for a coffee and a chat – her life's work had been undone. All that channelling of energy into her husband. All that intricate knitting together – managing him, she'd call it, manipulating, he might – had unravelled at the pull of a thread. Perhaps in the catch of an eye; a quick recognition of unhappiness on Maureen's part.

'And what does she want from this?' I asked miserably,

looking around at the fringed sofas, the tapestry cushions, the expensive oils hanging by gilt chains from the picture rail circling the eau de Nil walls.

'Oh, nothing,' he said cheerfully. 'Just to be mates, as it were. She's a widow, you see. Gets lonely, too. Just, you know, lunch. Scrabble. She's taught me crib.'

'Crib?'

'Cribbage.'

'Ah.'

'We play in the pub.'

Anyone would think my mother was being a spoilsport.

On the large tapestry stool between us was a pile of magazines. On top was a brochure for the Bunch of Grapes Inn: a pretty, rural pub in a row of Cotswold stone houses, with rolling hills behind. Ah. Not just scrabble. I seized it triumphantly.

'Love nest?' I asked grimly, flourishing it.

My father looked surprised. 'Oh, no, chap across the road. Dan, you know, married to Jennie. He brought it over. He stays there when he goes on his vintage-car rallies. Couldn't rave about it enough. He was here for a beer the other night. I've never been myself.'

I believed him. Put it down shamefully. It also occurred to me that Dan would never have come across if Mum had been here. He was a nice man, but a bit scruffy. Always mending old cars. And a beer, eh? He'd probably plonked himself down in that pink chair and had a lovely chinwag with Dad. I felt sad. For how many years would Dad have liked that? Other things, too?

'Although I don't think I could be blamed if I had,' my father said abruptly. 'It's not as if your mother enjoys that side of life. Hasn't done for years.' I realized suddenly where we were. Too much information, and yet . . . important information. Because, what the bloody hell did she expect? If she'd turned the tap off years ago. He wasn't a dog, my dad. Wasn't Buster, to be told what to do, but have no fun himself. Yet, my parents were in their late sixties. Was it right for Dad to expect it to go on and on? And, if so, maybe he had a point: maybe the modus operandi he was adopting, with him visiting Maureen and my mother turning a blind eye at home, was just dandy. Everyone was happy, and who cared about the neighbours? One thing was for sure. Mum moving out wasn't going to get my father begging her to come back. She and Ginnie had definitely miscalculated there. He'd just move Maureen in. I rubbed my temples nervously with my fingertips. Felt panic rising.

'OK, Dad,' I said quietly. 'I take your point about Mum. Being a bit – intractable. But don't do anything drastic yet, OK? Don't . . . you know . . .'

'Move Maureen into the master bedroom? Oh, no, darling, I wasn't about to do that. But we can surely share a little cheese on toast by the Aga, eh? Do the crossword together? Oh, look, here she is. Do stay. You'll love her.'

I rose, horrified, as, sure enough, through the front bay window, I could see a bouncy redhead with a wide smile and ample hips come swinging through the electric gates pushing a bike with a basket. She looked a bit out of breath. When she spotted Dad she waved madly and he waved madly back. She gave me a cheery, unabashed look too. Ma in *The Darling Buds of May* sprang to mind. She looked nice. Propping her bike against a tree, she took a package out of the basket.

'Um, I won't stay, thanks, Dad,' I said hastily, grabbing

my coat. 'I've got to get back. But I'm glad – well, I'm glad I came to see you.'

'Me, too, darling,' he said distractedly. His eyes were still shining delightedly through the window and he was hastening, not to escort me to the back door, which I was cravenly making for, but to the front, which Maureen was approaching. 'And give everyone my love, won't you?' he said absently as he hurried across the stone-flagged hall. 'Ginnie, all the grandchildren. Your mother, too.'

'Yes, and – any particular message? I mean, for Mum?' I hovered nervously, knowing he was about to swing wide the door.

'Darling!' he boomed, as I ducked smartly into the kitchen. 'You look ravishing, as usual!'

This, I suspected, was not the message to my mother.

I slipped away through the kitchen and out of the back, shutting the door quietly behind me, but not before I heard Maureen say, in what my mother would sniffily dismiss as estuary English: 'Ooh, Angus, you'll never guess. I found those soft herring roe you like in Morrison's. Seventy-five pence a pound!'

As I tiptoed around the side of the house to my car, it occurred to me that my Dad did like soft herring roe. Talked of them fondly from his days in the army, when he'd had them fried and on toast. It also occurred to me that, to this day, I still didn't know what they tasted like. In forty-odd years, my mother had never cooked them.

Chapter Nine

I went to the Rose and Crown for lunch, partly through need of a large drink and partly out of nostalgia. I'd done my first underage drinking in this pub; had wrinkled my nose in disgust at my first Dubonnet and lemonade with my friend Fi from down the road, hiding cigarettes under our stools so they billowed as if we were on fire, fearful our mothers would come in, even though they'd probably never set foot in here. The Snug Bar was much the same: low, bulging ceiling, faded sporting prints on dark-mustard walls, red Dralon-covered bar stools with lower ones clustered around little tables. The only comfortable seats were the worn leather armchairs by the inglenook fire, which blazed away even at this time of year, its chimney piece cluttered with horse brasses, tankards and country memorabilia. Occupying these two comfortable chairs, which, once I'd bought my drink, I'd been planning to head to, were, to my surprise, my nephew and a young girl.

Hugo had obviously seen me before I'd made him out in the gloom, and, having the advantage, had already arranged his features into a Greet The Aunt And Introduce The Girlfriend ensemble. He stood up as I came across with my gin and tonic.

'Hugo! What are you doing here? I thought you were doing some holiday job in London. Some internship?'

'I was but I jacked it in. And Frankie lives here so I pop

down periodically. Um, Ella, this is Frankie Parks. Frankie, my Aunt Ella.'

We shook hands, her shyly, me trying to hide my deep interest. She was prettier than I'd expected from Ginnie's description, with slanting green eyes, high cheekbones and long tawny hair, and if she was liberally pierced the holes weren't on display, except for the row up the side of one ear, which Tabs sported and were pretty much de rigueur for this age group. She was lovely, and as we chatted and made small talk about the village, I discovered she was Dan and Jennie's daughter and that she'd grown up here, as I had. She grimaced and said she didn't imagine much had changed since then and that the most exciting thing was still the mobile library rolling into the village and everyone taking bets on how pissed Odd Bob would be at midnight mass. I laughed, and thought how like Ginnie to be worried about what school she went to, rather than whether she had a sense of humour; although, actually, I was surprised at Hugo. So far he'd brought home textbook Sloanes, whom his mother had purred over and played the name game with: 'The Parker-Thomases? Oh, but Lucinda is my goddaughter . . . she's your mother's goddaughter, too? So you must go to Norfolk with them! Yes, exactly – Holkham! Ascot? Yes, we do, but not with the PTs, with the de Lyles. No! But I grew *up* with Candida de Lyle! Absol*utely*, we go to Fife – de Lyle heaven!' And so it went on.

This one was much more Josh's type, in point of fact. Oh, yes, he had a type already: a rather quirky, interesting one. And Frankie was much more in that mould. I sat on the chair Hugo had pulled up, deciding I wouldn't stay long: wouldn't intrude on their tête-à-tête.

'How's Granny?' asked Hugo politely, and I thought how handsome he looked in his blue-striped shirt and chinos, hair flopping over one eye like a blond Harry Styles. Although he'd lost a bit of weight.

'Oh, you know: stiff upper lip and all that. Didn't you see her when your mum brought her back to your place?'

'No, I've been staying at Frankie's. Seen a lot of Grandpa, though.' He grinned. 'He's having the time of his life.'

I was rather shocked. Even my children, who I thought were more liberal than Ginnie's, were shaken and saddened by their grandparents' separation.

'Well, I can see he is, Hugo, which is pretty alarming after forty-odd years of marriage, don't you think? Poor Granny!'

He flushed. 'Yes, but poor Grandpa for a lot of those forty years, wouldn't you say?' Despite his pink cheeks he looked me in the eye. 'I stayed with them, don't forget, all last year when I worked in the pub. And, trust me, you'd sympathize.'

'Well, yes, I know,' I said awkwardly, realizing he knew what he was talking about. There'd be no shaming him into being the outraged grandson. 'I've lived there too. She can be tricky.'

'Tricky? I swear to God, Ella, she rules his life. She tells him what to do, what to wear, what to eat, completely dominates him. He has to plant this, and mow that, chop wood and bring it in, and the only bit of fun, right, was this book club, run by Frankie's mum. And she was so down on that. She made him leave in the end.'

'Well, I think it all got slightly out of hand,' said Frankie nervously. 'Became an excuse for the repressed of the village to let their hair down, if you know what I mean.'

I didn't, but nodded, eyes large.

'Yeah, but it was like the scales had dropped from Grandpa's eyes – in a clatter. A glimpse of what he didn't have. He realized there was more to life than trailing round Waitrose ticking Granny's shopping list and being told which socks to wear. No joking, he had to go and change them once. He'd got his weekend ones on on a Tuesday. Anyway, after the book club, I reckoned it would be only a matter of time before he met someone like Maureen.'

'You've met her?'

'Oh, yes, he's often here in the pub with her. Everyone's met her.'

'But don't you see? That's so shaming for Granny! This is her village; she's queen bee!'

'I don't think it's like that, though,' put in Frankie, gently.

'No, it's not,' Hugo said. 'I've asked him.'

'Really?' I said, relieved. 'Oh, good. I wasn't sure. I mean, he told me it wasn't, too, but then he also said Granny hadn't been interested in – well . . .' Perhaps I wouldn't go into his grandparents' sex lives.

'No, it's platonic. They just laugh and play cribbage and cuddle a lot. All the things Grandpa really likes. And they go off looking for country pubs together, that type of thing.'

I was silenced. Nothing too terrible there, surely? And why couldn't my mother play cards and go to the pub occasionally? What was so ghastly about that? And I knew the life Hugo was describing at the Old Vicarage. When I was young, I couldn't wait to get away, particularly once Ginnie had gone. I imagine for Dad it must have been even worse when I left. I remembered his eyes filling up when he'd dropped me at the flat in London when I was eighteen. Driven away looking sad. How narrow his life must have become, how shrunken, so he could barely breathe. He'd loved having Hugo there, that I knew, but Hugo had only borne it because he'd fallen in love in the village. When I'd suggested to Josh he might do the same in his gap year, he'd looked horrified. Suddenly I felt rather grateful to Maureen for making my old dad, whom I adored, so happy. But what of my mother? What for her? A descent into becoming an even more miserable, bitter old woman? Minus Dad, who, I realized, with ever-weakening arthritic hands, at least held her reins to some extent. But now that he'd let go of whatever tenuous grip he'd had, who knew what sort of a monster she'd turn into, untethered? *And she was in my back yard!*

'Gather she's with you now?' said Hugo sympathetically, sinking into his beer.

'Well, no, not *with* me. Just staying for a bit,' I said quickly.

'Ah. Right.' He nodded politely, but looked unconvinced. It occurred to me she could be there for ever. What had I done? Been outmanoeuvred, that's what. I felt prickly with fear. I recalled my sister pretty much trotting back to her car having deposited her: driving away at speed.

'Well, I think it's jolly good of you, anyway.' He wiped some froth from his upper lip. 'Mum said she wouldn't have her under any circumstances.'

'I thought it was your dad!' I squeaked. 'Thought it was Richard!'

'Oh, no, Dad's pretty relaxed. Well, you know,' he grinned disarmingly, 'we all do as we're told. History repeats itself and all that.'

Except in your case, I thought privately. Richard and Araminta do as they're told, and you always used to, but recently you've broken out, Hugo: chucking in your much-trumpeted internship this summer, not working too hard at Cambridge – Ginnie had muttered something about end-of-year retakes, so quietly I almost hadn't heard – skulking down here with a girlfriend your mother wouldn't necessarily have chosen. No wonder you admire your grandpa.

I left them, after a bit, with mixed feelings. Grudging admiration for my father and Hugo and wonder at my sister's rigidity. What was her problem? Just because Hugo wasn't throwing himself into university life – and was on the darts rather than the cricket team, when he could have been a blue – so what? He had to be his own man at some stage. And what could be nicer than popping down here in his car, which apparently he did every weekend, instead of heading to the debating society as he had done at school? And this girl was lovely, surely?

As I left the village I drove slowly past the duck pond and then the gates to the Old Rectory. At that moment, I realized, they were opening by remote control. I hit the accelerator, not wanting Dad to think I was snooping – not that he'd mind – and in my rear-view mirror caught a glimpse of two bicycles emerging from the gravel drive. One was pedalled by the red-headed Maureen, skirt billowing, the other by my Dad, wobbling on unmistakably an ancient bike of Ginnie's, tweedy legs at right angles, bellowing with laughter. They were both obviously oblivious to me: off on some private, hilarious adventure of their own. It occurred to me that Daddy hadn't even mentioned Buster. He'd been devoted to that dog and it had been mean of my mother, who only ever complained about him, to take him. But perhaps he didn't need Buster now?

He'd been his companion, his solace in a cold home; but now he had a proper companion, one he could talk to. I left the village with a lump in my throat.

Arriving at my farmyard sometime later I realized I was shattered. Emotionally drained and tired out. Buckinghamshire and back was a long drive in one day and I was also starving, not having eaten at the pub, and dying for a pee. Ignoring the chickens, who, the moment they spotted me, charged, head down, clamouring to be fed, their rolling gait redolent of fat old women running for a bus, I belted for the back door. Polly, the Indian Runner, nearly caught me but I opened the door and slammed it firmly on her beak, only to run the dog gauntlet instead. Baying with delight, Maud and Doug leaped the length of the room to greet me – Doug, the mongrel, jumping so high he licked my mouth – whilst Diblet thumped his tail in his basket, too weary to move. I knew the feeling. Behind my pack of marauding wolfhounds, though, a far more intimidating welcoming committee was at my kitchen table. In my hurry, I'd missed the cars in the yard, but I spied them out of the window now, one of them being my mother's, which had clearly been collected from Ginnie's.

My mother and sister were both installed around the stripped pine, patently waiting for news. Newspapers and coffee mugs littered the table – they'd obviously been there for some time – and Mum's face was pale and tense. In the background, Joshua, in a dressing gown, eating peach slices straight from the tin, exited stage left. Giving me a faintly apologetic, 'Hey, what could I do, they like, barged in' shrug, he sloped off to attend to urgent screen-viewing business in the playroom. I couldn't help but think that for all my sister's angst about her own son, he had at least been up and dressed and in pressed chinos. You could take the boy out of his mother's house, but you couldn't entirely take the mother out of the boy.

'Well?' was writ large on Ginnie's and my mother's faces, but even they had the self-control to let me fend off the dogs, throw grain from a handy bin under the sink into the yard for the poultry – was that so difficult for anyone else to do? Couldn't swing their arms or something? – and duck smartly as one of the holiday guests, Mrs Braithwaite, clearly looking for me, peered in at the kitchen window. As I surfaced gingerly from under the sink, hoping she'd gone, I bumped into Ottoline, who came bustling out from the sitting room, a pile of clean linen under one arm, Horace, the cockerel, under the other.

'He's been raping Ladyboy again,' she told me, flinging wide the window and tossing him out, to indignant squawks. 'She sought refuge in the fireplace but he tracked her down, the little bastard.' She plonked the ironing she'd done on the side.

'Oh, thanks, Ottoline,' I said gratefully. The only person who actually helped around here and whom my family were regarding like the cleaning lady, clearly hoping she'd kindly leave the stage, so that they could interrogate me.

'Coffee?' I asked her rebelliously, filling the kettle to dagger looks from Mum.

'Why not?' Ottoline said after a pause, checking herself before exiting. We didn't often stop for coffee but she recognized the need in my voice.

Josh stuck his head round the door. 'Doug's done a turd in the playroom,' he informed me.

'Well, clear it up, then,' I said savagely, banging the kettle down on the hob.

'I would, but it's not, like . . . hard. Squidgy. You'd be better at it.'

I ground my teeth. Shut my eyes.

'OK,' he sighed. 'Let's leave it. It'll be hard in a few days.'

'Yes, but meanwhile I'll *know* about it, won't I, Josh?' I grabbed a roll of kitchen towel and stormed in. 'Can't just tiptoe around it in my dressing gown pretending it's not there, like you!' I yelled.

I dealt with it, flushing it down the lavatory, and whilst in the loo I pulled down my jeans for a much-needed pee. Obviously I hadn't shut the door properly so it slowly swung wide as I was in mid-flow, exposing me. I thus had a bird's-eye view of my son making 'She's stressy' eyes at his sister, who appeared to be curled up in her duvet in some dark corner of the playroom – she raised her eyebrows expressively back – and as I emerged, doing up my trousers, my mother and sister exchanged 'Is it always like this?' looks. Fury mounted.

'Well?' Mum demanded pointedly as Ottoline opened the back door and told Mrs Braithwaite I'd be with her in a minute. Mrs Braithwaite's face was stony and unamused, much like my mother's, but Ottoline firmly shut the door on her.

'Well, what?' I asked angrily, shrinking behind the dresser, out of Mrs Braithwaite's line of sight.

'Well, how is he? What did he say?'

I was aware that Josh and Tabs had lowered the volume on the TV in the next room. A bare toe pushed the door open a bit.

'Well, he didn't say a lot, Mum, really,' I said, struggling for control. 'What he did say was that he didn't think it was such a bad idea for you both to have some space. And, actually,' I added bravely, 'I rather agree with him.'

'Space!' she spat incredulously. 'What does he think he is, a teenager? He'll be saying he needs to chill next! What is this – a gap year? I hope you told him to jolly well come to his senses.'

I think it occurred to all of us that I probably hadn't been the best person to do this.

'Well, I – you know . . .' I scratched my chin. 'I – sort of – kind of suggested he think hard about what he's doing. About the situation. And his actions. But it's difficult, Mum. I mean, you don't own him, you know.'

There was a silence as we all absorbed this.

'HE'S MY HUSBAND!' she roared, making us all jump. Even the bare foot in the doorway. 'What d'you mean, I don't own him? I've been married to him for forty-two years! I surely stake some sort of claim, have some say in his conduct, particularly if it's as unbecoming as it is. Is he still seeing that tart?'

'Actually, I don't think she is a tart. Or not in the sense you mean. I think he's just having some jolly good fun with her. In a very Enid Blyton-type way. Cycling to pubs, playing cards, that sort of thing.' Obviously I wasn't looking at my mother as I said any of this. I wasn't that heroic. I pretended I had urgent business wiping down the front of the Aga, my face averted. I heard her silent incredulity behind me, though. Would have smelled it at twenty paces.

'Cycling to . . . playing . . . Ella, are you condoning your father's relationship with this woman? LOOK AT ME, PLEASE!'

I gripped the Aga rail in fright. Turned. 'No. I'm not. I'm just saying I think it's good clean fun, that's all. And that's what he lacked in his life. Some fun. A laugh.'

There was silence in the kitchen as I held my mother's icy, furious, pale-blue gaze. Ottoline and Ginnie studied their nails. My mother was coming to the boil.

'*I* played cards!' she stormed. 'I played bridge, every Tuesday! He never asked to learn, or to play with me!'

Because it was the one evening she went out, and he had the house to himself. We all knew that. The one evening he could watch any channel he liked on the television. Even rent a DVD. I massaged my temples. It was all so complicated, of course. Years and years of history, of disappointment, resentment, tempers held under pressure. Years of Dad biting his lip. It wasn't about playing cards.

'I think what Ella means,' Ginnie began, and I looked at her gratefully, thinking it was about time she effing well piped up, 'is that Daddy wants to – well . . . he wants to . . .' She lost her nerve. 'Just relax a bit,' she finished lamely.

'Relax!' Mummy turned on her furiously.

'And laugh,' I added. 'Laugh until his sides hurt and the tears roll, like he used to.'

I'd deliberately conjured up an image of my father which we were all familiar with, but hadn't seen for some time. My father could laugh until he cried, usually at something terribly silly. *You've Been Framed* on the TV: people slipping into ponds, being soaked by exploding hosepipes. An anecdote he'd tell and have to stop before he got to the punchline, unable to get it out he was laughing so much. Often at Christmas, at the head of the table, when Ginnie and I were younger: happier, less starchy times, when Mum had had a drink and would smile indulgently at him, not snap as she did these days. Once, when he'd been weeping with mirth, she'd leaned across and fondly mopped his face with a napkin. Not recently, of course. Recently she'd say: 'Oh, Angus, for God's sake, control yourself!' As if he was incontinent. He used to cry for other reasons – in church, at weddings; anything to do with the war. 'Two men coming to attention,' Mum used to scoff. He was an emotional man, and my mother wasn't.

'When did you last see him rock with laughter like that?' I persisted.

'Nothing's quite so funny as you get older,' she snapped.

'Yes, it is. It can be. What's age got to do with it? And, anyway, I saw him like that today.'

'With that woman,' she seethed, and I realized I'd gone too far. 'What sort of devoted daughter are you, Ella? You go down there as my envoy, to plead on my behalf, and see him having a laugh with some red-headed trollop who's not your mother and think: Ah, yes, *that* was the problem! That's what my father needed and wasn't getting – good luck to them! How *can* you be so heartless? So – so disloyal!'

I hung my head. Put like that ... If I'd thought the interview with my father had gone badly it was nothing on this. My mother got to her feet.

'You thought I was a drudge. A drag on your father, all these years.'

'No, Mummy, I –'

'I won't be staying here,' she said, trembling. 'I can't stay now, now that I see the way the land lies. Now that I know where your sympathies are.'

'No, Mummy, it's not like that,' I said desperately. 'I'm

trying to help, really I am. I'm just trying to be even-handed, that's all. To make you see that it's not all Dad's fault!'

'Oh, you always were a Daddy's girl. Always got round him. Always saw his point of view. Well, that's fine. You side with him. As usual.' She plucked her thin wool cape from the back of her chair, swept it round her shoulders and gathered her enormous navy handbag to her chest. Gripped it tightly. 'Come, Ginnie. I shall stay with you instead. Your spare room at the nursery end of the house, the one you keep for visiting children, will suit me perfectly well. I won't take the main one. I know you have lots of guests, but that blue one will do. And I'll manage very well sharing a bathroom with the children. Come along. We won't stay where we're not wanted.'

Panic had made my sister's eyes extra large. And she had a bit of a thyroid problem, anyway. She looked from me to Mum, then back again, horrified. But my mother was already making for the back door, which, on account of her regal bearing, Ottoline, in some spear-carrying capacity, was automatically swinging wide for her: almost snapping her heels. Mum swept through it without a word, scattering the chickens, who always dozed on the sunny back step having been fed, in her wake. Her cape, caught by the wind, shot out horizontally behind her as she strode across the yard to her car. All she needed was a broomstick.

There was a moment's silence, then:

'Shit!' Ginnie yelped. She got to her feet. Cast me a terrified look. Shot rigid fingers through vertical hair. I shrugged helplessly.

'But – but, Ella, this is a disaster! I can't – I mean, we can't –'

I made a hopeless face. Raised the palms of my hands to heaven.

Ginnie looked at Ottoline, in desperation. Ottoline shrugged vainly back.

'Fuck,' my sister was heard to hiss as she grabbed her car keys, took to her heels and hastened away.

Chapter Ten

Ottoline slid away tactfully. Ginnie and Mum stood by the car in the yard talking for a long time, as I knew they would: buffeted by the wind, talking talking talking. My sister, her cheeks pinched, entreated my mother earnestly, setting out her case, highlighting bullet points – what else? – with her finger in the air. But always with a look of caring concern. My mother's back, as I scurried around the kitchen throwing things in the dishwasher but still with one eye on the unfolding action, was stiff and defiant. Her hand was already on the car door handle. The next time I looked, though, her hand was off the handle and she wasn't staring haughtily into space any more; she was at least listening to what Ginnie was saying. Ginnie was going back over those crucial points, spreading her arms wide now for emphasis, even giving Mum's arm a little squeeze. And always the loving smile. I knew she'd prevailed. Knew, before she nipped round to release Buster – Buster! – from the boot. Before she'd carefully turned her elderly parent round and escorted her, one hand under her bony elbow, back to my door. She opened it. At least, I heard it open, but was busying myself at the Aga, wiping the hob lids, deliberately keeping my back to them.

'Mummy's had a change of heart,' Ginnie said gently.

'Oh, really?' I said lightly. I turned. 'I thought I was the disloyal, uncaring daughter? And you were the good daughter, Ginnie?'

'No, no, she realizes that was unjust, don't you, Mummy? And that you were only trying to help.'

'By driving all the way to talk to Dad at my busiest time in the holidays? With beds to change, the children at home and a million animals to feed? By installing her in one of my cottages, a cottage I've now cancelled the guests for?'

'Well, quite,' Ginnie purred. She pushed my mother bodily into the kitchen. Buster slipped in too. 'And she's just rather emotional at the moment.'

'I can see that,' I said testily. 'What's he doing here?'

'I'm so sorry, Ella, but he chases the cat. Constantly. Up the curtains, down the lane, into the woods. And you don't have one.'

'I've got everything else, though, haven't I?'

'I know, and I'm really sorry. But she disappeared for two days in terror. Araminta was beside herself. You know how she adores Bathsheba. Floods of tears and she was out searching with a torch most of the night.'

'Right.'

'And Mummy understands that it's only right that you should be supportive of both parents. That it would be very odd if you weren't. Don't you, Mummy?'

'As I said,' Mum said stiffly, face set, 'you always were a Daddy's girl. Bound to take his side.'

I felt my fists clench.

'Yes, well, be that as it may,' Ginnie went on smoothly, 'I think tempers are bound to be a little frayed at the moment, on all sides. And when that happens, people say things they don't mean. But, as I explained to Mummy, she really won't want to sleep near the children with their loud music and telephone calls at all hours. Much better to be here, in her own peaceful little cottage, and of course with her own independence.'

'Oh, I don't know, Ginnie,' I said, thinking she should surely have been a politician. 'What about that spare room at the top of your back stairs with the little sitting room next to it? That's nowhere near the children.'

'Except I'm planning to redecorate it,' said Ginnie evenly. 'And it's still not quite the same, is it? As having your own place?'

'It's quite clear neither of you wants me,' said Mum sharply.

'No, no!' we both said instantly.

'Of course we do, Mum,' I said quickly, ashamed. 'And Ginnie's right,' I added, swallowing hard. 'The cottage will be quieter for you.' I shot my sister a flinty look. She cast me a craven, obsequious one back.

It was always the way, though, wasn't it? Ginnie getting exactly what she wanted with none of the agro. I handed her the pile of sheets Ottoline had put on the side.

'Right, well, if she's staying, I'd be grateful if you'd take some clean sheets over there and put them in the ottoman in her bedroom. I've got a duck house to clean.'

Ginnie took the linen gratefully, sycophantically. She even executed a little bow before hurrying Mum away, shushing her as she asked imperiously: 'How often do they get changed?'

I set my mouth in a grim line. Flung my dishcloth in the sink. Then, as is so often the way, went to take it out on the Eastbourne residents. They were now in total cinematic darkness, with curtains drawn – if they'd ever been opened. It had obviously been deemed 'late afternoon': they were clearly planning to push on through until midnight. Horizontal on a sofa apiece, rugs up to chins, all three dogs snuggled in beside them, they were silent and inert, in thrall to the flickering screen. Buster, having come from a very different establishment, quietly licked an old crisp packet on the floor, wide-eyed, thinking it must be Christmas.

'*Oh, for God's sake, get dressed and open the curtains and bloody well clear up in here!*' I screamed.

The two of them raised their eyebrows incredulously at each other. The dogs slid down first, then the residents. They got languidly to their feet.

'Do pipe down,' Josh told me as he shuffled past in his rug. 'It's not really worth getting dressed, is it? We'll be going to bed soon.'

Realizing I'd lost whatever tenuous grip I'd once had on my household and sympathizing with any mother who resorts to physical violence, I watched them drip upstairs, knowing that if I opened my mouth I'd regret it. I went back to the kitchen, fuming. On the side were the remains of two enormous family-sized pizzas. They could have shared one, but clearly had both wanted different toppings so, hey, let's open two and leave what we don't eat. Without sitting down I rammed the remains of the cold pizzas into my mouth, chewing furiously and rhythmically like a cow – or even a pig – so hungry was I. I even ate a few handfuls of dry Coco Pops for pudding. Finally, sated and disgusted with myself but no less cross, I stalked back to the playroom and snapped the television off with a flourish. Any victory, however small, had to be celebrated with a flourish these days. The house was silent now, but with an annoyingly reproachful air to it as if I'd spoiled everyone's fun. Making a great deal of noise I threw sofa cushions on the floor to bash some life into them, brushed crisps onto the carpet, got the Hoover out and vrmm vrmm vrmmed around. Then I shut the dogs in the boot room – they'd crept there anyway – and savagely flicked up the dishwasher door with my foot, hurting my ankle. Breathing heavily from the exertion of all this and wondering if that was normal or if I should go to the gym – or even the doctor – I stomped upstairs to my room, and to what was laughingly called 'my work'.

Slamming the attic door shut behind me I leaned back on it and shut my eyes tight. Oh, to run away. To no longer be somebody's mother, somebody's sister, or somebody's daughter with divided and complicated loyalties. Not to mention somebody's wife, I thought bitterly, as, opening my eyes, and gazing through the famous north window at the far end of the room, I saw Sebastian emerge from the Granary, yawning widely. He stretched and glanced across to where Ginnie had disappeared into the Stable with her pile of sheets, installing them in the chest at the end of the bed. Oh, she'd be a veritable hive of activity now, working fast before Mum changed her mind. He frowned, but, being Sebastian, and not a great fan of Ginnie's anyway, was too disinterested to wander across. It occurred to me that I hadn't discussed this latest arrival, the newest addition to our ménage, with him; but although he wasn't necessarily an enthusiastic supporter of my mother, he was unlikely to object. Sebastian didn't object to anything as long as Majestic Wine delivered, he had a plentiful supply of oil paints, and he was left alone.

Miserably I peeled myself off the door. The once-lovely attic studio, earmarked for Sebastian years ago, was half full of rubbish now: more attic than studio. Suitcases, boxes of old toys I couldn't throw away, a dinner service I'd never used but which had been a wedding present, Christmas decorations in bags, broken lamps I'd been meaning to mend, children's books, were all piled down one side, the one with the sloping roof. At this end, by the door, was a large sash window, just as there was at the other, where I worked overlooking the yard. I crossed the room to hover over my desk. Gloria the Glow Worm was valiantly trying to stage a comeback under the pristine piece of paper I'd placed firmly on top of her, but I knew I must ignore her, as I ignored so many artistic impulses, if I was to feed this ever-increasing number of people and keep them in discarded pizza.

Instead I sat down and turned my attention to the juvenile delinquents of fictitious Huddersport. Leanne, and her dysfunctional family. I picked up my pencil to carefully draw Reg, the alcoholic stepfather, Arlene, the listless, drug-fuelled mother on the sofa, Dylan, the bullying, tattooed stepbrother. And always, of course, Leanne, the feisty young girl who would turn all of their lives around, in a mere forty-six pages, with her will of iron, her ponytail, her freckles, and her skinny frame. Feisty young girls always had skinny frames. I sketched and shaded away, telling myself that very few people did what they loved for a living, and I was lucky to be drawing.

When I glanced up an hour or two later, thinking at least I didn't have children who asked what was for supper, but foraged for themselves in the holidays, it was to see a man who'd managed to make a career out of doing what he loved best. Ludo's green Land Rover was bumping across what we derisively called the drive, and coming to a halt outside the house. A door opened. One long, jeaned leg was elegantly followed by another, then a denim shirt rolled to brown forearms, a mop of blond hair and, finally, those piercing blue eyes. Flashing up at me the briefest of glances, he walked round to the back of the house as I in turn got up and ran to the other end of my studio. I flung up the sash. As I leaned out, my heart did a little Irish jig in my ribcage. He looked up as he came round, saw me and grinned. His face creased delightfully and triggered a huge smile to break out on mine in true Pavlovian response. Even if I wanted to be cool about Ludo, that smile of his would render it impossible.

"Ello, missus,' he called up in a soft, mock-cockney accent. 'Prune yer creeper for yer?'

'Actually, my man,' I said haughtily. 'Ai thought I might grow it this yarr.'

'As you wish.' He doffed his forelock.

Ludo had long since ceased to have any gainful employment on my farm. Once the vegetable garden had been installed – and then shamefully neglected – his work had finished. I certainly couldn't afford to employ a gardener myself, let alone a garden designer, which, in the pantheon of countrywomen's indulgences, was up there with the personal trainer. But, since we needed to see each other, Ludo had invented the fiction that checking on the veggie garden was all part of the after-care service, which obviously no other customer received, but which enabled us to stroll around the raised beds together letting our hands brush over the overgrown parsley, thinking tender, wistful thoughts whilst Ludo murmured things like, 'Your fennel's a bit straggly.'

'I know,' I'd whisper back. 'And don't even look at my radishes.' We'd take a moment then to hold hands over the turnips, eyes locked.

As I raced downstairs, trying, for the children's sake, to look nonchalant and normal, I thought that, yes, I was a hussy, to have my heart turning somersaults thus for a married man, but that, actually, this man, and the feelings I had for him, were ironically the glue that kept this disjointed family together. Without him, I knew I'd be gone. Not physically, because I couldn't do that to Sebastian or the children, but, mentally, I'd be sunk. That's what I told myself, anyway. Without the green Land Rover, the long, jeaned legs, the sunny smile, the optimistic 'one day' that we always talked about but knew probably didn't exist, I'd be a crabbed old misery guts and of no use at all to my family, I thought defiantly, as I went sailing out to meet him, plunging my feet joyfully into my boots en route.

Having taken a fork from my tool shed and a battered old bag from the back of his van, Ludo was already making deliberately for the vegetable patch, so that the delight as we saw each other was shielded from view as I fell into step beside him. I had an old pink cardigan of Tabs's over my ancient summer dress, wellies on my feet. Hardly dressed up. God, he was handsome, I thought, as he grinned down.

'That was nice,' he said quietly.

'What?'

'Seeing you working at the window like that. Head bent, rapt. Totally absorbed as I drove in. I'd like to bottle that.'

I blushed and looked at my boots. 'Important to lose yourself somewhere,' I told him. 'Even if it is at the coal face of semi-literate fiction. What about you, Mr Pritchard? Busy day at the office? Half the women in Oxfordshire vying for your forking technique, as usual? All losing control of their beds?'

He sighed. 'I don't know about vying, but in these financially straightened times forking technique is certainly about the size of it. You can forget the landscaping. I can't remember when I last designed anything on paper – probably for Puffy Trumpington, and that was ages ago. These days all they want is their wisteria pruned or their raspberry canes cut back. Yesterday I spent the entire afternoon poo-picking at Longhorn Manor. There's very little creative impulse there, I can tell you. Speaking of which, is he still at it?'

He nodded his head towards the Granary as we approached.

'Of course. Is he ever not?'

'Well, not when he's in the Fox and Firkin.'

'True.'

Ludo lowered his voice as we went past. 'What's he painting at the moment, portraits still?'

'Nudes.'

'Oh. Right. Anyone in particular?'

'Ottoline, mostly. Who, of course, he's done a million times.'

Ottoline was indeed stark-naked and puffing away on one of her little cheroots as we passed the side window – reclining on a couch and reading *The Week*. No problems with nudity at all. And although usually a little flag was hung out if someone was posing, she gave a cheery wave as we went by. Ludo looked at the ground. Sebastian, if he saw, ignored us.

'Does she mind?' he whispered, when we were out of range.

'Not at all. She says it gives her a chance to catch up on world affairs.'

'And does he pay her?'

'For catching up on world affairs in the buff? No. And she wouldn't take it, anyway. She says it's a very good way of switching off. You can't move – can't scratch your bum without him harrumphing – so you just . . . unburden yourself. Mentally. Ottoline's very spiritual. She likes to let it all hang out. All she insists on, is that it's warm. She brings her heater because she said that once, in January, her tits nearly dropped off.'

Ludo laughed. 'And do you ever . . . you know?'

I smiled, knowing he was trying to be open-minded and avant-garde about it, as most people pretended to be, even though they were quietly agog.

'No. Not any more. I used to, of course. Just as he did for me.'

I knew a vivid mental image had reared up in his brain, which, if you've never painted from life, and most people haven't, is obviously titillating.

'What happens when you're drawing the – you know . . .' Lottie had once asked me, breathless.

'What d'you mean, what happens?'

'Well, d'you feel a bit . . . I don't know . . .'

'Randy?'

'Well . . .'

'It's just like drawing anything else, Lottie. You're so bloody intent on getting the proportions right, and the light, and the shade, and the form, you don't think: Golly,

I'm drawing his dick. Anyway, I always used to paint Sebastian from behind. He's got a lovely bum.'

Obviously I didn't voice this now to Ludo as we strolled on towards the lichen-covered steps which led down to the vegetable patch and the river, but I did think it was a very long time since I'd done a life drawing.

'Oh, God – duck,' I said quickly, seizing his arm and pulling him down. My mother was coming out of her cottage on the slope above us. She was shaking a bright blue rug covered in starfish, which I'd bought in Newlyn, in a disappointed manner. No dust at all flew up – hence her disappointment – because whilst I might be a slattern in my own home, any rented accommodation I leased out shone like a new pin. She sniffed it disparagingly and went back inside.

'Was that her?' whispered Ludo, as, shielded by the wall of the steps, we emerged cautiously.

'Yes,' I hissed back.

'Ah. Thought she looked like you.'

I shot him a horrified look. Realized he was joking and cuffed his arm.

'She looks like your sister, actually. Who I find pretty scary, incidentally.'

'Well, if you find Ginnie scary, this one will utterly terrify you. We're talking living daylights, here.'

'I ran into her in the fruit and veg section of Waitrose the other day – Ginnie, I mean. She asked me, in that loud, imperious voice of hers, if I'd "finished with her sister". My fingers plunged straight into the tomato I was fondling. I went the colour of it, too. Opened and shut my mouth like a goldfish. Eventually I spluttered, "N-nearly."'

I giggled.

'"Well, make sure you tie up any loose ends,"' he said, aping Ginnie's cut-glass voice. 'And all I could think of was your blonde hair, spread loose on your shoulders as you were hanging out the washing last week: how the sun had caught it.'

Ludo could say things like this: things that made your heart lurch, the lurching being all the more violent when it hadn't happened for some time. Years. Had probably given up all hope of it ever happening again.

'How's Eliza?' I said lightly, defiantly breaking the moment as we perched together on the crumbling bottom step, faded lavender bushes brushing our knees; deliberately bringing us to our senses, reality. I felt cruel as he swam back to the surface and sighed.

'Oh, same as ever. Planning a skiing trip at the moment. Méribel, apparently,' he said bitterly.

'Really? I didn't know you could afford that?'

'We can't. We can't afford to go to the pub for lunch. She wants to borrow. Says it's so cheap at the moment, we'd be mad not to, and that one day her parents will die and she'll inherit some money anyway, so why wait? Why not use it now? I think she'll be spiking their cocoa soon.'

'And if you object?'

'I do, mildly. And she points out that she's only trying to lead the sort of life she'd been led to believe she could expect from me. She sort of spits it. Savagely. Says that all the girls' friends go skiing and it's unreasonable to send them to a school where they can't join in the lunchtime chat.'

'But they go to the state school now.'

'I know. Apparently skiing trips still come down with the rations, though.'

'Not in this house they don't.'

We narrowed our eyes across to the distant hills beyond; to the ponies grazing in the steep field above the river. We sometimes spoke like this and I knew what we were doing: quietly wondering who was the most unhappy. Who had the most miserable marriage. I knew Ludo won by a country mile. The difference was that I still loved Sebastian. I didn't spit at him and he didn't really at me any more: also, he put absolutely no pressure on me. He was just there, getting more dishevelled and distant and dislocated from me by the day, in my garden. And I knew he loved me. We just couldn't do anything about it, because he despised me, too. And they were so close, weren't they? Love and hate. It seemed to me, though, that Ludo and Eliza didn't feel any strong emotion for each other at all. Just a weary indifference, which was surely worse.

Ludo's hand reached out for mine in the fold of my dress. Our fingers curled around each other's. We held on tightly, knowing we were unobserved, and knowing too that this was as daring as we got, apart from the uncharacteristically bold hug last week. That had been enough for me. It had got me through the rest of the day with a broad smile on my face, as I bounced around the kitchen, being pleasant to the children – which is what I mean by the glue. And for the next few days as well, still hugging the memory. But it had not been enough, I suspect, for Ludo. I think he went home happy, but yearning.

'Listen, Ella,' he said suddenly, turning to face me on the step. 'I know we both hate the idea of planning anything underhand, but it doesn't have to be seedy and Brighton-esque, you know. We could go somewhere pretty, Somerset, perhaps. I could be on a gardening course – there's a new one in Tavistock – and you could be looking for those Call Ducks you want, the white ones that mate for life. We could just happen to meet in the market square, you with your crate of ducks, me with my portfolio under my arm and with an "Oh, what a surprise!" look on my face. We could go for lunch at the local pub, have a bit too much to drink, and then I could discover the pub had rooms above and we could repair to one, with a dear little wrought-iron bed and a view of the Quantock Hills. It could all just unfold like that, in a flurry and a heap of clothes, so spontaneous, so joyful, so – loving. What d'you say?' he finished urgently.

I frowned.

'What about the ducks?'

Chapter Eleven

'D'you think you ever will?' Lottie asked me, when I popped in to see her on the way back from getting the milk and the papers some days later. I told Lottie pretty much everything. Had nothing to hide. Yet.

I sighed. 'I don't know. Some days I think: Oh, for God's sake, just do it, Ella Montclair. It's not as if you have a proper marriage. And other days I shrink from it, thinking: No, how *could* I? He's *married*. And he has more of a marriage than I do in some ways. They at least live together and to all intents and purposes are seen to be a couple: go to dinner parties as husband and wife and all that. Everyone knows Sebastian and I live next door.'

'So you're more honest,' she said, crossing the kitchen to let the cat out, wearing her Hobbs suit – she was off to work and her sartorial standards were high: no droopy ethnic skirts at the Holistic Centre for her. 'Or at least, Sebastian is. Since he was the one who moved out.'

'Yes, but not everyone has the luxury of various converted cattle sheds in the garden to facilitate an honestly broken marriage. Some people have to grin and bear it. Get on with having no married life, but still sharing a bed and a bathroom.'

She was thoughtful as she poured the coffee. 'You're having an affair with him, anyway, you know,' she said, casting me a glance.

'I know.'

'In all but —'

'Yes, I *know*, Lottie.'

'And, after all, you love him.'

'Yes, but I still love Sebastian,' I said quickly.

'Yes. But the distance between the two of you gets wider all the time. When did you last have a proper conversation with him, for instance?'

I narrowed my eyes at her pinboard on the wall opposite. 'Well, he came to supper last weekend. Tabitha had a friend and wanted it to look . . . normal. I asked, and he came. In a clean shirt, showered . . .'

I remembered turning in surprise as he came through the back door with a bottle of wine. A smile, even. Had flushed with relief and . . . something approaching delight. And he'd been sweet to Tabs and her friend, and even Josh had slunk downstairs fully dressed and displayed his best side, telling funny stories deadpan, being the cool older brother. I could see Tabs looking pleased as her friend was rapt, and then there'd been some brilliant father-and-son repartee as they sparred together. They could do a fine double act when they felt like it. But then, when the girls had taken the plates to the side and gone to watch a film, it had disintegrated. Sebastian had noticed a picture, a cheap print I'd bought recently, where, years ago, one of his had hung. I'd had to sell it to appease the bank, but for a long time had been unable to bring myself to replace it with anything. Except . . . the blank space had upset me too. Recently, I'd steeled myself and splashed out fifteen pounds.

'Nice to see I've been replaced with bland, derivative trash,' Sebastian had commented, amused, glancing at it.

I couldn't tell him I'd been unable to hang anything good, because nothing would ever be as good. That it would always feel like a compromise. Had deliberately gone for a cheap, John Lewis reproduction of sheep in a field, to replace *Girl with an Orange Bow*.

'Yes, I thought it was pleasant enough,' I'd said neutrally.

'Oh, it's pleasant enough. Although, frankly, I preferred the nasty mark on the wall. But if that's what you want, there it shall stay. We must, after all, dance to your tune.'

Sebastian had had quite a lot to drink by then and as he made a long arm for another bottle on the side, Josh made a comment to this effect.

'I think I'll be the arbiter of that,' his father had snapped back.

To change the subject – and getting up quickly to close the door to the playroom – I'd asked Josh how his A-level project on Laura Knight was coming along. Josh had inherited what remained of our genes. He'd shrugged gnomically and I'd offered to look at it after supper.

Sebastian had snapped: 'Don't bloody well help him!'

There'd been a silence.

'I wasn't going to,' I'd said, looking at his furious face across the table. 'I was just –'

'Just going to control, to organize, to manipulate,' he'd sneered, and I'd crumpled inside. Outside, too. There'd been tears, which, thankfully, the girls hadn't seen, but Josh had, and somehow he'd hustled his father away, back to his lair, and then been sweet to me, as Josh sometimes could. But I'd gone to bed very tight and very, very disappointed.

All this I didn't tell Lottie now. I know I've just said

I told her everything but sometimes it was bad enough living it, without having to *relive* it.

'Yes, he came to supper,' I said quickly. I fell silent.

'And it wasn't great?'

'No. It wasn't great.'

She was putting a series of *Vogue* prints into clip-frames to hang around her room at the centre to give it more of a chic ambience. Lottie was a very reluctant hippie. She believed in alternative medicine but didn't like the herbs and beads and sandals that went with it. She kicked against the womb music and the healing stones and clicked into work in high heels and as much bling as she could afford.

'I'm not advocating you have an affair with him, Ella. I'm just saying I wouldn't be judgemental if you did. I have a feeling that, if you did, you couldn't live in the crazy ménage you do at present, and maybe, just maybe, it would be good to rethink that.'

'What's wrong with my crazy ménage?'

'Everything. You think it's helping the children, but is it?'

'Oh, Lottie, I don't know. I don't know that shagging Ludo would help them either.'

'True.' She went quiet. 'It might help you, though. What's the plan, Ella? Really? The endgame? To live there for the next thirty years while Sebastian has affairs and you're celibate, catering to everyone's needs – your mother's included, now – the smell of burning martyr wafting from every orifice?'

'He hasn't had anyone since Isobel. I'd know.'

'I know, but it's only a matter of time, isn't it?'

'Oh, so we *both* have raging affairs, is that it?'

'No, you move out. Move on. Move away. Maybe with

Ludo. Maybe with someone *like* Ludo. But you move out of Limbo Land Farm with its life-sucking vortex which is dragging you down, and start thinking of pleasing yourself, instead of everyone around you.'

'But that's what I signed up to, didn't I? What we all sign up to when we marry. Pleasing husbands, children, in-laws – whoever. That's the deal.'

'He broke the contract, not you,' she said, abandoning the pictures and settling down to add a second coat of varnish to her already highly lacquered nails.

'Is this you in therapist mode, Lottie?' I asked admiringly. 'You're very good.'

'No, because, sadly, I'm just supposed to listen.' She shook the varnish bottle vigorously. 'Not supposed to advise at all. Particularly in the acupuncture world. I can't tell you how hard I have to bite my tongue.'

'And you really can't tell me anything about Eliza?' I hazarded, bending my head to meet her gaze as she attended to her manicure. I batted my eyelids wantonly.

'You know I can't.' She paused. Sat up a bit. 'I'll tell you one thing, though.' She looked me in the eye. 'She's not telling me the truth.'

'You mean . . . Ooh, Lottie! You don't think *she*'s got someone, do you?'

'No idea. All I know is that the spiel she gives me at the beginning of each session – because she has to say something, everyone does for five minutes – about her perfectly normal home life, is rubbish. I know that from you, obviously, but I'd know it was bullshit, anyway. Her headaches are worse than ever and that's not right. Even with my shaky paws they should be getting a bit better. Perhaps you're right. Perhaps she's got a guilty secret.'

We were quiet a moment: in silent, companionable contemplation of married life in all its various complex forms.

'Lotts,' I said at length, gazing as coat number three was applied. 'Do the long nails help?'

'What d'you mean?'

'Well, I can't help thinking . . . in terms of needle-grasping . . .'

'Oh, no, I'm used to them. And as we know,' she eyed me beadily, 'so much of my job is needle-retrieving. They come in very handy.'

I giggled. 'Is it getting any better?'

'Well, it's not quite so disastrous. But I did have a problem with the underside of Mrs Armitage's foot the other day. You know, she teaches Matthew. It was so horribly crusty – I couldn't get the needle in; it kept buckling. It's the people I know, Ella, who are the problem. Complete strangers and I'm in like a die. Anyway, you're coming in later, aren't you? Four thirty? I've got you down for half an hour.'

'Oh, yes. God, I'd forgotten.' I had. Had booked it ages ago. I'd been in once before, when I couldn't sleep; but, if I'm honest, it hadn't really helped. Lottie had been a bit flustered. I felt a shiver of nerves.

'Ottoline says you're brilliant,' I said to bolster her – myself, too. 'And you know *her*. She's not a stranger.'

'Ah, Ottoline.' She put down her varnish brush and smiled. 'She's different. She says things like, "Don't worry if it doesn't work, Lottie, I've only come for a lie-down and a chat." So I get it right first time. She puts you completely at your ease.'

'What does she come in for, though?' I asked, curious.

'Ah.' She tapped her nose. 'Hippocratic oath.' She smiled importantly. Annoyingly, actually.

I snorted. 'Anyone would think you were Christiaan bloody Barnard!'

'No, no heart transplants. But still. I have to keep schtum. Can't go spilling the confidential beans or I wouldn't have any clients.'

'I'll clearly have to get you drunk,' I told her, gathering up my shopping and making to leave, 'if I want any Eliza dirt.'

'Oh, stop worrying about Eliza and go to it, Ella. Go and get yourself laid. It's almost your *duty* to cuckold that husband of yours.'

I left, wishing I'd gathered just a tiny morsel, though. Wishing she'd just let slip that Eliza was having a sizzling affair, a glimpse of the green light I was looking for. Only then would I feel I could be the sort of woman who took another woman's husband, I determined, as I carried my shopping down Lottie's path and lifted it into the basket of my bike, which was leaning against the hedge. I knew that night I'd go to bed dreaming of Eliza entwined with a very beautiful Indian man from Swindon. All I knew about Eliza was that she used to make wedding dresses; she still did occasionally. Disappointingly this was not a career path many men naturally trod – I was keen for her to have an office affair – but I'd decided she must buy her silks somewhere and I'd plumped for the Indian quarter in Swindon. There she'd fallen in lust with a Mr Singh, who looked just like a young Imran Khan. He'd taken a roll of crêpe de Chine down from a rack in his shop, given her the eye, and shot out a length, as it were. Unfortunately the one and only time I'd had a proper conversation with Eliza, at a girly lunch at Ginnie's where, horrifyingly, I'd been placed next to her – I'd popped over unannounced with a birthday present for Araminta so Ginnie could hardly not say: 'Do join us' – when I'd asked where she got her fabric she'd said haughtily: 'I import.' Still, I persisted with the fantasy, as I couldn't see how importing could involve a likely male. Except perhaps the postman.

She'd been cold as a fish that day, I remembered, as I got on my bike and wobbled, basket laden with shopping, down Lottie's lane. Had obviously made up her mind I was infra dig, and had chummed up instead with Helena McCauley on her other side. The woman on my left had been pleasant enough so I'd chatted to her, but eventually she'd turned, keen to talk to her proper mates about GCSE results. I'd tried to catch the eye of the woman opposite and muscle into her conversation, nodding and smiling at what I thought were appropriate moments, but to no avail. In the end I'd stared straight ahead and concentrated hard on chewing my coronation chicken as if I was really interested in how it was made and which spices had gone into it. Ginnie had noticed, of course, and no doubt despaired, thinking: *That's* why I never ask her. I'd come away thinking eight women around a table of a Tuesday really wasn't for me. I preferred coffee with Lottie. A real chat, not a social event. Or even two minutes with Ottoline in the chicken house, I thought, as I wheeled my bike into the yard and saw her coming out of Mum's cottage.

'Just checking she's OK,' she called cheerily as she came across to meet me. She fell in beside me as I pushed my bike. 'And seeing if she wanted supper.'

'Oh, Ottoline, you are kind,' I said guiltily, thinking I wasn't. I was still feeling aggrieved at having her dumped on my doorstep. Had fled to discuss my love life with Lottie, rather than checking on her. I *had* asked her to supper a couple of times, naturally I had, and she'd come; but on the last occasion she'd criticized everything from the meal, hastily thrown together, to the dogs sleeping on the sofas, to Tabitha absently using her fingers to eat chips, to Josh looking at his phone while we were eating, to us not having any napkins, to – oh, everything. So I'd thought: Right. Not for some time.

Another time I'd popped in to take her some shepherd's pie we had left over, and she'd opened the door and told me that she was 'very disappointed in Tabitha'.

'Why?' I'd asked, bridling instantly, gripping my offering.

'The other day, I came back from Waitrose with my shopping, and she was lying on the trampoline in your front garden, sunbathing.'

'Yes, she does that.'

'She just about managed to raise her head when she saw me and said: "Oh, hi, Granny." Then she lay back down again,' my mother told me, outraged. 'Didn't offer to come and help with my shopping or anything! Can you imagine?' I could, actually. Had no trouble with that little vignette at all. 'And when I told Josh that at some point I'd like him to get the logs in for me, for the winter, and then work out a thrice-weekly rota so that my log basket is always full, he looked so startled you'd think I'd asked him to rub sticks together and make the fire himself. Presumably he gets the logs in for you, Ella?'

'Er . . . well . . .' No, of course he didn't. My children were bone idle. Wouldn't know a thrice-weekly rota if it bonked them on the head.

I'd been ashamed and read the Riot Act that night, so that Joshua had filled the log basket, even though it was only August, and Tabs had gone across and said, 'Sorry for not helping, Granny.' But the next time Mum came, for Sunday lunch, she'd been so critical of Tabitha's chipped black nail varnish and her unbrushed hair and the holes in her tights, that Tabitha had burst into tears. I'd been furious. And, actually, secretly pleased she'd behaved so appallingly. It gave me some vindication, I felt, for *not* popping round every five minutes. I'd surely done my bit merely *taking* her. Ottoline, though, would not be put off by a barrage of complaints or terse assurances that she was perfectly OK. She'd see a vulnerable old woman. The one I was pretending not to. I prickled with shame.

'She's tricky, Ottoline,' I said quietly, by way of explanation.

'Oh, I know. She pretty much told me to sod off. But I did ascertain that she'd found the butcher and doctor's surgery, et cetera. It's a blessing she can drive.'

'Well, quite,' I said, with a creeping sense of horror at the day when she couldn't. When I'd have to fetch and carry for her, when, God forbid, she'd have to *live* with me. An entire, dizzying screenplay danced luridly across the horizon, with Josh and Tabs at university, or, worse, in flats in London; Sebastian with a string of lovers opposite; me still delivering his clean linen and no doubt rubbing Vanish on the stains – and my mother in one of the children's rooms, berating me constantly. Me and Mum for ever. Oh, God. If anything was designed to make me run away with Ludo it was this. I had a horrible sensation of time slipping through my fingers: a sense that, in the blink of an eye, here I'd be – and there Mum would be. At my chair at the kitchen table. The more comfortable one at the head, with the arms and the cushion. I went cold.

'Ottoline, this is a mistake, isn't it?' I gabbled breathlessly. 'Having her here? She needs to go home.'

'Oh, no, I think it'll do her the world of good. I've already talked her into coming to my pottery group next week.'

'Really?' I was astonished.

'Well, she said no, but I insisted. She's got to get out, Ella. Can't stay cooped up in that cottage all day in her twinset and pearls, looking like there's a nasty smell under her nose. Even she can see that. Shall I feed the chickens?'

And she strode off in her puffa jacket to get the swill bucket from under the kitchen sink where I kept it. That was what I loved about Ottoline, I thought, watching as she added some stale bread from my breadboard and strode back outside. If something needed doing, she just did it. If Sebastian needed a sitter, she stripped. If a stubborn old woman needed bringing out of herself, she'd do it. If the chickens needed feeding, she'd feed them. She just got on with it. She was the sort of person who could probably plough a field with her bare hands if she had to. I watched her small, round frame march across the yard, pail swinging from her hand. She had no time for naval gazing, for gossiping, for chewing things over for hours with other women. Some would say she lacked sensitivity, but I thought she was ultra-sensitive. So sensitive she knew life just had to be coped with, whatever it threw at you.

In fact, she'd be a surprise hit at Lottie's touchy-feely Holistic Centre, I thought as I went inside. Whilst Lottie couldn't wait to wade in and give advice, had to sit on her hands and desist, Ottoline would be just the opposite. Would listen quietly, a hunched little figure in her faded jeans, patched sweaters and puffa jackets. Years ago, at the end of one of my classic, shoulder-shaking, cheek-soaking rants about Sebastian's infidelity, she'd handed me a man's spotty hanky and said: 'Yes, I do see. How awfully difficult.' Or something equally, marvellously, understated. Then she'd got to her feet, brushed down her denim knees and told me to follow her. We'd headed down the garden collecting a trowel apiece from the potting shed, and as we'd energetically weeded the lower bed together, I'd found myself almost embarrassed that I minded having a failed marriage, when, clearly, what mattered most was getting the bindweed out.

She was no thug, though. She threw the most beautiful plates and bowls in her studio at the Dairy: wide, slim platters which she glazed in subtle and translucent tones of duck-egg blue and green, or very pale white, when one thought white was just white. She could paint designs on them too, although she'd gruffly admitted to it only when I saw some at the back of a cupboard one day, before she'd quickly shut the door. Yet it was Ottoline who'd put down that paintbrush and defiantly take the tractor out in heavy snow to get groceries for the elderly from the village shop when the farmer said the road was impassable; or who'd dig an allotment when the tenant was in hospital, worrying about his cabbages. I suspected, too, that Ottoline made appointments with Lottie knowing her client list was thin. She took a rather dim view of alternative medicine but how like her to join the queue if necessary. I, on the other hand, although glad to support Lottie, had hoped for results.

As I gazed reflectively out of the window, mulling over all of this, my mother gazed back from her cottage. I jumped. Shit. You see? Always there! Panic-stricken I plucked my phone from my pocket and rang my sister. After the briefest of pleasantries, and going against everything I'd just been considering – and what Ottoline might hopefully have taught me – I said: 'The thing is, Ginnie, I think Mum could do with a break. Why don't you invite her round?'

'What, today?'

'Well, why not?'

'I've got the fair today, you know that. For Save the Children. It's impossible. I'm still here now, on my stall. Yes, those gloves are fifteen pounds, but they are pure cashmere.'

'Tomorrow, then,' I said, undeterred. 'Have her tomorrow, Ginnie. Maybe she could stay the night?' I was still at the window and could see Mum still hovering at hers. I knew she wanted a cup of coffee. Knew too, though, that if she came in I'd have to use all my life force not to scream as she picked holes.

Ginnie lowered her voice. 'Ella, I had her over last Monday, if you remember. And she criticized everything.'

'Well, she criticizes everything here, too!' I yelped.

'Yes, but in front of Richard.'

I shut my eyes. Always Richard. Always she wheeled out the husband. The trump card. Which I didn't have.

'Wanted to know why I had so many plates on the walls, and that stag's head over the Aga, which Richard shot in Scotland, and which she said was a dust collector. "When did you last get up there to do it?" she asked. And when I told her my girl did it, she wanted to talk to Linda about not just dusting it, but getting a bucket of soapy water to it. Trust me, Ella, Linda will leave if Mummy even speaks to her, let alone tells her off. She's terrified of her. No, I just can't risk it.'

Husband *and* staff. *Two* trump cards lacking in my hand.

'What – so you're not going to have her at all? Not ever?'

'No, of course I will! I'll take her out, like I said I would. But, you see, I've got the fair tomorrow and the next day, so I'm afraid this week is impossible. Yes, it's a little cot blanket. It is rather darling, isn't it?'

'Well, that's an outing in itself, isn't it? Take her with you to that,' I said angrily. 'It's at Celia's, isn't it? She'd love a snoop around Longhorn Manor.' I'd been to one of these fairs: lots of stalls filling the interior of a grand house, so plenty of nosing round the bedrooms. 'You can park her on a chair at your stall, get her to wrap stocking-fillers or whatever you're selling, surely? She'll love it. Love meeting all your friends!'

'It's too long a day for her, Ella,' she said patiently. 'I'm here until eight this evening – oh, hi, Lucinda! Two minutes. Literally, two minutes. Tonight? The Spencer-Cavendishes? Yes, we are! Oh, good!' She came back to me. 'And then tomorrow I'm here from ten until nine. Be reasonable.'

'She can drive herself. Come home if it's too long a day for her.'

'She'll get lost. It's all windy lanes. And she hates the satnav I bought her, doesn't like somebody telling her what to do, apparently. I'll have her next week.'

But I knew, with rising panic as I put the phone down, that next week would be Ginnie's turn to do Riding for the Disabled, or to sit on the Macmillan Cancer committee. Twenty women round a huge dining-room table in some other stonking great house, their credentials for raising money all indisputable, but . . . didn't charity begin at home? With her mum?

'She's a great do-gooder, isn't she?' said Lottie drily, some hours later, as I lay on her slab at the Holistic Centre. Lottie was clicking around her tiny consulting room in her L K Bennett's, fiddling with an Adele CD which she said soothed her, although I couldn't help feeling I was the one who should be soothed. She crossed to a trolley to line up her needles and then, worryingly, to consult the manual on her desk. Lottie could never resist a swipe at Ginnie, whose lifestyle she derided but probably rather envied. I realized I should never have said anything.

'Yes, and she's brilliant at it, actually,' I said, changing tack in sudden defence. 'I can't tell you how much money she's raised. Thousands. She works incredibly hard.' Funny thing, family. Fine for me to knock, as hard and as often as I liked. But not my friends.

'No one asks her to do it,' she said lightly. She turned. 'Didn't I say take your trousers off?'

'Um, yes, you did,' I said nervously. 'But I thought it

would just be in the ankles? Like last time? Fine to just roll them up a bit?'

'No, it changes now. I've got to do knees, and um . . . somewhere else.' She frowned back at her textbook, surreptitiously consulting it again.

'Right,' I said weakly, slipping out of my jeans. At least I had an afternoon slot. Lottie said she got better as the day wore on and I so badly wanted to believe her.

'Is she still doing all that charity-ball stuff?' she asked with a small, secret smile. Ginnie would send Lottie invitations to countless fairs and bazaars, but not the charity balls, which were very much for her own crowd, having a jolly time in black tie, outbidding each other for skiing holidays in the auction.

'Yes. That's where they raise the most.'

'I'm sure it is. It's just . . .' She wrinkled her brow thoughtfully. 'I think I'd have more respect for her if she worked in the Oxfam shop in town, like my aunt does. You know, for free. Sorting through people's smelly old jumpers and paperbacks.'

Well, of course Ginnie wasn't going to do that. Rather exhausted, I said surely it didn't matter how they raised the money as long as they did, and at least Ginnie wasn't lolling by her pool, ordering her staff around.

'No,' she said shortly. 'At least she's not doing that.'

And there we left it. With me wishing I'd never mentioned my sister. I knew Lottie felt aggrieved at never having once set foot in Ginnie's house, having heard so much about it, and in the very early days, when we'd just moved in, she'd even had Ginnie over to supper. She'd given Ginnie six dates so it had been impossible for my sister to refuse. Sebastian and I had been at the occasion

too, but it hadn't been a towering success. Lottie was a terrible cook and had only two dinner-party dishes in her
repertoire. One consisted of bits of anaemic chicken
floating in a creamy goo, which Sebastian christened
'Chicken in a Spunk Sauce', and the other was a sort of
brown slop, involving mince, strange pulses and God
knows what, which he called 'Labrador Sick'. That night
Lottie had surpassed herself. She'd done both. Labrador
Sick was served in ramekins to start with and Chicken in
a Spunk Sauce followed, on top of solid white rice. Lottie was also a very sweary cook, and after much clashing
of pans at the sink, and clouds of billowing steam as
she drained the rice, which burned her hands, she brought
the boiling plates to the table amid cries of 'Fuck! Fuck!
Fuckit!'

Richard, paling under a skiing tan, and used to lightly
grilled turbot or possibly partridge at this time of year, had
pushed the food around his plate in the tiny, steamy kitchen in wonder. Ginnie asked if she could open the
window and lunged to do so, and Sebastian and I did what
we always did and got roaring drunk so as not to notice the
food. Ginnie had never asked Lottie back, and even though
Lottie had invited her to numerous open days at the Holistic Centre, with special offers attached, she never came.

'Perhaps I should have her to supper again?' she'd
mused once, and before I could stop myself I'd said, 'No.'
Too quickly. Lottie's lips had pursed.

I knew she was hurt, but there wasn't much I could do
about it. Ginnie, like my mother, chose her friends forensi-
cally. She didn't deviate from a very narrow path.

'Your sister thinks I'm common,' Lottie had observed
to me once and I'd cringed with horror, because that very

morning, in my sister's kitchen, when I'd asked, with a smile, if she liked my lovely friend Lottie, Ginnie had wrinkled her nose and said: 'Bit common.'

'She does not!' I'd lied roundly to Lottie, remembering too the furious row that had ensued between the sisters over Ginnie's granite work surface. I'd told her our own family were no great shakes, look at Auntie Doreen. Hardly a countess. What gave *her* the right to say that?

In fact, it was probably that very insecurity which had prompted Ginnie to say something as snobbish as that, as she carefully covered her own tracks. But as Lottie picked up her needles and approached, I did hope she didn't have my sister in mind.

'Knees, you say?' I said nervously, although, actually, before I knew it, she'd popped one into my left one. Seamlessly.

'Well done,' I said admiringly, thinking: Good. I've picked a good day. I relaxed slightly as she moved around the end of the bed and popped another one in the other knee, again achieving that strange, slight tugging sensation which spread down the limb and meant she'd got it right. That it was working.

'Mmm . . . yes,' I murmured, knowing she'd like that.

'Good,' she murmured back.

Sometimes it was hard not to get the giggles with all the murmuring and the music. Me, that is. Not her.

'Those are your tension points for insomnia,' she murmured.

'Ah,' I murmured gratefully, shutting my eyes. 'So now I just lie here for, what? Twenty minutes?' As Ottoline said, this was the great thing about acupuncture. The little shut-eye one got after. The quid pro quo, as it were.

'In a sec. I've just got to put one in your head.'

My eyes snapped open like nobody's business.

'In my head? Why?'

'Because that's where it goes. Don't panic. I've done it heaps of times.'

'Whereabouts in my head?'

'In the middle of your forehead. Between your eyes.'

Shit.

She hovered, needle poised. Then she hovered some more. Came closer. If she couldn't see the fear in my eyes, I could certainly see it in hers.

'Um, Lotts, look,' I said quickly, mouth dry. 'The insomnia's not so bad these days. In fact, last night I slept like a baby. Nine hours. Surely the knees are enough?'

'They won't work without the head.' She was swallowing quite a lot. I could see her throat bobbing about.

'Well, never mind, they don't need to. As I said, nine hours solid and – *Christ!* What was *that?*' Something cold slipped down my face, just missing my eye.

'Sorry – sorry. Just slipped out of my hand. Your head's a bit sweaty, that's all. Couldn't get purchase.'

My fault, of course. The next attempt was on target, but we were both shaken.

'Thank goodness it was you,' she said, breathing heavily. Gustily, even. She stepped back from the bed as I lay there, pierced and immobilized, like William Tell's assistant on a bad day. She then got very busy, bustling round the room in her clicking heels to check heaters, the sound system – apparently I was to have Joe Jackson now – adjusting the blinds at the window.

'Don't move, will you?' she instructed, composure restored. Hers, not mine.

As if I could.

'And I'll be back later.'

Oh, splendid. Hopefully with more weapons of torture. The things I did for my friends. Which, as we know, is not quite true. The things I did to try to ease my mind, to still my buzzing brain. To shut it down and give me some respite from life. As I lay there, half naked and liberally speared, Lottie wobbled from the room in her heels, softly shutting the door behind her.

Chapter Twelve

'Meet me for a coffee?' Ludo was suggesting casually some days later, as I painted the broken fence at the bottom of the garden, mobile clamped between shoulder and ear.

I laughed. Oh, that it were that simple. 'Why not?' I agreed, entering into the spirit, although a bit of me knew he was serious. 'Or dinner at that new Italian everyone's talking about?'

'I hear the pasta is sublime. And the candlelight so flattering. Coffee might be less ambitious, though.'

I felt a frisson of excitement. 'I can't, Ludo,' I said softly, slapping paint generously onto the crumbling wooden slats in an attempt to hold the thing together and avoid buying a new one. 'I can't sit having coffee with you in some dark little corner of a cosy tea shop. What if someone saw us?'

'Well, then we're having a cup of coffee,' he said gently. Much lip-moistening at my end. 'Or a walk?' he suggested.

'What, with the dogs?' I enquired brightly. 'It went so well last time, didn't it?'

'Definitely without the dogs,' he said hurriedly.

It had been tried before, to disastrous effect. Ludo had brought Flossie, Eliza's precious cocker spaniel, and I'd stupidly brought both Maud and Doug, leaving Diblet behind. I should have left Maud, too; without her I might have coped better with Doug, but hindsight is a marvellous thing. We'd set off across the buttercup-strewn fields, Ludo and I, whilst the children were at school, Sebastian at the pub and Ottoline away, as if it were the most natural thing in the world for the gardener and his client to be dog-walking, but my heart was racing madly. In the event, everyone had behaved badly. Maud, a rescue mongrel who's needy at the best of times – she sits on your foot when you're watching television and if you ignore her she jumps on your lap, and if you ignore her still she trembles violently and looks as if she's going to pass out – was suspicious of Flossie, this rather glossy interloper, from the outset. After ten minutes, she decided she'd had enough. She sat down and refused to go any further, so that I had to carry her to prevent her going home and barking noisily to be let back into the empty farm, thereby alerting the whole village.

Doug, meanwhile, enchanted by the glamorous Flossie, was showing off horribly. A puppy of Diblet's, Doug had been A Mistake. Years ago Diblet had shagged an Airedale bitch at Longhorn Manor, mid croquet lawn, and mid smart luncheon on terrace. Celia had run from the lunch table screaming, shooing him away with her napkin, whilst her father, the Brigadier, had roared and gone purple, but, too late, the damage had been done. A terrific row had ensued with Celia shrieking down the telephone that Savannah was a show dog, worth a fortune, and any puppies would be worth a fortune too. Sebastian, with a straight face, had calmly told her that we waived any stud fee. 'Not if they're *your* dog's they won't be!' she'd spluttered back. Savannah had eventually had four puppies and I'd felt honour-bound to take one. I'd picked the one most like Diblet, except with corrugated Airedale hair like

Douglas Hurd, hence Douglas, which we'd hoped would encourage him to be urbane and diplomatic, in an Our Man At Netherby Farm sort of way. Obviousy he wasn't. Indeed, within weeks, it became clear that Douglas was a Doug, if not a Dug. Adorable and outrageous he might be, but he was also feral and untrainable and spent all day chasing squirrels, rabbits, his tail, the postman, cats – anything with a pulse. Naturally we had him neutered but the vet said at the time, looking a bit sheepish, that he'd never come across anything quite like Doug before – 'And the operation might not have been, ahem, an unqualified success. Bring him back if you're unsure.' He'd closed the surgery door quickly. He'd looked so traumatized – Doug and the vet – that I was loath to put either of them through that again, so I'd hoped for the best and ignored the signs. Of which there were many. Doug wasn't remotely interested in Maud when she came into season – but then hardly any dogs were, poor Maud – but then there had been the strange case of the Labrador bitch's puppies at Honeysuckle Cottage. With the Douglas Hurd curls. Then the Norfolk Terrier bitch's puppies at Burston Farm with – happily only to Sebastian and me – that distinctive, mad, rolling eye.

On the day of my walk with Ludo, everything became horrifically clear. My arms were aching from carrying Maud, and Ludo tried to take her from me.

'Here, let me,' he'd said manfully, taking the bundle.

'Oh, Ludo, I'm not sure. She doesn't really do strangers.'

Sure enough, she began to tremble violently, staring up at him with huge terrified eyes.

'Blimey, is she all right? She looks like I've assaulted her.'

'I think maybe put her down.'

He did, but too close to a puddle for her liking and she yelped as if she'd been kicked.

'I didn't touch her!'

'No, it's just she doesn't do puddles, either. She walks round them. I'll have to dry her feet.'

I did, on my jumper, whilst Ludo made soothing noises, which pleased me. Sebastian would be swearing: Bloody dog! Have you ever *seen* anything so wet! But consequently we took our eye off the ball, and when we turned it was to see Doug, in a state of ecstasy, humping a rather radiant Flossie in a mulberry bush.

'Shit!'

I lunged towards them, but it was all over bar the shouting, of which there was a lot from both me and Ludo. And violent tugging too, which apparently you should never do as you can injure the male; but frankly I couldn't care if I pulled it off, as I told Doug forcibly. Eventually we parted them, Doug looking smug and very much intact thank you very much; Flossie, shameless and thrilled, much as I imagined Eliza might look after a night with Mr Singh. It hadn't escaped my notice, either, that she'd wiggled her bottom in Doug's face at the start of the walk.

Ludo and I gazed at one another, terrified.

'Oh, God. D'you think . . .' I breathed.

'No, it takes ages with dogs. I'm pretty sure they have to stay locked together for hours and hours for it to work.'

'Still, we should probably get her the morning-after pill?'

'Is there such a thing?'

'Of course.'

'Oh – good plan, then. I'll go and get it. Except – oh,

Christ – Eliza knows the vet! Won't she put two and two together? If he says something about me coming in for it?'

We regarded one another in terror, our beautiful, sun-shiny morning amongst the cowslips and the buttercups disintegrating into dust and ashes as we imagined Eliza, like some avenging fury, hotfooting it straight from the vet's round to my place.

'I'll go,' I told him. 'I'll say it's for Maud. He won't know no one fancies her.'

And so we turned and headed for home. Obviously I didn't have to go instantly to the vet's, but Doug had cast a shadow over the whole morning. The prospect of Flossie in pup, and a whole load of Douglas Hurds emerging in Eliza's kitchen, filled us both with horror. We couldn't rest until the situation had been resolved.

As Doug gambolled happily ahead, Ludo remarked rue-fully: 'I'm not sure Doug getting his leg over was entirely the point of this walk.'

I giggled. 'No, although he was definitely provoked.'

'In what way?'

I told him about the bottom-wiggling and Ludo looked defensive. 'Well, she's never done that before,' he said shortly.

We walked on in silence. Our first row, I wondered?

'At least it's not me going to get the morning-after pill,' I told him at length, in a placatory fashion.

'Oh, quite,' he said with feeling, paling visibly at the thought. '*Quite.*'

So a walk definitely without the dogs, I thought, paint-brush in hand at the garden fence, mobile still clamped at my neck. But . . . wouldn't that look a little odd? We certainly couldn't go off the beaten track, where bona fide dog walkers might report back that Ludo Pritchard and Ella Montclair had been seen strolling in the wilderness, dogless. But neither, surely, could we walk casually through the village, where who knows who might drive by and think: Why are Ludo Pritchard and Ella Montclair walking shoulder to shoulder, he talking intently, she blushing madly, eyes lowered to her shoes? Body language was a very dangerous thing and impossible to disguise. Even Ottoline had given me an old-fashioned look the other day as I'd returned from the vegetable patch, fingers having been squeezed therein. But the vegetable patch couldn't decently be dug and titivated any more. It was becoming tidier than the house. Suspiciously overtended.

'Possibly a coffee,' I agreed eventually, faintly, into my mobile. 'Somewhere very public. So that, if anyone asks, we just – you know. Ran into each other.'

Ludo sighed. 'Yes, and we could wear badges, perhaps? That read: "Absolutely nothing is going on." '

'It isn't,' I said quickly.

'I know,' he said sadly, and recently that note of sadness and – no, not reproach . . . regret, had crept into his voice.

It made me feel . . . a bit guilty. As if I were leading him up the garden path, both literally and figuratively. After all, I'd been seeing him for ages now. But . . . what was the alternative? Booking into some ghastly motel in the next county and having a quickie? I shuddered. I just couldn't. The trouble was, I realized, as I resumed my brushstrokes having agreed to think about it, those sweet, tender moments when our hands brushed inadvertently, or perhaps even advertently, entwined under a coffee-house table, were almost enough for me. It was the intimacy I craved, and the love. The rest I'm sure would be marvellous too, but not the guilt afterwards. It simply wasn't worth it. Whereas for Ludo, I knew that little by little, as far as he was concerned, without pushing me in the slightest, this was where we were heading, unless he was to go stark-staring mad.

And then what? I put the lid on the tin of paint and pressed it down hard with the heel of my hand. Straightened up and narrowed my eyes into the sun. Then, when it had happened a few more times, would he leave Eliza? Would I leave Sebastian – such as I even had him – and set up home with Ludo, taking the children with me? But they were teenagers now. Might not even want to come. As were Ludo's girls. So – what, then? Ludo and I on our own? Where? I felt afraid. Neither of us had any money and I certainly wasn't going anywhere without the children. He was devoted to his girls too – which was probably why I loved him. I couldn't see him leaving them, either. So. An affair, then. With all the deceit and the guilt that involved. Whilst at the moment, I told myself, I was – almost – in the clear. I'd done nothing wrong. Well, break it off, then, Ella, I told myself angrily. Whatever it is you have here. This . . . friendship. Never see him again. He's only a man, for God's sake. Just a man. I marched back up the garden path, heart pounding.

My route back to the shed where I kept the paint took me past the Granary and after I'd dumped the tin amongst the others, I surreptitiously peered through the side window. At that moment Sebastian emerged via the front door and down the steps, which shook me. He was wearing a tatty checked shirt, jeans, and his feet were bare. So like Josh.

'What's this lunch, then?' he said crossly, but not menacingly.

For a moment I thought he'd said 'What's for lunch?' and lurched back a good few years. Then I realized. He wasn't too pissed, I decided, and it was after midday.

'What lunch?'

'I don't know. Some email,' he said, turning and going back inside. 'Come and see.'

He was making for his ancient computer on the table in the corner. I hesitated. I resisted going into the Granary as much as possible when he was there, getting the children or Ottoline to take the sheets. It was different when he was out, but when he was in situ I respected the privacy that he seemed to want – need. His paintings were stacked all around the walls: old ones I knew intimately, new ones I knew nothing about, all of which stirred so many emotions in me, I found it difficult when we were together.

'What email?' I said as evenly as possible, following him in, eyes front.

'Here.' He pointed at the screen. 'From the school. Tabs has forwarded it to me.'

'Oh.' I knew what it was. A school event; some sort of fete, just before the beginning of term, because when they'd tried to hold it at the end of last term the heavens had opened and for the next twenty-four hours the rain had reached biblical proportions. They'd had to call it off but, due to popular demand and some particularly pushy parents, it was to be held next week. It was the sort of thing Tabitha was usually dismissive of, would try to wriggle out of, too cool to be manning the tombola, preferring to be in Topshop of a Saturday. But recently she'd expressed a desire not just to attend, but to have us attend

194

together. A show of solidarity, perhaps: both her parents there. I read it and hesitated, wondering how to persuade him, feeling for the best way.

'Well, I know it's not your idea of fun on a Saturday morning but we don't usually go to these things and I think she feels that now she's getting closer to the top of the school, maybe she ought to go. I also happen to know some of her friends are going so –'

'Yes, fine,' he interrupted my gabble impatiently. 'If she wants, I can come.'

'Oh, good!' I purred, delighted. 'Oh, thank you, Sebastian.'

'You don't have to overdo it,' he snapped. 'I'm not some absent parent who has to be sobered up and wheeled out for the occasion, rictus grins all round.'

Well, that's exactly what he was, sometimes, I thought. I remembered one terrible parents' evening, years ago, at Josh's school, when he'd actually made the art master cry. The man was famously incompetent and a bully, but Sebastian had the sharpest of tongues. I kept my counsel now, however, not wanting to be on the receiving end of it.

'Great. Well, I'll tell her we'll all go. It's on Saturday,' I said.

'Yes, I can read.'

He flicked off the email. Without meaning to, I looked at his inbox – couldn't really read it and hadn't meant to spy, but he'd seen me looking.

'Paintings are looking good,' I blurted, to save myself, but stupid Ella, *stupid*. I knew never to comment on his work, particularly these days, but I'd been tripped into it. I braced myself. Waited, eyes half closed in defence against the scathing wit. The derision. The snarl to mind my own business. None came. When I allowed myself to look at him, it was a strange look I saw in his eye. As if he knew I was steadying myself to be verbally lashed, and was saddened. A mask came up in moments.

'Crap,' he said, more typically. 'All of it. Fucking crap.' As if to demonstrate, he strode to a portrait of Ottoline on his easel, unscrewed it, and tossed it at me. 'Here. You have it, if you like it so much.' He mocked me with his eyes. 'Add it to your collection.'

I hated our exchanges like this. This would rock me for the rest of the day, I thought as I went out, leaving the picture where it had fallen, face up on the floor, feeling his eyes in my back. This would make me shaky until bedtime, then unable to sleep, and then it would take two or three days to recover. Literally. That's why I resisted coming in here.

Mouth dry, I went back to the house and made myself a coffee with two spoonfuls of sugar. I knew what I really wanted was a drink, but I wouldn't have one yet. As the kettle boiled, I texted Ludo.

Yes, you're on. See you at the Copper Kettle tomorrow at eleven.

Then I picked up my coffee, went upstairs, and settled myself at my desk, where I gave Dylan spectacular acne, Leanne an overbite, and Leanne's mum, Arlene, love handles.

I put my pencil down an hour or so later, unable to draw any more hideousness. I felt a bit sick. Instead, and without thinking, I got up and went to the huge cupboard at the back of the room. I lifted the broken floorboard at its base, fished for the key, and opened it. The vast array of stacked canvases within stared back at me. Facing me was the one I loved best: a seascape of Sebastian's with bobbing boats and flapping sails, the light catching the water. It used to hang in the sitting room, but when Sebastian couldn't bear to look at it and threatened to burn it, even though he came into the room only on high days and holidays, I'd smuggled it up here so he couldn't. I knew exactly where and when he'd painted it: in Italy, on the holiday we'd taken when the children were small, on the cliffs above that little bay around the coast from Portofino. How he'd smiled with delight when it was finished. Happy times. I feasted my eyes a while, breathing it in. Inhaling its beauty.

The rest of the paintings I didn't look at. Some were mine, some were his. Some valuable, but not for sale. Yes, I'd sold *Girl with an Orange Bow*, or rather *we* had – he'd definitely been consulted – but only because it had been worth the most and meant selling just one. Later Sebastian had snarled that I'd forced him into it and he'd been pissed at the time. He'd said if I wanted to make so free with his work, why didn't I bloody well have done with it and sell the lot? Never. Not in my lifetime. When we were dead, Josh and Tabitha could do what they liked with them. For now, though, they were entombed up here, in limbo. My guilty pleasures, to gaze upon occasionally, when I felt the need. Felt low enough. And I did today.

Suddenly I started at a noise. I shut the door quickly and turned, pocketing the key, crossing to the window. Not Sebastian, thank God. Even though he wouldn't have seen me, the thought of him just outside, and me, crouched and looking in that cupboard, made me flush with fear. Instead, I saw my mother, stick thin – thinner than ever, actually – but still very much ramrod straight, in the ubiquitous blue cape, going into her cottage from her car with groceries. I popped the key back under the floorboard, flipped back the rug to cover it and raced downstairs in moments. Picking my way in bare feet across the pot-holed drive, I hastened towards her. She'd been to Waitrose – of course – and was coming back for the last plastic bag in the boot.

'I'll get it!' I called, seizing it and saving her the trip.

'Oh. Thank you, Ella,' she said, tight-lipped, as I sailed passed her and into the galley kitchen.

'Shall I help you put it all away?' There were a few bags on the floor.

'No, thank you. I can manage.'

'Right.' I turned at her tone. 'Shall I put the kettle on, then?'

'No, thank you. I had a coffee in Waitrose.'

Somehow this struck me as profoundly sad. My mother, sitting in an unfamiliar supermarket on her own, knowing she wouldn't bump into any of her friends, of which she had many in Buckinghamshire. Just whiling away the time. And my mother was a busy person: church-roof committees, bridge fours, lunch parties, choir practices. Her expression didn't invite sympathy, though. Chin raised, eyes cold, still in her cape, she was clearly waiting for me to go.

'Mum, how about coming for supper tonight?'

'No, thank you. I'm clearly a burden.'

'Of course you're not a burden! What on earth makes you say that?'

'I overheard your friend Lottie in the village shop saying what a saint you were to have me. And what a nightmare I was. Criticizing everything.'

I flushed. 'She's exaggerating. I'd probably just had a bad day and was having a moan.'

198

'Well, bad day or not, it's obviously not ideal. Indeed, the more I come to think about it, it's a terrible idea of yours and Ginnie's. It's not working, either, is it? As far as your father's concerned?'

I opened and shut my mouth. My idea? Ginnie's certainly, but never mine.

'Give it time,' I suggested. 'I'm sure he'll come round.'

In reality I was far from sure. I'd spoken to Dad a couple of days ago and I'd never heard him so chipper. He'd said he was just off to Zumba, had only got a minute.

'Zumba?'

'Yes, it's a sort of rock-and-roll fitness class.'

'Yes, I know what it is, but –'

'You'd love it, Ella. Great fun.'

'And – and Maureen goes too?'

'Oh, yes. But there's a crowd of us. We don't always dance together.'

'Dad, has Maureen moved in?'

'Well, she's here a lot, if that's what you mean.' He'd sounded surprised. 'But, no, she's got her own house. Why d'you ask?'

'Why d'you think I ask, oh, father of mine?' I'd said, exasperated. 'I've got your wife of forty years, mother of your two children, grandmother of four, going quietly round the bend in my back yard!'

'She can come back any time she likes, darling. I've told you that.'

'But you won't stop seeing Maureen?'

'No, I won't. She's my friend. And she likes me. I make her laugh.'

'Mum likes you.'

'She doesn't really, darling. She tolerates me. And she's

polite to me in public. Sometimes. She's not very polite to me at home.'

I fell silent.

'I won't move out of my own home,' he said, more seriously. 'Unless forced. Unless she wants a divorce. And I won't ask her to go. Wouldn't be so unkind. But if we're to live together under the same roof for the next twenty-odd years, it's got to be on my terms too, not just hers. We've lived under her regime for the last however many. I want to see my own friends, go out whenever I please, go to Zumba, or to the pub, or the cinema, without asking. And not necessarily go to choir or tend the garden. I'm sixty-eight years old, Ella, and I've worked hard. I will have what's left of the rest of my life.'

I'd put the phone down quietly. A few minutes later I'd picked it up again. 'Write to her,' I told him. 'Put it all down. Like you've just told me.'

And he'd promised he would. That had been Friday.

'Have you heard from him at all? Dad?' I asked casually, ignoring her refusal of my help and putting her milk and butter away in the fridge.

'Oh, yes. Some ridiculous letter this morning, about wanting to live his own life.' She snorted contemptuously.

'Is that so ridiculous?'

'Of course it is!' she scoffed. 'We're married! We don't just cohabit under the same roof and go our own ways; we do things together. And I do not want to take up cycling or go to murder-mystery evenings. Why should I!'

'No, but you could meet him halfway. Maybe find things you both like to do.'

'He *loves* the choir. He loves his garden and he loves all our friends. He's just being idiotic. Having a late-life crisis.

A last bloody hoorah.' She slammed two tins of Heinz tomato soup down hard on the counter.

Perhaps he was. And a bit of me thought: Good luck to him. It couldn't be much fun being Mum's prisoner.

I shrugged. 'OK. Don't.'

She swung around, furious. 'Oh, I wouldn't mind but it's not about that, is it? It's about that floozy of his!'

'Mum, I really don't think she's a floozy. Honestly I don't. I've told you before.' Neither did I see much point in continuing this. I changed the subject. 'I gather you're going to Ottoline's pottery group?'

'Yes, I said I would,' she said shortly. 'I've been to one already. I rather like Ottoline.'

I'd been putting macaroni away in a cupboard. I turned, surprised. 'You've been already?'

'Yes, I went last Thursday. I've been here for some time, Ella.'

Was it a reproach? Of course it was. Where had she been with me? Not even shopping.

'She's a doer,' she said defensively. 'Doesn't come in here telling me where I've gone wrong in my life, just fixes the broken drawer, tells me how to work the thermostat and goes away again.'

I ignored the barbed dart in my direction, pleased. 'Good. I like Ottoline, too. She's one of my best friends. In fact . . .' I was going to go on to say she was one of the reasons I'd stayed at Netherby, that she'd given me strength, supported me, but my mother had never invited this sort of confidence: Ginnie and I had always shied away from sharing, for fear of being derided. Of being told to buck up and stand on our own two feet. I wondered what my mother thought of my own situation. Of my husband in the barn. She'd never commented, never offered any counsel, any shoulder to cry on. Was she really so cold and hard? Did a heart beat within? It must do. It was just jolly hard to find. I knew I should have pressed her to come to supper tonight, perhaps even suggested a trip to Oxford tomorrow, to find her a new coat – she'd had that cape for years – but I didn't. In my heart I knew I'd never forgiven her for not being the mother I'd wanted. The one I'd seen other girls had. Cosy. Confiding. Forgiving. Was I punishing her? In her hour of need? I hoped not. But I had needs too. And, like I said, she was in my garden, wasn't she? Wasn't that enough? I left her to her unpacking.

Chapter Thirteen

In the event I rang Ginnie and suggested Mum needed a shopping trip. Ginnie, sensing I was now officially at breaking point and in no mood to brook an argument, promptly agreed, saying she'd pick her up at ten on Wednesday, falling over herself to say how grateful she was and how she knew I was carrying the can.

'It's fine,' I said wearily. Although it hadn't escaped my notice that Ginnie's charity fair had finished and she hadn't beetled round, as promised. 'She's no trouble, actually.' She wasn't. 'She keeps to herself.' She did.

'Yes, but it can't go on for ever. I saw Daddy yesterday and told him so.'

'Oh?' I said warily. At least she'd gone, made the effort, but I wasn't sure my father in his present state would respond to these sorts of tactics. 'And?'

'He told me to mind my own bloody business! Honestly, he swore, Ella, and you know he doesn't. Said he was having the time of his life and if she wanted to join in and have the time of hers that was fine, but if she was going to be a wet blanket she could stay away. Said he was having a dinner party and needed to get on and caramelize his brûlée.'

'Oh! But he can't cook, can he? Who was he having?'

'He'd made a casserole, he said. Told me he'd followed a recipe and if you could read you could cook and too much fuss was made about it. It's only the neighbours, I think. But the ones Mummy thinks aren't smart enough and would never normally have round. Not Angie, but, you know, Jennie, across the road and her husband, Dan.'

'With the old bangers?'

'Exactly. And that older lady, Peggy, who Mummy says smokes too much and floats around in bohemian coats.'

'Oh, yes. God, they'd never usually be allowed in.'

'Quite. And Peggy's got a boyfriend who's a horse dealer, apparently. Lives in some terrible shack surrounded by whisky bottles.' She shuddered tangibly down the line. I looked across the way to my own husband's shack, no doubt littered with bottles too.

'There's always another side to the story, Ginnie. He's probably perfectly pleasant. Anyway, take Mum shopping.'

Had I just given my sister an order? Must be a first.

'Will do,' she replied quickly, and I almost sensed her coming to attention. 'I'll be round first thing on Wednesday. I've got a totally clear morning.'

Morning, see? Not day. Nothing too protracted. I put the phone down. But then she was probably busy in the afternoon. Whereas, aside from attending Ottoline's pottery group on Thursday afternoon, which I'd decided to do so that Mum and I could be together but not, if you see what I mean, I had a totally clear week. Ginnie's life and mine were so different in that respect. Acres of white space gazed back at me from the calendar hanging on the back of the larder door. Except, of course, for something tomorrow that couldn't be written in. Not even in pencil.

I drove into Oxford the following morning having left a note on the fridge for the children, who still had a good few hours' sleep in them. When I arrived at the café in the

High Street, Ludo was already there, reading a newspaper. He was sitting at a corner table: very much a table for two. Not ideal, I thought, heart pounding as I muscled through the crowded room – this was a Carluccio offshoot and popular with yummy mummies, the better-heeled students and young professionals who flocked to its proper cappuccinos. Weren't we were supposed to be bumping into each other? Not sneaking off to some clandestine spot?

'You could have been a bit more central,' I whispered, hovering doubtfully. 'This looks a bit – you know. Pre-arranged. Lovers at the corner table.'

Ludo looked up from his paper in surprise. Blinked and gazed around. 'There wasn't another free table, otherwise I would. Sit down, Ella, it's fine. We could have bumped into each other at the counter.' He folded the *Telegraph* away.

I sat down. Didn't like it. Didn't like it at all. I got up and looked around wildly. 'There's one.'

A couple of middle-aged women were preparing to make a move: paying their bill, gathering their shopping. Slowly, though. I shot across, muscling in before a young mother with a buggy who'd also spotted it, and loomed over them, smile rigid. The two women looked startled, then smiled back and made faster tracks. The young mum shot me a filthy look as I sat down resolutely amidst the empty cups and saucers, the screwed-up napkins. Ludo came across with a weary grin.

'Happier?'

'Much. This looks a lot less – you know. Furtive. If we were having an affair, why would we sit slap bang in the middle of a busy café!' I gave a slightly hysterical laugh. A few people turned to look.

'Yes, well, you might want to keep your voice down,' said Ludo nervously. 'At this rate we'll be accused of something that hasn't even happened.'

'Well, quite,' I said hastily, glancing about. I cleared my throat.

'How is the gardening business?' I asked in a loud voice.

Ludo rubbed his temple with a forefinger and grinned. 'Good thanks. ARE YOU DOING MUCH PAINTING?' he boomed. People turned to look again.

'Why are you shouting?' I gasped.

'Because *you* are,' he told me. 'Now relax, Ella. And talk to me normally. I've missed you.'

When he said this he moved his foot to press against mine. I felt a million volts shoot through me, right up to my eyeballs, which could well be flashing like a fruit machine. But I didn't move my foot away. It hadn't escaped my notice that the blue linen shirt he was wearing was exactly the same colour as his eyes, and that he was tanned from working outside. A shaft of dusty sunlight from the window had settled on the top of his head, turning his hair to spun gold. Gradually, as he ordered coffee and we chatted, I relaxed; even managing to smile at a friend I recognized, who saw Ludo, did a bit of a double take, but then waved back as if it were quite normal. I breathed. This was fine. This could work. Occasionally. Not too often or people would most certainly talk, but I liked the fact that it didn't involve deception – unless you counted the double bluff. It was above board.

'Actually, how is the art going?' he asked when the table had been wiped and our coffee arrived.

'Oh, I've nearly finished. A few more illustrations of

a sink-estate staircase – you know, fag ends in lifts, beer cans lolling about in gutters – and I can send it off. Wait for the money to roll in. Well, pennies. It'll be a relief to see the back of it, actually. To unleash it on the prepubescent set.' I grimaced.

'Good. But I didn't mean that. I meant the real art.'

I paused, cup midway to mouth, regarding him over the rim. 'You know I don't do that any more.'

'I know. But why not?'

I shrugged. 'I told you, no time. I can't be setting up an easel in the fields when there are mouths to feed, can I?'

'But you sold quite a few pictures once. Got real money for them.' He grinned and tapped his nose. 'I know. I've talked to Lottie. I have my spies. Your secrets are not entirely safe, you know.'

'Oh, Lottie. She exaggerates. And, anyway, I haven't painted properly for years, wouldn't know where to begin. How are the girls?'

'Just because you haven't done it for years,' he said slowly, not so easily deflected, 'doesn't mean you can't still do it. And you must be good to have exhibited.'

'Not nearly as good as Sebastian,' I said quickly.

'Of course not. He was a great artist. Once. Everyone knows that. But it doesn't mean *you* can't paint, does it? Just because he's not coming up with the goods any more? Lost the muse?'

I'd had this conversation before, with Lottie, and felt my way as carefully as I had done with her. People who didn't create, didn't understand.

'You're right, he has lost the muse,' I said cautiously. 'I, on the other hand, have lost interest.'

'Ah. Right.' He didn't look entirely convinced, though. He took a sip of coffee. 'What sort of things did you do?'

I sighed, hating talking about myself. Some people love it, do it, all the time; you can't stop them. Lob them a personal question and you're there for the duration, no end to their autobiographical flatulence. I was the opposite. It was so boring. I knew all about me.

'Still lifes, chimney pots, skies – anything, really,' I rattled off. 'I was pretty amateur. Not very good.'

'Can I see them?'

I glanced up, alarmed. 'There's nothing to see.'

'But surely you've kept some? From your early days?'

I thought of the packed cupboard I'd only very recently opened.

'Not really,' I told him. 'Only sketch books. Anyway, enough of me. How *are* those girls?'

'Really well.' He smiled, his face softening, blue eyes crinkling at the corners, as I knew they would. He rubbed the side of his face with the flat of his hand as he leaned in and went on to tell me fondly about a hockey tournament he'd been to, in which Henrietta had done brilliantly: not boastful, just proud. How he'd got overexcited on the touch line when she'd scored a goal and she'd had to beetle across, stick in hand, to have a word. 'Dad – not so loud! Not so mental.'

I laughed. 'You're one of those competitive parents!'

'Can't help it,' he agreed ruefully, stirring the froth into his coffee. 'I so want them to win. In everything they do,' he said fiercely, and I knew about that strength of feeling. That love. About wanting one's offspring to achieve dreams that perhaps we hadn't. Thwarted lives and all that.

Living vicariously through them, easing our disappointments.

I wondered if hugely successful people were the opposite. Having achieved their dreams and made so much money, might they care less about whether their children did the same? The only truly successful person I knew was Richard, my brother-in-law, and he certainly cared. Was on the board of governors at Harrow, where Hugo had been at school, sponsored every cup in the Pony Club cabinet: oh, yes, he certainly wanted them to succeed. The only person I knew who didn't feel like that, at least in terms of measurable, tangible achievement, was Sebastian. If the children's reports were bad, he'd say, 'So what?' And toss them aside. Tabs's geography report had once said: 'Tabitha has not handed in enough work for me to comment.' Sebastian had roared. And Josh's first form teacher at secondary school had written: 'Joshua will either be very successful or be expelled.' It was the first time I'd seen Sebastian turn to his son with something like real pride in his eyes. Until then I'd thought he didn't care; he said that he did care, but that it didn't matter. There was a difference. More recently I wondered if this was true. That it didn't matter.

'What are you thinking about?' Ludo asked with a quizzical smile.

'Sebastian,' I said, without thinking.

He laughed. 'Oh, great!'

'No, I was just thinking . . . he says he only wants the children to be happy.'

Ludo made a face. 'Cop-out parenting. I dare say he says he wants to be their friend, too.'

'Yes, he does,' I said, surprised.

'They have plenty of friends. They only get one father. It's tough out there, Ella. You've got to enable kids. Set them up for the real world.'

This I agreed with too. In fact, I was a bit like that, I realized. Suggestible. Agreeing with whatever was last said, particularly if it was reasonable and persuasive. I wondered idly what Josh and Tabitha would have been like with Ludo as a father? More conventional; more focused, perhaps. Less . . . I don't know, wild? Unpredictable?

'Sebastian again?'

I was obviously staring into space.

'No, you, this time. I was wondering what it would have been like if we'd had children.'

Hard to describe the look of excitement and pleasure that flooded Ludo's face at this. He leaned forward eagerly, arms on the table.

'Ella, come away with me. Somewhere in the Welsh hills, perhaps. Walking in valleys by shimmering lakes, the sun on our faces. Then a cosy pub somewhere. I need you. I want you, damn it.'

Forcefully, in a coffee bar in Oxford. I nervously took a great gulp of cappuccino and singed my mouth.

'Ludo, I can't,' I muttered, paper napkin clamped to burned lips. 'Not yet, anyway.'

'Not yet,' he echoed with a yelp, slumping back in his chair in mock despair. 'When? I'm not getting any younger, Ella. Bits will start dropping off me soon. We'll be taking our teeth out as well as taking our clothes off if we leave it any longer.'

'But then what?' I said. 'I mean after? If we rush off to

the Gower Peninsula or whatever, what happens after that, when I'm a fallen woman?'

'Then I'll set you up in a charming little bordello in Cardiff and visit you regularly. You'll be in the window in a basque, winking saucily as I roll up in my jeep.'

'Obviously I'll have to get rid of Taffy first.'

'Oh, obviously. He'll be slipping out the back with the rest of the male voice choir.'

I narrowed my eyes thoughtfully. 'How many in a male voice choir?'

'About twenty-two. You'll manage.'

We both grinned, but, as ever, never really got to the bottom of what next. Never planned any further. Were both too scared to say: One day we'll run away together, rent a little cottage in the Highlands – and I so wished I could. But – what about the children? All four children? How could we possibly leave them? And, to be fair, I thought to myself, as we chatted on about this and that and then a bit later he paid the bill, how could we plan anything when we hadn't even been to bed together? When we may not be a perfect fit? When there was an outside chance he'd say, 'Good Lord, I'm sorry, Ella, but I had no idea you were a shrieker' – I'm not, incidentally. Or, 'Ludo, much as I love you, I'm afraid those star jumps you warm up with don't work for me.' Sex was surely a huge part of the equation.

And, anyway, not spinning dreams and not planning any Highland fantasies made us more realistic, I decided, as I drained my coffee. More truthful. And I was a sucker for the truth, perhaps because latterly I'd had so little – my fault, as much as Sebastian's. But, then again, surely fantasizing was part of being in love, which we undoubtedly were. Why were we so cautious, then? *Was* it the sex? Or lack of it? The proper intimacy? Ludo smiled up at the young waiter, a student probably in his gap year, giving him a hefty tip because he was no doubt skint, then pocketed his wallet, leaning back easily in his chair. Lean and chiselled, he was by far the most elegant man I knew. He passed a hand through his still-blond hair; hair I loved and wanted badly to pass my hand through too. I felt a surge of what I knew to be longing. Ludo folded his arms and fixed me with a crooked grin.

'All set?'

I thought he'd been about to try to persuade me again.

'All set,' I agreed, gathering up my handbag from the floor. I'd put it in a wet patch, which was unbelievably annoying. I surreptitiously wiped the bottom with my napkin, hoping Ludo hadn't seen. I realized, though, I was thoroughly out of sorts. That I wasn't leaving the café nearly as contented and glowing as I'd imagined I would. It hadn't served a purpose, the one I'd so smugly said was all I required. Ludo went to help me on with my jacket, then remembered and didn't, and a bit of play-acting ensued whereby we both agreed roundly that it had been great to bump into each other and gave our love volubly to each other's spouse. We left the café. Outside, he peeled off one way down the High Street towards the covered market and his car, and I went the other, towards the bridge. After a few yards, though, just before I reached the junction at Magdalen College, I stopped. Turned round. He was walking away into the distance, disappearing into the throng. I ran back through the crowds, handbag bumping against my side, dodging between students, strolling shoppers. As I reached him I seized his arm: he turned, surprised.

'Fix it,' I urged him breathlessly. 'Fix something and I'll make it. Whatever happens, I'll be there. I promise.'

Leaving him with a look of utter astonishment on his face, in the middle of a clutch of Japanese tourists, I turned and hurried off down the street again, his eyes on my back as I went.

Chapter Fourteen

'What were you doing with Eliza Pritchard's husband in the Copper Kettle yesterday?' asked Ginnie, when she called round the following day to collect Mum.

I dropped the wet dishcloth I'd been holding. Felt a gigantic menstrual blush course up my neck and flood my face. 'Having a coffee,' I whispered. 'I bumped into him in the street.'

'Oh, OK. It's just Sophie Bellingham saw you. I didn't know you knew him?'

'Ginnie, you gave him to me, as a present, remember? To do my garden?'

'Oh, of course.' Her face cleared a bit. 'I'd quite forgotten. That was ages ago, though, wasn't it? Oh, well, it's nice that you're friends. He's a bit of a lad, though; you know that, don't you?'

I turned to stone. Right by my own washing machine. It was a full few seconds before the rush of life returned to my congealed limbs. I gripped the work surface above my Bosch for support and we entered Final Spin together, both vibrating violently. 'What d'you mean?' I gasped, as even my face shook.

Happily Ginnie had bent down to greet Buster, who'd recognized her and come wagging up; she hadn't seen my tortured expression. 'Oh, no, nothing like that,' she said, tightening Buster's tartan collar. 'This is too loose, incidentally. Just flirts with his clients, I think. Goes with the territory with that sort of job, I should imagine.' She straightened up, hands on hips. 'Now, what d'you think about Country Casuals, for a change? Or should I just head her straight into Jaeger, as usual? I was thinking it might be a bit cheaper. I know she regards Daddy as a bottomless pit, but she should perhaps be a bit more careful at the moment, don't you think?'

I said something about Country Casuals being a splendid idea, but my mind wasn't on coats. A flirt. Of course I knew women flirted with *him*, but Ludo wasn't like that. What could she mean?

'She's jolly tricky, though, isn't she? Eliza? I wouldn't blame him if he indulged in a bit of banter occasionally, in his line of work,' I said, hoping I wasn't returning too blatantly to the subject.

'She can be,' she admitted. And this her best friend. 'Oh, I didn't mean he was a danger. He certainly hasn't strayed, if that's what you mean. Eliza would have said. And she would have kicked him out, too.'

She would. On both counts. Women always did tell their best friend, and, being Eliza, she'd have got rid of him, too. But some damage had been done, nonetheless.

That evening, after downing nearly a whole bottle of wine, whilst Tabs was at a friend's house and Josh in Oxford with his mates, where he spent most evenings in the holidays, I sent Ludo a text.

Really sorry to mess you about but can't do Wales for a bit.
There's so much going on here with my mother at the moment.
Will be in touch. x

I nervously dropped the phone on the carpet as if it were molten.

Then I knocked back the remains of the Chianti and waddled to the kitchen to drop the empty bottle in the bin. I'd lost it already, I thought, staring down at it. My bottle. Didn't take long.

No probs. Let me know when? x

His text had come back like lightning.

Soon. I promise. x

Then I hastened outside to shut up the chickens, which I'd forgotten to do, hunched in my old brown coat, deliberately leaving my phone behind.

Lottie was sympathetic when I told her the next day.

'You don't have to do it at all,' she told me, washing up at her kitchen sink as I hovered, hollow-eyed through lack of sleep, the papers and milk clutched in my arms. 'Just say no.'

'Yes,' I said miserably.

'But that would mean saying goodbye?'

'No. It wouldn't. I'm very sure of him, actually. I know he'd stick around whether I went away with him or not. It's just . . . I suppose I don't want to disappoint him.'

She shrugged. 'If he loves you he'll understand. Stop beating yourself up about it. Although, actually, I don't think he is a flirt. He doesn't seem the type. Are you sure Ginnie wasn't just saying it out of . . . you know.'

'Jealy-bags?' It had occurred to me. Ginnie had looked a bit miffed. After all, Ludo was her property. And pretending she didn't know I knew him – she'd bumped into him in the supermarket, mentioned the gardening.

'Possibly,' I conceded gratefully.

'He's certainly never flirted with me.'

'Really?' Lottie was much prettier than any of Ginnie's friends, his gardening clients.

'She's probably just lashing out, a bit piqued. We all do it. And, anyway, if it makes you feel any better, Eliza is seeing someone.'

I stiffened like a child playing musical statues when the music stops. Reached out and seized Lottie's hand. It was wet and rubber-gloved.

'She's *not*,' I breathed.

'She is, but I honestly shouldn't tell you, Ella.'

'Oh, for God's sake, you're an acupuncturist, not a neurosurgeon! Who is it?'

'I don't know. And that's all I can tell you. I've said too much already.' She went all pious on me, her mouth disappearing into a small line, but my heart was soaring.

Eliza was seeing someone. *Eliza* was cheating! On her husband, Ludo! Oh, joy of joys! Joy unlimited! She and Mr Singh were suddenly transported upstairs, she in his arms, to his little room above the fabric shop, except . . . might that be a bit – you know, seedy? No. No, they'd gone to India. On a covert trip, planned furtively together some time back. She, ostensibly to buy silk; he, ostensibly to see his family, but in fact – in *fact* . . . they'd holed up in a luxury hotel in Jaipur. There they were, lying on an exotic four-poster bed, silk canopy billowing, mosquito nets flapping, window open wide to the desert – or, no, was it the jungle? His brown limbs entwined with her ivory ones as they smiled secretly at one another, replete. Beads of sweat glistened on their upper lips and his arm was flung protectively over her pale breasts. 'Shalom,' Eliza whispered, fluent in Urdu now. Or was that Hebrew? Oh, well.

'Shalom,' he whispered back as the violins rose to an almighty crescendo and the camera panned away to the mountains – jungle – beyond.

I bounded out of Lottie's house with my milk and papers, bounced across the stream via the stepping stones, and almost skipped home through the village. It was the most heavenly late-summer morning: the browned-off fields shimmered under a pale lavender sky, which was saving itself for deeper colour later and the promise of intense heat, something we'd sorely lacked this summer. The ox-eye daisies, sodden with rain, were staging a heroic comeback in the hedgerows on account of the unexpected warmth, the wood pigeons were cooing in the tree tops, the swallows swooped and soared in the bleached sky. And so did my heart: right up to the heavens.

But I wouldn't text back and say: 'Yes! Yes! Any time! Any place! Anywhere on the Gower Peninsula!' I would just hug this to myself for a while. Play it cool. Play it my way. Be still, my beating heart, be still. The flaming crocosmia in the lanes nodded their heads approvingly, applauding my restraint: rows of tiny orange beads in hearty agreement as I went on my way, spirits high.

Ottoline's pottery group convened that afternoon in her studio at the side of the Dairy. Sometimes I had to steel myself to join this gathering, but today I nipped happily across to help. Up until recently, and out of the goodness of her heart, Ottoline had run a Women's Drop-in Centre in town, where she taught ceramics, sponsored by a charitable authority. In some dingy basement room below Asda, local disaffected women – abused, addicted to drugs and alcohol, out on parole – had come to take out their frustrations on a lump of clay, under

Ottoline's watchful, tutoring eye. She'd take their creations home, fire them in her kiln, then present them back to them the following week to be painted or glazed. Many a time I'd seen the products of weird and wonderful imaginations drying on Ottoline's workbench, and marvelled. Typically, though, when the recession bit, it was one of the first things the council insisted must go. The women had been upset: tearful, even, apparently. Characteristically undaunted, Ottoline had said she'd run the group from home, one day a week, if anyone was interested. They were. One or two men were interested too, which didn't faze Ottoline or the other women – the local authority would have had something to say about it had it still been under their auspices and their roof, but it wasn't.

Some people had come once, then couldn't be bothered to get the bus from town to the village again; but one or two stalwarts kept coming. It was a very mixed bag, and, in keeping with the sporting analogy, a rather gamey one too. There was a large, silent woman called Amy, in a vast khaki anorak that smelled as if a rat had died in it, a skinny teen-aged girl called Sam, a vocal and foul-mouthed girl called Becks and her equally foul-mouthed sidekick, Debs, and an extraordinarily well-spoken woman called Amanda. Most of the women had been in and out of prison but no one was quite sure what Amanda had done. We did know, however, that she loathed her husband. Had she tried to kill him? Spiked his Gentleman's Relish? It was a mystery. Everyone knew Becks and Debs had had their run-ins with the police, mostly drunk and disorderly, but I liked Becks. As I pushed through the stable door to Ottoline's bright, airy studio, I saw her stationed at the bench already. She made a startling apparition. Her short, hennaed hair was bright red and stood on end as if she'd had an electric shock, and she was covered in tattoos that crept up her neck. She wore a black shirt, combat trousers and heavy army boots. Beside her was small, dumpy, peroxided Debs, wrapped in a cheap market-stall cardigan, shoulders up round her ears. Incongruously, on the other side of the workbench, my mother was poised, silvery hair swept professionally off her forehead, fully made up, a pristine white apron over a crisp beige skirt and blouse.

I wasn't quite sure how this would go. As I slipped in beside her and grabbed an apron I said quietly: 'You do know, Mum, that the language can get a bit fruity in here?'

'Oh, I know. I was here last week, remember? I'm not that easily shocked, Ella. And, anyway, Ottoline has banned the C word. Apparently most people comply.'

'Yeah, but that's not the worst, is it?' argued Becks. 'To be honest, I'd rather be called a cunt than a fucking slag. That really pisses me off. Orright, Ella?'

'Fine, thanks, Becks,' I said breathlessly, one eye nervously on Mum, but she didn't flinch and carried on calmly kneading her clay.

Before us, behind a trestle table, was Ottoline, in habitual puffa jacket and jeans. She was outlining the plan for today and making sure everyone had a lump of clay, including the two men in the group, Ray and Charles. Ray was about fifty; small, round and leering, but so inconsequential no one cared. Becks and Debs could slap him down in moments if he was a pain and took great pleasure in doing so. Charles was a stately eighty-two and from the Hall at the far end of the village. A very grand old man – Sir Charles, no less – he was nearly blind. When he'd applied to join, Ottoline had been at great pains to tell him about the origins of this group; about its rehabilitative status and how those that came were often ex-cons. But Charles hadn't minded a bit.

'How marvellous,' he'd said. 'Good for you, Ottoline. Can't leave it all to the Salvation Army, can we?'

'Well, 'es probably lonely, isn't 'e?' Becks had remarked. 'Knockin' round that big 'ouse all day. It's not natural.'

And she was probably right. He seemed to treat the session as a social occasion and once brought fruitcake made by his housekeeper, which Ottoline had passed around, some of the women taking it in wonder, as if they'd never seen fruitcake in their lives before. But then the next week he'd brought a hip flask full of sloe gin, saying it was just like hunting, wasn't it? Frightfully good fun. Ottoline, of course, had to ban that, as the women swarmed. It wasn't Charles's fault, but he did tend to settle his hazy, sightless eyes at breast level as he talked to you, and keep them there. When I mentioned this to Ottoline she said, 'Oh, I don't think he's blind at all. Just pretends, so he can stare down women's tops.' Ray, of course, didn't pretend: he just stared anyway.

Leering aside, though, both the men were quite jolly, and somehow helped dilute the occasionally highly charged and decidedly hormonal, female atmosphere.

We were all encouraged to do our own thing by Ottoline and make whatever we liked. Most women indulged in fantasies. Some made little gardens with flowers when I knew they lived in high-rise blocks, or tiny models of thatched cottages with picket fences and smoke curling from chimneys. It was rather moving how often this bucolic theme cropped up. I was making jugs, thereby indulging my own fantasy, which involved my children sitting around a checked tablecloth at breakfast, pouring milk from them over their cereal, instead of drinking it straight from the bottle standing at the fridge, one hand plunged into the cereal packet.

I collected the jugs from the draining board by the sink, where Ottoline kept things stored from the previous week, and slid in between my mother and Becks. Becks was by far the most artistic of the group and had promised to help me with the handles. She was on her fourth ashtray, highly stylized and dramatic in the shape of a wave, the crest of which was breaking over to form the rim.

'How's tricks, Becks?' I asked cheerfully. 'What have you been up to this week?'

'I got arrested this morning, didn't I?'

'Oh, no. How dreadful! What on earth for? What did you do?'

'Nuffin' that wasn't justified,' she told me defiantly.

'Yes, I'm ... sure it was justified.' Ottoline and I exchanged a glance. 'What happened?'

'Well, my mate's pregnant, right, but it's not her boy-friend's baby.'

'I see.'

'So 'e gets out of prison this morning and comes straight round to mine, where she's stayin'.'

'Ah. Right.'

'So I opens the door –'

'What did you open the fucking door for?' interrupted Debs.

'Well, I didn't know it was him, did I?' she flashed angrily at her friend. 'So he pushes past me, right, into the kitchen, where my mate is, and he lunges at her, tosser. And I thought: I'm not havin' that.'

'So what did you do?'

'I knifed 'im with the bread knife.'

'Good heavens. Where?'

'Only in the calf. Stopped him, though.'

'Yes, I'm sure it did.' In his tracks, I should imagine. 'Where was your boyfriend, Becks?' Becks, rather unusually for her social circle, had four children all by the same man.

'Where 'e always is, in front of the telly, telling us all to calm down.'

'And he didn't interject?'

She glared at me. 'He's not a pervert. I told you, he was watching telly. Had all his clothes on.'

'No – no, I didn't mean . . .'

'Anyway, so the cops came – the neighbours called them cos of the noise – and I'm out on bail. They let me off wiv a caution.'

'Good. Excellent,' I murmured. 'And the boyfriend? I mean – the one with the leg. He's in hospital, I suppose?'

'Yeah, but 'e'll be inside again soon, thank God. 'E wrote off a car on the way over to mine, didn't 'e?'

'Heavens.' This man had been in the wars. 'But . . . why will he be back inside?'

'Well, 'e nicked it, didn't 'e? Knob'ead. What's that, then, Amy?' she asked cheerfully as Amy, silent, anoraked and hunched opposite us, put the finishing touch to something she'd been creating for a couple of weeks. Something we'd all been wondering about.

It was a large, hollow ball, one side of which had been moulded into a gruesome man's face, bald, huge ears, slits for eyes and mouth – Wayne Rooney on a bad day – and on the other side was an equally ghastly thug with bulbous nose and hollow eyes.

'It's my exes,' Amy told her quietly. 'Both bastards and you can see right through them.'

There was a silence. Ray and Charles looked a bit nervous. We worked on quietly for a while and I glanced to see what my mother was making. An oblong box, for tissues, perhaps. She was decorating it with a tool. Rather pretty. One of our number couldn't settle, though: Sam, the bleached, skinny girl of about fifteen, didn't know what to make. Eventually she decided to make something for her baby.

'Might make 'im Winnie-the-Pooh,' she muttered, biting a non-existent nail.

'That's a lovely idea,' agreed Ottoline, as she watched her break off a small piece of clay and roll it into an egg-sized ball. 'But obviously he can't . . .'

'Nah, I know. 'E can't put it in 'is mouf.'

'Good. Just, you know. Checking.'

Winnie-the-Pooh proved hard, though, and Sam got tearful, shouting at Ottoline when she tried to help. Becks stepped in and did the legs for her, and the face, and, after a word from Ottoline, made the whole thing a bit bigger. But, later, Becks decided her ashtray was rubbish and threw it on the floor, where it smashed, startling everyone.

'Crap!' Becks yelled, her face the colour of her hair. 'Fucking crap!'

Ottoline didn't rush over to soothe or cajole; she didn't pander to them. She just got the broom and swept it up. Wordlessly, she handed Becks another lump of clay. Becks seized it and pounded it hard on the workbench, pummelling furiously. I thought Mum would be watching all this with huge eyes, but she calmly got on with her box.

Ray sidled up to me, standing much too close, as usual, and breathing hard. He looked me up and down, sly and admiring, his eyes on my breasts. 'I like your jugs.'

I swallowed. 'Um, thank you, Ray. And I . . . like your egg cup, too. What are you making, Mum?' I asked, deflecting Ray.

'I'm helping Amanda,' she told me shortly.

'Right.' The box seemed to have a lid now. Not for tissues, then. And Amanda was making an identical one.

'What are they for, Amanda?' I asked lightly, as I passed en route to the sink to wash my hands. 'The boxes?'

'My shotgun cartridges.'

There was a stunned silence.

And so the afternoon wore on in the company of these eclectic, extraordinary, startling, sometimes entertaining people, the like of which, I thought, watching as my mother helped Sam with a tiny jar of honey, Mum would surely never have come across before. Nor me, either, if it wasn't for Ottoline. I knew better than to ask Mum if she'd enjoyed herself at the end of the session; she'd find it patronizing, which it probably was, but it was so difficult to talk to her without getting it wrong and her becoming irascible, that I ended up saying nothing.

When we were helping Ottoline to clear away, though – when the women and Ray had shuffled off to their bus stop, and Charles, his chauffeur having collected him, to his empty Hall – and when we were wiping down the plastic tablecloths together, it seemed odd not to talk.

'Did you buy anything with Ginnie in town?' I asked pleasantly.

'You mean, am I still spending your father's money with gay abandon? I gather you and Ginnie thought Jaeger too expensive for me. Perhaps you'd like me to shop at Dorothy Perkins? Or be a career woman? Earn my own money, is that it? After all these years?'

I gaped at her, J-cloth in hand. 'No! God, Mum, no. Of course not.' I was shocked by her hostility. She glared at me for a moment, her eyes very bright. Then she took her apron off and hung it on a peg. She thanked Ottoline brusquely, and walked out, full of the hauteur in which she specialized.

I went to the door and stared after her, baffled.

'She's still so hurt,' said Ottoline, coming to stand beside me in the open doorway. We watched her go back to her cottage. 'Can't you see that?'

'Yes, sure. But, God, Ottoline, we're doing our best, aren't we? Ginnie and me?'

She shrugged. 'Oh, you're ticking all the boxes. No doubt about that.' And she went back inside to clean the rest of the tables.

Chapter Fifteen

I brooded on what Ottoline had said for couple of days. Knew she was right. Knew, on paper, we were being the model daughters, sheltering our mother in a crisis, trying to mend fences between her and my father, but that because of the nature of our relationship, there were certain steps we weren't prepared to take. She was a guest on my farm as she was, occasionally, a guest on Ginnie's estate. We made time for her, rang each other to confer, to set aside mornings, or a couple of hours, synchronizing our diaries like a couple of board members. But we didn't fully integrate her. Why? In case we were rebuffed? Or in case we couldn't get rid of her? Probably.

Other cultures are scathing of our treatment of elderly relatives; cultures where elders are venerated and not only included, but regarded as heads of the family: Indian, Muslim, Mediterranean families. My own friends, however, had purred with admiration – gosh, you are a star to have your mother – so I thought I'd achieved. Done well. In my heart I knew I hadn't, though. Knew I was being shabby.

On the morning of Tabitha's fete, therefore, we were a party of five. Tabitha, her brother, mother, father and granny. I'd had to persuade Mum, who'd instantly said no, but Josh had sweet-talked her into it. Josh, who, in the first instance, couldn't believe he was being asked to attend himself.

'You're having a laugh.'

'I'm not, Josh.'

'What do I want to come to some rubbish fete for?'

'Because Dad's coming, and Tabs would like us all to go. I know she would.'

'What is this, *The Waltons*? Some cringy show of unity? Let's pretend Dad doesn't live next door and Granny hasn't been kicked out?'

'Something like that,' I said, keeping my temper. 'Think you can manage it?'

'For who, you or Tabs? I think you'll find she's not fussed about me or Granny coming.'

'You may be right. OK, Josh, you've got it. *I'd* like us all to go.'

'Do we have to hold hands? Pretend we're in love? Like politicians and their wives on holiday?'

'Quite possibly.'

'I'll dig out a polo shirt and tuck it into my jeans.'

'Look, Josh —'

'Yeah, yeah, all right. Don't go off on one. I'll come.'

And then, as I say, he'd persuaded my mother.

She'd arrived at the back door in her new coat and I did a double take. Looked her up and down.

'Is that the one you bought with Ginnie?'

She was wearing a very snazzy grey linen coat dress, with a full skating skirt and cream trim. Quite youthful and quite unlike anything she ever wore, but it suited her.

'Oh, no. Ginnie wanted me to buy some ghastly camel affair. In this weather. Ottoline and I found this in Monsoon.'

Ottoline and I. It hadn't escaped my notice that Mum was spending a lot of time with Ottoline. I hoped she didn't mind. It also occurred to me that Ottoline didn't do anything she didn't want to, so clearly she didn't. Lottie had spotted the pair of them coming out of the Playhouse together the other day. Laughing like girls, apparently.

'Really? What was on?'

'I'm not sure. Something Noel Cowardy, I expect.'

The next time I'd driven past the Playhouse in town I'd seen it was *Calendar Girls*. Great fun but, actually, not Mum's cup of tea at all. Something of which, latterly, she'd have given a thin smile and said, 'What fun,' but secretly disapproved. I knew better than to mention that, too.

'Right, well, come on, then. We're going to be late.'

Sebastian appeared from the Granary, looking surprisingly handsome in a clean blue shirt and buff-coloured linen jacket. His black hair was overlong, but clean and curling on his collar, and he'd shaved. I saw Tabitha smile in delight.

Once I'd shoed Ladyboy out of the car – if I left the window open she was inclined to roost on the back seat – I got into the driver's side. It was boiling hot and my legs were baking on the plastic. Sebastian was beside me, having lost his licence long ago, and, in the back, the children were either side of their grandmother. As I let out the handbrake I caught Josh's eye in the rear-view mirror, ironic and amused at this highly unusual family outing. I willed him not to say anything. Hopeless, of course.

'Do we have a packed lunch?' he asked politely. I ignored him.

'The sixth form are doing refreshments,' Tabitha told him, missing his tone.

'Your year,' I told him sharply, unable to resist the jibe.

'Damn,' he muttered. 'Didn't make the cut. That'll keep

me awake at night. Not to be trusted with a teapot, perhaps,' he mused.

'How ridiculous,' said his grandmother roundly. She turned to him. 'You can use a teapot, can't you, Joshua?'

'We don't have one, Granny,' he said truthfully and very sadly. 'So I've never tried. Mummy uses bags. Says it's quicker.'

My mother was horrified. 'For heaven's sake, Eleanor!'

I refused to look at Josh's smiling face in the mirror. As we drove on down the lane, browned-off fields frazzled under an increasingly simmering sun. The forecast had promised more rain; annoyingly I was in jeans. An error. On we purred. After a bit Josh cleared his throat.

'Does anyone know "She'll Be Coming Round the Mountain When She –"'

'Josh!' I interrupted sharply.

'Oh, let him sing it if he wants to,' Mum said, surprised. Tabitha tittered.

'That'll do, the pair of you!' I snapped. I wasn't sure who the pair were, but Tabs instantly assumed she was of their number and widened outraged and heavily made-up eyes into my rear-view mirror.

'Great! What have *I* done?'

'Not you, darling,' I muttered. As it dawned, my mother's mouth disappeared. She turned her head away, affronted. We drove on in silence. Sebastian brooded quietly beside me, looking out of the window. Josh shut his eyes and rolled his head back as if he were dying, and Tabitha continued to look hurt and pick her nail varnish. The school was still a good twenty minutes away. After a couple of miles I could bear it no longer and said the first thing that came into my head.

'Josh has got some artwork on display,' I told Sebastian

quietly, as if we were normal parents. 'We might take a look.'

'It's crap!' Josh exploded from the back, his head snapping upright. 'And why d'you have to say it in that conspiratorial way, like – let's see what the little chap's been up to?'

I licked my lips nervously. 'Josh, I'm just saying that, while we're there, we could take a look at your A-level work.'

'Well, don't. Keep your nose out of it, Ella.'

That helped. Oh, that really helped. The atmosphere in the car thickened and set. Sebastian still hadn't uttered a word and I knew it had been stupid to even mention art: Josh was genuinely cross.

We arrived at the school in complete silence, amidst other families cheerfully getting out of cars in the car park, chatting and laughing to one another, greeting friends. Tabitha looked anxious and pale.

'Why does it always have to be like this?' she muttered.

'I don't know,' I said sadly, but knew I was partly to blame.

I watched as Josh, hands thrust in pockets, shoulders hunched, sloped silently away to see whether any friends of his might also have been press-ganged into this arsehole event, and thence to commiserate and smoke in the woods.

'I've got to go,' Tabitha told me. 'I'm on the bring-and-buy.' She shot off to her stall, slowing down quickly when it became apparent her huge wedged heels and very short skirt couldn't cope with the grass. I remembered how, not so long ago, she'd speed across this stretch of grass when I dropped her, pigtails flying.

Right, I thought, slamming my car door. Since everything I said was wrong, I was damned if I was going to make the running. Feeling tears prick, I glued on a smile and turned to see Sebastian helping my mother out of the car.

'Thank you, Sebastian,' she said crisply.

Since he'd moved out of the farmhouse some years ago, she hadn't spoken to him at all. Other mothers might have tried to have a quiet word, get to the bottom of a daughter and son-in-law's separation, discovered his number from her grandchildren and picked up the phone, but not Mum. She'd instantly reverted to her well-I-never-liked-him stance. When she had to be, though, as she did now, she was studiously polite. I don't think Sebastian noticed her frost one way or the other, and he certainly didn't care.

As she turned speculatively, to survey the summer fete scene, handbag over arm, lipstick freshly applied, I noticed she had a horrible wet patch on the back of her new coat. With some sticky bits of shell attached. A glance back in the car confirmed my worst suspicions. Bugger. Ladyboy had laid an egg. *Bastard* chicken. She hadn't done that for months. She was supposed to be going through the change, for God's sake – a bloody sex change, at that! Just as I was summoning up the courage to tell Mum, with all the agro that would entail – taking her to the loo to sponge it down, or home, even, knowing my mother, because how was she supposed to walk around with a great wet patch on her backside – Tabitha reappeared, looking aghast.

'I'm supposed to have brought the kitty! It was my responsibility!'

Faced with this more immediate and potentially weightier problem I did what I always do and panicked. Shooting my fingers through my hair I cast around wildly, as if expecting loose change to rain from the sky.

'Typical!' I seethed. 'Tabitha, why can't you be just the slightest bit organized for once? I've got a sodding great jar of change sitting on the dresser at home, for crying out loud!'

'I didn't know!' she wailed.

But Sebastian was way ahead of us. 'Here.' He'd delved into the central compartment in the car, where, of course, I throw change, and was giving her a large handful. He added some from his pocket. 'Start with that and I'll change a tenner in a minute and give it to you.'

'Thanks, Dad,' she said gratefully. He then fished out a Tesco bag from the floor of the car, where any number floated about wantonly, and they tipped the coins in. She flashed him a relieved smile and took to her wedged heels again, bag in hand.

I missed that, I thought, watching her go. Sebastian never flapped. He had many faults but he was good in any sort of crisis. When Josh had fallen off his bike and his head had bled so much the grass had turned red, Sebastian had staunched the flow with his fingers and still managed to ring Lottie, who'd beetled round with Steri-Strips. They'd mopped my face with a wet flannel to bring me round but I was still sitting on the red grass with my head between my knees when Josh was in front of *Scooby-Doo* with a Fab. When they were even smaller it was always 'Daddy' they called in the night, as he went to clear up the sick and deal with the bed linen, ignoring me in the background as I flapped and wondered if we shouldn't call a doctor. Weren't they very hot? High temperature? Meningitis, perhaps? I flushed now as I remembered. The still small voice of calm had always been Sebastian's. I took a deep breath as we walked on in silence towards the modern school buildings in the distance, bunting flapping over the clutch of stalls in the courtyard, no children now to offer what shield they provided.

'I'm going to look at the cake stand,' my mother announced, and before I could open my mouth to tell her about the coat, she'd sailed off to check out the Victoria Sponges.

That left the two of us: my husband and I. I felt hot with nerves. We walked wordlessly across the hockey pitch. It was quite wide, the hockey pitch.

'How have you been?' he asked. The solicitude shocked me.

'Fine, thanks,' I said warily, waiting for the barbed remark to follow. None came. 'And you?'

'Oh, you know. Usual. I get my licence back soon, so that'll help.'

'Good.' I was astonished. This was verging on a normal conversation. 'It'll be a relief to get out and about a bit more, won't it?' I said, encouraged.

'What, like some day-release patient?'

Ah. Bullseye. But perhaps I had sounded patronizing. I hadn't meant to. Nerves again.

'Sorry,' he said quietly, knowing me very well. 'You didn't mean that any more than I did. And I'm sorry to always snap at you. You bring out the worst in me.'

I glanced up at him. He'd said it sadly. And I knew it was true.

'And we used to bring out the best.' It was the first heart-felt thing I'd said to him in a long time and his eyes told me he knew that to be true too. Our gazes fell to the grass.

'Ella, I've taken a job in Oxford.'

I looked up, astonished. 'A job!'

'Yes, they've asked me to be artist in residence at the university.'

My mouth fell open. 'Oh! Well, gosh, what an honour!'

'Yes, I suppose.'

His face hardened a bit. Perhaps I should have said: 'Lucky them to have you.' But artist in residence . . . heavens. Of course he was a famous name and his reputation went before him, still did, clearly; and of course what they didn't see was the alcoholic wreck shuffling from his lair at midday, throwing unfortunate canvases around, staggering drunkenly back from the pub at midnight, making the dogs bark, the cockerel crow, slamming doors. They – the powers at the university – saw only the work: and the early work in particular, one of which hung in the Ashmolean and which he refused to sell, despite our financial problems. Presumably he'd been for some sort of interview; but . . . perhaps not. If he had, they'd have seen this sober and attractive man in his crumpled linen jacket, faded shirt, jeans, which, I had to admit, we'd seen a bit more of recently. When he'd taken the children out to supper the other night, he'd looked like this as he'd called for them and they'd walked to the pub. I'd felt almost jealous as I watched them go from my bedroom window. But one clean shirt didn't make a pillar of the establishment, and it was a prestigious appointment, whatever he said.

'Well, it certainly will help having your licence back, then. To go back and forth.' And he'll have to stay sober, I thought with a stab of pleasure. To do that.

'No, they've given me a place in town. It's Christchurch. They're rolling in money. I've got somewhere in college.'

I stared in horror. 'You're moving out!'

'Well, I've moved out anyway, Ella. Let's not be stupid.'

I couldn't speak. Couldn't say: Yes, but only into the garden, where I can see you. Where the children can see you. Where I had – not control, of course not – but where there was a semblance of normality, however unusual it was. And how would he cope? Manage – I don't know – sheets, food? I bought his groceries, put them in his fridge, and he mostly had supper at the pub. Well, of course, he'd probably have a scout, I thought with a jolt. Someone who did all that for him, as they did at these grand Oxford colleges; he'd dine in hall, like the other professors, at the top table. They were all so clever that they weren't expected to get their own meals. Protected, venerated: an endangered species to be nurtured, set apart from the rest of mankind, by their talent.

'What about the children?' I gabbled, afraid. We'd come to a halt by an empty netball court. I gripped the wire netting. Held on tight.

'I've told the children. They're OK with it.'

My breathing became quite shallow. 'When?'

'At supper the other night.'

'They didn't say!'

'No, because I said I'd tell you,' he said gently.

It occurred to me that I was being treated carefully and gingerly. By my children and my ex-husband – for ex he surely was now. Don't upset Ella. And they'd discussed me the other night, over scampi and chips. But . . . I was the one who discussed their difficult father, explained how hard it was being Sebastian. Not the other way round.

'They'll miss you,' I whispered.

'Well,' he hesitated. 'Josh might come and stay.'

The blood left my face.

'No.'

'Just to stay, Ella, in his gap year, next year. He wants to work at the Playhouse. You know he does.'

Josh harboured an ambition to act and had already decided he wanted to do anything menial at the theatre to get a foot in the door: meet directors, actors, anyone.

'Oh, so Daddy's got the flash pad in town and they'll run like lemmings! Tabitha, too – all her friends live in Oxford. You'll have them both!'

My voice was raised, shrill. People turned to look as they walked by.

'No, Ella, it's not like that,' he said patiently. 'I told you, they might stay. Of course they live with you. I'm not try-ing to take them.'

But my heart was racing. I felt breathless. Could see it all panning out in a hideous screenplay before me: Sebastian, in some treacle-coloured Cotswold stone college, a set of rooms up one of those venerable staircases. The children with their own bedrooms, own keys, coming and going as they pleased, smoking inside, coming back from parties at all hours – Sebastian was much less strict than me. Which teenager wouldn't want that?

And then I saw me, at Cold Comfort Farm, in the tumbledown farmhouse. Alone with the dogs, the hens, the ducks, the sexually confused chicken, the slime in the yard, the poo, the broken fences, the escaping animals . . .

In the distance a figure in a grey coat raised a hand and came towards us balancing a cake.

And *her*!

'I thought I'd put this in the car,' she said as she approached. 'It hasn't risen as it should,' she remarked sniffily, 'but one must show willing. Haven't you bought anything yet, Eleanor?'

I wordlessly handed her the car keys and she went on her way, giving me only the briefest of looks as she took in my face.

'We'll have to get a divorce,' I said viciously, hoping to shock him now, as he'd shocked me. 'No question about it.'

'Of course,' he said solicitously, as if I'd said I had to have a new sofa.

I was rocked again. We'd never, ever mentioned the D word. Never.

'It makes perfect sense,' he said, almost in surprise. Almost as one would to placate a small child. 'We've had what so-called professionals would no doubt call a trial separation and it hasn't worked. But there's no reason why we can't be civilized about it, is there?' He regarded me with his brown eyes, genuinely anxious. As if I were the one to be handled with care. As if I were the one with the screw loose who could tip at a moment's notice, and throw things. I felt as if someone had scooped me out and deposited my insides in a pile beside me. Eviscerated. Of course: hence, gutted.

'No, no reason,' I said breathlessly.

Out of the corner of my eye I saw Lottie and Hamish coming from the car park with their two children. They saw us at the same time and approached.

'Hi, you two!' Hamish said jovially and in a surprised how-nice-to-see-you-together voice. 'Loving the principal-boy look, Ella!'

In an attempt to be trendy and please Tabitha, I'd got some of her boots over my jeans, but they were too long, to the knee, and didn't quite work. I'd also tied a scarf round my neck, which didn't help either. Hamish pecked my cheek and pumped Sebastian's hand. They genuinely got on and embarked on a bit of man chat. Lottie had seen my face.

'What's the matter?' she said in a low voice, taking my arm. We walked on ahead.

'Sebastian wants a divorce.'

'Oh. Well, that's . . . sort of, predictable, isn't it? Under the circumstances? I mean . . . where were you both going?'

'I didn't know it was where *he* was going!'

'But it was kind of what you wanted, eventually, surely? The situation couldn't have gone on like this for ever?'

'I don't know, Lottie,' I muttered miserably. 'I don't know anything any more.'

'Yes – just *wait*!' she broke off to say to Matthew, who was hanging on to her arm and leaping like a salmon, demanding money – 'Mum, Mu-um!' – for a stall. She found some in her bag and gave it to him. He sped off with Lil, his sister, at his heels. 'I've got my mother here somewhere too,' she said distractedly, glancing about. 'They've put her on a new drug and she's much better but as lively as a kitten. Must see where she's got to.'

'Not causing a stir in the Spar, then?' I managed, forcing a smile. Life mustn't always be about me. And Lottie clearly thought this news was predictable.

'Oh, she's still doing that, but in different ways. She picks arguments with everyone now, terribly punchy. Last week she made the girl in the bank cry. Sorry, Ella, I'd better find her. Please God, she's not at the apple-bobbing holding someone's head under.' She hurried off.

Sebastian and Hamish had peeled off to guess the weight

of a teacher, the marvellously game and rotund chemistry master, Mr Chivers.

'How dare you!' he bellowed cheerfully as a cheeky child guessed twenty stone. 'I haven't even had lunch yet!'

The audience laughed and, amongst them, I saw Ludo's daughter, Henrietta, pale, blonde and sensitive. Ludo himself was behind her, I noticed with a start. I saw him put his hands on her shoulders and throw his head back and roar as Mr Chivers made some other quip. They'd had to move Henrietta here for the sixth form, when the money had run out. Ludo's lovely face was wreathed in smiles. He hadn't seen me. Neither had he seen Sebastian, who was almost beside him. Same height, but much darker. In every way. Sebastian's face was, as ever, inscrutable, unlike Ludo's, which was an open book, showing every emotion. It was convivial now as he joked with Mr Chivers that his handle-bar moustache must surely weigh a few pounds? Sebastian would never have bantered openly like that in public, or had his hands resting on Tabitha's shoulders. Comparisons. Sometimes odious, but sometimes a good idea. If they helped. To see more clearly. I breathed a little more easily. A few paces behind Ludo, viewing the proceedings with disdain, was Eliza, in a prim summer shift dress I'd seen in the Boden catalogue. Navy blue with taupe trim. She was standing with Ginnie and Richard, I perceived, in surprise. But of course. Richard, despite having children at private schools, had been asked to be a governor here, as a man of some standing in the local community and a prospective high sheriff. He'd been rather flattered and said he'd think about it; he was obviously checking the school out. Ginnie, though, looked pained to be amongst us. She was fingering her pearls, a bright smile on her face, looking awkward. She'd got a pink embroidered coat on – no make-up obviously, and her hair was still on end – but nevertheless she made a complete contrast to the other parents here, who wore casual jeans or shorts. But perhaps that was the point. She cast Richard a meaningful look.

'She's foul to him,' Lottie hissed in my ear as she beetled back to my side. I jumped. Bit strong. Then I realized she was talking about Eliza, who she'd thought I'd been watching. 'And he holds the fort pretty much all the time these days. Any excuse and she's off to London.'

'London?'

'That's where her man is. I told you. And of course Ludo can't do a thing about it because she rules the roost.'

As if to demonstrate, at that moment, Eliza, looking exasperated, strode across to pull Ludo and Henrietta away, as if they were making spectacles of themselves by hooting with laughter. I saw Henrietta look tense as her mother had a low word, holding on to her arm, and then we all caught each other's eyes – Eliza, Ginnie, Richard, Ludo, Henrietta and me. As Lottie peeled off diplomatically, the rest of us converged, greeting each other enthusiastically, exclaiming about how wonderful it was to see each other, kisses all round.

'I don't know a soul!' Ginnie cried in mock alarm, a hand to her heart. It occurred to me that in the right social circles that would never usually stop her. She'd be in like a heat-seeking missile. 'Thank God you're here, I'd quite forgotten!'

'Forgotten where your nephew and niece went to

school?' I said, surprised, and quite sharply for me. Ludo and I ritually pecked each other's cheeks: the current coursed through me.

'I know! Too silly of me. I've brought mine, of course.'

'Why?' I asked in wonder, as indeed, my own niece and nephew, with a blonde girl I recognized as Frankie, hovered at a distance. They were in a rather awkward huddle watching the skittles, not knowing anyone.

'Because I'd like Hugo to try for an internship here, teaching cricket,' boomed Richard, who was sporting a bright pink shirt and yellow cords. He was a small man with no volume control. Perhaps that was why. 'Employers like to see some proper community work these days, not just building orphanages in Thailand.' Surely that was charitable work, not community? Was working at a state school now in the same bracket? 'And he needs to show he's capable of getting on with all types, if he's to go into the City eventually. It's much more PC to have something like this on your CV than, say, working at Summer Fields for a term.'

I cringed at the volume, and the content. Hid from one or two parents who'd turned to stare. Richard beamed and nodded genially at them in his loud clothes. He'd never quite got the country-squire look right, principally because he wasn't one. Had bought into it. For all his booming and his vibrant colours, though, I liked Richard. He didn't dissemble for anyone. Said exactly what he thought. And although he had his detractors, I wasn't one of them. His heart was in the right place.

'You mean next summer?' I asked.

'Exactly,' he said more anxiously. 'I'm already that far ahead, Ella. Have to be.' He glanced at Ginnie and I detected another agenda here. That, for once, the loud voice had been calculated: painting a picture to appeal to his wife. 'And cricket would be good for him,' he said in a lower voice. 'Working with children, too. More fun.' He meant than the internship Ginnie was lining up for Hugo at Deloitte's, courtesy of our uncle. I agreed, but didn't comment. I'd got involved once before, agreeing with Richard that working in the pub would be a good idea, and then been on the receiving end of Ginnie's fury.

'Except Uncle Bertie has gone to a great deal of trouble,' Ginnie told us now, muscling in, ears like Mr Spock's. 'He had to really persuade the board at Deloitte's. And Hugo's already had the interview.'

'Let's play it by ear, eh?' Richard told her gruffly. 'He doesn't like London very much. Prefers the country. And, anyway, there are other factors at play.'

'You mean the girlfriend!' she hissed.

There was an awkward pause. I couldn't quite believe my sister was getting so wound up about something a year hence.

'As I say, other factors,' Richard said in a placatory manner and I remembered Josh had told me Hugo wasn't sure he wanted to go into the City at all. Had said he'd been channelled all his life, from Summer Fields, to Harrow, to Cambridge; he wanted to make the next step himself. Might take another year off.

'Here they come,' I said nervously, as Hugo, Frankie, Araminta and Josh, who was of their number now, slowly left the skittles and ambled our way.

'I gather you've met her,' Ginnie muttered tightly.

'Yes, when I went to see Dad. I thought she was lovely. And Josh says she's great.'

The teenagers changed course suddenly, perhaps seeing their parents ominously huddled together. They headed off towards the hamburger stand.

'Sweet little thing,' said Ginnie brightly, but her eyes said: I'd like to poison her. 'Not a great deal of polish, obviously. But hey-ho.'

There was an awkward silence.

'Well, quite,' said Eliza, loyally. Henrietta crept away.

'Henrietta!' Eliza called after her, then made to follow, tottering in high heels. 'Henrietta, I thought we'd have a word with your English teacher!' Henrietta walked faster. 'While we're here. *Henrietta!*'

'Darling, leave her,' Ludo began mildly. She swung round furiously. 'Oh, you! A fat lot of help you are!'

He raised his eyebrows imperceptibly as she stalked away.

This was turning out to be such a lovely day. Meanwhile, happy, smiling people with fish in bags and toffee apples ambled past.

'She's upset,' Ginnie told Ludo, laying a hand on his arm.

'I know,' he said shortly.

'This can't be easy for her,' Ginnie went on in a low voice, still with the hand on the arm. 'It is so different from Musgrove Park.' My eyes widened. 'It's not just the children, Ludo, it's everything. The parents, the teachers, the buildings . . .' She gave a little shudder at the concrete block behind us, as if, at any moment, it might crumble, like in *King Kong*.

'Ginnie – *my* children are here!' I spluttered.

'Oh, I *know*.' She laid her other hand, the one that wasn't on Ludo, on me. All she needed was a white robe and a halo and she'd be Jesus. 'I know, angel, and, golly, they've done brilliantly. Apparently Josh's art is fantastic. I'm just saying that it must be awfully hard for Eliza, after lovely jolly Musgrove – speech days, tennis parties, that sort of thing. With people she's comfortable with.'

'I think you'll find there are plenty of people here to be comfortable with,' Ludo said stiffly, but I was speechless. And so embarrassed for Ludo, whose fault this terrible comedown surely was. This ghastly tumble from fee-paying perfection.

Even for Ginnie this was breathtakingly dreadful, but I knew she was upset about what Richard had just said. Her mind was still on her own children, which always brought out the worst in her.

'Mum's here somewhere, did you know?' I told her rigidly.

'No, I didn't.' She looked around, surprised. 'Oh, well done, angel. You are getting her out and about.'

I shut my eyes. If she called me angel again I'd slap her. In front of all these people. Instead, luckily, when I opened my eyes I saw my mother approaching. Ginnie released Ludo's arm to wave in greeting. As she went off to meet Mum I made a mental note to ask Ottoline, who had the most impeccable manners, whether it wasn't terribly naff to touch people quite so much. Holding on to them. I was sure it was.

As Ginnie departed I cast Ludo an apologetic smile on my sister's behalf. He shrugged good-naturedly, his eyes trailing me as I turned and went away. It occurred to me that, just for a moment back there, I could actually have plunged a knife into Ginnie. In cold blood. At a school fete. I knew I'd felt that about my mother recently, too.

What did that make me? Was there a word for it, I wondered? A mother-and-sister-murderer? Shakespeare would have one, I was sure. Why did I feel like that? Why? And then, as I turned the corner, I knew. It stopped me in my tracks a few metres short of the bring-and-buy stand. Knew that, just as my mother and sister lashed out when their worlds were rocked, so did I. And that, actually, neither of them mattered. What mattered, I thought, as I saw him hand a plastic bag full of change over the burgeoning stand to Tabs, and as she and her friend Meg then tried to persuade him to buy a cracked china piggy bank, was that my precarious world, the one that for so long had been held together with Sellotape and paperclips, had finally fallen apart. It didn't matter how much I patched and made do, Sebastian had removed the only brick in the wall that mattered. The vital component. The one that said that the man I'd once loved more than anyone in the world now hated me so much he wanted a divorce. *He* couldn't live with *me*. Not the other way round. As Sebastian's face creased into that loving, affectionate smile I hadn't seen for so long, and as Tabs gleefully handed him the piggy bank, a terrible, crushing sadness broke over me.

Chapter Sixteen

Ludo was waiting when I came out of the ladies' loo in the new modern block which housed the school gym. He'd obviously seen my face buckle as I stood and watched my husband and daughter. Had followed me here.

'What's wrong?' he asked quietly.

'Sebastian wants a divorce,' I said, putting the crumpled, tear-stained tissue in my bag and swallowing hard. I snapped my handbag shut and glanced around, blinking rapidly.

We were alone, but precariously so: in an empty echoing corridor, just shy of the boys' changing room. A few beefy-looking lads emerged in football kit, roaring with laughter, punching each other heartily. One of them gave my teary face a second glance.

'I can see that devastates you,' Ludo said quietly.

'Yup,' I gasped, thinking: Don't be too nice. 'Bound to, don't you think?'

'Of course.'

'Josh and Tabs –'

'I know.'

We didn't have to say any more. Had often talked about the children being everything. Regardless of how we felt about each other. How he couldn't imagine not seeing his daughters every day. I couldn't tell him about Josh. Knew I'd break down. A bit of my brain also knew that Josh was nearly eighteen. And that he wasn't exactly leaving home, either. That I mustn't overdramatize.

'Let's meet next week,' Ludo said quickly, as a clutch of parents approached.

I nodded. Needing it suddenly. 'Where?'

'I'll text you.'

'OK.'

We parted, and I walked quickly down the empty corridor, hugging my handbag to my chest for protection. Rows of empty pegs for younger children ranged down one side, sticky labels with names beside them. I was in the junior department, where both my children had started. Plimsolls left over from the previous term were still in lockers, and despite the fact that term hadn't quite started, the ubiquitous smell of soggy gym kit and school floor cleaner prevailed. A smell that children hated, but mothers, perhaps mothers for whom things had gone wrong, found nostalgic. I located Josh's old locker and was surprised I still could. Then Tabitha's. Remembered how she'd found this bit of school hard at first: how I'd had to persuade her into the classroom, find a friend for her to go in with, and how I'd always have to be on time to pick her up. How some boys had called her Tabby Cat. Not bullying, just teasing; but she hadn't liked it. Sebastian had said leave it, ignore it. I hadn't. I'd seen a teacher. Made it worse. Then the boys had called her Tubby Cat. She'd been a little bit plump at the time. I'd been beside myself. I'd seen the headmaster, the headmistress – the school sensibly had both – and had wanted to take her away. But it had all settled down eventually. In spite of me.

As I came out through the double doors at the far end

of the corridor into the sunshine, I saw Tabitha at her stall in the courtyard below. She was near the top of the school now: confident, clever, pretty. Well, I thought pretty; she still thought she was overweight. And she hated her curly hair; she straightened it constantly. And wished she had a boyfriend. We all ached for love in some form, didn't we?

From my vantage point, at the top of the steps, I watched as Ludo, who'd emerged at the other end of the corridor, rejoined Eliza, who was beckoning him impatiently, clearly itching to go. She asked him where on earth he'd *been*. She'd been waiting *ages*. I saw him shrug into her cross face, unaware he was being watched: not the charming man I knew. A bit bolshie, perhaps. Sullen. It struck me that he was just an ordinary man. Probably rather an irritating one, too, not unlike my husband. He wasn't really some romantic hero. He probably picked his feet. Left wet, winding towels on the floor. Got disastrously pissed at parties. Except . . . Ludo hardly drank and was always immaculately turned out, even in his gardening gear – in a Monty Don, *bleu-de-travail* sort of way. And I couldn't imagine towels on floor. Other annoying traits, then, but I couldn't think what. Snoring, perhaps. Not that I'd be sharing a bed with him, I thought quickly, descending the steps to the courtyard, so I wouldn't find out. I knew I was in trouble here, though, and that my heart was beating very fast. Rejection from Sebastian might be all I needed to have me rebounding faster than the speed of light into Ludo, and not just once, but ricocheting like a ball in a pinball machine, again and again, on a rather needy basis. Obviously that simply mustn't happen.

Anyway, I thought, trailing miserably round some stalls on my own, picking up hand-knitted scarves and wishing

I was at home, where at least I could throw myself on my bed and howl into my pillow, with this latest revelation I was unlikely to be in the mood to embark on a steamy affair. I'd be too busy clawing what remained of my family together. Even as I thought this, I saw them through the window, as I passed by the art block. Josh and Sebastian. And just as I'd seen Ludo unobserved, so I did my husband and son. They were in the spacious, airy room with a few other parents, looking at the pictures. Very much together, father and son were strolling around slowly, heads cocked appraisingly. They stopped at a particular painting, heads close, conferring quietly. It was a terrible shock. Without thinking, I pushed through the glazed door and strode across the room. Approached at speed as they admired a landscape.

'I thought we weren't going to do this?' I said, rather loudly. Emotion was exaggerating everything I said, so I was shrill, too. 'Thought you didn't want to be on display for us, eh, Josh?'

Josh wasn't often taken aback, but he was now.

'Oh, er, Dad was just wondering what the light was like in here,' he mumbled.

'Oh, really!' I said, aware I'd got him on the back foot for once. Pushing home the advantage. 'And if I'd *wondered*–' I made quotation marks in the air round the last word – 'would I have got the same film-star treatment? Would the red carpet have been rolled out for me, too?'

'Mum,' he said warily.

'And, no doubt, as you were discussing the light, you just happened to come across one of your own A-level pieces, hmm? Well, durrr!' I made an incredulous, Homer Simpson face, eyes wide and probably a bit mad, too.

One or two people turned, curious.

'Ella, calm down,' said Sebastian quietly.

'Oh, it's "Ella, calm down" now, is it? In a voice one usually reserves for the seriously unhinged? Ella, don't fly off the handle! Ella, don't make a scene! *Yes*, I'm leaving you, *yes*, I'm taking the children with me, and *yes*, I'm in charge of the school work from now on, what is your problem? *Is that it?*'

They looked at me, horrified. I'd said it at some volume. People were openly watching now and I knew I was about to either storm out or say more. Josh had the presence of mind to lead me by the arm to an easel in the corner. I was shaking.

'That wasn't mine, Mum; that was my mate Danny's. But this is mine, if you're interested.' He said it calmly. The painting was of a stubble field, lit by late-afternoon autumn sunlight: so mellow and beautiful and so fantastically good that, despite my highly charged state, I was speechless.

'Breathe,' he commanded in a more jocular, ironic voice. 'Breathe, Mum. You'll last longer. Nothing's ever as bad as it seems.' There was kindness there, too.

Sebastian had joined us now and they stood either side of me as I calmed down, protecting me almost. Waiting. I was grateful they didn't exchange 'Wow, crazy woman!' looks over my head. Believe me, I'd have known. Was grateful for their compassion.

'No, you're right.' I gulped. 'Nothing ever is. And this is good, Josh,' I said, recovering.

'Thanks,' he said briefly.

My breathing was coming down to a normal rate and I concentrated hard on the sunbeams hitting the stubble.

Lottie was in the room somewhere. I'd seen her out of

the corner of my eye as I'd stalked in. She was diplomatically keeping her distance, no doubt having heard my rant. But not so her mother, who'd spotted me.

A hand touched my elbow. 'It's Eleanor, isn't it?' A heavily lined face came round to peer into mine. Watery, pale-blue eyes, grey frazzled hair, wonky lipstick. All I needed. Really, all I needed.

'Yes,' I conceded weakly, forcing a smile.

'Are you all right? You've just made quite a scene, you know.'

'Fine, thank you,' I said, collecting myself and thinking she did look and sound a lot better than when I'd last seen her. Maybe I should have some of her pills? Perhaps she'd got some in her bag? I eyed it speculatively. Introduced her to Sebastian and Josh. She narrowed her eyes at Sebastian.

'You're the artist, aren't you?'

'So I'm told.'

'But haven't done anything for years. Painter's block, or some such excuse. Is that the party line?' I'd forgotten how direct she was. And how old age – and a touch of dementia – gave one carte blanche to say what one liked. It was rather like inebriation. And, paradoxically, with this unhinged abandonment came a superiority, since there was surely no stopping the intoxicated, or the crazy, or the old. They were in total command of the situation by virtue of not subscribing to the usual rules of self-control. I tensed, waiting for Sebastian's scathing response.

'That's right,' he said pleasantly. 'I peaked early.'

Even I couldn't detect a cynical tone. If anything, he sounded almost amused.

'Too much pressure, perhaps,' she said pensively, almost to herself. 'This is good, young man. Is it yours?'

'Yes,' admitted Josh, colouring slightly.

'I used to be a headmistress, you know. And before that, I taught art. Still paint, occasionally. There's an arts and crafts shop in Stroud where they hang them for me. It's all lesbians and goths in ghastly clothes, of course, but, still, they hang them. I'll get them to hang this too, if you like, if you want to make a few pennies. They're trying to get rid of me. Say I come in too often, make a scene if my pictures don't sell, but I know my rights. If they spent more time getting the lighting right and sweeping the pavement outside so the place looked inviting, instead of lounging behind the counter stroking their beards and fondling their worry beads, they'd sell more pictures. I take my broom regularly and sweep the pavement for them, lazy so-and-so's.' She raised her chin defiantly at Josh. 'I'm eighty-two, you know.'

'No, I didn't.'

'I didn't think you did. The young think they know everything, but they don't.'

'Um, Mum?' Lottie hovered nervously.

'What?' she snapped. 'I'm talking to this young man.'

I thought about the distressing scene in the Spar. This was no confused old lady running ketchupy hands through her hair. This was more Jeremy Paxman limbering up on *Newsnight*. Something had clearly kicked in hard. A powerful narcotic, no doubt.

'Your parents died in a car crash, didn't they?' She turned back to Sebastian, honing her interrogative skills. Lottie looked resigned as Sebastian agreed that they did. 'So you have no idea if you're long-lived or not. Mr Arbuthnot – next door but one – died last month, and he was only seventy-six. Imagine!' she said gleefully. 'Seventy-six! No age at all. And the woman who owns the gallery, Gwen Collins, is going downhill very rapidly, I'm pleased to say. She's only seventy-two.'

'It's all she thinks about,' Lottie murmured in my ear as her mother expanded on her theme to Sebastian, spitting a bit now, prodding his chest. 'How she's going to outlive everyone. She probably will, knowing my luck. She's frightfully competitive.'

'Perhaps it's all she's got left?'

I was grateful to her, actually. She was going some way to distracting my family and giving my own body and brain a chance to climb down. To retreat from the front line, regroup and regain some composure. As she rambled on, it occurred to me that one's whole life was a competition: who you married, how many children you had, the size of your house, your garden, what you achieved, what your children achieved. This was the final competition, then: all there was left to elbow-barge about.

'How old are you?' she demanded of my mother, who'd approached, clearly looking for us.

'I'm not sure that's any of your business,' my mother said tartly. She squared her shoulders, a match for any old woman. Horrified, Lottie and I grabbed a mother apiece as it looked as if they might square up, handbags at the ready. We turned them about – forcefully, in Lottie's case.

'We're going,' I told Mum. 'Tabitha's getting a lift back later, with a friend.'

'Who *is* that woman?' my mother asked, her head

swivelling a hundred and eighty degrees, despite being frogmarched away.

'Lottie's mother. She's only just come out of hospital. She's not entirely . . . you know.'

'No, I can see that! And I've a good mind to tell her my own mother made ninety-three, and my father ninety-four, so it's *extremely* likely I'll make *very* old bones myself!'

'Yes. Right. Marvellous.'

Somehow, though, that little episode had helped to distance the scary scene earlier. The one in which I'd been the protagonist. But only temporarily. As we walked to the car, I could see my own Oscar-winning performance roaring back to the men in my family in glorious Technicolor.

And the thing was, I thought, as I followed them across the hockey pitch, head bowed in shame, once it was out there – or they were out there, the words – it didn't matter how much you tried to retract them, claw them back, say sorry, sorry, that wasn't me at *all* – you couldn't erase them. They hung there, drying slowly on the mind, to be remembered for ever.

Stupidly, hopelessly, that evening, when the children were getting themselves some beans on toast in the kitchen, I nonetheless tried to do some clawing.

'Sorry about earlier, Josh,' I said brightly, muscling in to butter the toast he'd made for them, stirring the beans Tabitha had emptied into a pan. 'It was just a bit of a shock, that's all. Daddy saying he was moving into town and all that. I couldn't quite believe it, actually.'

Embarrassed silence.

'And obviously you both knew,' I went on breezily. 'Daddy had already told you at the pub. But for me, well, it as a bit of a bolt from the blue! I overreacted, I guess.'

They stared at the beans in the pan. Tabitha was quite pink. I wondered if she was tearful. I also wondered – shamefully – if she might be my bargaining tool here. My reason to block it happening.

'Tabs, I can see you're upset,' I said quietly. 'D'you want to talk about it? About Daddy moving out?'

'No.' Quietly.

I licked my lips.

'Come on, they're ready,' said Josh gruffly, meaning the beans. They weren't, they were lukewarm. His sister, however, took the pan handle gratefully and began ladling them out onto the toast I'd buttered.

'I'll have some,' I said desperately, grabbing a plate from the rack.

'There's no more toast,' Josh muttered.

'Doesn't matter, I'll have them on their own. Let's all sit down and talk about it.'

'What is there to talk about?' Josh said stiffly, his eyes on the counter.

'Well, maybe I can have a word with Daddy. Maybe I can persuade him not to move out. Maybe I –'

'No,' Tabitha said suddenly, her eyes coming up from the pan. They were glittering. 'It's what we want, too. What we all want. This is so – so odd, this situation. Dad in the garden, not living with us.'

'Yes, but at least he's there,' I said, shocked. 'At least we're all together.'

'Yes, but it's grotty for him, in that little hut. He can't live there for ever. He's not – I don't know – an animal or something. It's not right, Mum! And, anyway, lots of my friends have divorced parents. I'm cool with that. It's not a big deal. But this is just so weird and everyone says so. And I just *want it to be normal!*'

This was said at some volume. And there was no mistaking its message. We stood there staring at each other, my daughter and I. Her cheeks were red, her eyes angry. And then Josh took her away. He shepherded her with the crook of his arm, carrying both the plates, pausing to grab cutlery, into the playroom, their television room. Without turning round he shut the door behind them dexterously with his foot, so they could eat in peace.

Chapter Seventeen

Lottie popped round a couple of days later, in a break between clients. The children were back at school, all my holiday lets had gone apart from the Braithwaites, and I was alone in the kitchen. She bustled through my back door on a blast of cold air, bursting with barely suppressed excitement.

'I've had a bit of a breakthrough, Ella,' she said, as she shut the door behind her, turning to glow.

I was sitting at my kitchen table nursing a monumental hangover, head in hands. Harriet, my one remaining bantam hen, the layer, the only one the fox hadn't got this year, sat companionably with me. The dogs lay on my feet.

'Oh, really?' I raised my head. Such was her condition she didn't really register mine. She hastened across.

'Ottoline, OK, came in first thing this morning, for her session. And before I could get going, before I could even get the requisite needles out of their boxes, she sat bolt upright on the bed like Frankenstein's monster and said: "Lottie, would you do something for me?" "What?" I said, turning to stare. "Take off your shoes." "My shoes?" I said. "Yes, take them off." Well, obviously we all do as Ottoline says so I took them off, which was a bit of a relief, actually, because they were those new Topshop jobbies with the ankle straps which I can hardly walk in, and she said: "Now take off your jewellery." Mesmerized I removed my chains and bangles. "There," she said. "Now have a go."

'Well, Ella, I can hardly tell you the difference. I was skipping around that bed, firing in needles like Deadeye Dick, there was no stopping me. It's all to do with balance, Ottoline explained, which is pretty elementary when you come to think about it. How on earth could I pinpoint exactly where I was going, while subconsciously trying to balance in heels? Imagine Two Bellies Bill, or whatever that darts player's called, trying to score a bullseye in platforms? And obviously I explained about Sulrika – you know, my teacher – about how glamorous she was, with the nails and the heels and the gold chains and everything – totally unlike any other acupuncturist I've ever met, incidentally, literally no one does it glammed up – and Ottoline said: "So why do you?" I could only eventually stammer – "Because I wanted to be like her." And of course that sounded so lame and stupid I saw the light immediately. She didn't have to say any more. Look.'

She drew up a chair opposite, plonked herself down and put her hands on the table in front of me, palms down. Her short, scrubbed nails were a surprise even in my state. I stared. 'Golly. Will you miss them?'

'Not really. They were jolly time-consuming, if I'm honest. And I was so close to chucking it all in, the acupuncture, I mean. So nearly at the end of my rope. Something had to give. Last week that nice man from Park Cottages came in, although obviously I can't tell you his –'

'Mr Atkinson?'

'Yes, but for confidential reasons I can't tell you about his –'

'Impotence?'

'Exactly. So I had to put them in his –' She made a face.

'No!'

'Oh, no, not there,' she said hastily. 'In his perineum. But the needle sort of . . . skidded, and although he was terribly nice about it, it's not ideal, is it?'

'Not . . . ideal.' I winced.

'But, now? Now I've got *such* renewed confidence as I shimmy around on the balls of my feet. That's where most of our balance comes from, incidentally. The big toe. And the ears – so I've got rid of all my heavy earrings. And he's coming in again next week. I can't wait to have a go!'

'Good. Good, Lottie. I'm really pleased.'

It didn't sound like it, though, and she finally caught my tone. Leaned forward on the table, frowning. She cocked her head round and up to meet my eyes, which were gazing at the stripped pine. 'Ella? What's up?'

'Oh, ignore me. I'm fine. I did a bit of solitary drinking last night, that's all.'

'Why?'

'Oh . . . you know.'

'Sebastian?'

'Yes.' I struggled for composure. Found some. 'The children are fine about it all, you see, about him going. And that's rather . . . thrown me. I thought it was ideal for them, as it was. You know, the status quo. Apparently it wasn't.'

She nodded. 'Well, I imagine they see this as being more normal, if he goes. Children like that.'

She couldn't have echoed Tabitha more succinctly if she'd tried. I tried to speak. Couldn't. Did eventually. 'Did everyone think it so peculiar, then?' I whispered.

'Everyone?'

'You know. Round here. Local gossip.'

'Well, a bit,' she said uncomfortably. 'You must admit, it is a bit. This will be a much cleaner break for all of you.'

A clean break. Who said anything about a break?

'Is she still laying?' Lottie asked, nodding at Harriet on the table, current subject dealt with. I tried to concentrate.

'Um, a bit. The odd egg. Sometimes. She's a bit stressed, though, I think. All those cockerels. She escapes in here with Ladyboy because she gets pestered by them all the time. I've got too many at the moment.'

'Oh, we know. Half the village can hear them.' She laughed, but darkly.

I thought about this.

'Lottie, what else?' I asked, looking at her. 'Most people think my domestic set-up is peculiar and I'm waking all my neighbours with my cockerels crowing. What else haven't you told me? You're supposed to be my friend.'

I hadn't meant it to come out quite like that.

'Of course I'm your friend.' She looked surprised. 'And nothing,' she said quickly. 'Nothing else. It's just you're quite . . .'

'What?'

She hesitated. 'Well –'

'What?'

'Sensitive. So maybe I avoid saying things, occasionally. Sometimes. Don't want to upset you.'

'Oh.'

There was a silence. I was deeply upset. On the point of tears. Annoying.

'Lottie, telling me I've got too many cockerels is not going to reduce me to tears.' My voice wobbled dramatically.

'I know.'

'And, anyway, I've had a For Sale notice up in the farm shop for weeks,' I told her, blinking rapidly. 'With a photo of them and everything.'

'I know, I know!'

'I've told anyone who might be interested. I'd bloody *give* them away. I have tried, you know!'

'Yes, I know, Ella. Please don't get –'

'What? I am not upset! Why must everyone think I'm *upset* all the time! I'm just saying I know about the fucking cockerels!'

'OK, OK.' She got hastily to her feet. 'Sorry.'

'For what!'

'Nothing. I've, um. Got to run. Got my lovely menopausal lady coming in at two, and I've got to get Hamish some lunch.'

'See you later, maybe?' I said desperately, aware she was running away.

'Yes, definitely.' She turned before she got to the door. Smiled at me gently. 'See you later.' I knew she meant it.

'Sorry, Lotts,' I gulped.

'Don't say sorry. It's fine. You'll be fine.' She knew better than to give me a hug, though. Knew that was guaranteed to start the waterworks. 'Have you got your seeds in?'

'Seeds?' My mind flew to the garden. A little insensitive, surely? At a time like this? Quizzing me on my horticultural standards?

'You know. The ones I gave you. For your ears.'

'Oh. No, I haven't. I'll do that.'

'I would,' she said kindly. Then she was gone.

*

After a bit, I got slowly to my feet. I was cold. It wasn't the nicest of days. Autumn was in the air. The swallows were disappearing. Summer was over. Everything was over, I thought sadly and a touch melodramatically, perhaps. Acknowledging that, and determined not to wallow, I made myself go to the sink and wash up the pile of dirty saucepans from last night's supper. My hands were a bit trembly. I clenched them in the water. Sensitive. Was I sensitive? Perhaps. Did people tiptoe around me? It didn't feel like it. Felt like they trampled mercilessly, but perhaps they did. I recalled my children exchanging a glance as they stirred their beans the other night – don't upset her. And Sebastian wasn't like that. Oh, he had his moods, his rages, even, but it was all over quite quickly. There was no bite; he was all bark. It was nothing personal. Just the loosening of a valve, which had to be done occasionally, before he tightened it again. Like bleeding a radiator, perhaps. Unless he'd been drinking, which I'd noticed he wasn't doing so much recently. Although he hadn't given it up, that was for sure. How would he manage that, at Oxford, I wondered? The booze. Arrive to take a class stinking of wine, reeling everywhere? Would he even *take* classes? What *was* an artist in residence?

I went to the computer in the playroom and Googled it. It wasn't terribly informative. Just told me about past alumni, other famous artists who'd held the post. Rather impressive, actually. Well, bully for him. I got up and shook my head, trying to align my thoughts. Knew I was feeling pretty low. I went upstairs, opened my bedside drawer and found the seeds Lottie had been talking about. They were an acupuncture aid she'd given me some time ago, to combat stress. Goma seeds, from some tropical plant, on tiny bits of sticky tape which you peeled off plastic, then stuck in the tops of your ears. Apparently they gave off calming vibes. When you were feeling particularly anxious, you were supposed to press them, for an extra boost. I couldn't get the little bastards off the plastic for ages, which didn't improve my anxiety. Eventually I did, stuck them in – they looked like giant blackheads – and gave them an almighty squeeze. *Ow*. Then I went downstairs.

The house was very quiet after the long summer holiday. Ottoline was busy with her pots. Sebastian was painting. And I had my work too, of course, but – I hated it. I realized that was the truth. It came to me in a juddering jolt, like a lorry forced to stop abruptly at lights. Hated drawing things I didn't like. Ottoline was making things she loved. Even Sebastian was trying to do that, albeit failing. Lottie, too, now. I stared out of the window. Why did that make me feel panicky? I must stop relying so much on other people. For emotional security. Mustn't live through them. I needed to get a grip on my life, not just professionally – at least I *had* a job, even if I wasn't crazy about it – but emotionally. Must take the lead, before someone else did and bounced me into a position. Before I found myself somewhere I didn't want to be. I must go first.

With that resolve in mind, I turned. Stared at Harriet on a pile of old newspapers on the table. Suddenly I scooped her up. She was a sweet, obliging hen. That won't get you anywhere, Harriet, I thought. I took her back outside to the yard. She glanced up at me, beady black eyes alarmed. Surely we were happy where we were? Hiding away inside together? I took her to an empty stable, popped her in a nesting box with some food and water and shut the door.

Then I went out to where her tormentors were strutting around in the flower beds, as usual, deflowering my dahlias, preening themselves, crowing, picking fights with each other and wondering where the little bantam woman was. With the help of some grain I herded them into a loose box and stood looking at them, hands on hips. They cocked their arrogant little heads and stared back at me, eyes like dots of coal, red combs tossing.

Slowly I advanced on the one I knew to be the most tame. I knew exactly what I needed to do. For Harriet. Ladyboy, too, who was so desperate about the situation, she was trying to become a man. To fit in. How had I let their lives become this living hell? As I cornered Horace, the one I'd earmarked for selection, at the back of the stable, it felt as if I were doing this for the whole of womankind. Ottoline could do it, for heaven's sake, I thought, as I crept closer, so if I was to pass myself off as a countrywoman, chatelaine of this farmhouse, poultry farmer, even, I must too. Horace was taken by surprise as I scooped him deftly into my arms. Usually this woman was more fluttery, more hopeless. I put my fingers round his neck. I'd held him thus before, so he gave a bit of a squawk, struggled briefly, but then submitted, his beady eyes saying: OK, what is it? Wing-clipping? Toenails? Scaly leg? We eyeballed one another. For ages. At length I put him down. Couldn't even begin to tighten my grip on his throat. Couldn't begin to wring his neck, particularly not Horace, who, frankly, was a bit of a wimp. The most picked on and abused. The fall guy. Monsieur Blanc, perhaps, I thought, eyeing the pure-white cockerel, so-called because of his insouciant, Gallic shrug. I'd never liked

Monsieur Blanc. He was incredibly fond of himself — spiteful, too. He pecked my ankles even when I'd just fed him, chased all my visiting children, shat over all the windowsills and was very much the leader of the gang-rape gang. Him I could easily do without.

The dogs had pushed open the stable door with their noses and stood watching intently, tails wagging slowly. Go on, then, Ella. Kill a couple. Call yourself a poultry farmer? We'll watch. Help, even. The air seemed heavy with portent. Even the wood pigeons on the rafters appeared to pause in their cooing and wooing. Go on, Ella. It's about time. We all hate him. He's a bully. I seized Monsieur Blanc, knowing surprise was my only weapon, and, in a flurry of feathers and spurs, found his neck quickly. Speed was of the essence. I shut my eyes tightly and squeezed.

'Oooh, 'es lovely, isn't he?'

I swung about, eyes wide. Behind the dogs, Mrs Braithwaite, my one remaining holiday tenant, with her obese child, Jason, was watching.

'Was you giving 'im a cuddle?'

I stared. 'Yes. Yes, I was.'

'I was just sayin' to Jison, we must go and see the lovely chickadees today. Only we didn't get to see them yesterday and we like to visit them every day, don't we, Jison? Did you want to hold him, Jise?'

'Oh, er, well, I wouldn't, only —'

But Jason had already lumbered into the stable, a great child mountain of ten, who had a nasty cold according to Mrs Braithwaite, which accounted for his continued presence on my farm rather than at school. Within a twinkling he'd silently but forcefully wrestled the lovely tame chicka-dee from my arms, whereupon Monsieur Blanc, already thoroughly pissed off, pecked his nose sharply and drew blood.

'Arrghgh!'

Jason squawked and clutched his nose. The cockerel squawked as he was dropped. Mrs Braithwaite squawked and all was pandemonium as the dogs, seizing their moment, chased the bantams around the stable and out, scattering them to all corners of the yard. At which point I squawked.

'Buster – Doug – Maud – *come back right now!*' Even as I was chasing and roaring, though, I knew my outrage was slightly disingenuous. This was what I wanted, surely? Savaged cockerels? But perhaps not in front of the holiday lets.

Eventually, order was restored and I shepherded the dogs one way and the bleeding Jason and his mother the other, apologizing profusely for Monsieur Blanc, who was having an off day, and explaining to an incredulous Mrs Braithwaite that I didn't actually possess a first-aid kit, just a messy basket on the kitchen windowsill with empty Lemsip packets and Nurofen the dogs chewed, but that under the sink in her kitchen she'd find a pristine kit, with a red cross on the front. She scurried away, terrified for the life of her child, still shrieking about infection and tetanus injections and all manner of alarmist nonsense. Still apologizing – bowing, practically – I headed back to the house holding the dogs by their necks – no collars, naturally – scolding them roundly. Doug still had a few feathers in his mouth and looked very pleased with himself.

'But you couldn't actually do the deed, could you?' I reminded him softly as I shut them away with a sleeping Diblet. 'Couldn't finish them off, could you?'

It occurred to me that, under cover of darkness, I could just shut the dogs in a loose box with the cockerels for half an hour and they would indeed do the deed, even though I'd spent years telling them not to. Revert to type in moments. Be licking their chops in seconds. But then I'd have three bloodthirsty dogs on my hands and where might they look to sate their thirst next? The ducks? The sheep, even?

No. There had to be another way.

There was. Ten minutes later I was in my battered old Volvo, racing off in the direction of town, but actually bound for a smaller market town beyond, via the bypass. What a complete and utter blessing – what a coup, in fact – that it was today. I'd been pretty sure the market was weekly, but to pinpoint the very Monday was fortuitous, to say the least. This was surely meant to be. This was surely the hand of God, beckoning me on down the dual carriageway, saying: This is the way forward, Ella. The humane way. The Godly way. The righteous way. Find the boys some wives. Procure a little action for them, with some virile young birds who are up for it. Birds who are raring to go. Hot stuff. And let Harriet and Ladyboy retire in peace. I might even give them to Lottie, I thought, as I left the bypass at speed. She was always saying she'd love some chickens but didn't know where to start. Well, she could start with my old girls. They'd have a lovely, gentle time of it in a dear little coop on her back lawn, spoiled rotten by Matthew and Lil. Harriet might start laying properly. Ladyboy might even recover her feminine wiles and squeeze a couple out, whilst down on the farm, all sorts of gaudy action could be kicking off. I might even get the boys two girls apiece. See how the cocky white Frenchman dealt with that. Not to mention little Sarkozy, his poisonous sidekick. That should wipe the smirk off his face.

Historically the livestock market had taken place in the Cornmarket in the centre of town, but that was some years back. Now, due to popular demand, it had moved to the outskirts, where there was more space for the pens and enclosures and where the farm vehicles didn't impede the traffic so much. A large, flat field, prone to occasional flooding, with a central, breezy Dutch barn, was now the venue, and could easily accommodate any number of farmers who gathered, and less aggrieve shoppers and townspeople who'd complained of congestion. It occurred to me, though, as I got out of my car into a soggy meadow in the rain, that I hadn't really thought this through. I was wearing espadrille wedges and a rather tight denim skirt. Not my usual Monday garb, but an attempt, as I'd dragged myself out of bed this morning and recognized my mood, to look not like the downtrodden housewife I felt, but like the rather snappy yummy mummy I fully intended to be. Designed to psychologically give an edge to my day, my outfit, however, was drawing stares from my fellow farmers, who were, almost to a man – and indeed they were all men – uniformly in sludge green, with an occasional flash of tweed. I was certainly the only one clutching a Mulberry handbag with sunglasses on my head.

Having weaved my way through the bucolic scrum and located the makeshift office, which consisted of a trestle table manned by a couple of weather-beaten yokels straight out of central casting, I collected my order of sale card and number, and made my way to the steps which led to the raised platforms around the ring, where the animals were on show. I muscled my way through to somewhere on the third row, ignoring the nudges and stares. Sheep were being paraded round the sawdust circle below, looking lost and panicky and bleating forlornly. As I stood studying the race card, wedged between a couple of burly farmers, and as the droning voice of the auctioneer expertly took bids from the floor, I realized I'd timed it badly – if, indeed, I'd timed it at all. I'd have to stand through an interminable number of sheep, then ducks, then turkeys, before we got anywhere near the poultry. Better to stay, though, than go shopping, perhaps. I'd parked. I was here. Who's to say I wouldn't lose heart after an hour in the Waitrose café? Turn tail and head for home?

Two mind-numbing hours later, it wasn't poultry we were finally closing in on, but eggs. Boxes and boxes of them. Hotly contested, too. On and on it went. Fifty pence for six. Eighty-two pence for six. Seventy-three pence for six. Surely one could buy them for much the same price in Tesco? I ventured this to the farmer beside me. 'Not fer'ilized, you can't, love.' He beamed. 'Although you never know, these days.' He winked. He was a big winker. He'd winked at me a couple of times already. I didn't mind. I took my compliments where I could these days. As the hundred and sixteenth box of eggs was presented I wasn't sure I could bear the tension. Seventy-five pence? Seventy-six pence? No – eighty pence! It was a wonder I hadn't bitten through the strap of my designer handbag in excitement.

Finally, though, it was the chickens, which included bantams, and I woke up. Old English Game Bantams are rare birds, not easy to source, but I knew from Ottoline that the strain had been on the farm for ever and I wanted to keep it pure. I'd already ascertained that lot 257 was a box of fifteen such hens. That should keep the boys happy. Almost three to a bed. Cockerel heaven, surely? The crate was presented and a brown-coated chap took a bird out and held it aloft for us to see. She looked rather large to my reasonably trained eye as she was paraded around the ring for inspection, but my burly friend on my left assured me these were particularly fine specimens and he should know. His brother-in-law, Pete, had bred 'em, and a very fine bantam farmer he was, too. He'd snap them up like nobody's business if he were me.

Snap them up I fully intended to do, and if the last two hours had dragged, cometh the moment there's something terribly thrilling about bidding at an auction. I felt a frisson of excitement as I waved my number enthusiastically in the air, one or two florid faces turning to stare. So excited did I become that apparently I started bidding against myself and my burly neighbour had to stay my hand in a friendly manner. But no matter. I'd secured my girls for thirty-six pounds, a snip in anyone's book.

'Pleased with that, are you, love?' asked my new best friend beside me with a grin.

'Very!' I assured him as he winked at me, then at a friend in the crowd. Golly, I should do this more often, I thought as, flexing aching, numb feet I inched excitedly along the row to the steps. Yes, I should buy more animals. Restock my farm. In the correct gear, of course. Old Barbour, jeans. I could be just like Bathsheba, in *Far from the Madding*

Crowd. She'd been quite a girl, hadn't she? Well, I could be, too. Show everyone. Take control. Buy a few pigs, even. What had I been doing with my life? I lived on a farm, for heaven's sake – if anyone could have the good life, it was me! I tossed my head, hoping for a spot of Julie Christie verve.

I'd imagined it would take for ever to collect the birds, but, to my surprise, as I went round the back of the barn they were ready and waiting in their crate, just as soon as I'd handed over the readies to the greasy-looking individual behind the trestle table. He gave me a toothless grin and it occurred to me that in a matter of months I'd know him as Bob, or Bill, or Sid. Be on cheerful, livestock-bantering terms with him. The crate wasn't heavy, but it was square and awkward with no string, and I was aware of more stares and titters as I tottered with it in my arms to my car, overlarge handbag balanced on top, heels wobbling in the grass, rain soaking the rope soles as it started to drizzle again, the mud splashing up my bare legs. Nevertheless I was thrilled with my booty and stashed it in the back.

I'd decided I'd introduce the girls gradually to their suitors – I didn't want an ugly rush from the boys, who had absolutely no manners whatsoever. Once home, therefore, I took them to the loose box where Harriet was. I opened the box on the floor and they came out gingerly, stiffly, blinking in the daylight, glancing around cautiously, stretching their legs. They were sweet, brown, gentle and lovely. I'd give them a high perch in the rafters, I determined. Some cosy sawdust and a couple more nesting boxes for their smooth brown eggs, which had been in short supply recently. How nice for Harriet to have some company, I thought, as she left her box to investigate. No fighting, of course; hens weren't like that. Just a bit of soft clucking. It was almost like a knitting circle already. They'd be on dust-bathing terms in no time. I hurried about getting grain and water.

Ottoline happened to be in the yard, filling up the trough for the ducks – again, too many drakes, I decided firmly, eyeing the flashy green males. I'd tackle them next. She came across to the stable door. My mother was with her, weirdly dressed in jeans and a checked shirt. I'd never seen my mum in jeans before, and she also had a red hanky knotted round her neck at a rakish angle. I tried not to stare.

'What have you got there?' asked Ottoline, resting her plump arms on the door as I shut it behind me. I was lowering a tray of water – not too deep or they'd drown; they were still very young – to the floor in the corner.

'Well, poor Harriet was getting raped and pillaged at every turn,' I explained. 'And I tried to wring a few of the cockerels' necks and failed, so then I thought: Well, I'll get them some wives to take the pressure off. It'll also stop them crowing so much in the morning. I'm sure they're just frustrated.' I smiled a professional smile.

Ottoline burst out laughing. 'Providing them with more sex is only going to make them crow more, Ella! If you want to stop the noise you could try shutting the top of the stable door at night. They crow when they see daylight. I'm always up at dawn so it doesn't bother me, but I have wondered about the rest of the village.'

I stared. 'Right,' I said tightly. 'Why didn't you say?'

'Didn't want to interfere. Or upset you.'

'What d'you mean?'

'Well, I assumed you left it open so you didn't have to

bother to shut them up at night. Or let them out in the morning. I know you like a lie-in. And I've put a roosting bar up high so the fox never gets them. I imagined that's what you wanted.'

But didn't ask, because Ottoline always minded her own business. And didn't want to draw attention to my lazy ways. Or upset me. *Again.* That word.

'And, anyway,' she went on, coming into the loose box, 'aren't these hens going to be too big? They're not bantams, you know.'

'Of course they are,' I said testily. 'They're Old English Game. It said so on the race card, or whatever you call it.'

'Oh, it might have *said* that, but these are common or garden Rhode Island Reds, albeit young ones. They'll get as big as Pete Silkin's chickens down the road.'

'No!' I gasped. Pete Silkin's chickens were huge. Gargantuan beasts. Suddenly I remembered my burly friend's brother-in-law was called Pete. And when he'd winked into the crowd after I'd bought them, I'd spotted Pete Silkin, possibly on the receiving end. I clutched my head.

'Old Horace will never get his tackle in there.' Ottoline pointed. 'And as for little Sarkozy, he'll need more than a pair of platform shoes. He'll have to stand on a dustbin first!'

My mother cackled in a most ungenteel way for her. She rocked back on her tasselled loafers, thumbs in her hip pockets like something out of *Cannery Row*. And she didn't like smut. My left eye had begun to twitch manically. A recent problem, I'd noticed.

'Right,' I breathed. I surreptitiously reached up to both ears to press hard.

'And this one . . .' Ottoline went on cruelly, bending down to inspect it – she picked it up and turned it upside down. 'This one's a boy!' she cried. She pointed to another. 'And so is this one. Look, you can see the comb beginning to grow. Oh, Ella, they're *all* cocks, they're not even hens!'

They both roared. Roared and roared.

'Oh, Ella, you are *such* a ninny!' cried my mother, that's . . . my mother in the jeans, albeit pressed and from Country Casuals. 'You can't even go to an auction and buy a few chickens!'

At that moment, Sebastian, who never took a blind bit of notice of anything that went on at the farm, unless it was to do with his oil paints or his crates of wine – he barely troubled the yard except to go back and forth across it to the pub – returned from just this place. He sauntered across at the cackling.

'What's up?' he said, amiably for him. But don't forget he'd had a few.

'Ella went to buy some bantam hens and came back with giant cockerels!' spluttered Mum, who I actually hated, I decided.

Sebastian grinned. 'She never could resist a big cock.'

It was just a jokey remark, not a cruel one, and they all laughed good-naturedly, even Mum, who'd clearly morphed into some strange being who wore knotted hankies, went to *Calendar Girls*, and exchanged dirty jokes with her detested son-in-law. And, actually, if Sebastian wasn't leaving me, and if Josh wasn't drifting with him, and if my best friend hadn't said I was oversensitive this morning – Ottoline, too, in so many words – I might have laughed along with them. Been rather delighted everyone was getting along so famously. It was only a few chickens, after all. And quite funny, when you came to think about it. As it was, though, I pushed blindly through them, welling up as I went. I ran towards the house, wobbling in my stupid shoes. Safely inside I burst into tears and slammed the back door behind me. So hard, in fact, that the glass within the frame shattered, and fell, in a million pieces, on the floor.

Chapter Eighteen

A few minutes later, the back door opened. Sebastian appeared. Without even glancing in my direction he calmly stepped over the shards of broken glass and made his way through the kitchen and out to the front hall. I heard him go upstairs. Not long after, he was back, crossing the kitchen. I sat there, wet-faced, slack-jawed and incredulous as he went to step back over the glass and exit as he'd arrived, without saying a word.

'Sebastian,' I spluttered as he was almost out of the door. 'I'm not sure you can just wander in and out of here when you feel like it! I certainly wouldn't dream of invading your space without asking.'

A lie. I did. Frequently. On the pretext of taking linen and shopping across. Not when he was in, but sometimes when he was out. He never locked a door. I'd put the sheets on the side and have a quick tiptoe around the studio, see what he'd been up to canvas-wise – slightly more, recently, but not much. Obviously I'd never go upstairs. Well, I had once. Or twice. But never opened drawers.

'Tabitha rang to say she'd left a maths book behind,' he said coldly. 'She's got a test this afternoon and I said I'd drop it by for her.' He held it up in his left hand, having clearly just retrieved it from her bedroom.

'Oh. Right. Well.' I sniffed hard. 'Why didn't she ring me?' I wiped my teary face with the back of my hand, feeling a little foolish.

'I've no idea. Perhaps your phone was off.'

I sniffed again. 'Yes, perhaps.' I sat up a bit and held my hand out impatiently. 'OK, I'll do it.'

'No, I'll go.'

'How will you *go*?' I said witheringly, emphasis on the final word, waggling my head derisively.

'My licence kicked back in today. I'll take the car.'

'Oh. Right.' The car. My car. His too, though, I suppose.

Ottoline appeared at the back door. She looked down at the glass, dismayed, then up at me. Her face was full of anxiety.

'Ella, I am so sorry. I didn't mean to laugh. And, honestly, it's not a disaster. I can sort it out. I'll sell them on eBay, turn them into coq au vin or something –'

'No, Ottoline, it's fine.' I shut my eyes and held up the palm of my hand to her, something I didn't like when other people did it, as if they couldn't bear to look at one. But, actually, I couldn't bear to look at Sebastian's eyes, which were curious. Not concerned, more . . . intrigued. And not in a good way, more in an anthropological way. 'It's fine,' I said, into the darkness, still adopting the traffic-cop stance. 'I will sort the chickens out, and I will sort the glass out. But if I could just be left in peace for a *few* minutes, I would really, *really* appreciate it.'

Both disappeared at that. I felt them go, even if I couldn't see them. And, anyway, I heard the door close.

I opened my eyes and exhaled gustily. Sat there, fists clenched on my knees. I realized a howling gale was coming through the broken panes. I gave myself a moment.

After a bit, I got up and went to the mirror in the tiny downstairs cloakroom. Stared at my reflection. I'd run out of moisturizer a few days ago and, given the choice between Vaseline and fake tan, had chosen the latter as a lubricant, so at least I looked reasonably healthy. But my hair was sticking out of my head at strange angles and my eyes looked quite mad. I flattened my hair a little, fair and fine, and found a comb. Then I breathed deeply in and out, taking air right down to the diaphragm as I knew you were supposed to. I reached up to give the seeds another – ouch – squeeze. I couldn't help feeling Valium would be more effective. I kept the breathing going, watching my face, waiting for the eyes to calm down. Look less crazy. A bit of mascara would help, instead of the scrubbed look. Even a touch of lippy. What husband wouldn't leave a wife who looked like this? Ginnie always looked like this, I reasoned. Like an Englishwoman who doesn't give a damn, but no one would ever dare leave Ginnie.

Before the children came home I swept up the glass and rang a glazier – an emergency one, which cost the earth and I couldn't afford. I had the door sorted out in no time, which was most unlike me. Ordinarily we'd have a piece of cardboard taped to it for months – had done once, when Sebastian, as I recalled, had done the very same thing in a blazing temper.

Later, Ottoline put her head through the window to say that Lizzie Silkin, Pete's wife, had been round. Word had reached her that Pete had pulled a fast one and passed some chickens off as bantams and she was appalled. She'd taken them back, returned my money and Pete was firmly in the doghouse. Egg and chips tonight, instead of steak. I managed a smile. Thanked her, knowing, too, that I was the laughing stock of the village, but hey, who cares. I did, actually.

That evening I cooked a proper supper for the children. None of your beans on toast: meatballs, pasta and broccoli. Then I helped Tabitha with her homework. When, after a good fifteen minutes and with the help of a calculator, she'd finally explained to me what a vulgar fraction was, I snuck out to the yard. Got awfully busy in a stable. I reasoned the children had seen a lot of me tonight and probably wouldn't notice my absence. They didn't. Neither did they notice that I was strangely elated when I returned and sporting quite a few feathers on my jumper.

Since they both went to bed after me, I went upstairs early and set my alarm for two in the morning. When it went off, I awoke with a horrible start. I lay there wondering what on earth was going on. Was I going on holiday? Early flight? No. Hadn't had one of those for years. All at once I remembered. I was alert in moments. Stealing quietly downstairs, I threw my coat over my nightie, slipped my feet into my wellies by the back door and, hushing the dogs, who raised their heads sleepily, went out to the loose box where the cockerels were ready and waiting. I picked up the cardboard box I'd prepared earlier. Monsieur Blanc and his vicious friends were firmly within, the box taped shut, a few air holes punched in the top. Not Horace, though; he wouldn't hurt a fly, and, anyway, my girls had never minded his attentions. Feeling like a French resistance fighter, I put them in the back of the car and drove down the dark, empty lane, heading for the woods on the opposite side of the village.

When the bank of dark trees loomed I followed the road for a bit, then swung right, plunging down a narrow opening in the seemingly impenetrable lines of pines. The foresters drove their Land Rovers down tracks like this, right to the heart, to coppice and stockpile wood. I knew exactly where I was going, had walked the dogs here before. Nevertheless my heart was pounding as I bumped along, headlights bouncing up and down in the pitch black. At the end of the track, in a clearing, I stopped the car. Turned the headlights off. It was jolly spooky but I made myself get out, snapping on my torch and running round quickly to the boot, not giving myself time to be scared. I took out the box, set it on the ground sideways, and opened it.

The cockerels emerged slowly. They stood huddled together for a moment, blinking curiously into the night. Monsieur Blanc glanced up at me, then down at my ankles, as if he might have a go. I neatly sidestepped him behind a tree and shone the torch away into the distance. He cocked his little white head at the bright light ahead, assessing the situation. Suddenly he stretched out his neck and set off, taking the lead, as usual, followed by his merry men, who looked rather excited. Cyril, who was bone idle and very much the lounge lizard of the group, very nearly hopped off the ground and fluttered into flight, such was his brio. I watched as they disappeared into the wilderness.

The following morning, Ottoline popped her head round the back door. I'd just got back from the shops.

'You might want to stay inside,' she warned. 'I'm going to go and deal with the cockerels. Dispatch the little buggers.'

'It's all right, Ottoline,' I told her calmly. 'I've seen to it already.'

'Have you?' She looked startled. 'Golly. Well done.

Good for you.' My mother, still glued to her side like the Sundance Kid, and this morning, I kid you not, in dungarees, looked astonished. And a mite put out.

'*You* have, Ella? You've killed the cockerels?'

'Yes, *I* have, Mother. I live on a farm, remember?' Sometimes I wanted to slap her. Often, actually. Hard. 'Why are you dressed like that?'

'We're sorting out the rose garden today. Ottoline lent me some clothes. It's a terrible mess, you know,' she scolded.

I kept my temper. 'Yes, yes, it is. But obviously the holiday lets keep me very busy, Mum. And then there's that career of mine too, remember? You know, as an illustrator?'

She looked stung. 'There's no need to be fresh, Ella.'

Ottoline looked surprised too, and I realized there wasn't any need. Here was my mother, throwing herself into country life, being helpful, even looking the part, and I was sneering? What was wrong with me?

Later, when I went to the farm shop for Layers Pellets and dog wormer – I get all the glamour jobs – I bumped into two people I knew, both of whom asked me if I'd been on holiday. A glance in the rear-view mirror when I got back in the car confirmed my fears. Three days of sluttishly not bothering to buy moisturizer and being unable to cope with a tight face had deepened my complexion to a dark mahogany. This couldn't go on. I'd look like that man on that antiques programme soon, with the glasses on a chain. I couldn't be bothered to go into town, but I stopped at the village shop instead.

''Ello, luv, you look well. Been away?' asked Mrs Nicholls, who ran the store.

'Um, no. At least – well, you know. Country air, I expect. Er, I looked on the shelves but couldn't see any Nivea?'

'No, luv, we've run out. Try up the road in Hertsmere. We're waitin' for a delivery.'

Back to the car I went. Annoying. Hertsmere was hardly up the road. A good couple of miles up the hill. Nevertheless I got in and set off, bound for the next village, and then home, for three solid hours of work, I determined, during which time I would lose myself and not think about my marriage, my lover – who wasn't even my lover, I thought bitterly – my children, my parents, or my parents' marriage. I would just think about me and what passed for my career, but which, in the words of 'Desiderata', framed in the downstairs loo, was nonetheless a precious thing, in this ever-changing something something world. And which would become even more precious. Bigger and better, too, I decided, setting my mouth grimly. No, I would not be told glue-sniffing Gary was all I was fit for. I would create my own children's book, around characters I wanted to bring to life. Characters who would leap off the page because I wanted them to. I might even – and this was a bold thought, a really rogue one I hadn't had for years – I might even paint again. I swerved violently in the road. Since everyone else trampled all over *my* feelings, I thought, feeling terribly sorry for myself, I might not consider theirs so assiduously. I might get my jolly old easel out of the jolly old cupboard, set it up – under cover of darkness naturally, I wasn't that brave – and ... good God.

I screeched to a halt as I saw him on the edge of Hertsmere common. Braked so suddenly that I caused the car behind to swing past dangerously in an angry blare of horns and fists. But I was oblivious. I just gaped. There, in a lay-by, which was actually a bus stop, was Monsieur Blanc. Looking for all the world as if he were waiting for a bus. Behind him – oh, God – were his henchmen, in a row. A queue, one might say, even. Sarkozy, Oscar, Blenheim, Cyril – all the thugs. I stared, aghast. My window was open and I swear Monsieur Blanc stared back. To my horror, there was a flash of recognition. His beady black eye glinted at me and he ran towards the car with that fast, rolling gait, his cronies, after a moment's hesitation, firmly in his wake. I hit the accelerator. Shot off straight into the – happily empty – lane, and made a sharp left turn at the end. Not to the village and the Nivea pot, but straight home, glancing fearfully in my mirror as I went.

What were they *doing* here? I'd dropped them *miles* away. What were they, homing pigeons or something? They wouldn't actually *make* it home, I reasoned, my heart pounding. There was a fairly main road between them and our village, and quite a few fields, but still, they were having a damn good try. I went cold. Suppose they really did hop on a bus? Sail into town or something? Oh, don't be silly, Ella. It was hardly ideal, though, was it? If Ottoline saw them she'd know I'd lied to her. And my mother. I shrank from their disapproval and disbelief. Not to mention that of the village. I raked a nervous hand through my hair. I'd assumed they'd – you know – go native. Split up, run away, turn on each other, in a *Lord of the Flies*-type way. Get eaten by the fox, you mean, a little voice in my head said. Well, of course. I'd told myself that was a far more natural death than being strangled. It had been at the back, if not the very forefront, of my mind.

Over the course of the next few days, at least three people told me I was looking well and then asked me if I'd lost any chickens. No, I lied. Oh, it was just that, bizarrely, some walkers had come across some in the woods, on the other side of the village. How extra*ordinary*, I said, chickens in a wood! Most peculiar! I waited, dry-mouthed, like a murderer who hopes he's covered his trail thoroughly enough and the police won't come knocking. Yes, three chickens, in a clutch, Mrs Nicholls told me, when I went in for a pint of milk. *Really?* Two had gone, then, I thought, pleased but guilty, as I crept out. I'd released five.

Reports varied, as they do, when not much happens in the country. They weren't chickens at all, old Mr McEwen said, but wild guinea fowl. Nonsense, Mrs Appleyard told him, they could be heard crowing at night; they weren't guinea fowl, but they were a terribly rare species. Only seen in this country on two or three occasions and usually in Scotland. Even then, only on grouse moors.

'Were they grouse?'

'No, no. Much rarer than that.'

At this, Celia Harmsworth pricked up her ears. She had her man steal out at dusk in an estate vehicle, catch them up and bring them home, which he did easily, seeing as they were very tame. She was frightfully pleased with herself. Made them a special pen – or got her man to do it. She even informed the local zoo, until someone told her she hadn't got some splendid rare breed at all, but a few mangy cockerels, who were past their sell-by date and made a noise surprisingly like the ones that used to wake everyone up at Netherby Farm. Whatever happened to those, they asked me accusingly, when I was next in the shop. Those cockerels? At the mention of the C word, I couldn't speak.

'Mum wrung their necks,' Tabitha, who was with me, told them proudly, before I could stop her.

I crept away clutching my Wholemeal.

Ottoline, giving me a strange look, asked if I'd heard about the rumours of poultry in the woods? I lied and said I hadn't.

Numbers went down to one. One lone bird, a gigantic creature, vicious as anything, it was said. Pure white, who roosted in trees and dive-bombed walkers, screaming at the dawn, terrifying even the foxes, who wouldn't go near him. This monster molested rabbits, badgers, children. Quite true, I thought, remembering how he'd chased the holiday-let kids.

In a peculiar way, I found myself slightly rooting for Monsieur Blanc, who, in the days that followed, pretty much ruled the village, let alone the roost. Tales of his deeds got yet more dastardly, until one day the gamekeeper from the Longhorn estate – rather piqued at being made a fool of – went out with his gun and shot him. It was a fitting end, I felt, for one who had lived by the sword. Enormous, we were told this bird was, although, interestingly, no body was produced. His comb and spurs were apparently preserved in aspic for posterity and kept in the Harmsworths' game larder, where, renamed 'Napoleon', a label was stuck accordingly on the jar.

All this time, of course, real life was continuing apace and in earnest in my valley. By real life, I mean the only one that mattered: the one conducted in the secret chambers of the heart. Ludo's texts were getting more and more gently persuasive, urgent, even. Naturally they were. His wife was seeing someone – not that he knew, but surely every cuckolded man suspects? Sebastian was moving out. There was no earthly reason why the two of us should not be joined together in – OK, nothing holy, but certainly relief and abandon.

He'd write to my phone:

I love and miss you so much. Let's at least have some time together. I want to walk in the hills with you, lie in the fields, gaze up at the clouds with you.

Romantic. Persuasive. Seductive.

Without the bloody dogs

he added, and I smiled.

I rang him in a quiet moment; told him about the cockerels. He roared. Loved it. Loved me, he told me, all the more for it. Really? Not mad? I asked anxiously. No, not mad. Just lovely. I felt calmer. Happier than I had in weeks. I was loved for being me. Sebastian would have thought I was crazy; Ottoline, too. And recently even I'd worried that I was going a bit . . . odd. Apparently I wasn't. I was lovable. I felt something scrunched and tight inside me, like a ball of discarded paper, flatten and flutter gently down to rest. Nonetheless he needed to see me, Ludo said. Needed to love me properly.

He favoured the Quantock Hills in Somerset, for a long weekend. Or there was a delightful yet secluded little pub he knew called the Flower Inn, and which, in my head, I came to think of as the De-flower Inn. I dithered and prevaricated, not because I didn't want to, I did, but because . . . what then? Yes, Eliza was seeing someone, but would she and Ludo split up? Who knows. Did he want them to? Impossible to say. He always spoke of our 'one day' but family was everything too, remember? Like the Mafia. It was why I loved him. Did I *want* them to split up? Two weeks ago – not necessarily. Today? In the most clandestine cloister of my heart . . . yes. Of course. Because I no longer had a back-up plan. A plan B. With Sebastian out of the frame, what would become of me? Would I become – ghastly, red-letter word – the mistress? And all that that implied? Twanging suspenders, high-heeled shoes, a voracious appetite for sex and no thought for sisterhood? For the wronged wife? Except, she wasn't wronged, remember? She was twanging her own suspenders once a week in London. So . . . why didn't I tell Ludo? Nudge him along a bit, a little voice said. After all, he was carefully preserving something that didn't exist. Why go through the charade of staying together, when, unbeknownst to each other, they were pursing different lives and could both be happier elsewhere?

Henrietta's pale face at the fete, her eyes trained anxiously on her sniping parents as she scratched the eczema inside her arm, which I knew from Ludo to be a problem, came back to me. That's why. Sacrifices had to be made. For those we love. Whilst my own children, I thought, my heart clenching with fear, found the split infinitely preferable and were ready to jump ship to Oxford with their father at a moment's notice. Unfair, unfair, I scolded myself, as I walked in the damp fields with the dogs, Maud, who adored autumn, scampering through the yellow-gold leaves, scattering them in delight.

I texted Ludo back.

I love you, too. I just need a bit more time to think.

He replied:

Take as long as you like. My teeth may be in a glass by the bed
and you might have to help me on with my socks afterwards,
but I'll be there.

I smiled, loving the fact that he always saw the funny
side and would, I knew, wait for ever. My phone beeped
once more.

However, I do think we deserve it.

I pocketed it, thoughtful. Did we deserve it? 'Because
You're Worth It' went the famous cosmetics slogan, which
seemed to me to sum up this age: not of enlightenment,
but entitlement. We all felt owed. And, yes, I did too. Owed
some happiness. But if I felt like that now, how would I
feel six months into the affair? Entitled to a whole lot
more, surely? I sighed and trudged on through the swirling
sycamore leaves which fell softly to the ground, turning
my phone off as I went.

When I returned after a long and circuitous trek through
the woods, I came back down the hill, approaching the
farmyard from the rear. I paused a moment, taking in
the view. It was beautiful, of course it was. I should count
my many blessings. The huddle of stone buildings
crouched in the valley, their dark-slated roofs framed by
the hills in the background, the gently trickling stream,
the flat meadow freckled with sheep and not another
house in sight. Closer inspection would reveal that many

tiles were missing from the charming outbuildings and plenty of damp was galloping up the picturesque walls. However much I hastily painted over it at the beginning of each holiday-let season, it always staged a blazing comeback at the end, which, thankfully, was almost upon us.

Even Jason was going back to school next week, his cold subsiding to a few sniffles. Right now, though, down by the stream in the daisy-strewn meadow, he and his mother were feeding the ducks, which was a rather touching scene. As she'd told me cheerily the other day, 'Not many ducks in Streatham, luv.' They moved on to stroke Brodie, the donkey, over the fence. Error. Brodie was notoriously bad-tempered and Jason was picking grass to give him, but not holding it in the flat of his hand. I opened my mouth to warn him – too late. Jason let out a yowl as his finger was squarely bitten. Brodie looked at me innocently, as if to say: What? I ducked behind a chestnut tree as Mrs Braithwaite, fussing over her son, hastened him off for yet another visit to the medicine chest, surely about to demand a refund. When I was certain they'd gone I emerged to fix Brodie with a reproving eye. I knew full well he could take grass from a clenched fist if he felt like it, he just obviously didn't.

Following the stony path as it plunged down the hill, I came through the back yard, shutting the five-barred gate behind me. As I passed by the Granary I resisted the urge to look through the window, but, actually, even with eyes half averted, I could easily see the flag was flying from the mast, which meant Ottoline was sitting. Since Sebastian couldn't paint without natural light he didn't draw the curtains, but the flag of St George, hoisted and fluttering, at least let the rest of us know not to peer. As I opened my back door, though, I turned at the sound of a car crunching out of the yard. I frowned after it. Ottoline's red Clio was purring away, bound for the direction of town. I remembered that she and Mum had hatched a plot to go to Highgrove today, Prince Charles's garden, which occasionally was open to the public. Who could it be, then? Sitting for my husband?

Curiosity got the better of me. Within moments, and after glancing furtively about, I was tiptoeing across the yard. Sebastian always stood with the north window behind him, his easel facing it, so that was the one I chose, knowing I'd at least get his back. I flattened myself against the rough outside wall. Then, very cautiously and slowly, I inched along, turning my head when I reached the glass pane. The window was high, though, the Granary being raised on saddle stones, and I couldn't quite see without standing on something. I cast about. By my back door, an old terracotta pot with a dead geranium in it fitted the bill.

I ran to get it, tiptoed back, emptied the earth, which came out in a dry lump, and turned it upside down. Then I resumed my position, but higher now. Flattened beside the window I turned my head to look. It took my eyes a moment to become accustomed to the light inside, but then, sure enough, on the floor I saw a tumble of clothes: a bra – not old Mr Forester from the village, then, who sometimes did the honours – and the electric fire blazing for warmth. The tatty chaise longue where sitters reclined was slightly shaded by a screen, but if I edged to the side of the pot . . . and craned my neck, I could just see . . . painted toes, slim, naked legs . . . and working my way up a naked body . . . Shit! I gripped the windowsill, bug-eyed with horror. Wobbled, precariously. The old pot gave way under the pressure and one foot went straight through it with a crash. As I landed, both hands clutched my mouth in horror.

'*Mum!*' I gasped.

Chapter Nineteen

Within a twinkling, it seemed to me, certainly too fast for me to make a move in any direction, the Granary door was flung wide. Sebastian stood a short distance away, towering and glowering, terrible in his fury.

'What the *fuck* are you doing!' he barked.

I limped towards him, the flowerpot on my left foot hampering my progress, but, for once, not so terrified by my husband's temper as wanting to see for certain. To view, through the naked eye, without the possible distortion of glass, what I thought I'd seen. Ignoring Sebastian I ducked my head under his arm, which held the door open, and stared into the room. Sure enough, reclining on the chaise, but now with a shirt snatched up to cover what remained of her modesty, was my mother, looking astonished, but angry, too.

'Mum!' I inhaled sharply, jaw dropping.

'Eleanor. What on *earth* are you doing?'

Anyone would think I'd disturbed her having a nap.

'What are *you* doing, more like!' I spluttered, when I'd finally found my voice.

'What does it look like I'm doing? I'm sitting for Sebastian.'

'Yes, but –' I gaped, impotently. Many, many things sprang to mind. You don't like him, for one, but, chiefly, you don't *do* this. This was *not* my mother, sprawled naked and supine for her son-in-law's paintbrush, for heaven's sake.

'Mother, I am shocked!' I said forcefully.

'Shocked? Oh, don't be silly, Ella. I'm surprised at you. Do grow up. This is art, for goodness sake.'

Some confusion, surely. Had we swapped persona? Was there some sort of role reversal going on? A transubstantiation I hadn't noticed, which, courtesy of her imbibing the same air as me, rubbing along on the same soil, basking in the same sunshine, had caused metamorphism to occur? Could properties seep so insidiously to blur personalities thus? Art. How could I argue with that? With what had been my answer to everything since I was fifteen years old? It's art! You don't understand! My room, my clothes, my boyfriends, my way of life, my whole *raison d'être*. I'd have yelled it, no doubt, at full volume, through my purple-painted bedroom door, before throwing myself prostrate on my tie-dyed bedspread, surrounded by Andy Warhol posters.

Sebastian still towered above me, holding the door with outstretched arm, as if daring me to duck right under it.

'But you must admit,' I spluttered, half to him now, 'it's pretty bloody surprising!' My voice sounded weedy, though: pathetic with righteous indignation.

'Well, now that the surprise has sunk in, perhaps you could bugger off and leave us to it?' Sebastian said acidly. 'Sylvia and I have work to do.' He made to slam the door, but I stayed it quickly with my hand.

'I thought you were going to Highgrove!' I squeaked. 'With Ottoline!'

'Oh, gardens can wait,' she said airily, waving her hand. 'Once you've seen one, you've seen them all. Sebastian's work is far more important.' And with that she dropped the shirt – *Jesus Christ!* – and rearranged herself coquettishly into position.

As I clapped my hand firmly over my eyes, the door slammed equally firmly on my face. When I opened those eyes, it was to stare at dark, woodwormed panels. I stayed still, in shock, for a moment, one foot still wearing a terracotta pot. After a moment, though, I wrenched myself free. But not without injury. I jabbed my ankle on a sharp piece of clay in the process and limped quickly inside, bleeding. Sensing drama, Maud, Doug and Buster clustered excitedly as I ran for the phone, hands fluttering, and punched out Ginnie's number. She was obviously in her kitchen too, because she answered immediately.

'Oh my God Ginnie you will never believe what I have just seen!' I gabbled breathlessly, clutching the mouthpiece with both hands and glancing about furtively as if I might be overheard.

'What?' she demanded.

'Mum, OK, is sitting for Sebastian.'

There was a long pause. 'You don't mean . . . *sitting?*' she hissed at length.

'Yes, I bloody do!' I shrieked. 'Naked!'

Another silence. 'Good God,' she said faintly. I sensed her swoon.

'I know!'

'I . . . can't believe it. Mummy.'

'I *know*! Neither can I!'

Another silence ensued as the scene I'd just witnessed filtered through to my sister's brain, the full horror pictorial and penetrating.

'I'll come,' she said swiftly, coming to. 'I thought she'd gone off the rails a bit recently – wacky clothes, smoking –'

'Smoking!'

'*Yes!* I popped round the other day and she was puffing away at one of those mini cigars of Ottoline's. Cheroots or whatever, dressed in something long and floaty and ridiculous. She looked like something out of the Bloomsbury Group, like Vita Sackville-West. But this . . . this is something else. It's – well . . .' She lowered her voice. 'It's obscene. Isn't it, Ella?'

It wasn't often she deferred to me.

'Well . . .' I dithered.

'Of course it's obscene!' She pounced on my uncertainty. 'Richard would certainly think it was.' Richard. Always Ginnie's arbiter. Her touchstone. 'He's her son-in-law, for God's sake. It's downright creepy!'

'I know,' I said doubtfully, thinking I'd said the very same two minutes ago. Yet from Ginnie's mouth it sounded . . . prim. Reactionary. Yes, Sebastian was related by marriage, but Ottoline was his aunt. He her nephew. I'd never questioned that, had I? But Ottoline was different: she was bohemian, she was a free spirit; my mother certainly wasn't. It couldn't therefore be the same thing. Sylvia Jardine wiped assiduously under her pepper grinder, washed tea towels separately in a sterile solution, insisted on napkin rings. Ottoline had never done anything like that. She just didn't think like that. But . . . perhaps my mother didn't think like that either, any more? All of a sudden I regretted impetuously ringing Ginnie. It had been a knee-jerk reaction, one which would have my sister reaching for her car keys in moments, tearing round here to tell Mum her duties lay in National Trust membership, walking holidays.

'Ginnie – actually – I'll handle it,' I said, even though I knew it was useless.

'I'm coming!' she barked. And the phone went dead. So that was that.

I hovered nervously at the kitchen window, tending to my bleeding ankle with kitchen towel – no plasters, of course, and I couldn't raid the holiday lets and risk running into Mrs Braithwaite and the equally bleeding Jason – so I stuck a piece of paper on with Sellotape to staunch the flow. My eyes were on the yard, however, ears pricked for a vehicle. I did risk making a cup of coffee, but without taking my eyes off the window, running – limping – to put the kettle on. The moment I heard an expensive purr, I was outside.

'Actually, Ginnie,' I breathed, as she got out of her Range Rover, her eyes already far beyond me and fixed firmly on the Granary door, 'I've decided it's fine.'

I hadn't, really, if I'm honest. Still couldn't quite get my head round the disturbing scene, but had decided, in some weird way, that us *stopping* her was much worse. Public opinion would be very much on the arty side – I was very cowed by public opinion – and however nauseous Ginnie and I found it, we'd be branded spoilsports. Mostly, though, I feared Sebastian's scorn, as I'd always feared it. I wanted to show I could rise above this wide, bourgeois streak in my family, which I think he'd always suspected had percolated down to me.

'Oh, you have, have you? Well, I've decided it's very far from fine!' Ginnie declared, slamming her car door and striding – nay, marching – to the studio. I practically had to rugby-tackle her.

'No, Ginnie!'

'Get *off*, Ella!' she cried as I gripped her round the waist, my head in her huge chest. Was this how prop forwards did it? Lower, perhaps: her hips. I *had* to stop her. A short and unseemly struggle ensued.

'Oh my God – yuk – you're *bleeding* all over me!'

I was. My makeshift bandage had come off and my leg, as I tried to wrap it round hers and trip her, was gushing on her jeans, although, to be fair, her jeans were pretty agricultural already. This was a woman who wrestled sheep.

'Just come inside a moment!' I pleaded in a harsh whisper – we were perilously close to the Granary door. 'At least let's talk about it.'

She went limp in acquiescence, allowing herself to be led; succumbing to my strength of feeling, if not my muscle. Once she was safely inside my kitchen I shut the back door firmly, wishing I knew where the key was to lock it.

'This is all I bloody need, frankly,' Ginnie was saying as she swept a hand through precipitously erect hair and strode to my Aga to bang my kettle on the hob. Ginnie always took over in my house and I always let her. 'I've got Araminta wanting to change schools at the eleventh hour, Richard up to his eyes in work leaving me to run the entire estate single-handed, Hugo –' She broke off, unable, it seemed, to tell me the trouble with Hugo. She recovered herself. 'And now Mum,' she seethed, 'thinking she's some bloody Saga holidays centrefold!'

'Yes, well, it wasn't quite like that,' I muttered, making to get some mugs down from the cupboard, but Ginnie had already barged past; got them herself. 'I mean, it was an arty pose. Not a . . . you know.'

'Well, thank Christ for that!'

I turned. Cross. 'Well, *obviously* it was an arty pose, Ginnie.' Who was I cross on behalf of, I wondered? Mum? No. Sebastian? That he would in some way make a fool of our mother? Of course he wouldn't. How I wished I'd never rung her. 'And I think that maybe,' I cast about wildly, 'maybe she wasn't entirely naked.'

'Really?' She turned sharply, about to pour the kettle.

'Yes, I think there was – a thong.'

Her eyes bulged. 'A *thong*?' This snapshot of our mother was almost worse than the one of her naked.

'No, not a thong,' I said quickly, shaking my head and banishing the image. 'Some sort of . . . thing, though.'

'A thing thong?' suggested Ginnie drily and quite wittily for her. I knew I wasn't out of the woods yet, though.

'Yes, a wispy bit of gauze.' Now I was deep in an ancient Pete and Dud routine, two tramps in an art gallery. 'Covering her – you know.' I demonstrated low, with my hand.

'Oh.' She nodded. This helped. My lie helped. As lies often can, I find. Ease the way. Oil the wheels. Make life more comfortable. We both breathed a bit, for different reasons.

'And now that I'm over the shock,' I told her, forging on, 'I think it's fine. And you'll think so too, um, tomorrow,' I added, thinking the twenty-minute head start I'd had wouldn't be nearly enough for Ginnie.

'Don't bank on it,' she said darkly, although I could see she was simmering down a bit.

'Think of Lucian Freud,' I said encouragingly. 'God, he painted his entire family naked. And pregnant. You wouldn't mind if it was him, would you?'

She sat down heavily at my kitchen table, a black coffee before her. 'Would I mind if Lucian Freud came back from the dead and painted our mother naked and pregnant? Is that what you're asking me?' Despite the sarcasm she had clearly calmed down slightly. She looked all in, suddenly. Defeated. 'I don't know, Ella. Don't know anything any more.'

I frowned. Really? This wasn't Ginnie. Ginnie knew everything.

'What's wrong?' I sat down opposite her with my mug. 'I mean, apart from Mum?'

She looked at me, some inward battle going on behind her eyes. She seemed about to tell me, then changed her mind. 'Well, Daddy doesn't help,' she said caustically. 'I went to see him the other day, popped in unannounced. You know he's doing B&B?'

'*What?*'

'Yes, some government minister has said there are too many old people rattling round in enormous great houses. Says it's preposterous when there are so many homeless people. Daddy's taken it to heart. Taken in lodgers.'

'But – bed and *breakfast?*'

'Oh, he doesn't do the breakfast. They have to fend for themselves. And the whole place is in chaos. Dirty plates in the sink, cereal packets still on the table at midday . . .' We tried not to look at the array on mine.

'But – doesn't he need a licence, or something?'

'One would assume so, but I'm not even sure they *pay*, Ella. He airily said something about it all being above board and in return for favours, or something.'

'Favours!'

'Well, you know, gardening, getting the logs in . . . I don't know.' She really did look tired.

'Good God,' I said faintly, blinking into space. I tried to imagine the house. 'Does Mum know?'

'Of course not.'

'How many has he got?'

'Oh, two or three. All youngish, so the place looks like a youth hostel. Some South African's got his enormous great rucksack in the hall, then in the drawing room there's this Indian bloke with a laptop at Mummy's lovely walnut desk. And when I asked him – imperiously, I hoped – what he was doing, he said: "Working from home." "*My* home!" I roared, but it didn't seem to cut much ice. He just carried on tapping away. Then, in the midst of all this mayhem – there was a trainee hairdresser, incidentally, from Luton, in the kitchen, trying out new hairstyles on some bizarre life-size model with fake red hair – Daddy breezes in from the study where he's been working out to some keep-fit DVD.'

'Zumba,' I said abstractedly. 'It's a dance craze he's been doing at the village hall. Peggy got him into it.'

'Yes, but he was in *jogging* shorts, Ella. With a sweat band round his head. It was gross!'

I boggled, trying to imagine that. My dad mostly wore corduroy. Moleskin, occasionally.

'Was Maureen there?'

'Happily not, and when I mentioned her he said something about her dog-training and Zumba DVDs not really mixing. They howl, apparently, at the music. Her canine clients.'

'Well, that's a relief.'

'Oh, don't get excited. I think she's still very much on the scene. There were antimacassars on the backs of all the chairs and air fresheners everywhere.' She shuddered.

'But not actually living there?'

'Daddy says no.'

'Well, then it's a no. He wouldn't lie, Ginnie. Dad's not like that. And, anyway, in his present mood he'd be quite happy to tell us. Wouldn't spare us the gory details.' Rather like Mum, I thought. Not that he'd do it deliberately, of course. Was Mum? Doing it deliberately, to shock? No, I thought, not her, either.

Ginnie sighed. It was a heartfelt sigh, right up from the soles of her shoes. 'Maybe not.' She rubbed her forehead with the heel of her hand. 'As I say, I don't think I know anything any more.' She blinked hard, her eyes lowered to the table.

I bravely reached out and covered her hand. My sister and I don't cover hands. She flinched and I withdrew mine quickly.

'What is it, Ginnie?' I asked.

She didn't answer.

'Is it Hugo?'

If Ginnie had a soft spot in her seemingly reinforced-concrete underbelly, it was her son: her firstborn, Hugo. Bright, blond, beautiful, a sporting hero all his life, trophies and cups galore, captain of the first eleven, hitting a victorious century in the match against Eton in his final term – another mother I knew who was watching said she'd had to restrain Ginnie from running onto the pitch to do a lap of honour: had a nasty feeling she'd take her top off and wave it in the air. Normally Ginnie couldn't stop talking about Hugo. Araminta, too, of course, but Araminta wasn't quite so high achieving, so usually it was Hugo we heard about. But not recently.

'Is he still with . . . the girl?'

'Yes, he's still with Frankie.'

It was the first time I'd heard her say her name. I'd deliberately avoided it myself. Avoided pressing her buttons. I was surprised.

'And, actually, she's been brilliant,' she said quietly.

'Oh! Good. Because I thought you thought she was . . .' I hesitated.

'Not smart enough for us?' She raised her eyes from the table to look at me for the first time. Sad eyes. 'Perhaps I did. Not now. I'm very grateful to her.' She struggled with something. Herself, perhaps. 'Hugo hasn't been well, Ella. He had a bit of a breakdown.'

'Oh!'

'Nothing major, but, well . . . We had to take him to a doctor. In London. A . . .'

'Psychiatrist?'

'Yes. He said it was stress. Overdoing it.' She gave a hollow laugh. 'At twenty-one.'

I felt so sad. Rallied for her. 'It happens, Ginnie. These things happen.'

I knew she was blaming herself. For pushing. And, boy, could Ginnie push. Ringing him at boarding school – have you done this, have you joined that society, are you playing enough instruments, why aren't you doing fencing? Grandpa was so good at fencing. Well, surely you can fit cricket practice around the fencing? Surely you can do both? Why aren't you doing Greek any more? Josh told me.

'We were warned, at the end of his time at school, by his housemaster, but I ignored it. Richard didn't. Got him that job in the pub, near Mummy and Daddy. Away from us. Me, probably. Instead of going to the South Pole on that Quest expedition I wanted him to do. A good decision, in retrospect. And where he met Frankie.'

'Good.' The South Pole, for God's sake. Good for Richard.

'But it was all a bit late. A nice relaxed time, staying at Granny and Grandpa's, pulling pints, going out with a local girl. He was found crying in a bus shelter at five in the morning. Couldn't stop.'

I swallowed. Felt so sad. I was very fond of Hugo. I remembered thinking he'd looked rather thin when I'd seen him.

'And Frankie's been brilliant. I thought she might head for the hills when she heard, but she stuck right by him. Went to all his doctor's appointments with him. Her mother's been a brick, too. He stays there quite a lot. Feels happy there.' She gulped. 'There are younger brothers and sisters, which is lovely, of course. To mess about with. Tiny little house, but still. And he's never really had that. Well, Araminta,' she said, realizing. 'But away, at boarding school.'

She fell silent.

'This isn't your fault, Ginnie,' I said quietly.

'No. Maybe not. But . . . I don't know.' She heaved up another great sigh. 'So the upshot is, he's going to retake his first year at Cambridge.'

'Oh, OK.'

'Give himself a bit more time. To regroup. Start again.'

'Yes, good idea.'

It was. But this was all so hard for his mother. She gave me a level look. 'And I'm fine about it, Ella, really. Couldn't care less that he's behind his contemporaries. I want him to be well. Healthy. Happy. The doctor had a little word with me, too.'

'Right.' Because having got to the bottom of Hugo, he

no doubt felt the need to speak to the mother. 'But he didn't . . .'

'Blame me? No. No, this guy was the real deal. Cause and effect cod psychology didn't feature.'

'Good.'

She straightened up a bit. Nervously rubbed the handle of her mug with her fingertip. 'And, um, anyway, I'm starting a course of counselling myself. Next week, in fact.'

'Counselling?'

'Yes, it's what I want to do.'

'Oh!' I thought she'd meant she was *getting* the counselling. 'You mean . . . you're going to *be* a counsellor?'

'Well, eventually. It takes five years to train. But I'm definitely going back to work.'

'Right.' This in itself was an admission. That she didn't currently work.

Ginnie was always very busy, rushing around in a panic, but doing what? Nothing, Sebastian said. Chasing her tail. She had a man to do everything, he said; all she did was chivvy them and look harassed. But a *counsellor*? Surely she'd be rather brusque? Your marriage has broken down? Pull yourself together. Your wife doesn't understand you? Well, can you blame her?

'A lot of it's listening,' she told me, perhaps reading my thoughts. 'Not necessarily saying much.'

Oh, well, that was out of the question. Ginnie never drew breath. Had an opinion on everything. She'd never be able to sit on her hands without diving in with advice.

'Good, good.' I nodded encouragingly. 'I'm really pleased, Ginnie.'

'And, in time, I hope I can join the team down at the Holistic Centre. You know, where Lottie works.'

This had me getting to my feet and pretending to wash the mugs, I had to hide my face in the sink so badly. Ginnie with Lottie? Who was so socially inferior Ginnie could barely flick her a tight little smile? I turned to look at my sister, unobserved. She was staring out of the window now, her face collapsed. Shattered. People change. Of course they do. And if I couldn't see that, and couldn't help the transformation, I wasn't much of a sister.

'I'll mention it to her,' I said warmly, knowing that once Lottie had got over her shock and spat a bit of bile about frustrated housewives muscling in on what they saw to be an easy wicket, not to mention certain people only deigning to talk to her when they wanted something, she'd come round too. Lottie had a kind heart. And, after all, what was that Holistic Centre all about – teeming, incidentally, with women of a certain age – if not healing each other? Didn't it help Lottie and her terrible relationship with her mother? Hadn't she told me so herself? Perhaps I should be in another room down the hall, I thought gloomily: retrain as a reflexologist or something. Knead people's feet, so that between the three of us we could offer all-round treatment and be full of good karma ourselves.

'I'll sort Mum and Dad out,' I said shortly. 'You've got enough on your plate.'

'Thanks, Ella.'

She got wearily to her feet, and just a tiny bit of me thought I had quite a lot on mine, with my husband leaving home, but I wouldn't mention it.

'Oh, and such good news about Sebastian moving out. You must be delighted he's finally taken the hint. And he's a different man, don't you think?'

'What d'you mean?' I said carefully.

'Well, much more like he was before the painting all went wrong. More light-hearted. And, of course, it helps that he's not drinking. I ran into him and the children in Oxford the other day. They showed me the house. It's lovely, isn't it?'

'What house?' My mouth was very dry.

'The one the university have given him.'

House. I'd thought rooms. Up a staircase.

'I haven't seen it.'

'Oh, well, I only have because I bumped into them, outside Christchurch. They took me in. You have to go through the porters' lodge and everything, frightfully grand. It's off that huge great quad, then through some cloisters and at the end of a dear little row of medieval houses covered in wisteria. It's got a lovely garden at the back and all the space in the world at the front, with the whopping quad and everything. Christchurch is vast. Tabs showed me her room, and Josh has even got a little corner of Sebastian's studio. I had no idea he was so good at art. And of course the Playhouse is just up the road. Sebastian made me a cup of tea – can you believe it? – and because I had so much shopping and loads more to do, I left it all there and picked it up later. They were playing Perudo when I poked my head round the sitting-room door later on and said I was going. A really sweet little scene. Heads bent over the dice. And I couldn't help thinking how lovely to have a brother-in-law in town with a spare room – it's got four bedrooms – if Richard and I are ever there, at the theatre, or something. In his present mood I doubt he'll mind at all. Sebastian, I mean. Anyway, toodle-oo, Ella.'

She gathered her car keys from the kitchen table.

'I'm so glad I told you about Hugo. I'm over the shock

of it now and just so pleased and grateful he's on the mend. Nothing else really matters, does it? And I'm so pleased I told you about going back to work, too. I thought you'd laugh at me. You've always been the career girl in the family, the clever one. Golly, at one stage Mummy and Daddy thought you were going to be famous, remember that review in *The Times*?' She went to the back door. 'And don't worry about Mummy. How like you to exaggerate and say she was starkers when she was nothing of the kind.' She raised a weary smile as she turned to go. 'Anyway, good to chat and all that. You've made me feel so much better.'

And away she went to her car.

Chapter Twenty

I pulled out a chair and sat down heavily when she'd gone. Listened to the purr of her car leaving the yard. Even after the sound had faded into the distance, I stayed there motionless for a while. Eventually I got up and walked around the kitchen, arms tightly folded across my chest. Marvellous. She felt better. My sister felt better. That was splendid. Sebastian didn't just feel better, he *was* better, apparently. Excellent. The children were happy – of course they were: a ruddy great four-bedroomed house in town. How delightful. They'd be the envy of all their friends; think of the parties. Everyone was thrilled. And I was so very pleased for them all. Aware that my jaw was clenched and my nostrils flaring like foghorns, I stopped at the window to breathe. Relaxed my mouth and tried to gain control. Gave my ears a savage tweak. Hopeless. What were those breathing exercises Lottie had taught me? Not just down to the diaphragm, but further, right down to the tummy. Take it right down. I did, but felt a bit sick. Light-headed. I lay my forehead on the window pane to cool it. The moment it met the glass, though, I jerked it away, sharpish.

Mrs Braithwaite was emerging from her cottage, at the double, with her son in her hand, looking furious. Her mouth, if possible, was even tighter than mine. She held Jason's finger high and aloft, like exhibit A. As she marched very much in my direction I took an executive decision –

and dived under the kitchen table. I crouched there on my knees. Moments later, there was a sharp knock upon the back door. Rat-a-tat-tat. I sank lower, head almost on the floor, knowing she couldn't see me. I'd done it before when creditors had called and they'd all had a jolly good peer through the window – the electricity man had even gone round to the back garden – but, eventually, they'd gone away. And surely if Mrs Braithwaite didn't get an answer, she wouldn't just barge into my home?

'Blimey, whacha doin' under there, then?'

'Ah, Mrs Braithwaite. How lovely.' I crawled out. 'I, um . . . dropped an earring. Thought it might have rolled under the table.'

She drew herself up to her full height. Not for the first time it struck me that her eyes were very close together. Very proximate to her nose. She looked at me dubiously. 'You don't look like the earring type.'

'Ooh, I have my lighter moments,' I warbled girlishly, fondling my unadorned ears.

'Well, your donkey's gone and bit my Jison, look.' She jerked his arm up high, as if he'd won an Olympic medal. 'He's bin in terrible pain and there ain't no more Savlon in that tube, and not an aspirin in the packet, neither. Your animals have bitten him so much we've used 'em all. I came over here for something of yours. What with the cockerels and the ducks that chase us, this place is down-right dangerous!'

'Yes,' I conceded, brushing myself down – it was surprisingly dirty under my table – 'the country can be slightly hazardous, I do agree. And you're right about the cockerels, which is why I got rid of them. But the ducks only give chase if they think you've got food. I did ask you not to give them your sandwiches.' Chips, too, from a McDonald's carton, which I'd found billowing around the yard. I went to the windowsill to embark on what I knew to be a spurious and fruitless search in my messy basket. 'Aspirin,' I murmured ostentatiously, 'now let me see.' As I riffled amongst empty packets, a crusty old sachet of cystitis remedy materialized. I wondered if I could dissolve it in water and pass it off as aspirin? What would it do to a boy's waterworks?

'That'll do.' She snatched it from me.

'Oh, but –'

'And I'll take some of that, an' all,' she said, grabbing an ancient bottle of witch hazel.

'Help yourself,' I said wearily. 'Not only is it open house here at Liberty Hall but everything is free of charge.'

'And the sheep are a liability. They had 'im pinned in the corner the other day. Terrified, he was.'

'Yes, you told me.' I watched as she emptied the solid lump of crystal into a glass and added water. 'But, you know, sheep honestly won't hurt him. They're just nosy.'

'And as for those bulls you've got, all crowded in together –'

'They're long-horn cows, Mrs Braithwaite, and they're not even mine. They belong to the farmer next door, and, yes, they will be curious if you go into their field.' Don't go *in*, you silly woman, played on my lips.

'And in the brochure you say you're a kiddie-friendly farm.' I most certainly would not have written 'kiddie-friendly' but I refrained from correcting her. She made Jason gulp down the brew before I knew how to stop her. 'We came here expecting to stroke baby chicks, feed baby lambs, but there ain't nothing like that.'

'No, well, you see chicks and lambs tend to be born in the early spring and therefore in late summer they've grown into –'

'Didn't think we'd be the only ones here, neither. Thought there'd be loads of other kids for Jise to play wiv.' She glared at me accusingly as if *I* were the one who didn't have any friends. 'And now we know why, don't we?' she said triumphantly. 'Bloody dangerous animals. I'm surprised you've got any visitors at all!'

I'm surprised you've got any teeth, came to mind, but, happily, not to my vocal chords. Again, I wanted to slap her. I say again, because recently, if you recall, I'd wanted to do the same to my mother. Was this what was happening to me? Was I becoming violent? One did hear of such women, deserted and disaffected, who took to drink – I eyed the gin bottle on the side which, admittedly, had taken a bit of a battering of late – and ended up brawling with innocent bystanders. Except there was nothing remotely innocent about Mrs Braithwaite. I'd known her type the moment I'd picked up the phone to her: not wanting to pay a deposit; asking for a discount because there were only two of them; telling me the second she arrived she wouldn't be paying 'the full whack' on account of it not being quite what she'd had in mind: 'Being as it's so far from anywhere and the website said it was accessible.' Despite wondering if she'd expected a slip road to the M40 outside her front door, I'd wearily agreed to all her demands, knowing I wouldn't get anyone else at such late notice. Knowing she had me cornered.

'That's quite a nasty bite, isn't it, Mrs Braithwaite?' I said, looking at Jason's blemish-free finger. 'If I were you I'd take him down to the doctor's for a tetanus.'

This worked like lightning. She looked terrified. 'What – even though it's just a scratch?'

'Oh, yes. You can't be too careful. Especially in the country. We had foot and mouth here once, you know. It really can't be ruled out.'

That did it. With a yelp she was out of my kitchen and running fast for her BMW – no clapped-out Volvo for her – dragging Jason with her. I watched them go. Without an appointment they'd have to sit for ages in a crowded waiting room before finally seeing a nurse, who'd say that if the animal hadn't actually drawn blood there was really little point in a tetanus. Then they'd be back here in high dudgeon, protesting they'd lost a day of their precious holiday and wanted a refund, and their petrol money. Before you could blink I'd be paying *them* to take *my* cottage. But there'd been nothing else for it. I'd had to get rid of them.

All at once I felt terribly sorry for Jason. Why was he so large? That wasn't his fault, at ten, was it? He didn't buy his own food. And so silent? Was he permanently terrified? And where was Mr Braithwaite? Over the hills and far away, no doubt. Over the hills . . . I gazed at them as they loomed in the distance, framing my valley. They stared back. My eyes dropped to the Granary, where my mother and my husband would be ensconced for a good many hours to come. I tracked right to the Dairy, where Ottoline would be returning soon, to host another pottery group, with the flurry of oddballs who'd droop through my yard from the bus stop, swearing at the tops of their voices. Suddenly I knew I couldn't stand it any longer. I had to follow Mr Braithwaite. Had to head for the hills.

I thought about going to Dad, but Ginnie's description

of the ménage I'd encounter there seemed to rival my own. I felt a surge of panic. I couldn't even go home. When I'd first got married, I'd asked Sebastian if we could go home for Christmas – I was only twenty. He'd laughed and said, 'We are home.' But there'd been love in his eyes. And tenderness in the way he'd said it, which was what I missed, of course. As a lump of self-pity rose in my throat I plunged my hand into my pocket and, with the speed of Clint retrieving his Colt 45, pulled out my phone and scrolled down. As it rang, I put it to my ear. Ludo answered almost immediately.

'You know you said that one day we should spend some time together because we deserved it?' I gabbled with absolutely no run-up or preamble whatsoever.

'Yes?'

'Well, that day has come.'

It was a trifle melodramatic, I admit. A trifle – portentous. But that was how I felt. On the cusp of a pivotal moment. Like Madame Bovary had perhaps felt when she'd decided to cheat on her boring doctor, or Anna Karenina, on the point of fleeing to Vronsky. Unbridled – no doubt. Wanton – certainly. But with mind made up and very certain indeed. I realized I'd crossed a line. One I'd hovered and dithered over for so long, but had now leaped in one great jump, landing yards on the other side, in another country. A rather thrilling one. One that was totally devoid of energy-sapping dependants and where my own sap was rising so fast it was liable to bubble over into my Ugg boots. Everyone has their boiling point and I'd reached mine. No, I would not be chatelaine of this charming communal establishment with its marvellously eclectic jumble of freeloaders making constant demands on my time any more. I would have my moment in the sun.

Ludo's voice, when it came, was charged with excitement. 'You mean . . .'

'Yes,' I declared, equally excited. 'That is exactly what I mean. Where shall we meet?' Golly. I felt in charge for once. Liked it enormously.

'Wherever you'd like to meet,' he said tremulously. 'Do you mean a hotel?'

'I most certainly do.'

Blimey. Did I? And did I have to sound like a policeman?

'Well, what about the pub I told you about? The Flower at Micklehampton?'

Micklehampton. Quite close. And somehow I needed to be away, away.

'No, not there,' I told him. 'What about that place in Binfield that's supposed to be rather hidden away – all beams and log fires? The bunch of whatsits?'

'Grapes, generally. Although, at our age, it could be piles. Well, yes, we could, but it's too far to go today.'

'Then let's go next week,' I said, thinking that, for all my impetuousness, I did actually need to get my legs waxed. And maybe acquire some pants that weren't saggy and grey and came comfortably up to my waist. 'How about Wednesday?'

'Wednesday, it is,' he said happily. 'Eliza is visiting a friend in London then, or so she –' He broke off.

'What?' I pounced.

'Nothing,' he said quickly.

I'd caught it, though.

'Oh, Ella, how perfect. I can't tell you how much I've longed for this moment.'

'Me too,' I told him, actually meaning it now. Not just feeling cross and resentful and lashing out, which I knew I'd been doing when I'd plucked out my phone. I felt rather joyous. Yes, I was running away, with all the negativity that implied, but I was running away with Ludo, don't forget. Handsome, kind, in-love-with-me Ludo. Not just anyone. And, boy, it felt good. He was right: we were entitled to some happiness. I pocketed my phone feverishly. Not destined to dig gardens and run holiday lets for ever, whilst our spouses fornicated with whosoever they pleased.

As I went upstairs I tried not to think about the women Sebastian would fornicate with at Oxford: adoring young female professors, nubile students at the Ruskin, where he was probably on the syllabus, let alone the payroll. Art students were notoriously pretty. And he was on the wagon too, according to Ottoline. Not quite the alcoholic, shambolic wreck of yesteryear. He'd got himself together a bit. Wouldn't take long, though, I thought quickly, hating myself for the thought. But, nevertheless, it was true. Sebastian could only ever stay sober for three or four weeks at a time. It wouldn't be for ever.

Upstairs in my studio, I didn't even pretend to go in the direction of Leanne and the gang. Instead I went straight to my huge cupboard behind the door, lifted the floorboard in front of it and took out the key on the tiny piece of pink velvet ribbon. I hesitated, but only for a moment. Opened it. Riffling straight to the back of the stack of canvases I found the one I was looking for. Slid it out. Propped it against a wall and drank it in. It was a still life: wild flowers in a jug and a few pieces of fruit on a crumpled tablecloth. I'd painted it years ago, a good fifteen, but I liked it very much. I looked at it for another long moment, then put it back carefully.

My fingers selected another, a seascape, as yet unfinished. Most of it was done, but the boats in the foreground, which I'd sat on a harbour wall and painted in St-Jean-de-Luz in the very early days, when we went to places like that in the south of France and were feted and wined and dined by the wealthy aboard their yachts, were still unfinished. I could visualize the scene now, all these years later. Sebastian and I had got up early one morning and walked down to the harbour from the tiny apartment we'd been renting. Before anyone, aside from the fishermen, was up, we'd sat on the quay wall with Josh in a Moses basket, watching the boats come in with their catches. Then we'd set up our easels and painted together. I could still see that early morning light, lazy and languorous, rolling in from the sea, the sun's rays breaking through the mist and dancing gently on the water, glancing off the sides of the boats bobbing pink and turquoise in the foreground. Could still see the hills to the west with their clusters of red-roofed houses.

Within a twinkling I'd locked the door to my room but also pulled a chair across it. I set up my easel and screwed in the painting. Finding my palette, stiff with misuse, on the floor of the cupboard I squirted out a few blobs of colour. Just a bit, I wouldn't be here long. Then I got to work: cornering the memory in my head, reproducing it bit by bit, dab by dab. I'd thought holding a paintbrush in my hand during daylight hours – I had occasionally dabbled at night – after so many years would feel strange, nervous-making, but I was wrong. It was like holding a baby again: lovely, natural, familiar. I knew exactly what to do with it. And as that familiar feeling flowed in a circular motion from my brain, to my fingertips, to the canvas, then dipped back into my head for more inspiration, it became so absorbing, so automatic, I felt the years roll back. It was as if all the strokes I'd neglected to make in the long hiatus, the great yawning gap, had been stored somewhere, and were all the more concentrated and forceful in their surging comeback.

Three hours later I emerged from the room, shocked but sated. The painting was safely stashed away in the cupboard again, on top of the others, to dry. The door was locked, the key under the floorboard. And I was outside, walking, almost blindly, through the fields behind the house. My hands, hastily washed in white spirit, like a murderer removing all traces of blood, were thrust guiltily in my Barbour pockets; my face to the sun, like a salamander. I felt glorious. As if I'd been touched, or seen a vision. I imagined some sort of aura around me – like an angel in a child's picture book. Ridiculous, of course. A white light, then, at any rate. In reality I suppose it was just a middle-aged glow of satisfaction but there seemed so much more to it. I walked on, my face trained to the sunbeams in the west as if in a trance, as if I were walking across a desert barefoot with a cross in my hands. My eyes were half shut as I kicked up the leaves and laughed softly to myself. If anyone had seen me, they'd have thought me a trifle odd. Soft in the head. Either that, or in love. But no man, in my past life, or in my future life, could ever make me feel as I did at this moment. I knew I had never been happier. Knew it was euphoria in the truest sense of the word.

Sometime later, as I came back across the yard, I saw the school bus. It rumbled to a halt in the lane behind the hedge. A couple of boys who lived in the village dismounted, then, after a pause, Josh got off. I waited for him as he came through the yard from the opposite side, shoulders slouched, hands in pockets, dark suit that passed for sixth-form uniform tatty and frayed at the edges. His trousers dragged in the mud. With three terms to go I wondered if it would stay the course. I quickly shoved my hands back in my pockets.

'Hi, darling.'

'Oh. Hi.' He glanced up, surprised. He'd been miles away. Then he did a double take. 'What are you up to?'

'What d'you mean?'

'Dunno. You look . . . furtive, or something.' He grinned as he joined me. 'Like you've got a lover.'

I flushed. 'Don't be silly.'

He blinked. 'Easy. Joke. Have I struck a chord or something?'

I laughed gaily. 'Yes, that's it. Me and my lover have been rolling round the hay barn while you've been at school. What else would I be doing with my day?'

He shrugged, bored with the subject of his middle-aged mother, and quite possibly repulsed as well. We walked towards the house in silence.

'Dad says you might go to Oxford with him when he starts his new job,' I said easily, blithely even, congratulating myself on my phlegm.

'Yeah.' He shot me a cautious look. 'You all right about that?'

'Of course.'

'Only in term time,' he said hastily. 'It's just, it'll be so much easier than getting that fucking bus into town every day.'

'Well, quite. Except, he thinks you might want to work at the Playhouse in the holidays. Haven't you applied for a job there?' I helped him.

'Yeah.' He reddened. Unusual for Josh. He eyed me warily. 'Is that OK?'

'What, for you to apply for a holiday job? No, I forbid it. How dare you earn good money and get work experience too?'

He grinned. 'Cool.'

I could tell he was relieved. I really was doing terribly well. No twanging apron strings, no straining umbilical cord. That'll be the painting, I decided. The real work. Not the pretend work, with Leanne et al.

'It's just, Tabs and I thought you might be a bit – I dunno. You know.'

'Tabs and I?'

'Yes.'

'Well, Tabitha's not going.'

'Why not?'

'Because she's fifteen, Josh. A schoolgirl. She can't be swanning around Oxford at that age like a – a squatter!'

He gave me a 'you're weird' look. The one with the squinty eyes and the chin tucked into the neck. 'She's not *squatting.*'

'Well, living away from home!'

'Hardly. It's with Sebastian. Not in some fetid bedsit with drug fiends. And she'll be back in the holidays.'

'Will she?' I said, hyperventilating now. 'Oh, how marvellous. Oh, I am pleased to hear that. What – to visit her lonely mother at the farm?'

'Ella . . . Shit.'

This was awkward, clearly. A huge word in the teenage vocabulary. It simply didn't do to be awkward.

'It's out of the question, Josh. She stays here with me!' Panic was rising in my breast, but, even as I said it, I knew I couldn't stop her. He knew it, too, and didn't say anything. My breathing became laboured. My voice shrill.

'So you've decided all this, have you, the three of you, without even *consulting* me!' I shrieked.

Josh felt the injustice of this. 'It wasn't like that. We were going to ask you, talk to you about it. But it never seems to be the right moment. We didn't want you to — you know.'

'*What? Didn't want me to what?*' I yelled.

Fly off the handle. Like I was doing right now, in the middle of the yard: colour high, tears springing, bellowing at my son. But this had been sprung on me. And I was horrified. My baby. My Tabby. That she'd even want to go! But at the same time a tiny bit of me knew I'd want to go, too. And that she wasn't deserting me. She just wanted to be in town, with her brother and her dad — what fifteen-year-old wouldn't? It didn't mean she loved me less, but, boy, did it feel like it. As I trembled with fear I was aware of Mrs Braithwaite, back from the surgery, watching from the cottage window, brought to it by the raised voices. Jason was beside her. Ottoline had been drawn to her window, too, together with Becks and Debs and Ray and Charles in the pottery group, aprons on, clutching jugs and ashtrays. And at the Granary — oh, good. Even my naked mother and Sebastian had been roused from their artistic reverie. Mum was in some kind of paisley dressing gown as she peered out, wiping the grimy pane. I took Josh's arm roughly, to pull him inside. He shook me off, though, standing his ground. This left us mid-amphitheatre, the denouement to be played out.

'I won't have it, Josh,' I continued in a low voice, which, nonetheless, shook with emotion. 'And I cannot believe –' No, *don't* go there, my head shrieked, but still I went. 'I cannot believe you and Tabitha would do this to me. Cannot believe you'd be so cruel!'

There. It was out. Bad behaviour complete. Finish with a flourish, Ella: with the lowest card in your hand. Not with consideration for children old enough to choose which parent to live with, but with the most craven trick any separated parent can play in the divorce book. A plea to make the child feel guilty. To make them feel it was their fault their parents' marriage had failed and they could no longer live together as one happy family.

Josh was no fool. And he certainly wasn't going to fall into any guilt trap. Two bright spots of colour burned high in his cheeks and his eyes glittered furiously.

'Great. No, really, terrific, Ella. Thanks for that.' He shot me a venomous look, before turning to go inside.

Chapter Twenty-One

The Bunch of Grapes was off the cobbled high street and down a dear little country lane at the bottom of a no-through road. Rather appropriate, I thought, coming to a halt in the car park and turning off the engine to contemplate it. No way back. It was achingly quaint with a long, low, thatched roof under which poked the eaves of the bedrooms, like eyebrows, and which no doubt harboured plump little feather beds within, and all, I imagined, up some charming, old, rickety-rackety stairs that led up from the bar with its roaring log fire, from whence, after dinner, having got quietly plastered, one could retire.

I needed this, I thought fiercely, gripping the wheel as I looked up hungrily at the late Virginia creeper encircling those bedrooms. Needed it very badly. This week had been terrible. Ghastly. Particularly the day following the little exchange between Josh and me. On the night of the debacle, Tabitha had stayed with a friend in Oxford, so when she finally came home, and having had twenty-four hours to think about it, I'd determined to be reasonable. Reasonable, but firm. In fact, I had the whole evening planned. We'd sit down to a proper supper: spaghetti carbonara, her favourite. And then, as we were clearing the plates together – already a fairy tale: my children habitually bomb-burst from the table and when I shriek for them to come and help, take one plate each, their own, to deposit in the dishwasher at a strange angle – anyway, when we were washing pans at the sink, I'd carefully catalogue the drawbacks of the plan. The lack of support during her crucial GCSEs – Sebastian was famously disinclined to toil over homework, saying it was the teachers' job and when teachers became artists he'd swap roles too; the lack of creature comforts, home cooking, et cetera; the lack of a maternal presence. I wouldn't go so far as to say a role model. I'd thought about that, but decided not, on the grounds of derision. And gradually, as the two of us dried up together, I'd let her make up her own mind, which, naturally, would concur with mine. I'd reckoned without her and her brother texting, or even conferring at school, though. When she came through the back door that afternoon, on an earlier bus than Josh, resentment was already all over her face.

'It's fine,' she told me, marching across the kitchen and through to the front hall. 'I won't go. Josh has already told me you're stressed about it.' And on she flounced, upstairs.

I gave chase, abandoning the carefully concocted vinaigrette to go with the lightly tossed green salad accompanying the carbonara.

'I'm not stressed,' I told her, mounting the stairs two at a time behind her. 'I just think that, in the first place, you might have discussed it with me, and in the second, it's inappropriate for you to disrupt your studies in this way.'

'That's not true.' She swung round furiously on the landing. We faced one another in her doorway. 'That's dishonest. You think we're abandoning you. That's the reason you don't want us to go. And that is so insulting, Mum.'

'Is it? Is it, really? Without any warning or previous discussion I hear through your brother that the three of you are planning to up sticks and live in a cushy pad in town together, and that's not desertion? And, what's more, *I'm* insulting *you*?'

'Yes, because you're twisting things. All I wanted to do was be nearer school during the week – I'd be back at weekends – and be with Dad and Josh, and you're like – oh, poor me, they're running away. It's all about you, Mum, isn't it?'

I was speechless. Stung. I felt it *was* about me. And I hadn't been told she was coming back at weekends, just in the holidays. But I was too incensed to be reasonable.

'No, it is never about me, Tabitha. It is always about what you or Joshua or your father want. No one gives me the slightest consideration or even consultation –'

'Because we knew you'd be upset!'

'Too right I'm upset!'

'But that's not right, Mum. Don't you see? You're the adult, you should be like – oh, I must look at it from the children's angle. What's best for them. This way they get to see both their parents, how brilliant.'

'But we had that here, with Dad in the Granary –'

'But that's horrid for Dad, don't you see? It's no life for him!'

No life for him, again. And I thought I'd been so magnanimous, so gracious, by letting him stay, giving up one of the holiday lets. Everyone said I was marvellous to have him in the garden. Marvellous, Ella. I'd believed it.

'Right. Well, then you must go, Tabitha, I can see that. I can *quite* see that. I mean, it's no life for *any* of you here, is it!' Why? Why did I always *do* that?

'You see!' she shrieked. '*That's* why I can't! *That's* why I'm fucking well staying, because you make it impossible for me to do anything else!'

325

And with that she slammed the door in my face. But it didn't end there. Oh, no, I saw to that. Saw to hammering on it with both fists and yelling about her ingratitude, then collaring Josh when he came home, citing him as the ring-leader. At this Tabitha's door flew open and she screamed down the stairs, face tear-stained, that it had nothing to *do* with him. And then it had degenerated into the most unattractive, unpalatable scene imaginable. Which, actually, we didn't do, the three of us, on the whole. Had lived together – up to now – in relative peace and harmony. Oh, there was the odd niggle and sharp rebuke, but, in general, I was rather smug. Had listened when other mothers complained of surly, unpleasant teenagers and flaming rows but privately thought that although Josh swore far too much, generally their behaviour was good. Particularly for children of a broken home. But, then, it wasn't entirely broken, I'd think, looking out of the window as Tabs, say, emerged from her father's house. I'd been clever about that. But had this ugly scene been bubbling under for some time and I hadn't known? Had they, in fact, been unhappy but treading on eggshells so as not to cause a row? I had occasionally tested the water, said things like: Well, at least Daddy's only across the way. No response, if I'm honest. I'd laughingly told them about a television sit-com, back in the day, called *My Wife Next Door*, about a couple who couldn't live together, but had found a modus vivendi as neighbours. How funny it had been. Not much laughter from my offspring.

Later that evening, I'd had the biggest row of all. The obvious one. When the children were firmly ensconced in their rooms, doors shut, texting each other furiously no doubt – 'Cow' 'God, she's unreasonable' – or much worse, I stormed across the yard. Banged on the Granary door.

'Come in!' Jovially. As if, perhaps, expecting the children.

In I flew. Sebastian's head turned from his armchair. To my surprise, Ottoline was with him, watching the television.

'Oh, hi, Ella.' She smiled. Sebastian said nothing.

'Ottoline,' I said, wrong-footed.

'Just popped across to watch *Frozen Planet* with Sebastian. We love it. It's the penguins tonight. Pull up a chair.'

'Um, no, thanks.'

'Hello, darling.' Mum's voice, from the shadows. Lying on the chaise in the corner, in those flaming dungarees again. She'd be chewing tobacco soon. Oh, it was all very cosy, wasn't it? How many evenings were spent thus, I wondered? And why not at my place?

'Sebastian, can I have a word?'

We all considered this. How, exactly? Were Ottoline and my mother to leave? Was Sebastian to get up from his easy chair and retire – there was no other room, it was open plan – with me outside? In the garden? In the dark?

He regarded me coldly. 'Can't it wait?'

'Not really.' I was out of control. 'It's about you taking the children to live in Oxford.'

There was a long silence. Ottoline and my mother gazed at me. I couldn't read their expressions. Finally Sebastian got to his feet and I saw something I'd never seen in his eyes before as he joined me outside and shut the door. Couldn't place it. He listened as I gave it both barrels, firing first from one hip, then the other, then probably upside down and through my legs. He didn't flinch. When he'd heard me out, heard all about the injustice, the impracticality, the treachery, he responded in the same way as Tabitha.

'Of course,' he said evenly. 'I completely understand. The children must stay with you. I shall tell them so.'

And with that he went back inside and shut the door. I stared at the old oak panels he'd closed in my face. Felt very empty. Listened to the hum of the television within, still flushed and breathless with the exertion of shouting at him. Wondered if I could hear a murmured exchange? But not Sebastian's voice. He wouldn't discuss it, I knew. Ottoline, neither. And Mum would hardly talk to herself. I crept away, back to my house and the empty sitting room, feeling shattered, bewildered and very alone.

That had been a week ago. Since then, true to his word, Sebastian had moved out, minus the children. A removal van had come, just a small one, the sort you drive yourself, but that surprised me in itself. Sebastian had never organized anything in his life without me doing it for him. I couldn't imagine him on the phone ordering it. That evening he and the children had packed all of his belongings – precious few – his chaise, a table, a few easy chairs, but, mostly, his pictures, into the back of it. I'd watched from the kitchen window, a huge lump in my throat. When he was in the yard putting his easel in, and the children were inside packing books into boxes, I'd gone out. Asked if he'd like to take some furniture from the house. It was as much his as mine and he had a whole house in Oxford to fill. He thanked me but said no, it was fine. He had enough to be getting on with and Josh had gone on the net and ordered a fridge and a washing machine from John Lewis. Oh, and a kitchen table. He thought he'd be fine. I nodded dumbly. Josh had helped.

A washing machine. Sebastian had never used one in his life, but then Tabitha would no doubt show him how. His invisible support mechanism. Neither of the children had mentioned anything of this to me.

So this was it, then, I thought, as Sebastian and I stood facing each other in the yard. The end of an eighteen-year-old marriage. It seemed to rocket past like a high-speed train, each carriage blurred but full, breathtaking in its intensity and ferocity, but in its love, too. I felt rocked as I was left there on the station. Faint. I believe I might have physically swayed with emotion as I stood before my tall, inscrutable, hooded-eyed husband, soon to be my ex-husband, with papers to sign, nisi to decree. I wondered if he felt the profundity of the moment, too, as he regarded me with that level stare of his. Something registered, I was sure, behind the eyes, before he brusquely turned away.

That was some days ago, as I say. Since then, the children and I had cohabited ostensibly as normal, but it had felt strained. Josh hadn't gone, which had surprised me. After all, I hadn't quibbled about him defecting. But I didn't like to mention it. Perhaps he'd decided to see the term out and go after Christmas? Perhaps he didn't like to leave Tabs alone with the mad woman? I didn't ask. We became polite with one another, the three of us. A desperate – after you – situation developed if we met each other on the threshold of the only bathroom in the house. Over-bright smiles were exchanged and it occurred to me I'd won something of a Pyrrhic victory. My house was full of the children I'd demanded, but their hearts were elsewhere. Everything I touched turned to loneliness. The more I tried to engage them at the gastronomically laden supper table, the more polite and uncomfortable they became. Their days had been good. Lessons had been OK. Yes, they'd done some sport. Hockey. No, they wouldn't have another piece of home-made blueberry cheesecake, thank you.

Historically Josh and I would watch the ten o'clock news together and then *Newsnight*, debating hotly throughout. (We both regarded the television as a two-way medium.) Josh mocked anything vaguely right wing or establishment, supporting all revolutionaries or minority groups. It forced me into a more reactionary position than was natural – although I noticed I'd got much more conservative as I got older – and although it could get quite heated, it was all fairly tongue-in-cheek and amicable. Those days were gone now, I thought, turning the television off at ten thirty before the local news and climbing the stairs to bed.

All of which had brought me to the car park at the Bunch of Grapes. No, no qualms at all, I thought, getting out of the car and slamming the door. I crossed the gravel drive briskly, head down, shoulder bag clamped to my side. As I breezed through the oak-beamed reception, bestowing a bright smile on the girl at the desk, I ignored my heart, which was pounding. Through the glazed door I saw Ludo, already in the bar, on a bum warmer by the fire and reading a newspaper. I raised my hand in greeting. I *had* had qualms, years of them, but any niggling residual ones melted away at the sight of him. Satisfyingly tall and blond – he still had all his hair, thank goodness – with no visible sign of a paunch, he was a good-looking man. It helped that I saw a couple of middle-aged women having lunch in the window turn to look as I approached, pausing in their spritzers, clearly interested to see who he was meeting. He stood up to greet me with a smile, tucking the paper away, and I'd like to think I saw appreciation on his face too, because of course I'd tried. My hair was not tangled and hastily tucked behind my ears as it was in the vegetable patch; it was freshly washed with a few highlights. And despite the feasts I'd been cooking for the children this week, I'd kept away from the calories myself – more through unhappiness than design, it has to be said. I still had a good way to go, but I knew that the black jeans and tunic-style top I'd bought for the occasion were at least not too adhesive.

We sat and had a drink, and then we took the only available table, which happened to be next to the two women in the window, and ordered lunch. I couldn't touch it but Ludo ate and it was fine. Really it was fine. I told him about the terrible week I'd had because I couldn't not. It all came tumbling out. And he was sweet about it. Made me feel better. He frowned over his soup and said he couldn't imagine what the children were doing suggesting they move out; he was sure they'd regretted it the moment they'd said it. Sebastian, too, must have known it was a bridge too far and that was why they'd stayed. It was an impulsive decision and they'd all had second thoughts. I think we both knew he was lying and that the children had had eons of time to think, and the only reason they were staying was not because they regretted it, but so as not to upset me. But the catch in my voice and the wild look in my eye said: Be my friend, Ludo. And, as ever, he was. I knew that later we might revisit this topic. And he might gently ask me to reconsider. To see the situation through the children's eyes, and also, even more gently, put his point of view as a father. But for the moment, seeing that I was raw, bright-eyed, gulping down my gin and fiddling with a bracelet which was making the psoriasis I was prone to occasionally flare up on my arm, he was kind. Sympathetic.

'It'll settle down, you'll see. And then some sort of compromise could be reached, perhaps. A few days here, a few there? Maybe half the week with each of you?'

'Yes,' I faltered miserably.

'And maybe, if you suggest that, they'll be generous. You know what it's like if you drop the reins with children. They generally respond well. Rush to meet you.'

I nodded into my lap, ashamed. He agreed with Sebastian. He reached under the table and covered my hand in my lap.

'I'm not taking the Fathers for Justice side,' he said softly. 'I'm just trying to think of them. As if it were Henrietta and Chloe.'

'Yes, I know,' I said in a low voice. 'It was just . . . such a terrible shock, Ludo.'

'Of course it was. And badly handled by everyone. But then . . . there's no easy way to handle these things,' he said sadly.

Normally I would have asked him then about his own children. About Eliza. But I realized I was party to something he wasn't. Something Lottie had told me. And I couldn't possibly be the one to tell Ludo. It did occur to me, though, that recently, when I asked whether he ever wondered if leading such separate lives could lead to Eliza conducting her own, he hadn't dismissed it out of hand. Had even grudgingly admitted the possibility; had alluded to her going to London to see some friend more than was strictly necessary. So perhaps he knew, after all.

One gin and tonic led to another. I managed to share the cheese and biscuits he was having after his steak, but that was it. The women beside us had finished their salad long ago but were lingering, gripped, as Lottie and I would be, too, I thought, in similar circumstances. Ludo occasionally put his hand on my knee and was holding my hand under the table again. I saw the one in the pink cashmere jumper lean forward and whisper something in her friend's ear. Her friend with the pearls widened her eyes in agreement and nodded. I didn't care. I knew they knew he wasn't my husband, but I didn't care. I'd turned my phone off, too. It would be just like my family to decide that this was the day they *did* need me. For Josh to ring and ask if I could take his rugby kit in – despite his artistic leanings he was startlingly fast on the wing. Or for Tabs to fall out with her best friend and decide only her mother's ear would do at lunchtime. Oh, they could all revert to type at the drop of a hat, as could I. Become the dropper of whatever I was doing and picker up of everything else.

'OK?' asked Ludo, as we drained our drinks.

I nodded, and in the avid and fairly open stare of the women – one of them was having a hot flush in all the excitement, going the colour of her cashmere – we gathered our belongings and retired. To where? I wondered wildly as we threaded our way through the crowded room. Upstairs already? Had he booked the room for the entire afternoon? The handle of my bag felt sweaty in my hand. What *was* a dirty weekend? Was it dirty all the time? Or just in patches?

'I thought we'd take a wander down by the river,' Ludo told me easily, as he held the bar door open for me. He paused at the coat stand in reception to retrieve an attractively battered corduroy jacket. 'Binfield's only a ten-minute walk away and there are some lovely bookshops there. We could browse around for a bit. Take in an art gallery or two.'

'Oh – heaven!' I agreed, relieved.

'And then – and this might not be your cup of tea – but there's this tiny little picture house at the far end of town. It shows old black-and-white movies. Things like *Brief Encounter* and *From Here to Eternity*. I thought we could snooze in front of one of those and then walk back under the stars. I've booked a table in the dining room for eight.'

'Oh, Ludo, perfect! Yes, that would be absolutely lovely.'

It really would, I thought, and I should do things like this more often, I determined as we went through reception. Except of course, obviously I should be doing it with Lottie, like the two women in the bar. Having a trip away from their husbands and children, no doubt. But my trip only varied in one tiny respect, I thought, slightly drunkenly, as we made a detour to deliver my bag from the car to the double bedroom upstairs. I gazed at the floral counterpane on the pretty four-poster. Only one respect. Other than that, I thought, going a bit boss-eyed as I sailed downstairs full of gin and bravado – I caught my heel in the rail of the stair carpet on the way down and had to steady myself on the banister – it was really exactly the same. Exactly the same.

Chapter Twenty-Two

The river walk was lovely. The little town of Binfield was lovely too, delightful at any time of year, but particularly this one. The mellow, treacle-coloured Warwickshire houses seemed to lend themselves to the bosky mists and secrecy of autumn with their dark, hooded windows and cheerful lamplight within. It was like stepping into a Dickens novel, I decided, as we gazed through mullioned windows at pricey antiques, mingling with other tourists. We went in and enquired about the pretty Georgian card table in the window, for all the world like a proper couple, and then giggled as we left, on being told it was £5,000.

'We'll take two, shall we?' murmured Ludo as we shut the door behind us, little bell tinkling.

'Crazy not to.'

On the pavement outside was a clutch of upmarket garden statues, amongst them an extraordinary pair of stone warthogs, at least six feet tall, destined, presumably, for a castle.

'Are you all right for these?' Ludo asked me casually, pausing to pick up the price tag.

'Well, you can never have too many, can you?' I replied breezily as I read it: £8,000. 'Especially when they're such a snip. Either side of the drawbridge, d'you think?'

'Oh, no, darling. I think we want them in the minstrel's gallery, where everyone can see them.'

We laughed and sailed on down the high street, arm in

arm. Yes, arm in arm. Quite brazen, really, but then Binfield was a good couple of hours away from home and I didn't know anyone smart enough to live here. Except . . . Shit. Wasn't that one of Tabitha's teachers? It wasn't, of course, but I dropped Ludo's arm hurriedly, nonetheless.

In the little bookshop we browsed happily and separately for a good ten minutes. It appeared to be empty, no staff even: a trusting community, clearly. I managed to read at least the first chapter of the new Jilly Cooper whilst Ludo got stuck into some serious horticulture in the gardening section in the adjoining room. From my vantage point round the corner I was also sneaking the odd surreptitious glance over the pages of my book at him, enjoying the fact he was unaware. Impossibly boyish, he was leaning aesthetically on the bookshelves as he read, one long, lean leg slightly cocked as he paused occasionally to rake a hand through his hair when it flopped into his eyes. Yum.

'Can I help you?' An attractive, middle-aged woman, who'd appeared, presumably from a back room or the loo, obviously thought he was good news too. Having not seen us come in together, she was advancing flirtatiously, giving Ludo a full-on, pussy-cat smile. 'Oh, that's frightfully good. It's his new one. But then I find Alan Titchmarsh is always terribly reliable, isn't he?' She licked lipstick from her teeth and batted her eyelids wantonly. 'A very reassuring man to have at one's bedside.'

'I believe he is.' Ludo smiled. I saw her bask in his twinkly glow. She straightened her tight sweater over her ample bosom.

'But if you want something a little more cerebral, which I'm sure you do –' flutter flutter – 'might I suggest Rose-mary Verey? She used to live around here, you know. Had a fabulous garden at Bibery.'

'Yes, yes, I did know. I did some work in her garden once.'

'Oh, *did* you?' She settled in, fascinated, leaning against the bookshelves beside him, folding her arms so her bust went up a bit. I saw her tuck her tummy in, too. 'You're a garden designer?'

'Well, I'm a gardener.' Ludo caught my eye over her head.

'I keep meaning to go. I've seen loads of pictures, of course, and one does just salivate. All those lilies and azaleas and the *colour* schemes. Is it divine?'

'It is,' he said, amused. 'Darling, are you nearly ready?'

'Just coming,' I said lightly. I snapped Jilly shut with a grin. 'I might get this, though.'

I took the book to the counter and, as I did, our assistant hastened behind it, flustered now. Blushing, she got very busy with the debit-card machine, giving it her undivided attention, plainly deeply embarrassed. She popped my book in a bag as quickly as she could and gave me back my card without meeting my eye.

'She salivates,' I told Ludo when we were safely out of the shop, 'not at Mrs Verey's garden, but at something else.'

He threw back his head and laughed, but he didn't deny it, and the exchange, I felt, had been interesting. It wasn't just me, then. Who found him so attractive. I mean, obviously I already knew that. Ginnie had told me often about how her friends employed him not only for his green fingers but for the colour he brought to their back gardens as

337

he leaned languidly on his hoe, tousled hair ruffling in the breeze, smiling amongst the hollyhocks as his employer approached with a cup of tea, lipstick freshly applied. But I'd never actually seen him in action. Not that he'd been in any sort of action just then; he'd simply been on the receiving end of a charm offensive. But he couldn't be immune to it, surely? Or perhaps he was? Perhaps, if one was devastatingly good-looking, one naturally assumed the whole world trooped up the garden path smiling and bearing home-made chocolate brownies. Doors opened, everyone was pleasant, that was the way the world turned. I relaxed my facial muscles, trying not to frown. Straightened my shoulders and pulled in my own tummy as we walked down the street.

'Penny for them?' he asked, smiling.

I shook my head, lifting the corners of my mouth. 'I was only thinking, I've just bought a book which I have every reason to believe will already be on Tabitha's bookshelf!'

He stopped. 'Take it back?'

'No, no,' I said gaily, striding on. 'I can always give it to Ginnie for Christmas.'

Back at the hotel we sipped tea in the cosy bar, and since the whole place was full of squashy sofas and roaring fires, I slipped off my shoes and curled up. After the bookshop we'd had a relaxing couple of hours in the old cinema – or picture house as it liked to call itself – on the edge of town. There we'd watched the sweetly pretty Celia Johnson have a heart-wrenching time of it with suave, debonair Trevor Howard. But it hadn't perhaps been the ideal film for us – because, of course, once they'd hopped on and off dozens of trains and exchanged feverish stares over endless cups of tea in the steamy railway café, sweetly pretty Celia goes back to her rather dull but innocent husband who utters something knowing like: 'You've been away a long time, darling. But I'm glad you're back.' Then the credits rolled. So, no, not ideal. We'd emerged pensive. Thinking about Doing The Right Thing. Duty first. Making a decent fist of it, as they did in the fifties. But then, I reasoned, as we walked quietly back to the hotel, my husband was neither dull nor innocent. He was tempestuous and unpredictable and he'd had an affair, for heaven's sake. With the saucy Isobel. And what's more, *he* was divorcing *me*. What would Celia think about that? Might she not be frogmarching Trevor out of the steamy café and down the road to the nearest B&B? Tossing her prim little hat into a suburban front garden as she went, mentally shimmying out of her girdle and telling Trevor, in clipped little staccato sentences, exactly what she planned to do with him when she got him inside? Of course she would.

As we sipped our Earl Grey in the bar, dusk settled without. The night crept up to the windows, shrouding from view the trees opposite, dulling the silver shimmer of the river in the distance. It occurred to me that what I really wanted to do was have a little lie-down, possibly take an aspirin, and then have a bath before getting dressed for the evening. But that was quite tricky, wasn't it? How could I take a bath with Ludo around? But then, it shouldn't be tricky. Because later on we'd be ... you know. But that would all be so much easier after a romantic dinner *à deux* and lashings of wine. Swilling with tea and with a slight hangover from the lunchtime gins was no good at all. Happily Ludo seemed alive to everything.

'Right,' he said, glancing at his watch and folding in half the *Telegraph* he'd been reading. He tucked it away and got to his feet. 'This is where I love you and leave you, I'm afraid.'

I looked up, astonished.

'Didn't I say? I've got a prospective client round the corner. She wants me to talk through the drawings I've done for a knot garden with her husband when he gets home from work. Which will be,' he shot up his sleeve to reveal his watch, 'about now. I won't be gone long, my love, but it'll give you a chance to have a leisurely soak. Maybe even forty winks?'

'Oh,' I said, relieved. And, actually, it did ring a big bell. 'Do you know, I think you *did* say, but so much has been going on . . . Oh, well, that's great.' It was. I gave a ravishing smile, forgetting about the headache. 'I'll see you later, then. Whereabouts are they?'

'Oh, walkers. Just at the other end of the high street and then over the bridge. I'll see you in about an hour or so.'

He dug in his pocket and handed me the key to the room. Then, after bestowing one of his lovely smiles, he was gone.

As I watched him duck his head under the low door, I breathed deeply and easily, cosy and happy now. I'd finish my tea, I determined, and go straight up. I wiggled my toes happily under my cushion. Yes, a nice long bubble bath with some hotel smellies, and then I'd change into that rather clever blue silk dress I'd found in Coast. Clever in that it was definitely for my age, but not mumsy: was slightly edgy, actually, in its Chinese styling, the frogging down the front. A little bit like Mrs Middleton's coat at the wedding: a clever twist on a classic, although obviously not

340

in a mother-of-the-bride sort of way. More of a – well, dinner-in-a-candlelit-restaurant-with-an-attractive-man sort of way. Silky hold-ups instead of tights – which were great so long as you got the sticky bit at the top at the right tension. Too tight and circulation would be cut off and you could pass out, nose-diving the soup; too loose and within a few strides they were round your ankles, like Nora Batty's. I'd done both, to greater or lesser degree.

The Nora Batty occasion had been a scary dinner party at Ginnie's with all her smart friends. Sebastian, glowering and drunk, had insulted the woman next to him, saying that if all she did was shop and play tennis she was a parasite on society, all of which I could hear down my end of the table. Out of nerves, I'd proceeded to get disastrously pissed myself. I'd stumbled to the loo mid-pudding, not knowing my hold-ups were floating round my shoes. When I got back, amid concerned stares, I'd needed to blow my nose – it always runs when I'm plastered. Plunging my hand into my jacket pocket for a hanky, I'd found an egg. Naturally it smashed, and when I withdrew my eggy hand I wiped the goo and shell on my napkin, which the man next to me had seen and found startling.

'I'm her thister,' I told him in slurred tones, as if that explained everything, including collecting an egg from the hen house in a smart jacket, the first coat to come to hand on a kitchen chair.

'Ah.' He nodded nervously and turned to his other neighbour, clearly of the opinion I'd been let out for the day and would be driven back to the Home for the Bewildered later.

The next day, when I'd apologized to Ginnie, she'd been furious. She said I'd looked a sight as I'd gone to the loo in trailing underwear, and when I explained, she said no one minded being insulted by Sebastian; they expected it. It was all part of the fun and the glamour of meeting a famous artist. It was true, the women had swarmed around Sebastian as we'd arrived and he'd glowered back, in his Heathcliff way, to yet more fawning. But for *me* to get so pissed . . . Well, she said, I'd really let the side down. I recalled the flaming row Sebastian and I had had on the way home from that party. Sebastian insisting on driving, weaving down the lanes. Me, shrieking about how he played shamelessly on his creative credentials, flirting and insulting people. 'Well, which is it?' he'd snapped. 'Flirting or insulting?' And I couldn't decide, befuddled with drink and constantly escaping hosiery, which I began to rip off furiously in the car. Weirdly, we'd made love that night when we got home. Drunk and unhappy, desperate for something from each other. Anything. It wasn't long after that that Isobel appeared on the scene. I took a deep breath. I didn't want to think about any of this now. About the passionate rows and lovemaking with my husband, even whilst he was with Isobel. Like a child claiming it was *my* turn. I shut my eyes in self-disgust.

When I opened them, it was to see cars beginning to arrive in the pub forecourt. My vantage point on the sofa in the window gave me a bird's-eye view as they swung, one after another, in a string almost, onto the gravel sweep. They were a little early for dinner, I thought, but evening drinks, perhaps. This place certainly seemed to do a good trade. I watched as the headlights – more lamps than lights, actually: huge, round, old-fashioned things – dimmed slowly before going out. As people clambered out of doors that seemed to open the wrong way I could see that they were old. The cars, not the people. Vintage, was perhaps the word I was scrambling for. Like the ones in *The Great Race* but smaller.

'Oh, I see they made it, then.' A plump, rosy-faced waitress gazed over my head out of the window as she bent to collect my empty teapot, cup and saucer.

'Sorry?'

'Them old cars. They have a rally at the farm down the road once a month, and dinner here the night before. Sometimes one gets stuck along the way.' She chuckled. 'Many a time my Frank's had to get his tractor and pull 'em out. Get 'em here in time for supper.'

'Ah.'

Once a month. Right. As the pub door opened, heralding a blast of cold air and then the first clutch of motorists, one or two pennies began to drop. Quietly at first, but slightly disconcertingly nonetheless. Like the one which reminded me how I'd originally heard about this place. Where I'd picked up the brochure. As the second couple came through the door, another penny clattered down, slightly more loudly. I recognized them instantly, of course I did. They lived across the road from my parents in Buckinghamshire. I recognized the dog, first, actually. A huge great ginger thing, straining on a lead. Damn. They might not recognize me, though, I thought, quickly shrinking down in the sofa and pulling my fringe over my eyes. I reached for Ludo's *Telegraph* and put my nose in it. It was ages since I'd seen them and, without the dog, I'm not sure I'd know them either. After all, I glimpsed them only on the occasional visit home. Saw them in church on Christmas Day, or at Boxing Day drinks at that nice lady Peggy's. Out of context, it was unlikely they'd know me. Still with my head in the paper I found my shoes, wiggling my feet into them. When they'd turned to the bar for a drink, I'd slip away upstairs. It would be the work of a moment. I watched out of the corner of my eye.

She, the wife, looked harassed and windswept. She unwound a scarf from her dark curls, berating her husband, a rather attractive man with hair swept back like an ocean wave, for *always* having to have the roof down, *whatever* the weather. In flaming October, for heaven's sake!

'I feel as if I've been to Thorpe Park dressed as Isadora Duncan,' she wailed, but she was sweet to the waitress. My comely lady. Said how lovely it was to see her again, and how beautifully *warm* it was in here. And what a blessed relief to *be* here. One simply never knew with those wretched cars, whether they'd make it or not. She smiled broadly, thanking heavens for such a tolerant hotel that took dogs. There were so *few* these days, and the poor thing was simply no good at being left. Even with a house-sitter she'd eat the curtains, out of misery, until they got back. And my waitress beamed back, assuring her it was a pleasure to have the dog here, and how was the beauty, anyway? She bent to stroke her. Leila, wasn't it?

Jennie, as I now remember she was called, smiled and said yes, it *was* Leila and she was as naughty as ever. But she had calmed down a *bit* since she'd had puppies.

'We've got her son here, too, I'm afraid, and he is such a pickle. Hopefully he'll be on his best behaviour. He's coming in another car.' She turned to her husband. 'Dan, we must look out for Angus; that car he's in is worse than ours. I do hope he's OK, I thought they were right behind us.'

I went a bit cold. Let Angus be the dog.

'He'll be fine, love,' he soothed. 'He's been in one

before.' He headed to the bar, fishing out a tenner, but his wife looked fussed as she stared out of the window.

'Look, it's still got its lights on.' She reached out for her husband's arm. 'The car that pulled up literally just after us. That'll be him. Do go and rescue him, Dan. You know how the door sticks when you try to get out. They'll be having a hell of a tussle.'

As Dan agreed good-naturedly and shuffled towards the door, I prayed. Please God, let Angus be the son of Leila. Or, if not a dog, a friend of Dan's. A common enough name, surely? Yes, a friend of Dan's, whom he'd allowed to drive his car, as a treat. Chap from schooldays, perhaps, or the pub, or . . . oh, dear God.

The door opened before Dan got to it, and the wind caught it so that it banged back hard against the wall. Another blast of cold air rippled newspapers and napkins, sending the latter fluttering up in the breeze. Into the bar, ruddy and windswept, spluttering and roaring about how that had been the best fun he'd had in bloody years, bloody marvellous, in fact, his hair – what there was of it – standing on end, strode my father.

Chapter Twenty-Three

'That thing's got no ruddy door handles!' he roared, beaming around as he stood on the threshold, a scarlet-spotted hanky billowing wantonly from the top pocket of his tweed jacket. 'At least none that I recognize, anyway. Been trying to get out of it for five minutes!'

'Oh, Angus, I'm so sorry.' Jennie hastened across to greet him. 'They're silly little things, like hair pins. I can never get out unless someone helps me, but I was so desperate to get Leila out of the boot, I'm afraid we didn't wait. Dan, you are hopeless – I told you it was him.' She scolded her husband as he shrugged apologetically.

All this, I hasten to add, was happening firmly off stage as far as I was concerned. I took the odd peep, but, in the main, my face was covered by the *Daily Telegraph* crossword puzzle, two-thirds of which had been filled in by Ludo, and which I kept firmly pressed to my nose. My heart was pounding as I eyeballed one across. Bolt from the blue, he'd written. How apposite. And how stupid of me to suggest this place, which, of course, I'd first heard about when I went to see Dad: picked up the brochure from his coffee table.

'Well, he's here now,' soothed Dan. 'And I've seen the Hendersons and the Fields; they've gone up to see their rooms. And Peggy and Peter are on their way.'

'Peggy and Peter are here,' a gravely female voice assured

him, one that I recognized as belonging to a delightfully colourful lady, a widow, who lived down the road from my parents.

'That Humber's not as quick as your Morgan, though, Dan,' said a male voice I didn't recognize. 'I did my best, had my foot firmly on the floor, but I'm more used to getting power out of a horse than a carburettor.'

'That'll teach you to abandon your horse box to impress your lady friend!' boomed my father. 'Should have stuck to what you know, Peter!'

'Oh, I wouldn't want to show you all up,' said the male voice easily. 'That old lorry has got more age than most of these souped-up vehicles put together. And, I'll have you know, Peggy is more than just my lady friend these days. In a very rash moment last weekend she agreed to become my wife.'

Such ecstatic whooping and wild congratulating greeted this remark that I wondered if this was my moment? To escape? Surely the diversion caused by so much backslapping and cheering and clustering would enable me to creep, unnoticed, from the room? As the flurry of delighted good wishes continued I started my crawl around the room, sticking firmly to the edges. It was something of a steeplechase, however, as there were various stools and tables to negotiate, but I pressed on, newspaper to nose, making silent headway. As I skirted the throng at the bar I recognized Jennie's voice saying: 'Oh, Peggy, how *marvellous*. I am so thrilled for you both. And Peter, does Poppy know?' She was assured that Poppy did know, and was delighted, and had sent huge congratulations and masses of love from Italy.

'Don't tell me you'll live at Peter's place!' roared my father, who only has one volume. 'You'll be all right for whisky but not much else!'

Shrieks of mirth greeted this and Peter assured him good-naturedly that no, they'd be based at Peggy's, but his horses would remain at his yard. I, meanwhile, had the door in my sights. Corks were popping as champagne was ordered and I was just on the point of sliding out, literally almost home and dry, when the comely waitress popped her head round my newspaper.

'Everything all right, love?' she looked concerned.

'Yes, thanks,' I whispered, scared. Please go.

'Only, you went ever so pale a moment ago and I thought maybe you wasn't feeling well. Found a good article, have you?'

'Sorry?'

'In the paper?'

'Oh.' I lowered it an inch from my nose. 'Um, yes.'

'What's gripping you, then, love?'

'It's . . . about horses.' It had been the first thing to spring to mind on account of the conversation at the bar.

'Oh, horses! Lovely. Fond of them, are you?'

Shh, I implored her silently, but too late. Her voice had reached the recently engaged man and struck a chord, as shared enthusiasms often do. As this small, dapper-looking, older chap overheard, he smiled at me. My upbringing let me down. It was such a charming smile that I couldn't immediately flick the newspaper up again so, instead, I flicked the briefest of smiles back. The paper shot up, but too late. My father, taller by a head than the dapper man, and standing directly behind him, had caught it and was bearing down.

'Darling!' he boomed in astonishment as I turned to stone at the door. 'Good heavens! What on earth are you doing here?' He gave me a huge bear hug, delighted to see me.

'I'm, um – just here with a friend,' I faltered, when I'd finally located my vocal chords. Unwrapped them from round my tonsils.

'A friend? Oh, splendid. Lottie?' He gazed around the room expectantly. 'Or Ottoline, perhaps? Not Ginnie, I hope. She's frightfully cross with me at the moment! Ha!'

'No it's . . . not Ginnie.'

'Lottie, then, eh? Excellent! I say, cat got your tongue? Well, good for you, darling, you girls should get away more often. Do you good to get out of the sticks and away from all that mud. And there's masses to see in this little town. Where is she, love?'

'I'm . . . not sure.' The truth.

'Stuck in the lavatory, no doubt, like the three old ladies!' He nudged me hard in the ribs and roared. 'Seems to me you girls are never out of the lavatory! Beats me what you do in there. Applying your lippy, no doubt. Shame in a way it's not Ottoline, because did I tell you Peggy was at school with her? No?'

I confessed I didn't know that.

'Years ago – well, obviously years ago – but at the same convent. You remember Peggy, don't you? From Boxing Day shindigs and what have you. And Jennie and Dan from across the road? I say, Jennie –' And suddenly I was being propelled across the room to the bar, where my father insisted on introducing me to absolutely everybody in his vintage-car-rally group, something Dan had roped him into, he explained. Even lent him a car, which was super fun. 'My daughter, Ella. She's here with a friend. Amazing coincidence, but then it is the best place for miles around, so perhaps not? You've been before, darling? No? Oh, well, you're in for a treat, then! The chef is quite magnificent. You've booked into the dining room, I hope? Best tucker in the county! Go for the sole; he cooks it to perfection. My daughter!' he kept roaring, pleased as punch. 'Have you met Ella? My daughter!'

'Oh, married to the famous painter?' someone asked with interest and I had to agree I was.

'Sebastian Montclair,' the woman informed a friend beside her: an elegant, older lady with a purple velvet coat, bright eyes and high cheekbones, who I knew to be Peggy. She gave me a very beady look but Jennie, now with two straining dogs on leashes since Dan had brought another in from his car, had turned to me with real interest.

'Oh, but – hang on, you must be Hugo's aunt,' she said.

'Yes, that's right,' I said, determined to be polite but then to make my excuses and leave forthwith. My father, having had the pleasure of introducing me to all his friends, happily seemed to have forgotten about Lottie, and, seeing that Jennie had fallen on me, was pleased to break away from the women and into a more convivial male group at the bar, handing his champagne back to the barman and saying he'd prefer a gin and French, actually, if that wasn't too much bother.

'How is his mother, do you know?'

I gazed into Jennie's concerned eyes, all at sea. Suddenly I came to. 'Ginnie? She's fine.'

'Oh, good! Only I've been so worried about her.'

I realized she was referring to Hugo being ill. 'No, no,

she really *is* fine now,' I told her more earnestly. 'I mean, of course she's been terribly worried about Hugo, but she's pleased he's on the mend. She just wants him to get better and be happy, so she's not fussed about the university thing any more.'

'Oh, I am *so* pleased. Oh, I can't tell you what a relief that is.' Her hand went to her heart and her face relaxed visibly. 'Only, she finds it hard to speak to us, sometimes. For obvious reasons,' she added quickly.

'Obvious?'

'Well, you know Hugo's living with us?'

'I didn't,' I said, surprised. 'You mean at weekends? I mean, he's mostly at Cambridge, surely?' My mouth was forming the words, but in my head I was elsewhere. I was rapidly changing hotels. There must be another round here. This town was heaving with tourists, bound to be loads. I needed to text Ludo too, tell him not to return. Then I'd check out. Rather a lot to do, one way and another.

'Well, no, not now.' Jennie frowned. 'I thought you said his mother knew? Was fine about it?'

'Sorry?'

'Didn't you know? He's chucked the whole thing in.'

'Oh! But – but I thought he was just retaking the first year?'

'He was, and he started to do that, but still hated it. Hated the pressure. He's living with us now, has been for a bit. And I know how *I'd* feel about that, as a parent, and how your sister must feel – if she even knows! And I do *try* to encourage him to tell his parents. I tell him to take Frankie back with him if he needs moral support, tell them what's happened, or even just ring them. He doesn't have to do it face to face, but he just won't. And obviously I don't like to push too hard after all he's been through.' She looked desperately concerned.

'Gosh. No, I didn't know that.' Poor Ginnie. I was pretty sure she didn't, either. I'd only recently had that conversation with her.

'He'll come round,' said Peggy calmly, puffing on an electric cigarette. The end glowed red. 'He just needs to be given time. Let him go at his own pace and he'll slowly do a U-turn, you'll see. And maybe he's thinking of them? Maybe he doesn't want to give his parents a shock?'

'He shaved his head last week,' Jennie explained. 'And he's got a tattoo now. Right here. A dragon.' She pointed to the side of her neck.

'Oh!'

'Well, no, I wasn't thinking of that,' said Peggy. 'It's more – the whole sea change within him. What he's doing.'

'He's working at the livery yard,' Jennie told me. 'Peggy's fiancé's place, Peter Mortimer. Hugo's an excellent rider – well, of course you'll know that – and Peter's getting too old to fall off fresh young hunters.'

'*I* don't want him falling off fresh young hunters!' laughed Peggy. 'Although I still love him to ride. But it's a young man's game and Peter and I want to travel a bit. Go out and stay with his daughter in Italy, get some sun. Hugo wants to take over the yard.'

'Take over the yard!' I stared at her. 'But . . . he's so young.'

'I know!' wailed Jennie. 'And riding flipping horses for a living, for heaven's sake, instead of doing a Classics degree! What a waste!'

'But if it's what he wants to do,' said Peggy firmly. 'If it's helping. And, as I say, he might change his mind later.'

'But it'll be too late!' Jennie cried.

'It's never too late,' said Peggy with feeling. But I had a hunch she wasn't talking about university.

'Won't they be appalled?' Jennie asked anxiously. 'His parents? I know I would be.'

'They won't be thrilled,' I admitted nervously. 'Although, in a funny sort of way . . .' I gave it some thought. 'The thing is, Hugo's been brought up with horses. So at least it's a world Ginnie knows. Hunting and all that sort of thing. Her children have been immersed in it since they were tiny. I mean, it'll be a terrible shock to hear he's dropped out, but . . .'

'Perhaps he hasn't,' said Peggy. 'Perhaps he's just playing on a different field.'

What was it Ginnie had once said? That of both her children, Hugo was the one who had a special relationship with horses, even though it was Araminta who won the cups?

'And horses are great healers,' said Peter, the twinkly-eyed man, who'd appeared at Peggy's side. 'If he's not been well, it's the best thing he could do. He's a clever boy and he may well go back into the mainstream eventually, but at the moment this is helping him. He's spent a lot of time at my yard and I've seen him around the horses. They respond to his pain. They're the most sensitive creatures on earth and he's one of the most sensitive human beings. You'll laugh, but they talk to him. He's on the mend already, you mark my words.'

A mental vision of Hugo, Ginnie's golden boy, head shaved now, tattoo creeping up his neck, leaning over a stable door as a noble thoroughbred blew sympathetically into his hand, sprang to mind. It brought tears to my eyes.

'And there's a certain amount of brainpower involved in running the yard, too; I could never get it right. If he's got the nous he'll make a profit rather than a loss, and then hopefully he and Frankie can knock the house down and build another. Build a proper life for themselves. Oh, dear, have I said too much?' He saw my startled face.

'They wanted to get married,' Jennie told me quickly. 'So silly. Of course they're much too young and it's all too soon, and we've told them so. Told them to wait a couple of years, at least, but you know what the young are like. Impetuous. Think they know everything. Anyway, we've talked them out of it for the moment. I'm quite sure he hasn't mentioned *that* to his parents. And, of course, a bit of me just wants to ring her up and *talk* to her, but Frankie says no, and Hugo *really* says no. Looks horrified. And I've heard – well, I've heard stories . . .' She trailed off, embarrassed.

Heard stories of my sister's hauteur, her condescension, her arrogance. Rudeness as well, perhaps. But Ginnie had changed too. Hugo had seen to that.

'I'll ring her,' I told her. 'Or go and see her. But let me talk to her first. Break the various bits of news gently. Pave the way. And then I'll let you know. I'm sure it would be a good idea for you to meet, though. Have lunch or something.'

Jennie's face cleared as if a whole bank of black cloud had lifted. 'Oh, *would* you?' she said eagerly, gripping my arm. 'I'd be so grateful. I – well, I feel like I've stolen her child or something, like some ghastly kidnapper, and I know how *I'd* feel if someone took over Frankie. God, I'd be livid. She's my stepdaughter, by the way, but no different to my own. And so often my hand has hovered over the phone but I've stopped, thinking the last time we spoke we almost had an argument, when I suggested the psychiatrist was doing more harm than good, and she said it was none of my business and, anyway, her best friend saw him once a week and he was absolutely marvellous. Very highly regarded.' She swallowed as she recalled. 'But if you *could* have a word. Let her know I'm naturally as appalled as she is at the idea of them getting married, can't think of anything more silly, then maybe she won't think we're – I don't know – thrilled to bits to have bagged him. Which is what I suspect she thinks. They're determined to live together, though – at our place obviously, there's nowhere else – and there's not much I can do about that. And I don't want to make *too* much of a song and dance in case they run off to some ghastly registry office or something. Oh, I *would* so love to talk to her – here.' She whipped out her phone and I found mine and, together, we set about swapping numbers.

It was at that moment that Ludo, looking rather cross and wind-blown, came striding back into the bar, a good forty-five minutes earlier than I was expecting him. Our eyes collided in surprise across the crowded room and he looked more than a little taken aback to see me surrounded by a group of convivial new friends, apparently exchanging phone numbers. More than anything, though, he looked harassed and in a hurry.

'Forgot the bloody drawings!' he mouthed across their heads, pointing to the sofa where we'd recently been sitting and where, indeed, a blue folder was tucked down the side.

'Oh!' I felt my colour rise as I made to move round the group towards him; but the bar was crowded and it wasn't that easy. Jennie looked surprised as I left but it was my father's eyes which were of more concern. Very much attracted by developments and having seen our exchange, he was crossing to intercept me.

'You didn't tell me it was a foursome, Ella,' he boomed. 'That must be Lottie's husband, no? Ferreting about in the sofa?' Before I could stop him he was bearing down on Ludo, hand outstretched, all tweedy and avuncular. 'I say, I was just saying to Ella, I didn't know it was a foursome! You'll be the husband, no?'

Ludo turned from retrieving the folder. He looked startled to see this red-faced, cheery gent advancing with a beaming smile. He glanced nervously at me but could do little more than shake the hand that was being proffered.

'Husband . . . ?'

'Um, Ludo, this is my father,' I said, finally muscling through the scrum, face flaming.

'Oh!' Ludo reddened dramatically too.

'Angus Jardine, dear boy,' said my dad, pumping away at his hand. 'I say, is Sebastian about too, then?' He turned to me. 'Didn't know that was the state of play these days? But, good, why not! Have another go, that's what I say. These things need sticking at; it's all about perseverance. I should know – ha! Children all well?' He'd turned back to Ludo now, rocking back on his heels, hands deep in his trouser pockets, churning loose change. 'Got two, haven't you?'

'Um, yes,' Ludo admitted, on slightly firmer ground now.

Dad nudged me in the ribs. 'Impressed, eh, love? Oh, I keep abreast of these things. I might look like an old buffer but I do listen occasionally. Left the little devils at home, I suppose? You wouldn't want them tearing around a smart place like this, would you? Or are they a bit more grown-up these days?'

'They're – fifteen and seventeen,' Ludo said, bemused.

'As much as that, eh?' Dad's eyes widened. 'Golly, doesn't time fly! I seem to remember it wasn't long ago they were still in short pants. Well, you certainly wouldn't want them with you now, would you? Ruddy teenagers, they'd be running up an expensive bar bill and putting it all on your tab! But what have you done with the wife, that's what I'd like to know? Not still on the throne, surely!' He roared with laughter.

'My . . . my wife?'

'Yes, Ella said she was in the lavatory. Powdering her nose.'

Ludo looked aghast. He gazed at me, ashen. 'My wife is in the lavatory?'

'No – no, she's not. She – she's gone up to her room,' I said wildly.

'My *wife* has?' All the blood had left Ludo's face. But I couldn't help him. Couldn't help him at all. Not yet.

'Thought a little lie-down before dinner would do the trick, eh?' Dad nudged Ludo, who was so shocked at the thought of his wife being upstairs he nearly fell over. 'Well, better before dinner than after, laddie. You haven't come all this way and shelled out good money to have her fall asleep on you tonight, have you? That really would put the kibosh on the weekend!' He rocked with laughter. Then puckered his brow thoughtfully. 'Can't remember what it is you do, Ludo. Knitting machines, last I heard, I think. Still plugging away at that, are you? Making baby bonnets? Bootees and what have you?'

'I'm a – a landscape gardener.' Ludo said, terrified. He was inching towards the door, folder under his arm, giving me desperate looks. I was trying to give him reassuring ones back, ones that said clearly: Your Wife Is Not In The Building, but it was hard, given that I had only body language at my disposal, and was pretty wild-eyed and terrified myself.

'Ah!' Dad's eyebrows shot up. 'Gardening, is it, now? Well, why not, why not? You always were a man for a swift career change. Modelled for a bit, didn't you? Still do, I thought Ella said. Long johns on the back of the *Sunday Express* and what have you. Striking a pose in a posing pouch? Ha! This the sort of thing?' My father adopted a Mr Atlas pose, fists together, elbows at angles, muscles clenched. Ludo gazed at him, dumbstruck.

'The – the thermal-underwear ads you once did, remember?' I breathed, begging him with my eyes. 'Years ago? For the newspapers?'

Ludo looked horrified.

'Remember?' I implored him with my eyes.

'Oh! Um . . . yes. Thermals,' Ludo agreed dumbly, his eyes huge.

'Not much of a shelf life in modelling, though, I imagine? I mean, as a career?' hazarded Dad, dropping the pose and picking up his drink again. He leaned on the wall and folded his arms, really settling in to get to the bottom of this modelling lark. Here for the duration. 'All right for a few years, but there's always some young stud coming up behind you, eh? Well, not literally, one hopes! Ha!' He snorted with mirth at his own joke. 'Although, I dare say, in that world you have to keep your back to the wall at all times!' He slapped his thigh and nudged Ludo again, who, this time, really did topple.

'Y-yes – I-I mean . . . no,' Ludo faltered, desperate with confusion as he righted himself.

'So it's gardening now, is it?' Dad gulped his gin and French. 'Well, good, that's good. There's always going to be a demand for that, and, I must say, it's a great deal healthier to be out in the fresh air rather than flouncing around in your shreddies. To tell you the truth, I wouldn't mind getting someone to look at the old herbaceous borders myself. They took a hell of a battering in those storms. I say – you haven't even got a drink, dear boy, what can I get you?'

'N-no, I won't, thank you. I have to go.'

'Yes, he has to go,' I echoed faintly.

'Back to the wife, eh? See how the land lies up there. Not a bloody headache, I hope. That's all you need! I say, why not give her a call and see if she fancies a glass of champagne? That'll set her up for the evening. Ella, you give her a call, see if she'll come down for a sherbet. I'd love to see her. Still sticking pins in people, is she?' He swung abruptly back to Ludo.

Ludo blanched. 'P-pins?'

'Yes, I thought Lottie was into all that mumbo-jumbo?'

'Lottie?'

'Your wife,' I told him, wide-eyed. Quietly praying. Ludo stared back at me. We communed silently. There was long silence. Endless, it seemed. Finally he spoke.

'Oh! Yes! Lottie. Yes, she is . . . still sticking pins in people.' He licked his lips. And such was his relief that his real wife wasn't in the lavatory, or even upstairs, and that he was, in fact, married to Lottie, he became verbose. 'And of course it's not all mumbo-jumbo, you know. Witchcraft goes back centuries.'

Dad boggled. There was a startled silence.

'Not those sorts of pins,' I spluttered. 'He means acupuncture. Lottie's acupuncture!'

'I say, old boy, I knew she was a bit alternative,' Dad murmured doubtfully, 'but witchcraft? Bit rum. I'd nip that in the bud, if I were you. Leave that to Johnny foreigner. The voodoo boys might know what they're about, but you don't want to be messing around with all that funny business.'

'No – no, quite,' Ludo said hurriedly. 'I – I meant acupuncture. Forgot she did that. No, not forgot, obviously. How could I forget? I just – just call it witchcraft sometimes. To – to, you know –'

'Tweak her up?' Dad's face cleared in a jiffy. He looked delighted. 'I say, splendid! Couldn't have put it better myself! Load of old tommyrot, eh?' He clapped Ludo enthusiastically on the back. 'First class! Witchcraft – ha! You and I are going to get on famously. Let me get you a drink.' He tried to frogmarch him to the bar.

'No – really, thanks awfully, but I must go.' Ludo hastened door-wards. 'I've got a client who's waiting to see my drawings for their garden and I'm terribly late as it is. It was lovely to meet you, Mr Jardine.'

'You, too. You, too. Witchcraft! Capital!'

And leaving my father gazing delightedly after him, Ludo fled. Dad rocked back on his heels. Thrust his hands in his pockets and jingled his change some more.

'Nice chap, that,' he told me reflectively. 'Lottie's husband. Don't think I've met him before. Bit tongue-tied occasionally, but a good sort.'

'Yes,' I breathed. 'He is. And um, no. No, you haven't met him. I'll – I'll be back in a mo, Dad. I forgot to tell him what time we're having dinner. Back in a jiffy.'

And feeling as if my nerves had been scrubbed to a glaring sheen with a Brillo Pad and then hung out to dry, I left the bar, hastened through reception, and bolted after Ludo.

Chapter Twenty-Four

Ludo was already hotfooting it down the road, head bent against the drizzle that was accompanying the wind, folder tucked under his arm, as I ran after him. 'Ludo! *Ludo!*'

He swung round halfway down the street: face cross, hair wet. He waited for me to catch up. 'What the hell was all that about?' he demanded as I reached him.

'Ludo – I couldn't help it!' I gasped, keeping pace as he turned and hurried on. 'He just arrived, with all his neighbours, vintage-car enthusiasts. So *stupid* of me not to think! It's where I first heard about this place. It's a regular haunt of theirs apparently, but I couldn't say: I'm here with my lover, could I?'

'No, of *course* not.' He shot me a horrified look. 'But all that Lottie's husband business and the underwear modelling. I don't know, Ella. I hate lying.'

'So do I!' I squealed angrily. I pulled him to a halt in the street by his arm. He turned round and we stood regarding each other, the rain soaking our faces. 'So do I, Ludo, but I had to think of something, didn't I? Don't you see?'

'Yes, of course, my love, of course you did. I'm sorry. Didn't mean to snap.'

'And we *are* lying, anyway. At least – you are, to Eliza.' I wasn't, actually. Would tell Sebastian if he asked. Although maybe not the children.

'Yes – yes, I know,' he said quickly, clearly not relishing being reminded. He hastened on again and once more

I kept up, but it occurred to me we were in a bit of a pickle here, and he was still very keen to keep his business appointment. But men were like that, weren't they? Work came first and women were . . . what, a distraction? No. That was uncharitable.

'We'll change hotels,' I was telling him now as I leaped a puddle at speed. I didn't quite make it to the other side and one foot got soaked. 'I'll go to the car and ring a few places.'

He stopped abruptly. 'Do you really think that's necessary?'

I blinked at him. 'Ludo, if you think for one moment I'm conducting a steamy affair with my father down the corridor. Christ – he could be in the next room or something!'

The prospect patently alarmed Ludo. He rapidly capitulated.

'Yes, yes, of course. I do see.' He made tracks again. 'But it's such a bore, isn't it?' he said, almost petulantly. 'It was so cosy there. At the Bunch of Grapes.'

Was it my imagination, or was this my fault? For running into my father in the bar? I kept my temper, because perhaps it was.

'No, no, it'll be no trouble,' I soothed, as I'd soothed countless times in countless situations over the years. Children, husband, family. I sped on beside him. Dodged round a couple coming arm in arm towards us. 'I'll find a really nice little place in the centre of town. The Crown, perhaps. I hear it's good. Or what about the – Ludo, could you please slow down for a moment! You're late already, so please just give me two minutes of your time!'

He halted immediately. 'Sorry. So sorry, darling.' He opened his arms and pulled me hard against him, right there in the middle of the street. Our hearts pounded fast together. My feet were sopping wet because I'd got the wrong shoes on, and Ludo wrapped his arms round me tightly and lifted my heels off the ground. 'I'm really sorry. I'm being foul and it is absolutely not your fault,' he whispered into my hair. 'I'm just disappointed. Do you want me to cancel this appointment?' He stood back and whipped his phone out of his pocket. 'Find a place with you?'

'No, no,' I said at once, immediately placated. 'I can do it, I promise. I'll arrange it all and let you know where we are. Honestly, it's not a problem.' We kissed then, rather fiercely, on the lips. In the rain. A bit like in a Richard Curtis movie. Eyes shut, wet through, not caring. Energized. I wondered if I looked like Julia Roberts? Probably not. It was the first time we'd ever kissed like that, though, and the passion surprised both of us. We parted, panting. His eyes were on fire and I had an idea mine were too.

'See you later,' I said in a whisper.

As I turned and bolted back up the high street I was aware that he was watching me, appointment momentarily forgotten.

Despite my protestations to the contrary, though, finding a hotel was a bit of a problem, after all. In fact, it was downright impossible. I sat in the car in the car park, sopping wet, ringing every establishment in town. But it was very short notice and there were a lot of tourists in Binfield, all jockeying for rooms. I put the phone down on my last hope, the Swan, who'd almost laughed at me. Everywhere was full. Even the neighbouring villages. No room at the inn. Perhaps we should just drive on, go north: try somewhere further afield? Take our chances? I suspected it would be some seedy dive, though, some ghastly motel.

Which wasn't what I wanted at all. Home, then? I swallowed a great lump of disappointment, opened the car door and limped damply from it. Yes, home. I'd sneak into the hotel first to collect my things, put them in the car, and then mull it over for a moment before breaking the bad news to Ludo. We'd just have to try again another weekend. Damn.

The bar was mercifully empty now. Just a few people huddled around the fire in Aran sweaters, orange cagoules steaming dry on the backs of their chairs, walking sticks resting against the wall. My comely currant-bun lady was clearing tables. She saw me looking round.

'Oh, they've all gone to their rooms, luv. We always put them in the annex across the yard, there's that many of them. They're very self-contained over there. Course, they eat in the restaurant, but they always retire over there early because they've got the rally in the morning, see. Like to be fresh. They'll all be gone by eight o'clock tomorrow.'

I gazed at her. Earlier, of course, I'd been to our room. Unpacked. It was directly above the bar, in this small, very old section of the pub. Totally separate, were they? In the modern annex? Almost . . . well, in a different hotel. And if I found a different restaurant, which I was sure wouldn't be a problem . . .

'Everything all right, luv? Have you lost your key?'

'No . . . no. I've got it. I – I just wondered if you'd got a *Daily Mail* or something?'

She had. And I took it upstairs. Stopped, though, en route, halfway up. From the landing window I could see the wooden-clad annex, like a row of chalets, but it was quite a distance away. Across a cobbled courtyard and a car park too. Virtually in a different street. Also, we could order breakfast in bed. Never even trouble the dining room. What's more, there was a back entrance to this old part of the hotel; I'd passed a door that led straight up these stairs. We wouldn't even have to come in through the front door. Wouldn't trouble reception, perchance they were in the bar later.

I locked the bedroom door firmly behind me, had a hot bath and emerged steaming. Then I put on a white towelling dressing gown I'd found on the back of the door and sat on the four-poster to text Ludo the good news. Just. My phone was low on battery, a light told me.

He texted back.

Great! So they're almost in a different hotel!

Which, up to a point, they were.

Heaving a great sigh of relief I changed into my Chinese dress – no time for forty winks – put on some make-up and waited for Ludo to come back, trying not to think that a gin and tonic in the cosy bar downstairs would have been nice. We'd find another elsewhere.

We couldn't. When Ludo returned, he was not in the best of humours – the husband, annoyed at being kept waiting and wanting to get to his supper, had found fault with Ludo's design: couldn't understand why there was so much box hedging, even though his wife patiently explained that was the essence of a knot garden. He'd ended up saying that he hadn't really been consulted about all this garden-design business and wanted to give it some thought. 'Tantamount to saying: "Not today, thank you",' Ludo said gloomily as we trudged back up one side of the high street, having already exhausted the other, shoulders hunched against the persistent drizzle, not a brolly between us.

'Not necessarily,' I urged, slightly disingenuously, as we peered through Café Rouge's window at the crowded restaurant; a queue about ten deep had already formed inside the door. 'He may come back to you when he's had some time to think about it.' And when the wife picks a better moment, I thought privately. I imagined her disappointment as a project she'd nurtured and mulled over in the bath, chatted to friends about for – ooh, months now, had come crashing down because of a late contractor and an irritable husband. She'd lick her wounds and lie low for a bit, then start campaigning again in a few months' time. Return to the knot garden in the spring. But, of course, with a different contractor.

'No, that's dead in the water,' he said bitterly. 'Another two grand down the tubes. Another wasted drawing, too. A complete waste of time, in fact.'

I bristled, because, for some reason, I felt he was blaming me.

'Such a shame you forgot the folder,' I said lightly.

'Such a shame your father was in the bar. That ridiculous conversation delayed me another ten minutes.'

We walked on in silence but I was quietly simmering.

'Sorry to be so gloomy,' he said suddenly, hugging my shoulders as we walked towards the last pub in the high street, a nice-looking place called the Bear, complete with thatched roof. 'The whole thing, as you say, was my own stupid fault, not yours.'

I brightened instantly, marvelling at my mercurial nature. I'd been about to snap, but I was sunny now. One minute everything was roses, the next, bindweed, and then – oh, hello – roses again.

We finally ended up in a half-empty Pizza Express at the

wrong end of town. Half empty because it was in a patch of ribbon development on the edge of an industrial estate, which we agreed wasn't quite what we'd envisaged, but better than nothing.

Frankly I was just glad to get in from the rain and get a large glass of Merlot to my lips, even if it was freezing cold. The wine and the room. But love would keep us warm, I thought, as I glowed at Ludo across the Formica table. I wondered if I should say that? Ironically, of course? No. Bit cheesy. And his demeanour, somehow, didn't encourage it. He was looking around in a disgruntled manner. There was a hen party at the next table, the only other occupied table in the room: ten, overly made-up women were shrieking and laughing and making a great deal of cackle.

'Very conducive to the romantic atmosphere,' he remarked drily.

I laughed, as if he'd made a terribly funny joke.

When the pizzas arrived, tempers improved, and draining the bottle of wine helped too. Then Ludo asked nicely if they could possibly put the heating on? He rubbed his cold hands together with a charming smile.

'Ees broken,' a young Polish gentleman explained, spreading his hands helplessly. 'The engineer, he come tomorrow.'

'Ah.'

No matter. We ordered a hot cappuccino apiece after our pizzas and, as we were drinking it, mulled over the last chaotic hour or so. We even managed to giggle about Ludo being married to Lottie and how that might work.

'You'd have a lovely easy time of it,' I assured him. 'You'd loll around in your pyjamas all day while Lottie brought in the bacon. Wouldn't have to poo-pick at the manor any more.'

'I'm warming to this,' he said. 'Lucky old Hamish.'

'Although she is a bit chaotic in the kitchen. You wouldn't be fed as well as you are at home.'

'Who's says I'm well fed at home?'

'Ooh . . . Ginnie says Eliza's a terrific cook!'

'Ah, yes, you might be right.' He grinned. 'Well, if I'm lolling around in my jim-jams I can rustle up supper myself, can't I?'

I smiled and sipped my coffee. And then, as the cup met my lips, something the Jennie woman had said came back in a rush. Probably at the mention of Ginnie. I put my cup down in its saucer with a clatter.

'Oh – Ludo. Jennie, who I met in the bar – you know, mother of Frankie, the girl who's going out with my nephew – said that Hugo was seeing a psychiatrist in London. Said he'd been recommended by Ginnie's best friend. That's not Eliza, is it?'

The two spots of colour I'd seen earlier in the bar returned to Ludo's cheekbones now. He cleared his throat. 'It is, actually.'

I blinked. Leaned forward. 'You're kidding. Eliza is seeing a shrink?'

'Yes, she's . . . she's been finding life a bit tricky recently. She finds it helps.'

He sipped his coffee placidly. Was that it? I waited. Shook my head in bewilderment.

'In what way?'

'In what way is life tricky or in what way does it help?'

'Well – both, really.' It occurred to me he was being somewhat evasive about this.

'Oh, well, you know.' He ran a weary hand through his blond hair. Leaned back in his chair. 'Time of life, that sort of thing, I suppose. Children growing up. Women's problems.' He shrugged. Gave a disarming smile. 'Who knows?'

He should, surely?

'Ludo, you don't go to a psychiatrist about women's problems. You might pop down to the Holistic Centre, or even the doctor's, but not to a psychiatrist. There must be more to it than that?'

'Perhaps there is. But, as you know, Ella, we don't have the best of relationships, so I don't really know.'

They didn't talk at all. Which struck me as being very different to me and Sebastian, who yelled and screamed far too much. But we did at least communicate. Something else struck me too. I rolled it round in my head before I said it, like a ball of pastry gathering flour on a board.

'Ludo, Lottie also told me – and of course she shouldn't have done, Hippocratic oath and all that – that Eliza was seeing someone in London. She assumed – well, we both did, actually – that she meant a lover. Could it have been this doctor? If she goes up regularly?'

Ludo shrugged miserably. 'Blimey, what is this, Ella, the Spanish Inquisition? I don't know. Perhaps.'

'Perhaps?' I felt cross. 'And yet the other day, when I tentatively asked whether you ever wondered if Eliza had another life, a man on the side, you said you didn't know. Let me go along with it. Sort of led me to believe she might, which, of course, gave you the sympathy vote. When all the time, in fact, she was seeing a shrink? Getting her head sorted out?' He glanced up, alarmed at my tone, which was, what – combative? Accusatory? 'And how come you never told me this? We tell each other pretty much everything, don't we? At least, I do.'

'Now, hang on a minute, Ella. Eliza's her own woman. How do I know what she gets up to in London? I wasn't hoodwinking you, if that's what you mean. Perhaps she has both? A shrink and a lover? And perhaps I was protecting her, out of loyalty? Perhaps I didn't want the neighbourhood knowing she had mental-health problems?'

That I could believe. That rang true. Except . . . this was me, Ella, not the neighbourhood. He trusted me. I knew, too, that his trite throwaway line about her possibly having both was nonsense. She was hardly going to see a psychiatrist and then leap into bed with her lover, as, to assuage my guilt about seeing her husband, I'd had her doing. And Lottie said she came for acupuncture every week now. And we knew money in that household was tight. Acupuncture *and* a shrink. She must be desperate. Suddenly I realized she was incredibly unhappy. She must be. I recalled her tight, pinched face at dinner parties opposite the gorgeous Ludo. She had probably once been very attractive, in a thin, gamine sort of way, but she'd aged considerably; she was much more lined than the rest of us. Once, years ago, when Ludo and Eliza had given a drinks party and invited pretty much everybody, including Lottie and Hamish, Ludo had answered the door to the pair of them and gestured to Eliza, standing behind him, saying, 'Hi, there! You know Eliza, don't you?' Hamish had bounded in in his Tiggerish way, saying: 'Of course! I met your mother at the school play!'

Eliza's mouth had all but disappeared.

371

Lottie was mortified, but, later, we couldn't help giggling guiltily. '*So* stupid of Hamish, but she *does* look old,' Lottie had insisted.

'Or he looks young,' I'd said. I'd been at the party too: it was the first time I'd seen Ludo. I remembered watching this floppy-haired man with the megawatt smile distractedly pouring Pimms in the garden for shiny-eyed women. Distracted, but surely not entirely oblivious to his charms?

At that moment I imagined Eliza, hunched and gaunt opposite some psychiatrist in London, huddled in that camel coat she always wore; Liberty's headscarf round her neck, like someone from another generation, Lottie and I would whisper. Ludo wore pink trousers, velvet jackets, patterned shirts with mandarin collars: we'd all felt rather sorry for him with his frumpy wife. But had she been, rather desperately, staking her claim? As his wife and the mother of his children? Pearls. Sensible skirts. Be *sensible*, Ludo, her clothes seemed to say. Whistling in the wind.

I watched as he smiled at the pretty waitress who'd arrived, in place of the Polish gentleman, with the credit-card machine. He punched out his number. I thought he'd singled me out. Thought I was special. Perhaps I was? Just because his wife was mentally unstable and rather conventionally dressed, it didn't mean he'd had heaps of affairs and that she was suffering the after-effects, did it? The waitress departed. I took a deep breath.

'Ludo, am I the first woman you've ever had an affair with?'

He looked surprised as he pocketed his wallet. 'Ella, you know you are. You've asked me that before.'

'I know. It's just . . .'

Just that you've been economical with the truth, I thought. You didn't let me in. Didn't tell me your wife was seeing a psychiatrist in case I felt sorry for her. So sorry, in fact, that I might have felt a complete heel about seeing you. Might have thought twice. And very occasionally you've dropped tiny hints that Eliza might have her own romantic life. Perhaps used it as leverage to push me a little further into having an affair.

We walked quietly back to the hotel, once in a while remarking on a window display, or the fact that the rain had abated slightly. We gave a brief laugh now and again at nothing in particular, desperate for levity. He had his arm round my shoulders, but it felt odd. Unnatural. I gazed in a cook-shop window as we passed. Some gadget for squeezing lemons caught my eye. I'd recently taken to doing that like Jamie Oliver, letting the juice slip through my fingers, leaving only pips in my hand. Why should that image spring to mind? Of something slipping through my fingers, only sour pips remaining? We walked on in silence. I felt sad. For me, partly. I'd wanted my moment in the sunshine. Knew I'd needed it. Had wanted to love and be loved. But most of all I felt sad for all middle-aged women. Single ones, obviously, but particularly those with charming, youthful husbands. Was Sebastian in that category? He was certainly very good-looking, but in a more craggy, unusual way, and he didn't do conscious charm. Conscious insults, more like, I thought with an involuntary smile. Any charm he had was surely a by-product. A mistake.

We went round the back of the hotel to the entrance I'd told him about – the fire escape, as it turned out, which had certainly escaped me – and tried the door. It was locked.

Ludo rattled the bar, irritated. 'Oh, well. We'll just have to go round the front.'

'Yes, I suppose,' I said nervously. 'Only, I just hope Dad –'

'Oh, bother your flaming dad!'

I turned, astonished. He looked furious. Something of the man I'd seen at the school fete, bad-tempered and disaffected as Eliza had admonished him, came back. That rather did it for me. That show of temper. I felt the colour rise in my own face; his was still taut and pale. Without a word, we turned and stalked round to the front of the pub in silence. As we went through reception, a young man on the desk glanced up from his BlackBerry with a smile. Neither of us acknowledged him. I stopped at the foot of the stairs.

'Look, Ludo, you go up. I'm going to have a drink in the bar.'

'Oh, darling, I'll join you. I'm so sorry. I didn't mean to say that. So stupid.' He took my hand, shamefaced.

'No.' I regarded him rather deliberately. Retrieved my hand. 'You go up.' I said it slowly.

He tried to laugh it off. 'Our first row!' he said lightly. 'Had to happen.'

I didn't reply. But he knew I meant it. I saw realization pass across his eyes. Realization that I wouldn't be coming. At all. At least – not in that capacity. In what capacity, then, I wondered desperately? After all, my things were in that room. Were we to lie beside each other like statues all night? I was certainly too pissed to drive home. But I'd think about that later. Right now, all I wanted was some time alone to think, and a very large drink. I was aware of the young man behind us listening possibly. Or possibly not. Possibly texting his mates and not giving a damn about a middle-aged couple having a tiff.

'I've got a key,' I said firmly. 'I'll be up later.'

'Don't be ridiculous, darling.' Ludo laughed lightly. He riffled a hand through his blond hair. 'I'm not going up without you. This is absurd! Come on. I'll tell you what – we'll both have a drink. I could certainly do with one.'

He took my arm and made to move me through the open doorway into the bar. It occurred to me that through sheer force and my innate inability to make a scene, I was being outmanoeuvred. It also occurred to me that, with a couple of Cointreaus inside me, a warm fire, some loving words, perhaps even a few tears . . . well, who knows what might happen? But even as I was being propelled into the room, happily, God was on my side. My trump card, the one Ludo really didn't want to turn up, was on his own at the bar. Dad. He was waving a tenner at the barman to get his attention, his back to us. Suddenly the prospect of being Lottie's husband and getting his kit off for the *Sunday Express* on a regular basis loosened Ludo's grip on my arm. It was all I needed. I shook him off in a twinkling – and sailed away to join my father.

Chapter Twenty-Five

Dad glanced across as I approached and his face suffused with delight as he saw me. He waved the tenner even harder.

'Darling!' he boomed. 'How marvellous! Come and have a drink.'

'Thanks, Dad. I'll have a Cointreau.'

'Lottie's husband not joining us?' he asked, as Ludo turned hastily and headed towards the stairs.

'No,' I said shortly.

My father was by now giving his order to the barman, instructing him that the whisky should on no account be mixed with anything other than tepid water and that the Cointreau should be on ice. Crushed ice, that is.

'And, actually, Dad,' I said, as we waited for our drinks, 'he's not Lottie's husband. He's someone called Eliza's. And he doesn't model underwear, or make baby bonnets. Although he is a landscape gardener. We've been having an affair.'

There was a silence.

'Ah.' That was all he said. Another long pause ensued as we both gazed fixedly at the row of optics behind the bar. The barman was busy at the far end, crushing the ice. At length Dad spoke. 'I did wonder.'

'Did you?' I was surprised. Managed to look at him.

'Not at the time, but when you'd gone. Couldn't see

Sebastian in a place like this. Bit bijou for him, somehow. And I thought a threesome a bit odd.'

'Right.' I swallowed.

The barman came back with our order and when Dad had paid – which took a while because the chap had run out of change and had to go and get some more, which gave me a moment to collect myself – but when it was all sorted out, we took our drinks and sat by the fire. We were the only ones in the bar now. I was glad I'd got that little revelation over with.

'Where are the others?' I asked lightly.

'Early night. They take this car-rally business rather seriously. I fancied a nightcap.'

My father sipped his whisky thoughtfully.

'Over now, is it?' he asked. 'The two of you?' I was surprised. On two counts. I didn't know it had been that obvious, or that he could be so matter-of-fact about it.

'Yes, I think it is,' I said sadly. 'Although, to be honest, it never really got going. I mean, we certainly had a love affair. But we never actually . . . you know.'

He nodded. Put down his whisky. 'Rather like me and Maureen.'

'Oh?' It had occurred to me earlier that she wasn't with him.

'Yes, awfully fond of her and all that, great fun, but it never really got off the ground. All got a bit much, if I'm honest. I had to escape to the pub a lot. And I'm running away this weekend. Dan and Jennie suggested I get away. Sweet of them.'

'You mean . . . Maureen is at the Old Rectory?'

'Yes. Can't seem to – you know . . .' He hesitated.

'Get rid of her?'

'Well, it's so tricky, Ella.' He looked upset. 'I mean, I was all for her coming, and having the lodgers and everything –'

'That was her idea?'

'Yes, and, as I say, I was all for it. The house was so empty without your mother and it seemed sort of charitable. And I thought we would give the money to charity or something – Lord knows, it's not as if we need it. But Maureen saw it more as a business, and before I knew it, was charging commercial rates to all those people. And we're not even a registered B&B or anything –'

'Good grief, Dad. Get out now!'

'Well, I can't – it's my house!' he yelped, his rheumy grey eyes popping.

'No, I mean, get out of the situation!'

'Yes, well, quite,' he said emphatically. 'Quite. But you know I can't exactly *shop* her, Ella. I'm fond of her. And it's not all bad. We've had heaps of fun.'

'Yes.' I could see that. Ludo and I had, too, I thought sadly.

'And she's opened my eyes to all sorts of things.' I wasn't sure I wanted to know. 'Cycling, hill-walking and whatnot.'

'Ah. Right.' God, this Cointreau was good. I took a great gulp.

'But there are still going to be irritants, aren't there? Things that get on your nerves.'

'You mean, whoever you're with? Yes, I suppose.' I was still thinking of Ludo. His pale face. White with . . . was it anger? 'Such as?'

'Oh, I don't know. She licks her teeth an awful lot – well, she plasters on the lipstick so it gets stuck there, has to get cracking with her tongue. And she uses a great deal of cheap bath essence so the bathroom pongs for hours afterwards, smells like a tart's boudoir. And she puts all these teddies on the bed – pink ones. Expects me to *buy* the wretched things, too. Ghastly things with "I Love You" on their T-shirts, and they're made with so much nylon I'm completely static by the time I've delved through them and got into bed. You could plug me in and I'd light up the entire house.'

I chuckled in spite of myself.

'And then there are the air fresheners in the lavatories. More than two to a bog, sometimes!' He leaned forward earnestly. 'Quite frankly, Ella, I prefer the smell of shit.'

I grinned. The party was over, clearly.

'And I do *not* want a cockapoo,' he said petulantly, sitting back and folding his arms.

I damn nearly spilled my drink. 'A cocka *what?*'

'Poo. Cross between a cocker spaniel and a poodle, apparently. She's mad for them. But, to be honest, I just miss Buster. Would like him back.'

'With pleasure,' I said with feeling. 'I've got him, surprise surprise. Does Mum know about all this?'

He sighed, his shoulders sagging forward dramatically. 'Ah. Your mother.' He adopted a dark, sepulchral tone; rubbed his brow with his fingertips. 'That's another story.'

'Is it? I'm all ears.' I was, surprisingly. And, surprisingly, not too distressed about Ludo. Thoughtful, but not distressed. I mean, it would have been heaven had it been right, complete heaven, but I realized – and I knew I didn't have time to analyse it now but would later – that for some reason it wasn't. And at my age, and at my stage in life, it had to be absolutely perfect. I wasn't eighteen any more: couldn't afford to kiss a few frogs. If I was going to kiss again – if, indeed, I was – it had to be the prince. I hadn't got time to get it half right. Or even three-quarters. Would rather be alone. And yet . . . I'd loved Ludo. Genuinely. I felt a lump come to my throat. Did love, even. I shook my head. No. If I was honest, that wasn't entirely what was in my heart right now. I was being disingenuous. I was sad, but for other reasons. For nostalgic, sentimental reasons that had more to do with the lack of love than the lack of his presence. And, anyway, my father was talking.

'Yes, I saw her yesterday.'

I swam to the surface. Came to. 'Really? You saw Mum?'

'Yes, we went to Daylesford together for the day. You know, that chichi, upmarket Chelsea-in-the-country farm shop. In the Cotswolds.'

'Yes, I know. *And?*'

'Well, we sat there for hours, having lunch. Hours and hours. Talking talking talking. It got dark, as a matter of fact.'

'Oh! How lovely.'

'Well, it would have been lovely except . . . ' He swallowed. 'Well, I went there, you know, to say I'd made a complete mistake with Maureen. Couldn't cope with her pink fluffy slippers and loo-seat covers and all that, and that I missed your mum.'

'Excellent, Dad!'

'Wanted her back.'

'Yes?'

'But, of course, I did have with me a list of things that had annoyed me about your mother.'

I eyed him warily. 'Ri-ight,' I said nervously.

'Which, naturally, I gave to her.'

Christ. Men. 'You handed it to her? When, at the end of lunch?'

'No, just after I told her I'd be happy to have her back, but on certain conditions. She read it at the table, and then immediately fished in her bag for a pen and paper and, totally off the top of her head – and I'd spent ages writing mine – wrote down her *own* points about me! She also said that she'd Found Herself – whatever that means – and was perfectly happy where she was. Said she wouldn't be coming back to the Old Rectory in a hurry, thank you very much.'

'Oh!' Suddenly snapshots of Mum feeding chickens in her dungarees, posing for Sebastian, helping at Ottoline's pottery group sprang to mind. 'Yes, she has a bit,' I agreed. 'Found herself, I mean. She's done a lot. And she's made great friends with Ottoline.'

'And someone called Charles, evidently,' he said bitterly.

'Charles?' I blinked. 'Not *blind* Charles?'

'Is he?' My father boggled.

'Well, no, not exactly. He sort of pretends. But . . . Golly.' I was stunned. Then thoughtful. Mum and Charles. At the Hall. Not so inconceivable, actually. My mother was a very good-looking woman. I'd wondered where she'd been recently, when Ottoline had been buzzing around on her own, saying Mum was busy. I stared at Dad.

'But . . . she said she would *be* coming back, surely? At some stage? Surely she was thrilled?'

He sighed. 'I don't know. I really don't, Ella.' He looked shifty. 'Her list was longer than mine.' He said in a small voice.

I frowned. I'd always sided with my dad. Had felt his life

was tough. And yet Ginnie had often sided with Mum, who I found indefensible.

'OK, what was on hers?'

'Oh, ridiculous things,' he snorted. 'Not clipping my nasal hair any more, which she found disrespectful. Said she didn't like the way it grew out in clumps, from my ears too. Oh, and giving a little fart just before I get into bed. Picking my feet in the bath and lining up the bits of toenail on the side. Always buying her lavender water at Christmas because it reminds me of my dear mama, when I know she doesn't like it and my mother's been dead twenty years. She said she doesn't want to smell like a corpse, thank you. I mean, I ask you!'

I shifted uncomfortably in my seat. 'Right. What else?'

'Oh, the usual tommyrot about slurping my tea – behavioural issues, she calls them, which, according to her, mount up. Apparently I always call her old girl in public and slap her bottom when I make a joke. She said she didn't want her bottom slapped. And she didn't want to sit behind me freezing to death on a shooting stick every Saturday, either. It seems no other wives are forced to these days. But your granny *always* sat behind my father. And she said she didn't want to cook or eat any more game, because she hates the smell, especially jugged hare, my favourite, which, as you know, is made with the blood of the hare, just like Aunt Hilda made it, slitting the throat first. But, more than anything, she said didn't want any more fucking lavender water. She actually said "fucking", Ella!'

He looked shocked. I was too.

'And your list?'

'Well, obviously I hate being bossed around all day and I hate bridge. Hate hate hate. And I don't want to go to choir on a rainy Monday when I could be watching *Last of the Summer Wine*, which she loathes, apparently. How can anyone loathe Compo and Foggy? And – oh, I don't know. I just want to be treated like an individual, I suppose,' he finished miserably.

'Yes,' I said sadly.

I thought back to Mum, rather happily – and usefully – showing Sam how to make a tiny mug for her baby son. Feeding the sheep. Releasing Curly, the goat, who always got his head stuck in the wire. Putting a bell on him so that when he was frantic and struggling, we'd all know. How, the other day, I'd found her helping Tabitha with some dress she was trying to shorten for a party. But really showing her: not just snatching it and doing it quickly, as I would have done. Getting Tabs to neatly hem it on the machine as she stood over her. How she wanted to be an individual too. Very many years ago she'd been a nursery-school teacher. Obviously she'd given up when she married my father. Women did then.

'Anyway.' Dad heaved up another great sigh. 'We're meeting again soon.'

'Oh, are you?' I was encouraged. 'Not all doom and gloom, then?'

'Oh, I wouldn't get excited. As I say, I don't think she's coming back. And of course I haven't told her about the lodgers. Although she knows about Maureen. She was jolly scathing.'

'I bet she was.'

'Despite the fact that there's this Charles fellow,' he spat.

'It won't be like that, Dad.' It wouldn't. And Dad knew that too. Whatever Charles might hope, he would be very much A Walker.

'She's talking about going to Tuscany, with Ottoline. Painting, for God's sake. Because she knows some chap who runs courses out there, an ex-solicitor married to Peter Mortimer's daughter, Poppy, who she's kept in touch with. And I would have loved that,' he said petulantly. 'You know how I love dabbling with watercolours. But oh, no, I'm the one left behind with Maureen and the lodgers to deal with.'

I looked at him squarely. 'Maureen is your problem, Dad,' I told him firmly. 'You got yourself into this pickle. You started that relationship and you jolly well have to finish it.'

'Yes, yes, of course. Although . . .' He hesitated. 'I suppose if your mother's *not* coming back . . .'

'No, you *can't* go hedging your bets!' I said, cross, for once, on Mum's behalf. 'If you want her back you've got to get rid of the sodding girlfriend first. You must see that. And not just run away on a vintage-car jaunt. Tell Maureen properly.' Men. *Again*.

'Right.' He gulped. 'And the lodgers?'

'Leave that to me,' I said grimly. 'I know just the man – or girl – for the job.'

His old grey eyes cleared as they communed silently with mine. We could already see her rolling up her sleeves, brandishing her rolling pin, flashing her signet ring as she cleared Forest Glade and Essence of Pine in one clean sweep of her arm.

'Ginnie.'

'Exactly. I'll ring her tomorrow.'

He breathed out happily. 'Oh, good plan. Thanks, darling.'

Our eyes spoke again, but more guiltily this time, knowing what was left unsaid. That neither of us liked confrontation. Both ran away. Left it to the Sylvias and Ginnies of this world. Well, they were so good at it, weren't they? Never shrank from it. We were alike, Dad and I. Shirkers. It did occur to me to wonder if Ginnie would want to do this with so much on her plate. So much sadness with Hugo. No. She'd love it. It would take her mind off things. She'd be livid not to be asked.

We left it there, sipping our drinks in silence. But I realized that, actually, there was something else I really couldn't shirk. Something else more pressing. Like, where on earth I was going to sleep tonight? I voiced it to my father in nervous tones.

'Oh, that's not a problem, love,' he said airily. 'My room's got twin beds. Take the other one.'

'Oh!' I could have hugged him. Instead I fell on the offer. 'Has it really? Thanks, Dad, I will. How marvellous.'

He shrugged modestly. 'Oh, you know me. Anything to oblige the womenfolk in my family.'

In the event, however, it wasn't quite so marvellous. When I crept upstairs to the *salle d'amour* I was to have shared with Ludo, to collect my things – I'd decided, after a certain amount of dithering, that I really *did* have to collect them, that it would be awfully cowardly not to – I was naturally hoping against hope to find Ludo diplomatically asleep. Or at least pretending. Disappointingly he wasn't. Instead, as I softly softly put my key in the lock, quietly quietly opened it . . . there he was: propped up in the huge four-poster, bedside light on, John le Carré in hand. He was bare-chested too, which gave me a bit of a jolt. He gazed at me wordlessly over reading glasses. Reading glasses. I didn't need those yet. They didn't quite go with the surprisingly hirsute chest. Really hirsute. After all, he was blond.

'Um, Ludo,' I faltered, as I tottered in, cravenly leaving the door ajar behind me to facilitate running. 'I've um . . . found a bed.'

'Excellent news.'

Was it my imagination or was there a touch of sarcasm there? I ploughed on. 'Yes, you see, my father's got a spare one in his room.'

'How very cosy.'

'Well, no, not really. But, it would be so difficult, to – you know . . .' I gulped. Gestured to the bed but didn't look at him. 'Anyway,' I rushed on after a pause. 'I – I thought it would be for the best.' I was already tiptoeing around the room now, seizing my overnight bag, my hair-brush, nipping into the bathroom for my sponge bag, snatching up my jeans from a chair, like a professional cat burglar. 'So I'll be over there, in the, um, annex. Should you – you know – need me. Not that you will!' This was beyond awkward and I couldn't find my shoes. Under the bed, maybe? I didn't want to get that close to the bed, though. Let alone rummage beneath it. His eyes, behind those strange, gold-rimmed specs, followed me round the room. So much hair. Did he shave his neck, I wondered? I'd never noticed it before. Was it on his back? I felt damp. Clammy. Ah – *there* were my shoes. I snatched them up.

'Ella.' It was said softly. Beseechingly. I glanced up. The glasses were off now. I averted my eyes so I wouldn't feel the pain. Catch the blue rays. Feel the sadness. Remember the stolen moments in the vegetable garden, or the rose garden, holding hands. Our feet touching under café tables. Pressed close. Hearts beating.

I took a deep breath. 'I can't do it, Ludo,' I said to the floor. But also to Eliza. And perhaps my children. Certainly her children. Maybe even my ex-husband. And then I looked up. Made myself meet his eyes, which were indeed very sad. And then I turned and went, clutching my belongings, closing the door quietly behind me.

Down the stairs I ran, my heart pounding. I hurried across the courtyard in the drizzle, my arms full, and entered the annex like a thief, clattering through a modern glazed door. Climbing some rather nasty stone stairs – but, oh, I was so pleased to see them – I hastened along the corridor, pushed open the door, which had conveniently been left ajar, and into my father's room.

Pushing the door shut with my bottom, I heard him gargling noisily in the bathroom. It was something he'd always done, and something Ginnie and I laughed about and said you could hear across the landing. But maybe Mum didn't? Laugh? And maybe I wouldn't either, I thought, with a jolt. If he were my husband.

'Hi, Dad,' I called.

'Hello, darling!' he gargled back.

I quickly got changed into my brand-new silky nightie and slipped into the spare bed, thinking I'd get up and brush my teeth later, when Dad was asleep. It wouldn't be long because Mum used to say he'd be snoring before his head hit the pillow. I waited as he peed noisily, door wide open, then emerged in his stripy pyjamas, top tucked right in, cord tied up underneath his armpits. He gave a great belch and went to sit down weightily on the side of the bed, but just before his bottom made contact with it – he farted. I winced. Then he rolled heavily under the bed-clothes and turned out the light.

'Night, darling.' he muttered.

'Night.'

I lay there staring into the darkness. Sure enough, within moments, one rhythmic snore followed another. They gradually gained momentum until the room fairly shook. I lay still, listening to the monstrous cacophony, feeling the hotel vibrate, and wondering if the people next door could hear? Of course they could. Finally I got wearily to my feet, not even bothering to be quiet. I knew I could turn on the bathroom light, brush my teeth with brio and even pull the chain and he still wouldn't wake up. I did all of these things and crawled back to bed, bits of sodden loo paper stuck firmly in my ears. It muffled the sound, but certainly didn't keep it out. As I shut my eyes tightly and tried to pretend I was on a ship and it was merely the noise of the engine, it occurred to me that Mum used special ear defenders, ordered in bulk, from America. It also occurred to me that only I, Ella Montclair, could come away on a dirty weekend, and end up sleeping with my father.

Chapter Twenty-Six

The next morning, feeing horribly fuzzy-headed, I tottered down to reception. I'd left it late, knowing my father would be up early and away to the rally, and in fact I'd heard him moving laboriously around the room. I couldn't miss him, actually, clearing his throat and humming. Did he have to make such a din? I thought, slightly uncharitably – after all, he'd kindly let me share his room – but still. When he'd gone, saying, 'Cheerio, Ella!' in a loud stage whisper, just to make sure I was well and truly awake, I lurched out of bed, turned off the light, lunged to switch off the radio he'd left blaring, then went back to sleep for an hour.

Nine o'clock, therefore, saw me creeping downstairs with my bag. There'd been a slightly awkward moment earlier when a chambermaid had popped in to clean the room – clearly reception had told her the occupant had paid the bill and checked out – so, assuming the room was empty, she'd barged in with her bucket and mop and found me in my bra and pants.

'Oh!' She'd frozen to the spot, eyes wide. Then, in broken English: 'Oh, so sorry – they say the gentleman had gone!'

She looked me up and down in astonishment. Such an old man. Such a young woman. The man was surely old enough to be . . .

'He's my father,' I told her quickly, snatching my dressing gown to cover myself.

She blinked. Then gave me an old-fashioned look. 'Of course, madam.'

'No – really, he is! I mean, I'm sure you've heard that line a million times before, but honestly –'

The door was shut. She'd gone.

Right. Well, of course. This was the ultimate irony, wasn't it? I tossed my dressing gown on the floor, bitterly. For it to be put about that I'd had a steamy night of passion, when in fact I'd done nothing of the sort? Had resisted manfully.

By the time I reached reception, word had indeed spread. My comfy, currant-bun lady had a very different look on her face as I wondered, tentatively, if I had anything to settle up?

'No, madam,' she said icily. 'Your husband saw to that.'

'Oh – he's not my husband,' I said instinctively, then realized that was worse.

'Your – ahem – friend, then. Mr Pritchard in room seven. Your friend in room twenty-three, Mr Jardine, has also settled up.'

'Yes, he's my father,' I said, feeling a little faint.

'Of course, madam,' she said smoothly. 'Both gentlemen have paid their bills. And yours,' she added pointedly.

There didn't seem to be anything to say to this, and, actually, I was really rather exhausted and it was only nine o'clock. I crept away under her censorious gaze, vowing never to return to the Bunch of Grapes at Binfield as long as I lived.

I perked up when I neared home, though, thinking that as long as my own conscience was clear, which it was, the rest of them could go to hell in a handcart, as my Auntie Doreen used to say. I squared my shoulders defiantly at the wheel. I felt a pang of regret and remorse for Ludo, of course I did, not for last night – that was never destined to be – but for the future: for the fun and the love and the laughter we'd never have. But I wouldn't let my mind go there. Instead I made myself sing along to Westlife on the radio. Wouldn't indulge. I'd made a decision, I'd stick to it. Nevertheless I found myself sighing pretty deeply as I got out of the car and slammed the door, but I was fairly sure that had more to do with the mud in the yard, the dogs barking for attention and the chickens running out to be fed – where have *you* been, you hussy, written all over their faces – than anything else.

As I put the key in the back door, I turned at an unfamiliar noise. Then gawped. A Bentley was gently purring through the open gateway, into the yard. It stopped outside my mother's cottage. A chauffeur appeared to be getting out. He knocked on the Stable door. After a moment, my mother answered, looking drop-dead gorgeous and swathed in a mink she hadn't worn for years. Her heels were high and black, her stockings sheer, and diamonds were sparkling in her ears. Agog, and as if drawn by a string, I went in a trance towards her.

'Hi, Mum.'

'Oh, hello, darling.' She smiled across the car bonnet.

'Off somewhere?'

'Yes, Charles and I are going to the Fat Duck at Bray for lunch.'

'Oh! How lovely.' I peered into the car. Sure enough, Charles, looking very fat-catish and wrapped in a covert coat with velvet collar, rug over his knees, brigade tie firmly knotted, was in the back. He gave me a friendly smile and a fluttery wave of his liver-spotted hand. I fluttered back.

'Um, Mum.' I sidled round the car and stood beside her as she fished in her bag for her key. 'I saw Dad yesterday.' I said it softly, hoping to bring her back down to earth as she locked her front door.

'Oh, yes.'

'Yes, and, you know, I think he's really regretting his – well . . . His actions. Especially, you know . . .'

'Maureen?' She turned, pocketing her key. She looked lovely: lightly made-up, her hair softly waved.

'Yes,' I said eagerly. 'Maureen.'

'Well, if you saw him you'll know I've seen him, too.'

'Yes, and you're meeting him again soon. And – well, the thing is, Mum,' I lowered my voice further, although I was sure Charles was fairly hard of hearing as well as seeing and the windows were up, 'I think if the two of you were to iron out a few creases, just tiny ones, there's every chance for the pair of you. I really do. And it would be crazy to throw – what, forty-odd years of marriage? – down the drain, wouldn't it?'

'Would it?' She smiled. Snapped her bag shut. 'How was Rebecca?'

'Rebecca?' I came to with a jolt. Remembered I'd told her, and the children, that I was going to stay with an old schoolfriend of that name last night. I coloured and realized she was watching me closely. 'Fine, thanks.'

'Good. Sorry, darling, what were you saying? About throwing away years of marriage?'

I opened my mouth. Shut it again.

She regarded me sagely. 'I don't know the answers, darling. Wish I did.' It wasn't said snidely. Or nastily. Or bitterly. Just slightly sadly and genuinely. She got in the car as the chauffeur opened the door for her. In the back I saw Charles reach across and squeeze her hand.

The car purred expensively into life and, in a daze, I watched them go. Blimey. Bentley. Fat Duck. Profound remarks. You had to hand it to the old girl, didn't you? She hadn't lost her touch. It also occurred to me that throughout mine and Ginnie's young lives Mum had always been the one to prod and question and challenge whilst Dad took the back seat. The easy seat, if I'm honest. I'd always resented it, but . . . maybe it made us what we were? Maybe, without Mum's constant intervention and probing, I'd have ended up in bed with Ludo last night? Had her influence on my life stopped me? In some distant, hazy place to do with upbringing, perhaps I'd done the right thing because of her rules and maybe I shouldn't resent her so much? Years ago, when I'd left home at eighteen for art school, her one piece of advice to me had been: 'Trust your instincts.' Not 'Don't do drugs.' Or 'Don't sleep around.' Just 'Trust your instincts.' Was that because she knew she'd shaped them? Formed them? And knew she could rely on them, and therefore my moral judgement, to be good? Without her knowing – and certainly without crediting her – I'd quietly held on to that piece of advice all my life.

Ottoline came out to join me from her studio, covered in clay. Stood beside me.

'How long has this been going on?' I jerked my head in the direction of the Bentley as it disappeared down the lane into the distance.

Ottoline wiped her hands on her apron. 'Oh, he's been pursuing her for ages. Flowers are delivered practically every day. Her place looks like a film star's dressing room. Didn't you know?'

I turned and peered through Mum's sitting-room window, cupping my hands around my eyes to see better. Sure enough, white lilies and gardenias abounded.

'No. No, I didn't.'

She laughed. 'Too busy with your own life, I expect. How was your night away?'

'Good,' I said shortly, avoiding her eye. She didn't try to find mine.

'Excellent,' she said lightly. There was a silence. 'By the way, I've got Becks and the gang coming round soon – do you want to join in? Or would you prefer not to hit the ground running?'

Already, round the corner from the village, the small green bus from town was trundling into sight, laden, no doubt, with Becks, Amy, Amanda et al., and, actually, it was the last thing I needed right now. I opened my mouth to say no, thank you, to make an excuse – then shut it again. I'd taken note of Ottoline's last remark. Too busy with your own life. Me again, see?

'Lead on, Macduff,' I told her, as she turned and went back into the Dairy. 'Let's shape that clay.' Something more apposite about feet of clay becoming pliant came to mind, but I couldn't quite articulate it.

Later that day, when the children came home from school, I hadn't prepared blueberry cheesecake, or even a spaghetti Bolognese: there was just a hastily opened tin of beans and some bacon burning in a pan. They looked a bit relieved that the table wasn't laid with a cloth, as it had been for the last week or so, and glugged happily from the Tesco Smoothie carton as they stood at the open fridge.

'You know this hasn't got much fruit in it,' Josh observed, reading the label. 'You should be buying Innocent Smoothies, like Rob's mum. Looking after our five-a-day.'

'Except Innocent Smoothies are about three times the price, so I wouldn't be looking after your inheritance, would I?'

'There is one?'

'Of course. There's a massive debt for you, Josh, and Tabitha gets the chickens.'

They grinned. Almost back to old times, I thought, as they drifted towards the playroom to await supper on their laps. I took a deep breath. 'Darlings, I think I've been a bit of an idiot.' They turned; looked at me in surprise. 'I over-reacted when you told me about Dad's place the other day. Shock, I suppose, but it was stupid and totally out of order. I've had some time to mull it over and I think you should both go there for a bit.' I couldn't help that 'for a bit'. 'Your school's in Oxford and it makes perfect sense if he's there. And it's not like I'm a million miles away. You can pop home for a square meal whenever you feel like it.' We all tried not to look at the square meal burning on the stove, but I could feel the room relax a bit: the air was not so taut.

'I don't know,' began Tabitha. 'You'd be on your own. I'd feel bad about that. I was being selfish too, wasn't thinking of that.'

'I wouldn't be on my own!' I said, realizing Ludo had been so right: drop the reins and it brings them up short immediately. 'Blimey, it's like a commune here. I've got Granny and Ottoline – and I could pop into Oxford whenever I felt like it, for lunch.'

'And Dad says you can come to the house if you want,' said Tabitha eagerly. 'See us there.'

'Did he?' I was surprised. But then not, when I thought about it. Sebastian had so little feeling for me; he neither loved nor hated me. It wouldn't matter to him if I popped in and out. It would be a matter of complete indifference, which was sad. Indifference was sad. I, on the other hand, couldn't possibly do that. I'd feel stirred up for days afterwards if I set foot in a house we no longer shared: had no history in together.

'Or Wagamama? Or, as I say, you can come here. But the point is, it's not a separation, as I so stupidly suggested it was. It's just the next phase in a very sensible and fluid arrangement. Sensible geographically, and fluid because, who knows, one day you might both be itching to come back here when you decide you want to be sheep farmers!'

They both laughed, but I saw proper light return to their eyes, which I hadn't seen for a while, and it made me ache. How wrong it had been to insist they stay. This would hurt so much, I couldn't pretend it wouldn't: couldn't even think of them packing up their things – not too much at once, they'd be subtle, I was sure of that – but still, their clothes would have to go, books, make-up, guitar, CDs. Yet how much worse to have those polite, subdued children around, who might – and this chilled me to the bone – have ended up hating me? I almost wanted to run upstairs and pack their things now.

In the event, we did it at the weekend. That gave us a few days to acclimatize ourselves. Not that I'd ever acclimatize, I thought, running periodically to the loo to take a moment to steady myself as I gripped the washbasin, but time for them to talk to Sebastian, transfer a few things after school, tidy the stuff in their rooms upstairs into piles.

I watched them get excited and try to hide it. I saw them both glancing at me anxiously, looking for signs of a nervous breakdown. Tabitha took her favourite posters off her walls – then put them all back. I think the Blu-Tack-stained room upset her. She threw her arms around me a lot. Squeezed me tight. She'd prattle away about how much she'd be back. And I did terribly well, too. Josh would tell me I'd probably take a lover and I'd agree that seemed to be the sensible course of action, and he'd suggest likely candidates, favouring the landlord at the pub, mostly: over seventeen stone and with boils on his nose. I'd give Ron serious consideration and we'd laugh. But when they weren't there, at school, usually, I'd run to Lottie's practice and tell her to stick needles in me, anywhere, the tears rolling down my face.

'Just stop it hurting.'

'I can't really do much about the pain,' she'd tell me sadly, holding my hand. 'But, for what it's worth, I think you're doing the right thing. They'll be back. You'll see.'

I'd gulp, still dripping, and then climb up on her couch anyway and she'd stick a few needles in my ankles for form's sake. And, actually, I usually did feel a bit more relaxed – exhausted, probably – on the way home.

Ludo texted after a few days, saying he'd been a prat and he hoped we could still be friends. That sort of thing. I didn't answer for a while, but then in a very weak moment texted back: 'Of course.' I didn't want to put a kiss but it looked so weird and cold without, to my lovely Ludo, so I did.

On the Saturday I drove the children into Oxford. We turned off the High Street and wended our way down the tiny cobbled back streets which lay behind some of the more beautiful ancient colleges and quads. As we drew up at the porters' lodge of, arguably, the grandest of the lot, the porter, having checked our names on a list, took out a huge bunch of keys and opened what looked like a draw-bridge gate for us. As we drove slowly and rather reverently into the other-worldly, hallowed grounds of the famous college, a shock of vivid green quad in the centre, the children were on the edge of their seats, unable to contain their excitement.

'It's over there, I think,' pointed Tabitha, across the other side of the quad.

I duly navigated the gravel path round the square and pulled up outside a beautiful terrace of Cotswold-stone Georgian houses, dripping with late roses and wisteria. Sure enough, as if he'd been at the window, Sebastian emerged from the front door of the end one, wreathed in smiles.

I almost passed out when I saw him. He was smiling, as I say, which was unusual in itself, and dressed, not in his usual baggy, crumpled, paint-splattered ensemble, but new black jeans and a proper shirt with a collar. His hair was cut quite short and freshly washed. It gave him an achingly vulnerable look, which was so unfamiliar I couldn't help but remark on it as we got out.

'Good heavens, what's this? The new boy-band look?'

He looked relieved at my light tone: not tight-lipped and resentful. But he had no idea what it was costing me. Actually, though, as he caught my eye, I saw that he had.

He ruffled his shorn locks ruefully, keeping up the jocular charade. 'She did go a bit crazy, didn't she? I just asked for something slightly neater, and of course I normally do it myself. But I didn't want to look like one of the students.'

'Have you met them yet?' I asked as we unpacked the back of the car, the four of us, my heart pounding.

'Oh, yes, I took a class on Monday. They're a nice bunch. Very talented, too.'

'Oh.' I lowered the bundle of duvets I was carrying. 'You're actually teaching? I thought artist in residence meant – I don't know, something more reclusive. On more of a pedestal?'

'It can be whatever you want it to be, but I want to teach. I'm loving it so far, but it's early days.' He strode on into the house with Josh's computer printer in his arms, but I stopped in my tracks. Sebastian loving something? And, what's more, saying it? I had to take a moment before I moved on, following them all inside.

It was lovely, of course it was. A college house – which was rare, usually they were sets of rooms – was obviously not huge, but still with a staircase that managed to curl round a tall narrow hall, a domed skylight above. There were a couple of small but perfectly proportioned Jane Austen-style rooms downstairs, plus a more modern kitchen at the back with a sunny conservatory, and four bedrooms upstairs. But it was the garden that took my breath away. I hung out of what would be Tabitha's bedroom window and gazed down. A long, narrow, leafy, walled enclosure, its borders full of tasteful blue and white colour even at this time of year and, near the bottom, a round pond with an elegant nymph statue pouring water from a jug into it. Beyond was a gorgeous weeping willow, swaying gently in the breeze. It was so beautiful it made me realize what they must think of Sebastian to give it to him. As I drew in my head I felt humbled.

'It's lovely,' I said, clattering downstairs, but knowing I mustn't stay: knowing the floodgates would open before long. 'And where do you paint?' I gabbled, even though I already knew. Had peeked inside.

'Upstairs,' he told me. 'In one of the spare rooms. But also outside, which I haven't done for years.'

'Bit chilly for the sitters?' I joked, keeping a breezy smile going.

'Oh, I haven't started doing that yet. Just a landscape, that's all, that sort of thing.'

Our conversation drew to an abrupt halt at this point, as it did when we talked about painting.

'Right, well, I'll be away, then,' I said lightly. I gathered my keys from a table, and my bag, glancing, for a final time, around the pretty, putty-coloured walls, hung already with Sebastian's paintings, but others too: friends' paintings – famous ones, mostly. It occurred to me I'd been wrong to tell Josh he didn't have an inheritance. There was surely one here.

The children were outside, unloading the last of their stuff onto the grass quad, from whence they could transport it later.

'I'll just say goodbye to the kids.'

Sebastian put a hand on my arm. We were alone in the hall. The first time he'd touched me for years.

'Thank you, Ella,' he said, his hooded eyes heavy with meaning. 'For doing this.'

I averted my eyes first. Nodded at the carpet. Knew he wouldn't be so crass as to explain I wasn't really losing them, that they'd be back all the time, and that by doing this I was enabling them in so many ways. Or that I'd done a wonderful job as a mother, or anything patronizing like that. Some sort of gross golden handshake. But it was all there, in the eyes. His gratitude.

I turned to go, feeling old and tired. As I walked down the gravel path flanked by late hollyhocks and roses, I held my arms out dramatically to my children, big beaming smile in place. Tabitha left what she was doing and ran to hug me, squeezing me hard. Even Josh gave me a clap on the back as he hugged me and said, 'Cheers, Mum,' in a gruff voice, which bloody nearly tipped me over the edge.

I quickly got into the car, turned the ignition and gave them all a cheerful, overenthusiastic wave as they stood together, the three of them. I didn't buzz down the window in case I choked. Only the porter gave me a second glance as he let me out, opening the gate, and as I blindly scrabbled for my sunglasses in my bag. I shoved them on my already damp face. A blue car, which had followed us down the cobbled street as we'd arrived, was now parked outside the college gates. I saw the back of a woman in a camel coat getting into the driving seat, but I didn't wait to see what she thought of my demeanour. Instead I drove past at speed, swung into another cobbled side street, and parked abruptly at the end of what turned out to be a dead-end lane. Then I switched off the engine and howled.

Chapter Twenty-Seven

I think I must have sat there for quite some time, because when I looked at my watch it was one o'clock. I didn't want to go home, I decided, when I'd recovered. Or as much as I was likely to recover, anyway. I sat up a bit at the wheel. Didn't want to go back to an empty house. I felt drained and limp and it occurred to me the best thing I could do was go to a restaurant and try to eat. I wouldn't, I knew, but I could have a drink, read a newspaper or something, ring Lottie. And then go and spend a great deal of money I didn't have in Brora.

I knew Sebastian wouldn't have any food in the house and since it was lunchtime they might well do the same, I realized. If I wanted to avoid bumping into them, I'd have to go to the other end of town. Even as I thought it, though, even as I was driving back down the High Street, crawling along in heavy traffic, I saw them. The back of them, anyway. Sebastian, tall and dark with his long, lanky stride, between the two children. Tabitha, in a tiny skirt, was almost hopping beside him, excitedly, like a child; Josh, telling his father something, his face as I passed, glancing in my rear-view mirror, alight, on fire, as they turned into that huge buzzing brassiere, the Quad, for some lunch. Half of me wanted to vomit, but the other half, I was relieved to note, loved them enough to be glad. I hadn't seen any of them looking so happy for a long time, I reflected sadly.

I went right to the other end of Oxford, to Browns, which was equally buzzing and cheerful, I thought defiantly, as I was shown to one of the few remaining tables for two. Newspapers were available in a rack, so I spread out *The Times*, ordered a glass of wine and an omelette, and made myself read and eat. The drinking came more easily. When I'd drained my glass I wondered if they'd thought to send me a little message? Tabitha might have done. I checked my phone. Well, of course not; they've just arrived, Ella, don't be foolish. Tonight, perhaps, as she was going to bed. 'Thanks, Mum, you're a star. Hope you're OK?' Or something like that. There was one from Ludo, though.

Are you all right? Big day. Thinking of you. x

I'd texted him, finally. Properly. In response to about eight of his, telling him what was happening today: needing his love, somehow. Just as a friend. Some show of support. He'd been brilliant. He hadn't rung, he'd just texted some really lovely words of encouragement, saying I was doing the right thing and that the children would benefit hugely from my big-heartedness. I didn't feel big-hearted. I felt shrivelled. But I wrote back now:

Yes, I'm OK. Don't worry. Thank you. x

As I paid the bill and closed my newspaper, I noticed that Jude Law, who was on the front page, pictured at some film premiere in an open-necked pink shirt, had a hairy chest too, which was interesting.

Brora was at the other end of town, the Magdalen Bridge end, the Sebastian and the children end, so I couldn't go there. But Clarendon Street had a few boutiques and I made myself browse for an hour, just as I'd made myself eat. As I paid for a pair of velvet palazzo pants, which I could neither afford nor imagine where I was going in them, some feather earrings too, I resolved that it was important to make oneself do things. And that when I got home, I would tidy the entire house and maybe even paint the sitting room, which I'd been meaning to do for some time. Had even bought the pretty yellow Farrow and Ball paint, just hadn't got round to it. I certainly didn't want to go back to Leanne and the gang upstairs. The very thought of them made me want to join Leanne's mother, Arlene, comatose on the sofa. Copy a few of her over-imbibing techniques. The thought raised a smile, which was progress, I decided, as I walked back to my car, which was on a meter, opposite the Ashmolean, in Walton Street.

As I went to open it, though, someone across the road caught my eye. My smile faded. Eliza was coming out of the museum, a glossy catalogue in her hand. With a friend? No, on her own. I wondered, with a jolt, if she'd seen me. If I could get away quickly, but she had. She was coming towards me.

'Hello, Ella.'

'Eliza!' I flushed. 'How are you?'

'Fine, thanks, and you?'

'Yes, really well, thank you. Haven't seen you for ages.'

'No, that's right.'

She was looking drawn, but slightly better than usual, I thought. Quite a lot of make-up. Her hair was still scraped back off her face in that severe manner and the Liberty scarf was firmly knotted round her throat. My mouth felt a bit dry and I scrabbled for conversation.

'Have you been to look at the Peruvian Statues?' I nodded at the posters advertising the exhibition on the railings across the street.

'No, not yet.'

'Oh, it's just . . . I saw your catalogue. Thought – Oh, sorry. Won't be a mo.' My phone was ringing in my pocket. I plucked it out and went to switch it off, or quickly answer if it was the children, but it stopped ringing anyway before I could get to it. I glanced at the number, which was one I didn't recognize.

'It's me,' Eliza said quietly. She drew her hand out of her own coat pocket, holding her phone. 'I'm ringing you. Which means you're having an affair with my husband.'

She gave me a level stare. It seemed to me that she gazed into the depths of my soul. I gaped at her, horrified. Felt the blood drain from my face.

'I took his phone while he was asleep,' she went on. 'Saw a number that kept recurring in his send box. I didn't recognize it. It came up far too frequently. I suspected it was you. He talks about you too much. Mention-itis, I believe it's called.' She was still holding my eyes. I couldn't speak. There was so much pain there, in that heavy hazel gaze. 'It's happened once before, you see. Years ago. Oh, he's not a serial adulterer or anything like that, but he talked a lot about her, too. Just after we were married. I'm asking you not to do this, Ella. My family won't survive it. The girls won't survive it. Particularly Henrietta. I'm pleading with you to leave him alone.'

I felt as if someone had driven fast down the street and knocked me flying off my feet. I was hanging on to the bonnet.

I gulped, horrified. Still couldn't say anything. Useless to deny it. To say that nothing happened. It had. We'd fallen in love. Nothing had happened in bed, but pretty much everywhere else.

'He's a romantic,' Eliza continued. 'I knew that when I married him. Romantics fall in love. More than once. They like to be in love. At all times. And you're very lovable, Ella. Pretty and vulnerable in your charming, tumbledown farm, with your famous but arrogant husband who no one can believe can't love you and could leave you. There you are, beautiful and dreamy, in your sweetly chaotic inherited farm and your flowery dresses and your wellies, surrounded by ducks and chickens, with your talented, clever children. You live the dream. All it really needed was for Sebastian to give you a black eye and the vulnerability would be complete. I knew when we first met you that Ludo wouldn't be able to resist you. I hoped you'd resist him.'

I found my voice. 'I have, up to a point,' I managed. I didn't recognize this person. This girl she was describing, like someone stepping out of a Cath Kidston catalogue.

'Yes, I thought you might have done. A lot of frantic texts from him, but not so many from you, recently. But don't backslide, will you, Ella? Now that Sebastian has well and truly abandoned you? Don't weaken. Trust me, there will be plenty of men sniffing round your door, but there will never be any round mine. You'll be fine, Ella. Men will always want women like you. Pretty, soft, disarming women. But they won't want me. I'm too prickly. I wasn't always, but it's become my defence mechanism. My armour. I'm begging you,' she gave a strange, twisted smile, 'in the immortal words of Dolly Parton, not to take my man. He's flawed, for sure, but I love him. And the girls love him. And we can get over this, as a family, if you let us. If you leave us alone.'

I opened my mouth to speak but she'd already turned away. She didn't want to hear my denials. Or my apologies. Or know about my shame. She was already walking fast down the street in her camel Jaeger coat, the sort my mother used to wear, her hands stuffed deep in her pockets, no doubt clenched hard. I felt as if the vehicle which had knocked me off my feet had suddenly stopped and flung me from its windscreen into the gutter. As if in a daze, I watched as she stopped a bit further down the road. She fished a key from her pocket and, without looking back, got into a bright blue Polo, which, of course, I recognized. The one parked outside Christchurch: the woman in the camel coat. Moments later she'd driven away.

I stood there for a good few minutes after she'd gone, transfixed to the pavement. Turned to stone. Then I quickly got into my own car. My hand was trembling as I turned the ignition. As I pulled out I nearly ran over a traffic warden who'd appeared beside me, smiling at me through the window.

'Just in time, luv!' he observed in a friendly manner, but I ignored him. His face changed when he saw mine. Stricken, no doubt. I drove off.

With complete disregard for the speed cameras on the Banbury Road, I drove fast towards the ring road. I felt numb as I left it and headed for the lanes, but then abruptly, as if a switch had been flicked in my brain, my mind started racing at breakneck speed. I was the Jezebel. The predator. The sort of woman I so despised. The sort who stole other women's husbands. Of course I was. But, somehow,

I'd persuaded myself I wasn't. After all, I'd rejected Ludo when I'd discovered Eliza wasn't having an affair, but . . . that had been a shock, that discovery. And shocks pass. Fade, after a while, as we get used to them. How long would it have been before I'd persuaded myself that she might not be having an affair, but she'd still brought it upon herself? By dressing like my mother? Staking her claim in a territorial way, in what I now realized was a desperate way, deserving of pity rather than contempt? The only way she knew how? Everything about her, her clothes, her stern, disapproving demeanour, screamed: '*No*, Ludo, stop it! *I'm* your wife! Come back!' Misguided. Badly judged. Unlikely to endear herself, or even engender success, but heartbreaking, surely?

And how brave, how much in love, to confront me in the street like that. To follow me all morning in her car. Had she followed us from the farm, I wondered? Or just chanced upon us driving into Christchurch? How hard would *her* heart have been beating, behind mine? How tightly would *she* have been gripping the wheel of her Polo, waiting for me outside Sebastian's college, then Browns? Picking up a catalogue at the door of the Ashmolean, holding on to it tightly as she waited in the portico. And she was so right. Now that Sebastian had gone I could easily have drifted down the slippery slope towards Ludo again. Had already replied to his texts, when I'd told myself I wouldn't. Had added kisses. Had admired Jude's chest. How long before I was sitting in a different cosy hotel bar, miles away from Oxford this time, in Devon, perhaps, where circumstances were finally more conducive, and where we laughed about our hilarious escapade in Binfield?

Ashamed and humbled, I drove down the lanes that led to the farm. I felt, not a liking exactly for Eliza, but more than a sneaking admiration. A bloody great bucketful of admiration, actually. And a huge amount of guilt. My father used to say that the worst thing you could hear, the worst thing anyone could say to you, was, 'Shame on you.' I felt it very much upon me now.

I purred slowly down my lane, shoulders hunched, not even wanting to go home. Just wanting to hide. But, just as I was convinced that my day could surely not get any worse, I swung through the farmyard gate and it took another dive. There, in the muddy cobbled drive, was my sister's car. I shuddered to a halt, dismayed. Then I turned off the ignition and moaned low. All I needed right now. Really, all I needed. I slumped, defeated, at the wheel: even rested my head on it for a moment. Oh, God. Had Eliza phoned her best friend already? Told Ginnie, in no uncertain terms, that she was sorry to be the bearer of bad news, but she'd just confronted her little sister, who, for all her artful, whimsical ways, was actually a scheming adulterous witch? An arch, manipulative husband-stealer? I raised my head.

Ginnie was waiting for me by her car. Even she wouldn't break into a locked house. As I sat up and trembled she peeled herself off her car and bore down on me. And she didn't just bear down, she hastened, almost breaking into a run, hair vertical, lips tight, eyes madder than ever, full, it seemed to me, of homicidal thoughts. Slowly, I got out of the car to face the music. Braced myself inwardly. But I'd taken my sister's grim demeanour for anger, when in fact it was intense, euphoric, satisfaction. An easy mistake to make with Ginnie.

'I've done it,' she told me tersely, chin jutting out trium-phantly as I emerged. 'I've dispatched the silly cow.'

I gazed at her. It took a moment, but slowly it dawned. And with it came relief. Not me.

'Maureen?'

'Exactly. Maureen. Not as quickly as I'd have liked, because what I thought I'd achieve in a day turned into a week-long campaign – the woman showed some metal, which surprised me. Don't let the fluffy slippers fool you, incidentally. But it's done. The deed is done. She's gone.' She clenched her teeth, almost quivering with satisfaction.

I felt such profound relief that I was out of the frame I could barely stand up. Victory was surely all over my sister. In her eyes, her hair, even down to the battle scars on her scruffy trousers. Any minute now she'd burst into her very own St Crispin's Day speech. I turned away so she wouldn't see my face and she followed me eagerly into the house.

More than anything in the world I wanted to be alone. To lick my wounds, to look at my trembling hands, recall Eliza's contempt and pain in private. Recoil from it on my own. But Ginnie wanted to share. To tell me everything. She'd been fighting hard and she'd had a major coup. Dis-patches would necessarily follow. As I put the kettle on it made me realize how alone we all are. I hadn't given Gin-nie a thought for days. She hadn't me. No one really considered each other, did they? No one was truly sensi-tive to each other's needs. Fleetingly, of course. Guiltily, if we knew there was distress in their lives. But we were all so parcelled up in our own, we became distracted. Yet this was my parents she was talking about. I forced myself to listen, to concentrate as I opened the boot-room door and greeted the howling dogs. Ottoline would have walked and fed them, but I needed their unconditional, uncomplicated noses in my hand right now, their crooning whimpers of delight. And then again, I thought as I straightened up, maybe Ginnie was also what I needed right now? Someone to prattle on, someone who was pleased with themselves, so wrapped up in themselves, they wouldn't give me a second thought?

'She resisted, of course. Oh, boy, did she resist.' Ginnie was saying as I gave Ladyboy some grain in a saucer. Even as she talked, I realized I wasn't listening. I was outside the Ashmolean. Talented, clever children, Eliza had said. Were they? I knew Henrietta struggled. Ludo had told me she was borderline Special Needs. I never quite knew what that meant. 'No, you wouldn't,' Ludo had said with a sad smile when I'd voiced it, tentatively. Mine had never struggled, so I'd naturally found other things to worry about. Tabitha's lack of confidence about how she looked – much better now, since she'd lost some weight. Josh's sharp tongue, which got him into trouble at school. But maybe I should concentrate more on the things they could do? Paint? Act? Always come near the top of the class? But it came so easily to them, like flopping down horizontal on a sofa, which they were so good at too, but . . . why didn't I celebrate success more? Sebastian didn't either, I knew. Just took it for granted. Josh was obviously clever and sharp, precocious, even, for his age, but Ginnie had nearly fallen off her kitchen stool at Tabitha's straight A stars in the GCSEs she'd taken early. Why hadn't I *told* her, she kept saying, almost petulantly.

'Told you what?'

'That she's so clever!'

'I – I don't know,' I'd faltered, confused. Should I have

done? Was I surprised myself? No, not really. Tabs had always had pretty good reports, though they said she could speak up more in class, be more confident. But I hadn't thought it was so important. Not as important as other things. But I wondered how all-consuming it would be if my child had special needs? Like Eliza's? Severe dyslexia? It also occurred to me that she, Eliza, must have known I'd lost my own children this morning. She'd seen me take them to their father's. She wasn't to know it was permanent, of course, although if she'd stuck her nose round the college gates she'd have seen us unloading a laden car. But if she had thought it a big day for my children, might she also have thought: 'So what? Hers can take it. They're robust, clever. Mine can't.' Own worlds again. Tabitha would give all the A stars in the world to have a boyfriend, like Chloe, Ludo's youngest, who was so pretty. Yes, perhaps that's what Eliza had thought.

'Picture the scene, OK, Ella.' Ginnie was planted firmly on a chair at my kitchen table, sleeves rolled up, knees apart. 'She comes to the door, like some fishwife, cigarette in mouth, those wretched slippers, and says, "Yes?" In an imperious way. Like I'm a bloody tradesman!'

'Oh. She didn't look like that,' I said absently, handing her a coffee.

'Well, OK, she might have said hello first,' admitted Ginnie, never one to let the truth stand in the way of a good story. 'But she was jolly abrupt. So I gave her the good news. Told her who I was. That rocked her back a bit, I can tell you.'

'I can imagine.' One could almost feel sorry for Maureen, who had, after all, lifted Dad's spirits considerably, I thought. I recalled how I'd gone to the Old Rectory and they'd been cycling together, making biscuits. But I hadn't liked the B&B idea. 'And where was Dad?'

'At the rally – you rang and told me, remember? This was a few days ago – I'm just filling you in. So, anyway, she wouldn't let me in, said she didn't like my tone. So we had some argy-bargy on the doorstep with me telling her exactly what I thought of *her* tone, and of her making money out of my parents' house. The place is full of dogs, incidentally, let alone lodgers.'

'I know. She's a dog psychologist, remember?'

She snorted. 'Or some such bollocks. Anyway, I warned her I was going to take legal action and I clearly put the wind up her because, when I went back today, there'd been some progress. The lodgers had gone – there were only three, but at least their ghastly bicycles and rucksacks had gone from the hall – and she was there on her own.'

'Where was Dad?' I asked again.

'He's been staying with Peggy and Peter.'

How like my father, I thought. To run a mile. To leave it to someone more capable to sort out. As, perhaps, I would, too.

'Anyway, Hugo and Frankie were with me.'

I jumped. 'Oh?' Even in my sorry, shell-shocked state I could raise some interest at this. 'Really? You've seen his hair, then? His tattoo? Piercings?'

'Oh, yes, but it's all superficial, isn't it?'

'Yes. Yes, it is.'

'And he's so much better now he's working with horses. I don't know why we didn't think of that.'

Yet again I'd underestimated her. Yet again. Big strong Ginnie. I looked at her as I sat down across the table from her with . . . yes. Love. Loving her gumption, which could always be relied upon, and could be deployed in all manner of ways.

'They came to help. Hugo's been worried about his grandpa; the whole village has, apparently. Daddy's just been completely taken over by this woman. And, actually, I didn't have to say anything, Ella. I mean, I tried to, but Hugo told me to leave it to him. We went inside – just me and Hugo, Frankie decided it was none of her business – and went to sit in the drawing room. And Hugo – well, he was obviously much nicer to her than I would have been. And every time I tried to interrupt and have my two pennyworth he'd say: "Mum, hang on." Quietly. But he told her – this Maureen – how Daddy had felt compelled to move out because he couldn't handle the situation. And that although Maureen had been a terrific friend to Daddy, he was a bit out of his depth now. There's something about Hugo, Ella.' Her eyes shone with admiration. 'A depth. A sincerity. People listen to him. Something to do with his gentleness, which certainly doesn't come from me.' Certainly, I thought fervently. 'And, somehow, that shaved head, the piercing, it *really* doesn't matter: almost helps.' She struggled to explain. 'Like – some sort of hair shirt. It was such a shock, of course, when I saw him, but it's still the intelligent face, the same soft brown eyes.'

I nodded. I could see Hugo handling it brilliantly. Sensitively.

'He talked a bit about how he'd recently lost his own way. I couldn't believe he needed to tell this woman all this, but he did. And how he was pleased he hadn't lost touch with the person he was meant be.' I didn't look at my sister at this. Could see this was hard for her. 'And how he hadn't, in the end, become the person everyone expected him to be. He said he'd liked Maureen when she'd taken up with Grandpa, played cribbage with him in the pub, but he didn't want to watch her become someone she wasn't. Someone defensive and defiant, just because she'd made a mistake with the lodgers. Just because she'd gone a step too far. "Hang on, Mum," he kept saying, as I kept trying to butt in and point out that, in *my* opinion, she'd gone a *lot* more than a step too far. He made me go to the kitchen, put the kettle on. But I didn't, I loitered in the hall. Heard him saying it would be so easy for a witch hunt to ensue, especially in a village like this. How Maureen could become vilified, which would be wrong, because, in fact, she was a very nice person. At which point Maureen burst into tears.'

'Oh!'

'And Hugo was brilliant. Let her cry a bit, then went to sit next to her on the sofa. Patted her hand. I did go and make some tea at that point. Felt a lump in my own throat. Felt a bit of a heel, too, if I'm honest. But while the kettle was boiling I crept back to the hall and I heard Maureen say that it had all just got out of hand. That what had seemed a good idea – one lodger – had escalated, and she'd got carried away, but she never meant any harm. She *had* made a bit of money from it, but not much, and she'd been washing sheets and serving breakfast like nobody's business. I have to say the house was very tidy, despite the desperate pong of whatever it is she spreads about. Anyway, I was quietly hoping Hugo would cut to the chase and politely show her the door, but he just said that with his grandpa staying down the road, he could see how she'd got herself backed into a corner. That he'd made it even harder for her, by not publicly supporting her, and would she like to stay on a while and think things through?

'Maureen looked up at him – I was peering round the door at this point – and she dabbed her eyes with a tissue and said: "No, thank you, Hugo." Quite sort of . . . proudly. She said this might be the nicest house she'd ever stayed in and was ever likely to stay in, but she had a little house of her own and she'd go back to it. She said she wished Angus had come back and been as nice as Hugo had, and if he had she might have listened to him, instead of which she'd dug her heels in in defiance: adopted a sort of siege mentality, which wasn't her at all. She said she hadn't recognized herself these past few days; but that cometh the hour, people divided into two categories, didn't they? Fight or flight. And she was a fighter. Unlike Angus, who had chosen flight. At this point I felt compelled to come back into the room, minus the tea, and say that, actually, I was a fighter too, and I sort of understood.'

'Good for you, Ginnie,' I said quietly.

'Could sort of see how she'd got herself into this pickle. But I did say "sort of" a lot.' I smiled. 'There were an awful lot of ghastly teddies around to temper my sympathy. On Mummy's walnut desk, for heaven's sake! A huge pink one!'

'But you had *some* sympathy,' I urged, bringing her back.

'Yes. A bit. Anyway, Hugo and I finally left and went to the pub and Frankie joined us. She's lovely, incidentally. So funny and quick and Hugo just lights up at the sight of her. It's heaven to see. Like he used to when he'd hit a six, or went up for a prize at speech day, remember?'

'Yes.' I smiled. I privately thought Frankie was his real prize. First prize. Ginnie looked so much happier, too.

'And we chatted for ages in the pub. A lot about Maureen, about how she'd backed herself into a corner, but also about what he, Hugo, wanted to do. I didn't suggest anything, I swear to God, Ella.'

'You know about Cambridge?'

'Of course. In my bones, if I'm honest, I knew months ago.' She swallowed. 'Was just in denial. I knew he wouldn't stay. But we didn't discuss that. He just talked about the horses down at Peter Mortimer's, and how much he was enjoying it. He's got quite a lot of responsibility there, you know. Peter still owns the yard, obviously, and all the livestock, but Hugo's very much acting as manager. There's a string of fifteen hunters and eventers.'

'But Hugo can cope with that.'

'Oh, God, yes, with his eyes shut,' she said, with a flash of the old mother courage. 'But what I mean is, it could be a proper business.'

'In time,' I said gently.

'Yes, I know. In time. And actually Frankie was the one putting the brakes on. Saying he shouldn't increase the yard just yet, should keep it the way it is for a year or two. Work his way in. Just as she puts the brakes on the wedding.'

'Oh?'

'Not that she doesn't want to get married. She does. But she told me quietly, when he'd gone to the loo, that she's persuaded him to wait at least three years.'

'Oh, that's good.'

'Exactly.' Ginnie's eyes shone. 'By which time he'll be twenty-four and she'll be twenty-one. The same as Richard and I were. She's a jolly sensible girl, actually, Ella. Adores him, but doesn't want him to feel pressured into marrying just because he's asked her. He gave her a ring but she wears it on a long chain round her neck, under her clothes.'

'Sweet!'

'Yes, she is,' Ginnie said gratefully. 'He's very lucky to have her.' She gulped. 'And I . . . sort of, told her that.'

'Did you?' I felt my eyes well up.

'I did. I think even you might have been proud of me, Ella.'

She looked at me tentatively. Almost nervously. And so many years rolled back: years of being very different sisters. It was like the tide shrinking away to reveal a beach of gnarled, distorted pebbles, each with their own history. Each pebble a fight, or a sulk, or a slammed door. So many injustices felt, because we couldn't understand one another. Couldn't fathom each other out. But, at this moment, I felt we did. In my eyes she'd always been a bit of a bully. Whereas she probably felt I was a coward. That she was strong and I was weak. But perhaps we were neither, except when pushed to take up positions. Like Maureen. And Eliza. So that the small streaks became broad strokes. Perhaps, at heart, we were a lot more marginal and blurred.

We each took a very deep breath. Let it out simultaneously with a sigh – and then laughed. These two middle-aged women, slightly careworn – more than slightly – very much frayed at the edges, but still drinking coffee together, as we had done for many years, in each other's kitchen.

'Maureen said she'd be going in a day or two, but in fact, when we emerged from the Rose and Crown, she was packing her car in the front drive.'

'No sign of Dad, of course?'

'Of course not. He'll wait till the coast is very clear.' But Ginnie didn't say it bitterly, as she might usually. Or add: 'Leaving someone else to do his dirty work.' She just ran her hands through her hair. Tried, unsuccessfully, to smooth it down a bit. She smiled. 'And meanwhile I gather Mummy's had a date?'

'One or two,' I told her. 'With the not-so-short-sighted Charles.'

'Ah. Not a blind date, then.'

We giggled.

Ginnie sighed. 'Well, I know you always support Daddy, but, you have to admit – good for her, in a way.'

'Oh, I agree.'

She looked surprised. 'Good.' She pulled a face. 'Apparently, there's a chauffeur and Mummy and Charles look like royalty in the back.'

'They do. You've seen them?'

'No, Eliza said she saw them driving into town the other day. Anyway, enough of our blasted parents and my blasted kids, what about you? I haven't asked you a thing about your life, Ella. How are you?'

Chapter Twenty-Eight

I'd already risen quickly at the mention of her name. Gone to the sink, ostensibly to rinse my mug, but in reality to hide my face.

'Me? Oh, I'm fine.'

'Sure?' Ginnie got up to join me. Rinsed her own cup. Then peered right round to inspect me properly. 'You look – well, you've gone a bit ashen, actually. Like you've seen a ghost.'

I shook my head dismissively. 'I took the children to Sebastian this morning, Ginnie. Feel a bit – you know. Bereft.'

It was true: I missed them more than ever now. Wanted to draw my clan round me after that ghastly scene at the Ashmolean, say: Well, *these* are mine. But I was being disingenuous, too. It was the content of the scene that had sent me flying. I wondered if I should tell Ginnie? Before Eliza did? But then . . . I had a feeling Eliza wouldn't. Even though I told Lottie pretty much everything. Pretty much. Not the whole lot. I turned to dry my hands on a tea towel.

'Ginnie, you couldn't give me Eliza's mobile number, could you?' I said in what I hoped was a reasonably normal voice. 'Only I bumped into her in town today and she mentioned an exhibition she was going to. I can't remember where it was and I thought I'd get out a bit more now that . . . you know. Empty house and all that.'

'Sure!' She whipped her BlackBerry out, pleased. With

lightning reflexes she began to tap her friend's phone number into mine. I had a vague idea it was in my phone already, since she'd rung me, but I wouldn't know how to retrieve it; I'd only just grasped predictive texting – Ludo had shown me – but Ginnie had been at the cutting edge of technology for years. Sebastian, of course, didn't even have a mobile, I thought fondly. Far too fondly. Don't think of him standing there looking expectant as he awaited his children, hair short and clean, pink shirt pressed, like a small boy at boarding school awaiting his parents' first visit, and then looking completely thrilled and open-faced as we rounded the corner, as he could occasionally. On our wedding day. At the births of both his children: standing by, gripping my hand. Bounding up five flights of stairs in London with Diblet in his coat. Don't think. I shut my eyes. Hoped I wasn't going to faint. Wondered why I'd been such a fool. But I knew why. I opened them again. Ginnie was happily still engrossed in her textual transaction so didn't see my face and I'd re-arranged it by the time she looked up.

'There. Good idea, Ella. And there's a fantastic new play on at the Playhouse, apparently, Millie Saunders told me. Richard won't be interested because it's a musical, not his cup of tea at all, but maybe we could go? I know about the bereft thing, incidentally.' She added, her face momentarily saddened. 'With Hugo.'

'I'd love to,' I told her, meaning it. 'And we could have a bite to eat first.'

'Good idea. I'll get tickets. Oh, God – look at the time! And the piano tuner's coming – I must fly.'

And seizing her keys she scurried off to her car, happier than I'd seen her look in a long time, I thought.

I watched from the window until her car had left my drive. Then I sat down and texted Eliza.

> I will never see Ludo again. You have my word.

She came back within moments.

> Thank you. I would be grateful if you didn't tell him – or indeed anyone – about our conversation this afternoon. It will only make him hate me.

My heart lurched for her at this. I frantically texted back.

> I will never breathe a word.

I knew now she wouldn't be telling Ginnie. Wouldn't want it spread any further. I sank back in my chair. Lady-boy was gazing at me from a pile of old newspapers on the kitchen table and Diblet's dear old head was on my knee. My troops. My arch defenders. And I was still armed. Still dangerous. Even though my weapon lay limp in my hand. I regarded it a moment, then raised it. Texted another number.

> Thank you for asking how I am, I will be fine. But I can't see you ever again, Ludo. You cannot be my sticking plaster. I'm changing my number. Please don't get in touch with me. I mean it.

And this time there was no kiss. I didn't even find it hard to resist. And that way, he'd know I meant it.

I thought I'd feel cold and numb and miserable after that, but, strangely, I felt better. Almost energized. Control, I suppose. That elusive old chestnut. I got up and went outside, pausing only to plunge my feet into my boots. Odd socks again, I noticed. Then I whistled to the dogs and went out to feed my sheep. As I passed the water butt by the old barn I took my sim card from my phone and threw it in. I didn't even stop to see if it sank to the bottom. Just walked on by.

Ottoline, of course, was already one step ahead of me on the animal front, her priorities being ever practical. I found her pouring meal into a long, galvanized trough at the far end of the field, the ewes, running up to push their noses into it hungrily, bleating balefully.

'Thanks, Ottoline,' I told her as she straightened up with the sack and turned at my approach. 'You've been doing far too much for me lately.'

She smiled. 'I enjoy it, you know I do. But nice to have you back.' She looked at me properly. 'You've been away a long time.'

How strange. It was the same line that Celia Johnson's husband had delivered at the end of *Brief Encounter*, the film Ludo and I had seen so recently.

'Well, I'm back now,' I said shortly and indeed self-consciously. I was pretty sure it had been Celia's response.

Ottoline gave her small, enigmatic smile. She didn't ask me how my night away with my friend Rebecca had been. Ottoline had a sixth sense about so many things.

We left the ewes eating happily and walked in silence to the feed shed, where she deposited her sack, but it wasn't an uncomfortable silence. Then we delved into the bin to collect a scoop apiece of Layers Pellets to give to the chickens.

'I see Sebastian's gone,' she said lightly as we made our way across the yard.

This stopped me in my tracks. 'You mean he didn't say goodbye?'

'Oh, yes. In a manner of speaking. A week or so ago. He just didn't say when exactly he was going.'

'Ah.' We walked on. It occurred to me that Ottoline would miss him almost as much as I would. She'd miss the children too, which I couldn't bear to mention. But Ottoline wasn't quite like other budgerigars.

'I like my own company,' she told me, second-guessing me. 'It's you I'm worried about.'

'Me?' I gave a tinny little laugh. 'Oh, don't worry about me. I'll be fine,' I warbled, thinking: *Don't* be nice, Ottoline. Not someone as bluff and straightforward as you. Don't sympathize.

'The ex-girlfriend is about, you know that, don't you?' she said, typically wrong-footing me. No flannel there, then.

'Isobel?'

'I don't know her name. The blonde.'

'Yes, Isobel.'

It hadn't escaped me. Not that I'd seen her, but somehow I'd known. Had always been aware of Sebastian's pulse. His heartbeat. And, on a less visceral, more tangible level, had been aware of comings and goings at the Granary recently, too.

'I didn't see them,' she went on. 'Someone just told me they'd seen them in town together.'

'I know.' Why was she telling me this? My heart began to clench in that horrid, familiar way.

'But Isobel isn't a threat, Ella.'

I stopped again and turned to look at her. 'I know that, too. Sebastian's deliberately gone for someone he won't fall in love with, I know. I understand that man right down to his little finger, know him inside out, but we've separated, Ottoline. Christ, he's moved out! We're even more separated than usual, than we have been for years. What is it to me who he sees?'

'I just don't want you to use it as an excuse, that's all. To throw up your hands and say, "Oh, well, he's with Isobel again, what can I do?" There's a lot you can do.'

My heart began to hammer fast in my chest. 'What d'you mean?'

'Ella, why d'you think Sebastian has gone?'

'Well, to – to give us both some space. Some finality. Closure, I believe the Americans would call it.'

'And to work,' she said softly.

'Yes,' I agreed tautly, trying to keep my voice steady.

'Which he can't do here, with you.'

I swallowed. Did she know? No one knew. She gave me a flinty look.

'Ella, I know what happened. Why it all fell apart.'

I had to hold out a hand to steady myself. The flat of it found the rough brick texture of the barn wall. After a moment, eyelids lowered against her in defence, I made myself look at her.

'He told you?' I said, aghast.

'Yes. He did. Years ago, when you first came here.'

'Right.' Years ago. Christ.

'And I didn't say he'd gone to Oxford to paint,' she went on quietly. 'I said he'd gone to work. To inspire. To teach. Something he *can* do without you around.'

I averted my gaze to the feeding ewes in the distance. Couldn't look at her. Unsteadily I removed my hand from the wall and carried on walking. She fell in beside me as I stared resolutely down at the two pairs of boots on this damp, October day, concentrating hard on the way they splashed through the mud, the puddles in the yard.

'The new chickens have settled in well,' I said conversationally, keeping my voice steady. 'I thought they'd fight at first, but they haven't.'

'Bugger the chickens.'

I stopped. Touched my forehead with my fingertips. It was damp.

'We're over, Ottoline,' I said quietly. 'Sebastian and me. Well and truly. You know that.' I gave a hollow laugh, raising my face incredulously to the heavens. 'He doesn't even love me, for one thing.'

She seized my arm and swung me round to face her. She looked furious. 'How can you say that? How *dare* you?'

I gazed, astonished, into her blazing eyes. Ottoline didn't do emotion. 'Well, he doesn't. He hates me.'

'Oh, hate, sure, which is precariously close to love, isn't it? A very fine line. Like the one between passion and art. Which – and I know it wasn't your fault, Ella, wasn't ever how you wanted it to be – he was forced to choose between.'

My mouth was so dry I had to work my tongue hard to produce saliva.

'I didn't ask him to choose between me and art, Ottoline. Christ – we wanted both!'

'Yes, but he couldn't have both, could he? Couldn't finish a picture. It didn't mean he stopped loving you; he just hated what he'd become. A has-been. A failure. Yesterday's man. In some ways I wish you'd carried on painting, Ella. Buggered off to France or somewhere inspirational. Done your own thing.'

And with that she stomped off, bucket swinging from her hand, gripping it tightly: a short, stumpy figure in faded denim, disappearing into the distance. I gazed after her.

'Instead of doing *his* thing,' I finished for her softly, and to her departing back.

Chapter Twenty-Nine

The first time it happened it had been a joke. A laugh. Stumbling up the five flights of stairs to the attic flat in Cadogan Terrace shortly before we were married, fresh from a party in a restaurant, San Lorenzo's, I think – roaring with laughter at some joke: some fellow painter who'd slid clean under the table he was so drunk – clutching each other as we remembered. Sebastian was in his huge brown overcoat, me in some arty flowing number, something I'd seen on another girl on the tube and copied. Engaged, happy, pregnant. Sebastian had probably been a bit worse for drink, but I wasn't because of the baby. Just high on life. We'd had to shoulder-barge into the flat, as usual – the door always stuck – making 'Don't wake the neighbours!' faces at each other and then, once our hilarity had died down, Sebastian, as always, had gone to his easel to wind down whilst I'd disappeared into the galley kitchen to make some tea. His current canvas was a landscape, almost finished, but not quite. I knew what he was going to do with it, though.

'What?' he asked, amused, rising to the bait, eyebrows cocked as I returned, handing him a mug of tea.

'Oh, the yellowish-brown, ploughed field at the bottom will turn dramatically to a brilliant wash of yellow ochre in the left-hand corner, as bright as the sun but with just a hint of green. Then a characteristic touch of red will appear in the distance. Probably on the handle of the plough, to draw the eye.'

He roared with laughter, right up to the rafters, not a bit offended. Asked what else. I told him – adopting a camp tone peculiar to one particularly obsequious art critic, one Simon Monk, employing his ridiculous use of random emphasis. I said that in all proba*bility* it would veer *seamlessly*, and in an intensely *Faust*ian direction, towards the obs*cure*, thus achieving, in its *fi*nal execution, a per*ceptive* perspective on the human cond*ition*, despite the over*whelming* pastoral content. Simon wasn't hard to ape and I was a good actress. I squirmed and contorted my face, wringing my hands like Uriah Heep on drugs. Sebastian doubled up.

'You've got him in one!' he yelped.

'And, of course, it'll all be *ex*ecuted with the in*trins*ic Sebastian Montclair *brush*strokes, which have become such a *key*note of his con*temp*orary *rep*ertoire.'

'Oh, will it?' said Sebastian with a grin. He handed me a brush. 'Go on, then, show me.'

He ignored the tea and opened a bottle of wine instead. Handed me a glass. I did allow myself one now and then but it always went straight to my head. Giggling, I waved the brush about, eyeing up Sebastian's canvas and pretending to dab at it, imitating his stance at the easel. The way he rested on his back foot as he surveyed the painting, his other leg slightly at an angle. The way he raised one eyebrow just before adding a brushstroke, then looked almost in pain as he dabbed, eyes half shut. As I said, I'm a good mimic, and Sebastian hooted as he flopped back down on the sofa.

'Oh, I think you should go all the way, Ella!' he said, wiping his eyes. 'Go on, live a little. Have a go.'

'What, on this?' I turned, grinning.

'Why not?'

'But you like this one!'

'I don't, actually.' He made a sour face. 'Was going to ditch it tomorrow. I've fallen out of love with the hay bales in the corner; they're a bit too regimented and anal for my liking. I'm throwing them over for the sumptuous, rolling flesh of my nude tomorrow.' He sipped his wine.

Sebastian always had more than one picture on the go. More than a few, in fact, and the nude behind us was one of many works in progress.

'I'm not sure Mrs Archibald would like to hear herself described as rolling flesh,' I told him sternly. But, rising to the challenge, I picked up his palette. Then I switched the brush he'd given me to something a bit thicker and started to mix white with cobalt blue. The palette was very much his colour scheme, not mine: strong and forceful and quite dark, but I knew how he'd use it. Still imitating his stance to make him laugh – he quite often put his hand in his back pocket – I added a few strokes to the canvas. Sebastian settled back on the sofa behind me, shifting a cushion behind his head, putting his feet up, fuelled with his wine.

'Go *on!*' He laughed.

And so I did. And it was fun. Fun not to be me, to be painting in someone else's style, which came easily, because I didn't have to think. I knew, you see. Didn't have to invent. Or use my brain. I just became another person. Emboldened by grunts of admiring laughter behind me, I played to the gallery and added some trademark strokes which he'd employ only very occasionally, like punctuation marks, and which were greeted with howls of delight. The picture was almost there, anyway – seven-eighths finished – so it wouldn't take long, I reckoned, an hour or so, to cover the blank canvas at the bottom and add some finishing touches.

In the event, though, it was completed much later than either of us imagined, any sort of creative process being like that. Hours pass very quickly. When I turned round, he was fast asleep, the best part of a bottle of wine gone too. I woke him up to show him and, bleary-eyed, he staggered to his feet. He almost gagged with laughter as he prowled round it, roaring with glee, at which point we decided it was time for bed. Arms round each other we stumbled drunkenly away.

The next morning we were still highly delighted and I could tell Sebastian was impressed.

'You'd never know it wasn't me,' he said, standing back and viewing it from all angles, smiling critically.

'Oh, you would,' I said, thinking: Well, no. You wouldn't, actually.

So that was that. And nothing like that happened again for a while. But then, just before we got married, for a laugh, it did. We'd giggled at the still life of flowers and fruit which he hated but had spent ages on, and which I'd finished in an evening just to get rid of it. He laughingly suggested we give to Javier, his agent, for the next collection.

'Don't be ridiculous!' I said, tossing it in the corner.

Around the time of our wedding, though, it happened more often. Sebastian had a one-man show in Cork Street – exhausting. Masses of paintings were required and he was under huge pressure to deliver. A deadline of three weeks hence loomed, and, whilst he had quite a lot of finished pictures, there were an awful lot of unfinished articles too: an awful lot of pictures on the go. Maybe I'd just complete one or two, we thought? We discussed it together over a bottle of wine. Neither of us needed persuading. Indeed, after another bottle, we both thought it a hoot. And an arresting idea, too. It rather cocked a snook at the art world, we felt; the pretension behind all those snooty critics who were so quick to pour scorn, but hadn't an ounce of talent in their little fingers themselves. And, after all, I did it so well. Sebastian marvelled when he came across to my easel.

'Only because you've done three-quarters of the work. The quality work,' I'd say, slightly uncomfortable. He'd look a bit unconvinced.

Javier, however, was delighted.

'Finally you get a beet of a wiggle on!' he declared in his outrageous French accent when he came round one day to flush Sebastian out of his studio, demanding to know how he was getting on. He hustled the paintings down to his van to take them to the framers, which, left to his own devices, Sebastian would take ages to organize. 'Finally,' he called up the stairs, 'I can get them 'anging on the gallery walls!' The door slammed shut behind him.

To show Sebastian, though, I brought home a friend's picture from art school. An unfinished one. One that had been abandoned.

'You see? I have no talent,' I said, finishing Tobias's picture one afternoon in the same way, but in a nineteen-twenties, cubist style quite unlike Sebastian's. 'Can't do anything myself, but give me something to copy and I'm away.'

'Yes, but you're not copying,' he said, as he inspected it, his eyes narrowed, head cocked as he scrutinized. 'You're imitating. That's much better.'

I made a dismissive face. 'It's still pretty uninspired.' I played it down. Right down. Knew I had to.

And, anyway, it wasn't a problem. We hugged the secret to ourselves. It was our special bond. And when the cameras flashed at his one-man exhibition in Cork Street and the champagne flowed and the red stickers flew to the bottom right-hand corners, we just toasted one another quietly, from one end of the crowded, brightly lit room to the other. He'd been under far too much pressure with the scale and size of this exhibition, that was all. Expectation had been immense. And Javier had been too greedy. We'd be wiser next time. Wouldn't agree to so many pictures. Then it wouldn't happen.

This, by now, was unspoken between us. We didn't talk about it. And, yes, I helped out now and again, but not often. And, actually, creatively, who didn't? We had a friend, a writer, whose wife edited his manuscripts before they were sent to the publisher. It wasn't unusual. And it wasn't necessarily wrong. Look at T. S. Eliot, I told myself, with Ezra Pound. What was that, if not an artistic collaboration? And you're not telling me Michelangelo didn't have other artists up there on the Sistine Chapel with him? Lying on platforms, filling in the rather boring bits of sky? And what about Damien Hirst, with a team of artists, mass-producing dots in a factory, for heaven's sake?

But then Sebastian had a bit of a block when Tabitha was born. Artistically. A bit of a barren period. It lasted on and off for a few years. Well, five. It didn't really matter, though; his reputation went before him, and it happens to a lot of painters, everyone knows that. By now, however, we had the house in Flood Street and huge bills to pay, not to mention school fees. We'd overstretched ourselves.

Over a drunken lunch with a gallery owner in Le Caprice, Sebastian agreed to do another large one-man show, this time in Pont Street. When he told me I went quiet. I knew we needed the money, but I also knew he didn't need that sort of pressure. He needed to work quietly, at his own pace, and then, a few years down the line, put on a show when he was ready. In retrospect, we should have moved house. Gone to Clapham, somewhere cheaper. We didn't. Instead, Sebastian worked day and night on the Pont Street exhibition whilst I tried to keep the children quiet. He'd emerge from his studio white and exhausted: the worse for drink often, too. He'd look scared. We both knew what was happening. He was losing his confidence. He'd start one picture, declare it was bollocks, and then frantically start another. And whereas a few years ago it would literally be a few finishing touches that were missing, almost as if he were savouring the moment of finally adding them, going, 'Ta-da!' – and which, that very first time in the attic studio, I'd felt he'd almost given me as a gift, an act of love – now it was more. Now a quarter would be missing. A half. Sometimes more. Sometimes, if I were to finish a canvas, which I did one night, it would be three-quarters empty. Sebastian had been desperate that time. He'd woken me at four in the morning, sober for a change, but ashen-faced. His shoulders had sagged and he'd howled. The one and only time I'd ever seen him cry. I'd knelt up on the bed and cradled his head, appalled. Not at the crying, but at what was happening to him: to my beloved man. My Sebastian. He'd begged me just to get him going again, even though we'd tacitly agreed I couldn't: that it couldn't go on. He was like a junkie begging for a fix. Just a few strokes, then hand the brush to him. He was sure he'd be fine. We tried it. Me in my dressing gown; him, dishevelled and unshaven, in what he'd been wearing for the past four days; the children asleep. It worked. I passed him the brush after half an hour and – almost in a trance – he took over.

We breathed at each other at the end. Met one another's eyes, relieved, but didn't say a word. Finally we went to bed exhausted, and slept. Well, he did, for hours and hours, the sleep of the utterly burned out and spent, but for me it was a new domestic day and the children were waking. I remember being shattered: physically, but emotionally too.

The Pont Street exhibition was almost upon us. It was terrifying. There still weren't enough pictures. Press releases had been sent out and previews were appearing in newspapers full of expectation: a lengthy piece by Brian Sewell in the *Evening Standard* wondered what we would be seeing from the young gun? Something to stun a generation, perhaps? A generation. Christ. So we did it a few more times. Always in the dead of night, always at four in the morning, as if we were burglars. Or traitors. We never named it. Never spoke of it. Just went back to bed, exhausted.

And the exhibition was deemed a success. Perhaps not as explosive and headline-making as Cork Street a few years back, but Sebastian was established now and could afford to deviate from his traditional path. Even have a few duffs. I was secretly pleased that the ones I'd done fifty per cent of *were* the declared duffs.

'Odd, how he's slightly lost his touch in that one,' I heard Simon Monk murmur to Brian Sewell as they stood shoulder to shoulder that night in the gallery, regarding a canvas.

'Mmm . . . Almost as if he's lost heart. Or changed his mind. Changed horses mid-stream.'

I passed on behind them with my drink, my heart pounding.

'See?' I said to Sebastian while we read the papers avidly the next morning, as soon as the newsagent's was open and we could run down and get them. 'They love yours, think they're terrific. And they hate the ones I've . . . you know . . .'

We did.

After the show we were both utterly exhausted. So, sensibly, we went away. We took the children out of school – they were so tiny it didn't matter – and we went to Portofino for three weeks. No one mentioned painting, or art, or exhibitions, and we swam and sunbathed and let the glorious Italian heat and light filter right through us, right down to our very bones: nourishing us, restoring us. Actually, I lie. Sebastian did sit on the cliffs one day and paint the most beautiful picture he's ever done, the one of the boats in the bay which is still in my cupboard. We had a lovely villa, right up in the hills with a view of the sea – we deserved it, we felt, and hang the expense – and it was probably the most luxurious holiday I've ever had. We made love a great deal, whenever the children weren't around – as soon as they'd gone to bed at night, or for their afternoon naps – but, if I'm honest, there was a desperation to our lovemaking: as if we were hungry for something from each other. I think we both longed for another baby: an Italian-holiday baby, something a world away from the pressure of work and the art world. When I miscarried three months later, we were devastated. His face collapsed as I wept silent, shivering tears.

After that, Sebastian couldn't do it. He couldn't paint. And we'd have the most terrible rows. I'd try to bolster him, cajole him. I'd tell him he was the most talented person I knew, the most talented person *anyone* knew, and that he just had to believe in himself. I said anything I could possibly think of to make it better, but, somehow, it made it worse. Sebastian would put his head in his hands. Then he'd put his hands right over his ears to shut me out. And when I wouldn't stop, would still be there talking when he'd withdrawn his hands, he'd turn terrible eyes on me. Eyes that said: 'Go away. You've stolen my soul.'

Only then did I shut up.

Eventually we ran away. We fled the circling, curious critics, the newspaper reviewers who wanted to know what had happened to Sebastian Montclair, the supremely talented art sensation, the golden boy? Why he'd dried up? We fled the gallery owners who hadn't been lucky enough to stage his exhibitions: Ah, they'd say privately, we wondered if he could keep it up.

We thought the change of scene, the slower pace of the countryside would do us good. Do the trick. Any trick. It was desperation. More than anything, though, we were desperate about ourselves. About what was happening to us.

We still loved each other passionately, but it was driving us apart. We drank. We rowed. We behaved badly. I, in particular, behaved very badly. I wouldn't leave him alone. Kept pushing him to have another go. I created the studio upstairs at vast expense, with money we didn't have. He rejected it. When he set up in the Granary I constantly roused him from where he slept on the sofa during the day and told him he had to get up, keep going. I was like a mother pushing a stubborn child through hated exams. I should have left him to his own devices: let him work his own way through it, even if it took years. But I was desperate for him to regain his self-esteem, for us to be happy again – to be normal. But what is normal?

I was full of guilt, too. Brimming with it. I knew that if I'd never showed off that night after the party in San Lorenzo's, if I'd kept to myself the knowledge that I could paint like he could, not been some ghastly little confidence-basher, the muse might well have returned a few days, or perhaps weeks, later, of its own accord. And even if it hadn't – so what? It would have been Sebastian's business, not mine. Nothing to do with me. It was that terrible fear that I'd ruined everything which compelled me to make him paint. And, in actual fact, to ruin things entirely. Finish the job. The marriage, the art, the whole shooting match. Sebastian was essentially a kind, sensitive man, but through sheer force of will, and to assuage my own shame, I succeeded in turning him into another person. I'd messed with his mind.

Years later, as I stood with my back to the Granary wall, the building I'd yet to go inside now that it was empty, deserted by Sebastian, I raised my eyes to the middle distance where the ewes were contentedly licking their empty trough, replete. The years had flashed past me at the rate of knots, but now it seemed the brakes were well and truly on and everything was screeching to a shuddering halt. Right where I stood. Outside an abandoned studio, on a deserted farm. Everything was about to disintegrate for ever. With, no doubt, a pen in hand, a signature apiece, and a document called a decree nisi.

I turned my gaze from the ewes and sought out Ottoline, on the horizon. Her small, solid figure was administering to the goat now, remonstrating with him, unravelling Curly, from the hedge where he'd got stuck, freeing his horns, his bell tinkling. So she'd known all along. From the very moment we'd arrived. But had loved us enough to stay silent. Had never mentioned it to me. Had hoped we'd work it out. Alone. Which was all we could do. She'd known why Sebastian had derided me as I'd copied her bohemian style in the house. Known why he'd screamed at me to stop as I helped Josh with his homework. Had known, as she'd kindly posed for him, why he could never finish a picture. Why I couldn't work in oils ever again; kept a secret cupboard, where, very occasionally, I'd dabble at night, unable to stop myself, while he was blind drunk and comatose. She knew why I was an illustrator and, as I laughingly once admitted to her after a long day, not a very original one at that, but an illustrator after a long-dead French one I'd discovered in a Provençal bookshop, whose style I admired. She knew where Josh got his acting skills from. She knew why Sebastian and I couldn't live together and why we couldn't live apart and why neither of us painted properly and why he drank. And yet she'd never said a word. Not one. For some reason I found that astonishingly lovely.

Yet there'd been real and rare anger when she'd turned on me just now. As if I'd betrayed Sebastian, somehow. As if I'd left *him*, rather than the other way round. What else could I have done? I'd have done anything, surely she knew that? My heart was in pieces, surely she knew that too? I'd tried everything to claw our love back. What hadn't I tried, for heaven's sake, over the years? I almost said it out loud,

incredulously, to her back, as she straightened up from dis-
entangling Curly. It was as if she'd been *forced* to say
something – finally – by me. By my treachery. Treachery to
love, she seemed to suggest.

But what on earth did Ottoline know about love? I
watched her squat, solid figure stomp away from the goat,
pail swinging from her hand, trudging off into the distance.

Chapter Thirty

A week passed. Two weeks. Ottoline and I lived politely and silently side by side, each in our separate houses. I thought she'd break the ice and come to me, have a cup of tea, talk about the animals; I thought we'd move on, but she didn't. And I didn't quite know what to say to her. Was unnerved by her silence. I could have gone across and helped with her pottery group – it would have been the natural icebreaker – but something stopped me. If I'm honest, I was a little afraid. Instead I pretended I was busy. Even to myself. I took the lid off the tin of paint and told myself I'd paint the sitting room, as Becks and the gang appeared. I quietly replaced the lid on a full tin that evening. Not a word of reproach was exchanged between us, not a sullen look, but not a particularly jolly one, either. Thus, we quietly coexisted. Meanwhile I bought a new sim card. I texted the children, telling them I'd dropped my phone, broken it and bought a new one, and gave them my new number. I asked how they were getting on.

'Fine!' they enthused. 'Really good!' And they'd so meant to come back last weekend, they said, but there'd been this concert, at the Round House, on Saturday, and then they'd totally overslept on Sunday, but they'd be back this weekend.

'Not for me, you won't!' I laughed, doing rather well on the phone to Tabitha when she rang. 'I'm fine, my darling, honestly. And so pleased you're having fun.'

'Yes, and it's not all fun. Daddy makes us work,' she told me quickly. 'He's really strict about homework. I promise you, I'm never allowed to go anywhere until I've done it.'

'Good. That's brilliant, Tabs, I'm pleased.'

'And Josh is out tonight, he's gone to *Henry V*, but he's going to ring you tomorrow. He said.'

I couldn't speak. Told her the dogs were barking at something and I'd better go. Said I'd see her very soon. I put the phone down and tottered to the bathroom, wondering if I was going to be sick. I wasn't. I just sat on the closed lavatory seat holding my knees, knowing I was a responsibility now. That my daughter was reminding her brother to ring me. That they were looking after me. That the roles had reversed, as they did in every parent–child relationship at some point, just a little early in mine.

In the sensible, rational part of my head, though, I knew this wasn't true. Flushed with the euphoria of city life, of being at the centre of things, away from the mud and isolation of our village, they were just busy. It had nothing to do with me. If I'd gone with them and Sebastian had been left here, they'd be the same. Reminding each other to ring him. But they'd be back. My children loved me very much, I knew that. I wasn't going to overdramatize here and think they'd defected or rejected. They wouldn't be back for the mud and the isolation – that, they could do without – but they'd be back for me. One day. I got up stiffly from the loo and told myself to stop feeling sorry for myself and go and feed the chickens.

My mother was still with me, of course, in the cottage, but even she – the one I'd been afraid would be welded to my side for ever – was only around in a very temporary fashion. A few days after her second lunch with my father, she came to see me. She wasn't wearing the dungarees and the knotted hanky she'd been affecting recently, but neither was she in a Jaeger twinset and pearls with her hair blown terrifyingly off her face as if she'd been caught in a jet stream. She had on a loose blue cotton shirt, which hung outside grey linen trousers, and her hair was done differently: not glued into position with hair spray, but very definitely styled in soft waves round her face. No colour, though: she was letting the silver shine through.

'You look terrific, Mum,' I told her as I opened the back door to her. She'd knocked, you see. Hadn't barged in, as usual. 'And how was lunch with Dad?'

'Very good, actually.'

I smiled. Had sort of thought it might be. Had indeed spoken to my father the other day. She sat down and told me what I already knew: that they'd stayed for hours in the restaurant, until they were politely asked to leave by the waiters and staff.

'Honestly, Ella, I felt about nineteen.'

'Good.'

She looked so well. Obviously not nineteen, but younger: lighter.

'We both brought our lists,' she told me, 'as I'd asked your father to do, although he'd originally said, "Yes, all right, Sylvia, but as long as that's not an order."'

'Oh!' I laughed, wondering how she'd take this.

'I know,' she told me, cradling the mug of tea I'd handed her. 'I am rather bossy and I can't change that overnight, but I can try. It was top of his list, of course.'

'Naturally.'

'But then, at the top of mine was: "Stand up to me a bit" – which took him by surprise.'

I smiled. Sat down opposite her with my mug of tea. 'I like "a bit", Mum.'

'Well, I know.' She looked sheepish. 'As I say, we can't either of us change our spots just like that, we're only mortal. But, d'you know, Ella, we don't need to. I don't want him to turn into a sergeant major. I know he's a kind, gentle man. I just don't want him to be meek. It brings out the worst in me. And he knows I'm strong and sparky; it's why he married me.'

'He just doesn't want you to be domineering,' I said, mentally ducking: couldn't believe I'd said it.

'Exactly,' she said calmly. 'And as you get older, traits you had when you were younger, ones you've always had, get exaggerated. You need to watch that,' she told me as she regarded me beadily over the rim of her cup, briefly reverting to type.

'Oh, I know,' I agreed, for once meaning it. I knew I was inclined to get things out of proportion. Needed more perspective. Was prone to being oversensitive, too. I did need to watch that. Amongst other things, of course.

'Like that famous blind eye of yours.'

'What?'

'Oh, you know.' She busied herself brushing imaginary crumbs from the table. 'How you and your father push things underground. Pretend they're not there.'

'Right.' He did. I didn't. And I wasn't sure I wanted a pep talk. This was her coming-of-age story. Old-age story. Not mine. I told her so – rather bravely. Well, not in quite so many words. But, to my surprise, she laughed.

'Yes, well, that was number three on his list. Don't lecture. Or preach. Be less of a know-all. Even if it's something I reckon I know a lot about.'

I grimaced. 'Well, that's got such deep roots, Mum, how are you ever going to dig those up? Those go right to your very core. What else was on his?'

'Oh, more important things, actually, which seem tiny, but are the stuff of life. Don't brag about the children – that's to me – it's embarrassing. Don't crack your knuckles in public – to him – I can't bear it. I suppose it sounds trivial but it's about respecting one another. Or at least, one another's wishes.'

'Right. And where are these wish lists going to be, by the way? On the fridge door? Presuming there is going to be a shared fridge door?'

'Yes, there is. But not at the Old Rectory.'

'Oh!'

'I can't go back there, Ella. Not after . . . you know. Everything that's happened.' She meant Maureen.

'Mum,' I said gently, 'I don't think Maureen was ever anything more than a friend. A good friend.'

'No, maybe not. I don't think she was, either, actually. But it's not just that. Not just the neighbours. It's the huge-empty-house-in-the-country bit. Although I love it – have loved it – I feel . . . *we* feel that it's time to move on. I know it's your childhood home, Ella, yours and Ginnie's, with so many memories, but it's dragging us down. Has dragged us down terribly, recently.'

It had been my home as a child but it hadn't felt like that for many years. Guiltily I realized I hadn't felt pangs of nostalgia or longing for it, even when I was little. Coming home from school with my satchel I remembered a sense of dread, wondering how tight-lipped she'd be. What I'd be told to do. Happy days, too, of course, but not Home Sweet Home. As a teenager I'd definitely been dying to get away from its echoing, draughty rooms. Did my own children feel like that, I wondered with a lurch? About Cold Comfort Farm? Probably. These days, I went to the Old Rectory dutifully, on high days and holidays, to see my parents. Not nostalgically. Did Ginnie? I wasn't sure.

'Well, I think that's a good idea, actually,' I said at length. 'Dad does love it, though. The whole village bit. The social life. You both loved that.'

'Oh, it was his idea. We think we'd like art galleries, theatre, the ability to walk into town and have lunch. A smaller house and a smaller garden, where he's not constantly chopping logs and bringing them in. One where we can throw a match at a gas log fire.

I nodded. 'Oxford.'

'No, we thought London.'

'London!'

'Well, why not? We've always loved it. Lived there when we were young, when we were first married, and we've always hankered for Chelsea. We'd like a small place there, rather like the one you had once, Ella, remember?'

Of course I did: the pretty, pink, Georgian doll's house in Flood Street. The one I'd so adored, had been so happy in initially, but where everything had turned horribly sour. I was pretty sure I'd find it hard not to be envious if she bought one of those.

'But, actually, we thought modern,' she said, thinking aloud. 'At any rate, your father does. Or maybe a modern conversion. Somewhere, at least, where the windows don't rattle and everything opens and shuts. Something we can turn the key on. And we've never lived in that part of London.' Mum and Dad started life in Finchley. 'We'd like to explore the parks, join clubs, go to museums – start again.'

There was a light in her eyes I hadn't seen for so long. Not for years. And it wasn't an ambitious glint, either, one that said, 'Dress *this* way', or 'Marry *that* way', or 'Take *this* career path' – to her husband, her children. It was more a light for herself. I realized Mum had subjected herself to an extent. She was so ambitious, but she'd forgotten to be ambitious for her own happiness. She might be going to live in Chelsea – no flies on her – but she'd consider a small, modern house. She didn't need to be in the smartest, prettiest street; she'd done that. Had been the lady of the manor in the biggest house in the village. Dad, I suspected, would have gladly given up the struggle long ago; when he retired, probably. I wondered if he'd ever suggested it? No. He would have been too scared. And it would have been rejected out of hand. Any suggestions, particularly life-changing ones, had to come from my mother.

'So – what, you'll join the V & A appreciation society? Go to arty lectures, that type of thing?'

'Perhaps, but your father wants to do it himself.'

'Do what?'

She swept on, ignoring the question. 'And he wants us to go away a lot more, learn new skills. Not just appreciate other people's, as he puts it. Although I dare say we'll do a bit of that, too, go down the culture-vulture route.'

I frowned, confused. 'Right, so . . . what are we talking here – cruises? Pyramids and things?' And of course Mum loved bridge. Lots of that on board ships. With kindred spirits.

'No, we thought more courses in Tuscany. You won't remember, but a lovely girl in the village, a young widow, went to Tuscany with her new husband, a solicitor. Anyway, he's a painter now and they run watercolour courses from their farmhouse in Umbria. They last about six weeks. We thought we'd start there.'

'Oh, yes. Dad mentioned it, actually. Lovely!' I got up from the table, jealous suddenly. Turned to straighten a tea towel on the Aga.

It was lovely, of course it was. And I'd always known where my own talent had come from. From the pair of them. Knew, as a child, that if I sat down at the kitchen table and asked them to draw me a horse, a dog, they both could. But my mother hadn't looked at me when she'd said it. I turned back to her slowly.

'It's OK, Mum. Painting's not a dirty word. We're allowed to say it.' I gave a tremulous smile. 'Do it, even.'

She nodded. Knew better than to pursue the conversation, though. Ask about mine.

We were silent for a moment as she gathered our cups and took them to the sink to rinse. I bent to stroke Diblet, who'd got up briefly from his basket and stood swaying beside me on shaky legs, tail wagging slowly. I hid my face in his rough old coat and inhaled his comforting smell. Sometimes I wondered if I'd be able to go on when he died. When I raised my head, Mum was at the sink, her eyes narrowed out of the window to the yard and the Granary opposite.

'He's gone, then, I see?'

I straightened up. 'Yes. He's gone.'

She put the cups away without looking at me. Then turned. Her eyes were kind. 'D'you want to talk about it, Ella?'

Blimey. What next? Holding hands across the table, like me and Ginnie? I quickly went to the Aga to rearrange the tea towel yet again. Felt the familiar lump in my throat.

'No. If you don't mind, I don't.'

I abandoned the towel and grabbed a dishcloth; wiped down my tiled surfaces with rare efficiency. Mum didn't reply. But she didn't leave, either.

'And the Charming Charles?' I said eventually, when I trusted my voice. Quite cheerfully, actually. And quite neatly turning the tables. 'What about him, Mum? On the slag heap?'

She laughed. Sat back down at the kitchen table. 'Charles has been a brick. We've had some very nice times together, he and I, and I've been thoroughly spoiled. But he's not your father, Ella. He's a bit . . . Well. You know.'

I did. Everyone around here did. Arrogant. Full of himself. Which Dad never was. For all his faults – which I now knew to be multitudinous – hubris was not amongst them.

'And he does so love the sound of his own voice,' Mum said, warming to her theme. 'Honestly, darling, I found myself surreptitiously looking at my watch at lunch the other day. It made me miss your father. He's certainly never been a bore.'

I smiled, delighted. 'Better the devil you know, eh?'

'Most definitely,' she said with feeling.

'Good. Oh, Mum, I'm so glad.'

I swooped, on an impulse, to hug her: to have the moment she'd looked for a second ago, perhaps. But she was sitting and I was standing and this was something we didn't do, so it was awkward. She briefly squeezed my arm round her neck, but we broke away quickly. I think it had been enough, though. Better than nothing. Briskly, she got up to go, brushing her grey trousers down.

'I won't clear out immediately, though, I mean from the cottage, if you don't mind. But it won't be long. The plan is to rent somewhere in London until we find somewhere to buy, but that won't take long. I mean, finding somewhere to rent. The estate agent's already rung me about somewhere furnished in Limerston Street, which we can move into the week after next if we like it.'

'Oh! That soon?'

'I don't want to go back to the Old Rectory, Ella. Not at all. I feel a bit . . . bruised. I want to go straight from here to London.'

'Yes, but . . .' So many friends in that village. Lifelong friends. Not to say goodbye?

'I'll say goodbye when we have a proper base in London. Our own house. When I'm feeling a bit stronger. Have them all up for lunch. A buffet party, perhaps – Angie, Peggy – you know, the girls.'

I did. Vaguely. Not well. They'd been shadowy figures in my young life, but they'd been the bedrock of hers. But it was time to leave them. I saw her bustling around a smart modern Chelsea kitchen brimming with flowers and shiny crystal, showing off to her friends as she opened the front door to them – that wouldn't change. But life went in cycles, didn't it? And if my parents weren't to get sucked into the vortex, it was time to invite them all to lunch, but then say goodbye. I realized Dad had always known this, in his quiet way, but if anyone had ever asked Mum if she'd leave the Old Rectory she'd put her chin up and say shrilly: 'Only feet first!'

And now she was leading the way. Or – no. He was beside her, I hoped. Naturally there'd be no minor miracles, I was aware of that – they'd been married for over forty years, for crying out loud – but there would be a subtle shift in balance. She'd still tell him what to wear and he'd still embarrass her at parties, but, hopefully, they'd catch each other's eye across the room with real meaning when it happened and regroup. Think: 'Right, rein in, Sylvia.' Or 'Don't be a prat, Angus.'

'Well done, Mum.' I walked her to the door and we went out into the weak sunshine together. The sun was quite low in the sky now, just skimming the tops of the beech trees. 'I'm really proud of you.' I stared into the distance as I said it, but I said it.

'Thanks, darling.' She didn't look at me, either. As I said, no minor miracles. We couldn't possibly look at each other and say things like that: things we'd never said before.

'And good luck to you,' she told me, turning briefly. 'Do what you know you have to do.'

I'd swivelled my eyes from the distance to meet hers and opened my mouth to speak, to enquire what the devil she meant, but she was already on her way: a wispier, less brittle silhouette, skirting her way expertly round the puddles, the craters even, in her new suede ballet pumps, en route to her cottage. I stared as she shut her front door firmly behind her, without looking back at me.

Do what you have to do. What on earth could she mean?

Chapter Thirty-One

By the time I left Oxford the following day and turned for home, the city was heaving. Chock-a-block with tourists and traffic and I was frantic. Frantic to get away. Desperate to escape. For some obscure reason – if pressed I'd say it had something to do with Ottoline's fury, her eyes blazing into mine, together with that strange, oblique instruction of my mother's, which I'd stupidly interpreted as some kind of divine sign, as if she were a legitimate oracle instead of an unsound know-it-all – I'd driven into town as if drawn by a star dangling over a stable, or, more pertinently, over a Georgian house in Christchurch.

In keeping with the biblical analogy I'd had to tend the sheep and donkeys first, it being my day for chores – no sign of Ottoline – and, irritatingly, Curly had escaped, so I'd spent a good hour chasing and untangling him from the bushes before I set off. Heart hammering with nerves and hardly pausing to shed my wellies – just – or pick the bits of straw from my dress – I did that as I drove along – I'd sped into Oxford. Despite, or perhaps because of a sleepless, floor-pacing night, I was at fever pitch. Fizzing with excitement. A fuse had been lit. Embers had been prodded. Something I hadn't entertained for years, had pushed underground, as Mum had perspicaciously observed I was wont to do, had surfaced like a sea creature emerging from the depths. Ottoline had said it clearly – it rang in my head right now, even though at the time it had just sounded dully somewhere distant and remote – then she'd underlined it by her silence. My mother had reiterated it, albeit in a more obscure way, but, somehow, that obscurity had been the final, thought-provoking push. Ottoline had done the spade work, digging around the wreck of my marriage, worrying it, hassling it, but it hadn't budged. Then along had strolled my mother and given it a sharp little nudge with her shiny red fingernail and up it had rocketed like a submarine, scattering me and everything else, in its wake.

Could it be true? Could it really be true? That Sebastian had chosen to teach instead of paint, out of some strange, warped love for me? He couldn't paint and be *with* me, that much we knew. He'd tried it for the last ten years but I'd been a constant reminder of his failure. It hadn't worked. I'd been the chain round his ankle. His impediment. His shackle. At one time he'd talked of going to Newlyn, alone – just for six months – a place he and Ottoline adored for the light, but that had never come to fruition. Why? Because he couldn't bear to leave me? Well, he's left you now, another, slightly more rational, voice had said, but I'd ignored it. Had driven doggedly on, over Magdalen Bridge, its imposing tower looming above me, my mind racing. And I'd ignored one or two other tiny details, too: like the fact that he could barely speak to me these days, or how happy he'd looked when I'd taken the children to him, having left me for good: having set up home elsewhere. Instead I dwelled on how nice he'd been to me that day. I wondered, perhaps, if he'd been hoping I'd stay and have lunch with them all? Rather than dashing off like that? If he'd been about to suggest it – since I'd had quite a morning of it, packing them up and driving in – about to suggest we all went to the Quad together? Yes, quite possibly.

Parking in a little-known spot behind a restaurant where, as long as you popped in and had a coffee and collected a token, you could get a space, I walked quickly and determinedly, head down and on a mission, towards Christchurch. There was no mobile I could reach Sebastian on and I didn't want to leave a message on his answering machine in case the children picked it up, so, instead, I'd decided to pop a letter through his door. Yes, I could have sent it, but, on the other hand, the chance of bumping into him was too good to pass up. As if I were just shopping in town. Which I rarely did, but still. I'd made an effort too, despite Curly's attempts to sabotage it. Had on a dress I knew he liked. He'd said so once, about two years ago, when it was new and I'd come running out in it to feed the sheep, plus wellies, of course: he'd said: 'That suits you.' At that time in our marriage it was high praise from Sebastian and I'd nearly fallen over. He'd coloured up slightly as he'd seen my reaction and we'd both gone awkwardly on our ways, me putting it down to an aberration on his part. But . . . why hadn't I considered it more at the time? He was still noticing you, Ella, I told myself now, hurrying on and feeling the letter in my coat pocket. Still very much aware of you and, no, not immune.

The letter was simple and short. It just said that now that he'd moved out, I thought it might be easier for us to be better friends. That perhaps we could meet for lunch occasionally, with the children. Or even without! I'd thought long and hard about that exclamation mark. If he hated me, it showed it was only a joke. If not – well, then the sentiment was there, and I'd made the first move. Towards some sort of date. With my husband. Bizarre.

Hastening on and feeling about nineteen, licking lipstick off my teeth – I rarely wore it; never wore much make-up at all, in fact, because Sebastian didn't like it . . . oh, you idiot, Ella – I stopped abruptly. On the brink of the huge, walled college, just before the gates, I ducked behind a postbox. Pulled a mirror from my bag and a tissue. Not that he'd be about, I thought, rubbing away at my lips. Probably in some studio, or taking a class in a lofty lecture theatre. I paused, lowering the mirror a second, to imagine that. I bet the pretty girls at the back – or even the front – were impressed by him. Sebastian *was* impressive; it was one of the words you could use about him. You couldn't say warm, or cosy, or comforting, or any of the words I associated with Ludo, but you could say towering, glittering and, oh, a whole host of other things, which, once you'd got through, made the essence of the man more desirable, being so hard won. I licked my lips and put the hanky in my pocket.

Ludo. I'd been left surprisingly still and calm after talking to Eliza. I didn't hate him for once having had an affair and being economical with the truth; he wasn't a serial adulterer or anything horrible, but Eliza was right: he was a romantic, and Sebastian wasn't. Romance sustained Ludo. It kept him going. The thought of a woman brightened his day. People like Sebastian were different. They rarely fell in love – couldn't be bothered – but when they did, they fell headlong, for ever. But they could live without it. Would much *prefer* to live without it, rather than cast around for another romantic chapter, as I knew Ludo would. Oh, not now; he'd be genuinely sad at my text.

Would miss me terribly, as I had him initially, although not as much as I'd imagined. But in a year or so, he'd move on. Find some other, pretty, vulnerable girl to wholeheartedly transfer his affections to – yes, wholeheartedly; there was nothing fake about Ludo. And poor Eliza, I thought, sadly, would become even more desperate and wretched. I hurried on, slipping through a conveniently unmanned side door by the porters' lodge. Whereas Sebastian, who undoubtedly needed the comfort that couching up to a fellow human being provided – he was no monk – would not look for love, but be content with a girl like Isobel, who catered to all his needs except his heart, which was not something he gave lightly or easily.

Once inside the imposing walls I tiptoed through a formidable arched colonnade. Centuries of clever, quick feet, gowns flying, had no doubt trodden up and down it; famous ones, too. My famous husband amongst them now. Feeling like a spy, out of the shelter of the arched walkway I slipped and into the sunlight, stealing round the gravel path that skirted the vast grassy quad and led, ultimately, to his front door. But then I thought: No, why steal? If he's at home, so much the better. Maybe here, in these courtly surroundings, I glanced about at the looming, treacle-coloured architecture, we could have a civilized chat, as we had the other day; only, this time, minus the children. I raised my chin and marched up the path to the black front door with the shiny brass knocker and, when I put the letter through, let the letter box clatter noisily back into place. I waited on the step a moment then thought: What are you doing, Ella, knocking? Hastily I turned and scurried away, wondering why I was always in such a state of flux and full of contradictions? Do this – no, do that.

Think this – no, think *that*. Confusing. For everyone. Most of all, for me. As I reached the arched colonnade again, I heard a sound behind me. I turned. Sebastian's front door was opening and a woman was appearing from within. With a gasp, I hid behind an enormous pillar. Then peered back in horror. Isobel?

It was a blonde, for sure. Tall, beautiful and reed thin, with nothing like Isobel's comforting curves. She glanced about, clearly wondering who'd made the letter box clatter. She was wearing skinny black jeans and a grey jumper, which, even at this distance, I could tell was cashmere. Could almost smell the Jo Malone. As she bent to pick up the letter from the mat, she had one last glance around before she shut the door. Silky, blonde hair swinging, she pulled a strand away from her prettily painted lips to stop it sticking. I saw her face clearly. Caught her limpid blue eyes. The years rolled back. By now I knew for certain it wasn't Isobel, but what I hadn't been expecting, by any stretch of the imagination, was Celeste.

Like I said, leaving congested Oxford was hell and I was frantic. Desperate to escape. Hot, sweaty, my mind in turmoil, I was stuck in heavy commuter traffic, praying the car wouldn't overheat, heading by infinitesimal degrees up the Banbury Road. Nothing was moving and I was so desperate for distance that – oh, sod it – I swerved in panic into the bus lane and roared on, amid an angry blare of horns. When the black front door had closed I'd run, breathless and shaken, my feet echoing through the arched colonnade, out of the college and down the cobbled street to the restaurant and my car, my mind a blank, focusing solely on getting away. Hand trembling, I'd turned the ignition and kangarooed out of my space, forgetting the coffee I was supposed to buy. The barrier wouldn't go up in the car park without a token. I'd had to run inside, buy a coffee and run out – whereupon I'd found an angry man in a car behind mine, which I'd deserted at the barrier, blocking his. Bleating apologies, I'd then had a horrid exchange during which he called me a selfish cow and I'd burst into tears. He'd looked aghast and retreated rapidly to his vehicle, before I finally drove off.

All this had served to distract me to some extent. Now, however, alone in the car, speeding up the empty bus lane, the full horror loomed. Celeste. *Celeste.* Who had surely been a true love, a proper love. The only one before me, the only one *besides* me, and from whom – well, let's face it – I'd stolen Sebastian. It had been fairly uncontroversial back then, no one was married, but I'd never forgotten her shattered face as she'd left Sebastian's first private view at the gallery in Ebury Street that evening, knowing she'd lost. Heartbroken. Devastated. But what style and grace she'd adopted in defeat. Smiling beside him, still the designated girlfriend, the partner elect; only her sad eyes giving her away. And never a cold glance at me, the incumbent. Certainly never a snarl. Dignity and poise at all times. And now, here she was, with all that dignity and poise still firmly intact, back on my doorstep, or, more literally, Sebastian's. Was she divorced? Widowed? Or perhaps she'd never even married, I thought with a heart-stopping lurch, having never got over Sebastian? Or perhaps they were having an affair? After all, we all did it. I cringed. But a proper one. Not a half-baked one, like I'd attempted with Ludo. Sebastian would never stand for anything pathetic like that. It would be the real thing or nothing. Her face flashed before me again at the moment she'd taken the strand of hair from her lips. Still beautiful, of course, with her chiselled face, high cheekbones, beautiful blue eyes – if anything, more stunning than ever: this top *Vogue* model, who'd graced more covers than any other English model of her generation. Still utterly gorgeous.

I had to tell myself to breathe, to loosen my knuckles on the wheel. My fingers were going white. Oh, I'd been so smug, hadn't I? About Isobel. With her comely, barmaid figure, her slightly raddled face. I'd known I'd had the upper hand. But this was like a slap across the face. A door had opened and not just a beautiful, if slightly older, woman had gazed out, but the bogey man too. It was as if Celeste's face had morphed into that of a ghastly grinning gargoyle's, like the ones overhanging the quad through which I'd run. I could almost hear the nightmarish, mocking laughter following me. Taunting me. I knew I was in shock. Knew, after something so unimagined had happened, I'd been left reeling. Revenge, they say, is best eaten cold, but I'd never really understood that platitude. I did now. It would taste so much sweeter the longer it was waited for. Not that Celeste would be interested in revenge. Life wasn't always about me, as Tabitha had so succinctly reminded me recently: no, this was her own personal story, playing out on her own stage, which I'd just happened to stumble across: interrupt.

That she was living at Sebastian's, with him, was beyond doubt. I swung through the farmyard gate, almost scratching the side of the car on the post, scattering ducks and chickens in my wake. It was obvious by the proprietorial way she'd opened the front door. The elegant yet casual clothes which said: 'At Home'. She'd no doubt gone back to the kitchen, where she'd been having her lunch and reading the paper, letter in hand, thoughtful. No, of course she wouldn't open it, Ella. What, steam the envelope and read it? Of course not. But she'd put it to one side, thoughtful. Then probably dismiss it as a handwritten note from a professor or a student, which, I was sure, was very Oxford. Very normal. And then Sebastian would come home tonight, after his lectures, his classes, and as he opened it and read it she'd watch his face, which would be – what? Thoughtful? Incredulous? *Derisive?* Yes, the latter, I thought in horror, as I flew into the house and slammed the back door behind me, instinctively locking it for privacy, not wanting my mother or Ottoline. Would he share it with her? The letter? Would they discuss me, the little woman, abandoned and feeling a bit desperate? Writing letters to her ex about the possibility of having lunch? Feel sorry for me? I threw off my coat and ran into the sitting room, slamming yet another door and leaving the dogs shut up and whining in the boot room, not even wanting their company, the reminder of what I had: dogs, chickens, sheep . . . *animals*. Not people. Wanting to hide.

I curled up in a corner of the sofa in the gloomy, north-facing room, dragging a cushion onto my lap. It was spotless, the room: I'd had a thorough spring-clean. Had thought it would be cathartic, but the result had been the opposite. A sad, immaculate reminder of where the children used to lounge horizontal on a sofa apiece and throw crisp packets and biscuit wrappers on the floor, fighting over the remote control. The children. Why hadn't they told me? Suddenly I startled in recognition. Sat up a bit. They had. Tabs had tentatively asked, a month or so ago, if I knew Dad was seeing someone. Yes, I'd answered with a bright smile – we'd been going through the freshly-baked-cheesecake stage – I did. Even Josh had grunted something about Dad's squeeze. I'd thought Isobel. Squeeze surely meant comfort. It meant curves. And sex. So *stupid*, Ella! So patronizing.

I raked a hand through my hair and, at that moment, saw myself very clearly. And what was stretching ahead. I'd always been happy on my own, in my own company, but there was a big difference between solitude and loneliness. I ached with the latter and the promise of more. I also felt the groundswell of a terrible, terrible jealousy. Bitterness is common to many abandoned wives, particularly those who've been replaced, and the knowledge that Celeste and Sebastian were sharing a bed hurt more than I can say. But a breakfast table, a supper table with *my children*. A life . . .

The idea that the two of them, Sebastian and Celeste, would be walking arm in arm through sun-dappled quads, no ducks to feed, no scaly chicken's feet to wash, no sheep with poo-coated bottoms to clip, no Cold Comfort Farm, was bad enough. But the *four* of them . . . At plays, concerts, which they'd doubtless done already. My mind raced ahead. I saw Celeste listening as Josh explained in the interval how he interpreted the play, in that intense, glittering way of his, so reminiscent of his father. Celeste, who was beautiful but no fool, chipping in, discussing it; bringing Tabs in, making sure she didn't feel left out. Then later, in some trendy Oxford restaurant, laughing over a bottle of wine, this arty, golden, dynamic family. People noticing them. Thinking: How lovely – what a good-looking family.

By now my breath was coming in little bursts if I was

lucky enough to inhale at all. Hyperventilating, I believe it's called. I'd never done that before. Image upon image piled into my brain. I remembered the first time I'd seen Celeste, as I'd bumbled up to my flat in my old blue coat: they'd been coming down from Sebastian's, going out to dinner or a party. She'd been wearing a black velvet mini-dress and I recalled thinking I'd never seen such a vision in all my life. I sat for a long time on that sofa, gazing into space, eyes wide, reflecting. And then I put my head in my hands and cried.

At length, I noticed it was dark. The murky autumn night had gathered quickly outside the windows and pressed against the glass and my legs were stiff from being curled for so long beneath me. I was cold. The dogs, who'd been whining for ages at being deprived of my company – and their supper – were barking now, or at any rate Doug was: always his last resort for attention. I slowly unwound my legs and went to the window to draw the curtains, knowing I had to light the fire, have a drink at least. Move on. But, as I went to pull the drapes across – I screamed.

A face was pressed right up against the French windows, or so it seemed to me. I shrieked and lurched backwards, falling over a low stool. In the dark outside, a man threw up his hands, exasperated. Sebastian. Christ Almighty, it was Sebastian. I stared in disbelief for a moment. Then stumbled to my feet. With cold, fumbling fingers, I undid the French-window lock. The door flew open.

'What the fuck did you scream like that for?' he demanded, furious.

I gaped, astonished.

'What are you *doing* here!' I gasped, when I'd eventually found my voice. 'You frightened the life out of me!'

'Well, I couldn't get in through the back door, you'd locked it, so I came round here. What the bloody hell are doing sitting here in the dark, Ella? Like some little gnome? I thought there was no one in. Could barely see you.'

'I – I, well, I . . . was tired. Must have dropped off,' I gabbled, staring up at him as he came right in now, on a gust of cold air, shutting the door behind him. He bent down to switch on a lamp. My heart was still banging with fright but the first thing I noticed was more nice clothes: a navy-blue moleskin jacket, which he'd never choose on his own, a crisp white shirt, clean jeans. Not the grey, shambling wreck I was wont to see shuffling through this sitting room. I took a breath and straightened up. Found some steel.

'What are you doing here, anyway? In my house?'

He gave this last remark the derisive look it probably deserved, then whipped my letter from his jacket pocket.

'You came to see me,' he told me coldly. 'Celeste said she saw you deliver this by hand.'

I flinched. Brazen. Just mentioning Celeste like that. *So* Sebastian. So forthright. And I'd thought I'd got away with it. Thought she hadn't recognized me. I'd ducked pretty smartly behind that column and our eyes had met only very briefly. I'd seen no recognition in hers and I'd had longer to study her. I must have been wrong.

'Um, yes, yes, I did. Because I just happened to be in town. Shopping. And I thought I'd just scribble you a note. In Waitrose. Which was where I was shopping. Not – scribbling as I shopped, I didn't do that, but – in the café. Just to say, if we ever needed to meet to discuss the children, or – or have a kind of – meeting – we could maybe have lunch. But now I see that lunch is not a good idea. So – so maybe a coffee or something to – you know. Discuss.'

'We've never discussed the children in such a corporate-sounding way, Ella.'

It was true, we hadn't. We just sort of muddled through. Didn't, as I knew other parents did, go to parents' meetings together, discuss their aims and ambitions, their problems, their potential. We just let them flow on around us in what Lottie told me was a rather haphazard fifties fashion, rather as her parents had done: never knowing what exams Lottie was taking, who she was going out with. Nowadays parents were much more watchful, more involved, she'd tell me. But mine had been much *too* watchful. My mother, certainly: way before her time. So maybe my inclination was a reaction against that? And it certainly wasn't in Sebastian's nature to be remotely vigilant.

'N-no, we haven't done that,' I faltered. 'But now that they're getting older, doing more important exams, and now that we're – you know – separated, geographically – well, in every sense – there might be a need to, I don't know, touch base. As it were. Occasionally.'

We were standing before one another in the sitting room. Sebastian towered above me. I was in my socks, my stockinged feet, and I wasn't tall. Not like Celeste. He scratched his head.

'Right,' he said shortly. 'I thought it might have been more than that.'

'No, no,' I said quickly. 'No more.'

He nodded slowly. Took a moment. 'Well, in that case I'm . . . sorry I frightened you.'

'Oh, no, don't worry. It was silly of me to be sitting here in the dark.'

'You're free to do what you want in your own home.'

He was looking at me carefully now. Scrutinizing me. Clearly he did think it was a bit strange. I gulped. Moved on conversationally; groping my way.

'And – and, Sebastian, we must start to think about – you know . . .' I floundered.

'What?'

'Well, a more . . . permanent . . . situation. Obviously.'

'What d'you mean?'

Still I couldn't say it. Then I managed: 'Divorce.'

'Oh.' His face was inscrutable. 'Obviously.' There was an edge to his repeating me. A snideness.

'Well, yes. I mean – I'm not going to just potter along behind at *your* speed, take my cue from you. I have to take some initiative here. And now I know the lie of the land, I'm inclined to force the pace a bit.' I felt my chin jut. Good for that chin. I pushed it out a little further.

'Why now?' Was it my imagination, or did his eyes look strained? 'I thought things would be easier now?'

'Well, for you, maybe,' I spluttered. 'Since you're living with someone!'

'How d'you mean? Who am I living with?'

'Oh, come on! You just told me she saw me. Celeste!'

'Celeste?' He frowned. 'I'm not living with Celeste.'

I stared. 'You're not?'

'No.'

I regarded him for a long moment. Blinked. 'You're lying.'

'I'm not. I don't lie. I'm not living with Celeste.'

We regarded one another. He didn't lie. I did, small, white ones, but . . . he didn't. And as we stared, various respective pennies began to drop. At length Sebastian found his voice. 'Ah. Right. So – you thought . . .' He stopped. Regrouped. 'Celeste came for lunch. With Hugh. Her husband. I was burning something in the kitchen, attempting to feed them, and the soup was boiling over, and we heard the door. She went to get it.'

I stared. 'With Hugh!'

'Yes, the banker husband she married seventeen years ago. You remember?'

I didn't. Or did I? Hugh. Hugh Hugh Hugh. Oh, *that* Hugh. Did she marry him?

'They've got a son at Magdalen School, a chorister. I bumped into them last week in town. He's only sixteen, the boy, but Celeste is already thinking about university. He's very bright, apparently, and you know Celeste. Ambitious. I think she thought I might be the way to some admissions tutor's pigeon hole in a couple of years' time, but perhaps that's uncharitable.'

I gaped, trying to absorb this information. 'No. No, not uncharitable.'

'At any rate, he's nice, Hugh. Despite being a bit of a stuffed shirt. And it was nice to see her.'

'Yes.' I felt breathless. 'Yes, it must have been . . . nice.'

He frowned. 'You didn't seriously think . . . ?'

'Well, I didn't know!' I squealed. 'I mean – she came to the door! Your door!' I turned away, needing some time, some space. But there wasn't any. I walked around the sitting room, which was tiny, trying to get some purchase on the situation. Not Celeste. Thank Christ for that. Thank the frigging Lord. I couldn't compete. Just couldn't. But – what, then?

I stopped by the bookshelves. Turned. 'Sebastian, are you still seeing Isobel?'

'Isobel? Well, yes, I paint her. See her quite a lot, in fact.' He glared at me. 'What is this, the third degree?'

Suddenly, though, it was important. 'I – I sort of need to know. Really know. You just paint her?'

'At the moment, yes. But she's a friend, too. And she has been more.'

'I know. Yes, I know.'

'And Ludo?'

It was said abruptly. Uncharacteristically. Sebastian didn't ask questions. Ever. He never pried.

'Over,' I said quickly. 'Almost before it had begun.'

He stared, assimilating this. Nodded briefly. 'Right. Well. Here we are, then.' He gave a short laugh.

'Yes,' I agreed. It felt like a play. Like two characters on stage. 'Here we are.'

In the home we'd shared for ten years. Brought the children up in. But not a happy home. We shouldn't be here. It was wrong. I ached to be elsewhere. Anywhere. Because we *had* been happy once, in other places. Blissful. So blissful it hurt.

'Ella, much more pertinently,' Sebastian said, and this in a much lower voice, 'are you painting?'

I flushed, found out. 'Occasionally,' I admitted, knowing he meant proper painting. Knowing it would pain him.

'In the middle of the night?'

'Yes.'

A dark shadow passed over his face. I hung my head.

He moved a hand across his eyes. Sat down on the arm of the sofa and shook his head. 'That's terrible.'

'Sebastian – only very occasionally, and only –'

'No, terrible that you have to steal around doing it at night. To spare my feelings.'

'Well – I . . . well, obviously,' I floundered, surprised.

To my even greater surprise he stood up, came across and took my hand. He looked levelly at me. 'I know all about that feeling, Ella, of course I do. What d'you take me for, a bloody fool? About not being able to help it. When people say to me in amazement – because I haven't produced anything for so long – "Are you still painting?" I look at them bewildered. Think: Of course. It's like breathing. I *have* to do it. And I've stopped you doing it. You haven't been able to breathe.'

I gazed beyond him, to the dark night outside: over his shoulder. I didn't look at him.

'I've seen the attic light on at night,' he went on. 'Four o'clock in the morning, sometimes. I've imagined you unlocking some secret cupboard, getting your easel out, feeling like a thief as you frantically screw in your canvas, glancing over your shoulder to make sure all's dark and quiet at the Granary. But once you've got your brush in your hand, once you're painting, in your dressing gown, maybe, forgetting everything. Feeling . . . easier. At peace. Flowing. I've thought of you like that, Ella and I've loved you for it.'

I gazed up at him. 'For being like you?' I whispered. 'For not being able to breathe without it? Or for sparing your feelings?'

'Both.' He took my other hand. We stood there facing each other in the dimly lit sitting room like a couple about to dance, about to perform some very formal, country dance. Which had intricate, precise steps. This was to be no impromptu shuffle. 'And it occurred to me too, that you must surely love me, to do that. To deny yourself air during the day.'

'Of course,' I said in wonder. Wonder, because about that there had never been any doubt.

'Yes,' he said sadly. 'Of course. You got there before me. Have always been there before me.'

'What d'you mean?'

'Ella, we both know creativity can soothe the soul and I used to think it the best balm in the world. The only one, possibly. When it's going well, it's euphoric. When it's not, it sends you crazy. And I have been crazy, for a long time. Because a better balm had been staring me in the face. I think I chose painting above you, Ella. I thought it was what made me tick. But you make me tick.'

I stood still like a statue. Didn't want to break the spell. Didn't want to breathe. I wondered if we'd embrace. Kiss. We didn't.

'We have to be so careful,' I whispered eventually into the silence, knowing it to be true. Knowing what was stopping us.

'I know. Which was why I came in response to your note. About lunch. I think it's a good idea.'

'You do?'

'Yes. Assuming you don't want to discuss the children's exam results.'

'No. I don't. I thought . . .' I hesitated.

'Little by little?'

'Yes.'

'Bit by bit?'

'A beginning.'

'Exactly.'

'But still in separate houses?'

'Yes.'

We both agreed. Our eyes communed silently.

'You need to paint here, Ella. In the light. In the fields. Amongst the sheep and the goats. To your heart's content. Set up your easel outside and feel the sun on your face: have the dogs at your feet. And I need to find another way.'

I squeezed his hands hard. Another way. 'What about breathing?' I whispered.

He smiled. A rare, lovely, heartbreaking smile. 'I'm going to see how I get on with an oxygen mask.'

Teaching, he meant. And I knew it was the ultimate sacrifice. By choosing to become an academic, he'd chosen me. I knew too that he could have gone away and tried to paint elsewhere: moved to France or somewhere. I'd known that for years, but he never had. In my heart I'd known he'd loved the children too much to do it, but I hadn't known it about me.

'How do you rate our chances?' he asked softly, this time opening his arms for me to walk into. I did. We held each other close. I could feel his heart beating against mine and knew mine was racing, too.

I pressed my head against his shoulder. His moleskin jacket was unfamiliar but his smell was just the same. I inhaled it greedily. 'Our chances of just having lunch?' I asked.

He gave a laugh. 'Yes.'

I pulled away and looked up: his eyes were soft and our faces were both suddenly wreathed in smiles.

'Not good, Sebastian. Not good.'

Look out for

Catherine Alliott's

new novel coming
Spring 2015

A house in the south of France. A party with family and friends. What could be nicer? What could possibly go wrong . . . ?

Catherine

We donned our wellies and
trudged through the mud to catch up
with Catherine about reading,
writing and life in the country . . .

Chatting with

Catherine

Q: It's been twenty years since your first book was published. What changes over the years have affected your stories since then?

A: Over the years my books have included a wider age group of characters: I'm writing about grannies, mothers, teenagers – all sorts!

Q: Which book have you found most challenging to write?

A: *One Day in May* was probably the most challenging to write. I knew very little about the Bosnian war and had to do quite a lot of research, which was pretty harrowing. I had no idea . . .

Q: How have your protagonists changed and developed since you started writing?

A: Since I started writing twenty-three years ago my protagonists have definitely got older! Perhaps a little less scatty, but then again, perhaps not.

Q: How do you choose your characters' names?

A: I'm going so fast I just chuck anything in and think -- I'll change that later. Unfortunately by the end I can't think of Mavis as anything other than Mavis, so it sticks.

Q: What book are you reading right now?

A: I found a John le Carré in my son's room; it's called *Our Kind of Traitor*. V. good. I read anything that's lying around.

Q: If you couldn't be a writer, what would you like to be?

A: A painter – as in artist, not decorator.

Q: When you need to escape from your everyday routine, what do you do?

A: Light the fire, watch daytime TV and eat chocolate.

Q: What is your favourite food?

A: In – macaroni cheese. Out – Dover sole.

Q: What would your super power be?

A: I'd like to be able to imagine supper – and there it is, on the table. Oh, and all cleared away, too.

Q: What is your idea of perfect happiness?

A: So corny. All my children plus boyfriends, girlfriends, any other friends and of course my husband, eating around the same table. Or actually, a table somewhere hot, on holiday, abroad, i.e. without me having to cook. Oh – and grandparents too.

Q: What is the trait you most deplore in others?

A: Deplore. Golly. Quite strong. Well, I'm not mad about bad manners, which come in many guises.

Q: When did you last cry and why?

A: Two weeks ago, at Badminton Horse Trials, watching a great friend's daughter jump round the cross-country course. Amazing. I've known her since she was seven.

Q: What has been your most embarrassing moment?

A: I suppose it has to be when I fell in the freezer in Safeway on the King's Road many years ago, a scene which later featured in *The Old-Girl Network*.

Q: What single thing would improve the quality of your life?

A: Training our Border Terrier not to fight other dogs and not to chase deer. I sound like a fishwife in the woods.

Q: What do you consider your greatest achievement?

A: Training our last Border Terrier. (Up to a point. She really did hate poodles.)

Q: What is under your bed?

A: So much embarrassing rubbish. Old sofa cushions, bags of material I intend to make into things and never do, loads of old clothes, a broken lamp, stacks of paperbacks I've run out of space for on the shelves, the odd mousetrap . . . I could go on.

Q: What is the most important lesson life has taught you?

A: Try to laugh it off.

Twenty years of

Catherine Alliott

Now discover Catherine's other books . . .

Going Too Far

'You've gone all fat and complacent because you've got your man, haven't you?'

Polly Penhalligan is outraged at the suggestion that, since getting married to Nick and settling into their beautiful manor farmhouse in Cornwall, she has let herself go. But watching a lot of telly, gorging on biscuits, not getting dressed until lunchtime and waiting for pregnancy to strike are not the signs of someone living an active and fulfilled life.

So Polly does something rash. She allows her home to be used as a location for a TV advert. Having a glamorous film crew around will certainly put a bomb under the idyllic, rural life. Only perhaps she should have consulted Nick first.

Because before the cameras have even started to roll – and complete chaos descends on the farm – Polly's marriage has been turned upside down. This time she really has gone too far . . .

The Real Thing

Every girl's got one – that old boyfriend they never quite fell out of love with . . .

Tessa Hamilton's thirty, with a lovely husband and home, two adorable kids, and not a care in the world. Sure, her husband ogles the nanny more than she should allow. And keeping up with the Joneses is a full-time occupation. But she's settled and happy. No seven-year itch for Tessa.

Except at the back of her mind is Patrick Cameron. Gorgeous, moody, rebellious, he's the boy she met when she was seventeen. The boy her vicar-father told her she couldn't see and who left to go to Italy to paint. The boy she's not heard from in twelve long years.

And now he's back.

Questioning every choice, every decision she's made since Patrick left, Tessa is about to risk her family and everything she has become to find out whether she did the right thing first time round . . .

Rosie Meadows Regrets

'Tell me, Alice, how does a girl go about getting a divorce these days?'

Three years ago Rosie walked blindly into marriage with Harry. They have precisely nothing in common except perhaps their little boy, Ivo. Not that Harry pays him much attention, preferring to spend his time with his braying upper-class friends.

But the night that Harry drunkenly does something unspeakable, Rosie decides he's got to go. In between fantasizing about how she might bump him off, she takes the much more practical step of divorcing this blight on her and Ivo's lives.

However, when reality catches up with her darkest fantasies, Rosie realizes, at long last, that it is time she took charge of her life. There'll be no more regrets – and time, perhaps, for a little love.

Olivia's Luck

'I don't care what colour you paint the sodding hall. I'm leaving.'

When her husband Johnny suddenly walks out on ten years of marriage, their ten-year-old daughter and the crumbling house they're up to their eyeballs renovating, Olivia is, at first, totally devastated. How could he? How could she not have noticed his unhappiness?

But she's not one to weep for long.

Not when she's got three builders camped in her back garden, a neighbour with a never-ending supply of cast-off men she thinks Olivia would be drawn to and a daughter with her own firm views on . . . well, just about everything.

Will Johnny ever come back? And if he doesn't, will Olivia's luck ever change for the better?

A Married Man

'What could be nicer than living in the country?'

Lucy Fellowes is in a bind. She's a widow living in a pokey London flat with two small boys and an erratic income. But, when her mother-in-law offers her a converted barn on the family's estate, she knows it's a brilliant opportunity for her and the kids.

But there's a problem. The estate is a shrine to Lucy's dead husband, Ned. The whole family has been unable to get over his death. If she's honest, the whole family is far from normal. And if Lucy is to accept this offer she'll be putting herself completely in their incapable hands.

Which leads to Lucy's other problem. Charlie – the only man since Ned who she's had any feelings for – lives nearby. The problem? He's already married . . .

The Wedding Day

Annie O'Harran is getting married . . . all over again.

A divorced, single mum, Annie is about to tie the knot with David. But there's a long summer to get through first. A summer where she's retreating to a lonely house in Cornwall, where she's going to finish her book, spend time with her teenage daughter Flora and make any last-minute wedding plans.

She should be so lucky.

For almost as soon as Annie arrives, her competitive sister and her wild brood fetch up. Meanwhile, Annie's louche ex-husband and his latest squeeze are holidaying nearby and insist on dropping in. Plus there's the surprise American houseguest who can't help sharing his heartbreak.

Suddenly Annie's big day seems a long, long way off – and if she's not careful it might never happen . . .

Not That Kind Of Girl

A girl can get into all kinds of trouble just by going back to work . . .

Henrietta Tate gave up everything for her husband Marcus and their kids. But now that the children are away at school and she's rattling round their large country house all day she's feeling more than a little lost.

So when a friend puts her in touch with Laurie, a historian in need of a PA, Henrietta heads for London. Quickly, she throws herself into the job. Marcus is – of course – jealous of her spending so much time with her charming new boss. And soon enough her absence causes cracks in their marriage that just can't be papered over.

Then Rupert, a very old flame, reappears, and Henrietta suddenly finds herself torn between three men. How did this happen? She's not that kind of girl . . . *is she?*

A Crowded Marriage

There isn't room in a marriage for three . . .

Painter Imogen is happily married to Alex, and together they have a son. But when their finances hit rock bottom, they're forced to accept Eleanor Latimer's offer of a rent-free cottage on her large country estate. If it was anyone else, Imogen would be beaming with gratitude. Unfortunately, Eleanor just happens to be Alex's beautiful, rich and flirtatious ex.

From the moment she steps inside Shepherd's Cottage, Imogen's life is in chaos. In between coping with murderous chickens, mountains of manure, and visits from the infuriating vet, she has to face Eleanor, now a fixture at Alex's side.

Is Imogen losing Alex? Will her precious family be torn apart? And whose fault is it really – Eleanor's, Alex's or Imogen's?

The Secret Life Of Evie Hamilton

Evie Hamilton has a secret. One she doesn't even know about – yet . . .

Evie's an Oxfordshire wife and mum whose biggest worry in life is whether or not she can fit in a manicure on her way to fetch her daughter from clarinet lessons. But she's blissfully unaware that her charmed and happy life is about to be turned upside down.

For one sunny morning a letter lands on Evie's immaculate doormat. It's a bombshell, knocking her carefully arranged and managed world completely askew and threatening to sabotage all she holds dear.

What will be left and what will change for ever? Is Evie strong enough to fight for what she loves? Can her entire world really be as fragile as her best china?

One Day In May

May is the month for falling in love . . .

Hattie Carrington's first love was as unusual as it was out of reach – Dominic Forbes was a married MP, and she was his assistant. She has never told anyone about it. And never really got over it.

But years later with a flourishing antiques business and enjoying a fling with a sexy, younger man, she thinks her past is finally well and truly behind her.

Until work takes her to Little Crandon, home of Dominic's widow and his gorgeous younger brother, Hal. There Hattie's world is turned upside down. She learns that if she's to truly fall in love again she needs to stop hiding from the truth. Can she ever admit what really happened back then? And, if so, is she ready for the consequences?

A Rural Affair

'If I'm being totally honest I had fantasized about Phil dying.'

When Poppy Shilling's bike-besotted, Lycra-clad husband is killed in a freak accident, she can't help feeling a guilty sense of relief. For at long last she's released from a controlling and loveless marriage.

Throwing herself wholeheartedly into village life, she's determined to start over. And sure enough, everyone from Luke the sexy church-organist to Bob the resident oddball, is taking note.

But just as she's ready to dip her toes in the water, the discovery of a dark secret about her late husband shatters Poppy's confidence. Does she really have the courage to risk her heart again? Because Poppy wants a lot more than just a rural affair . . .

Welcome to

Alliott
Country...

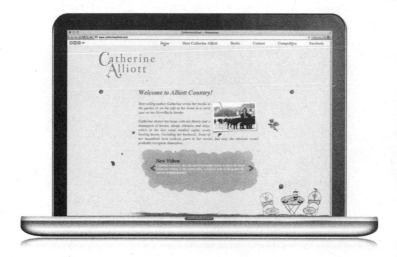

www.catherinealliott.com

Check back regularly for the latest news from Catherine,
extracts of all her books and behind-the-scenes
content all about life in Alliott Country

Like Catherine on Facebook:
www.facebook.com/AlliottCountry

He just wanted a decent book to read ...

Not too much to ask, is it? It was in 1935 when Allen Lane, Managing Director of Bodley Head Publishers, stood on a platform at Exeter railway station looking for something good to read on his journey back to London. His choice was limited to popular magazines and poor-quality paperbacks – the same choice faced every day by the vast majority of readers, few of whom could afford hardbacks. Lane's disappointment and subsequent anger at the range of books generally available led him to found a company – and change the world.

'We believed in the existence in this country of a vast reading public for intelligent books at a low price, and staked everything on it'
Sir Allen Lane, 1902–1970, founder of Penguin Books

The quality paperback had arrived – and not just in bookshops. Lane was adamant that his Penguins should appear in chain stores and tobacconists, and should cost no more than a packet of cigarettes.

Reading habits (and cigarette prices) have changed since 1935, but Penguin still believes in publishing the best books for everybody to enjoy. We still believe that good design costs no more than bad design, and we still believe that quality books published passionately and responsibly make the world a better place.

So wherever you see the little bird – whether it's on a piece of prize-winning literary fiction or a celebrity autobiography, political tour de force or historical masterpiece, a serial-killer thriller, reference book, world classic or a piece of pure escapism – you can bet that it represents the very best that the genre has to offer.

Whatever you like to read – trust Penguin.